# STARGATE

**Also by Pauline Gedge**

Child of the Morning
The Eagle and the Raven

# PAULINE GEDGE

# STARGATE

THE DIAL PRESS
NEW YORK

Published by
The Dial Press
1 Dag Hammarskjold Plaza
New York, New York 10017

Manufactured in the United States of America
First printing
Design by Francesca Belanger

Library of Congress Cataloging in Publication Data

Gedge, Pauline, 1945–
Stargate.

I. Title.
PR9199.3.G415S7   1982      813'.54      81-19473
ISBN 0-385-27420-3          AACR2

*For Elisabeth, my sister and my friend.*
*With love.*

Thank you, M.R.S.

# ONE

# 1

Ixelion stepped under the archway of his Gate, the box clutched tightly in his hand, and the guards with their silver wands and stiff capes of scales greeted him with soft, deferential voices. He smiled at them briefly and absently, passing them to walk quickly along the causeway, lit now by the fire that welled up through his pale skin and conjured reflections on the mottled surface of the river that flowed through the tunnel. Ixel the fair, he thought with a burgeoning relief. Ixel the pure. There is no water in the All like the waters here on my world. I feel as though I have been away on a long journey fraught with terrible dangers and have come home exhausted and changed, but of course that cannot be. You change. I do not. To right and left the rock tunnel curved, throwing back to him the constant low rumble of the flowing water, and as he paced he brushed the familiar wall carvings which invited his fingers to move along them with the same slow, majestic weight of the river itself. He bent and saw his likeness fragmented by the water. He held out a hand in a gesture of reassurance, spreading his fingers to see the delicate, opalescent webbing between them, and then went on until he came to the mouth of the tunnel, where the river foamed out to spread like gray twisted tresses laid upon the flower-burdened earth. Here he sat for a moment, wetting his feet, closing his eyes and inhaling the damp coolness. She thrust it at me, he thought. I did not want to take it. With a shudder of distaste Ixelion opened his eyes and looked down at the pale-blue wood of the box, and its tiny runnels of gold winked back at him his own fire. Not now, he thought, rising. Now I simply wish to go home.

He skirted the massive, motionless forest from out of whose wet trunks and dripping leaves the ever-present mist seeped. He soon could see the pinnacles of his palace, reaching up to be lost in the grayness of the heavy sky. As he came to the ramp over which another river poured he met a group of his people emerging from the forest, nets full of flowers slung over their shoulders. When they saw him, they ran to him, calling with their light, high voices, and he was quickly surrounded by cool, naked bodies and questioning eyes.

"Sun-lord! It is the sun-lord. Ixelion has come back!"

He stood still while they reached to touch him, unconsciously cradling the box in both arms so that they might not brush against it.

"You have been gone for many years, sun-lord," one of them said when they had all drawn back a little and regarded him. "Look. My son has left the water!"

Ixelion bent and put his hand on the boy's shoulder. "And have you given up chasing the fish entirely," he asked gravely, "now that you have hung up your tail?"

The boy laughed. "No, sun-lord. The fish gather on the beach outside my house every morning. They would be disappointed if I did not chase them away again."

"The sun has sulked since you went away," a woman remarked. "We have not seen his face once."

Ixelion talked to them a moment longer and made his farewells, and immediately they picked up their nets and left him. He went up the ramp, crossed his terrace, and entered the green dimness of his hall. Water from the room's many fountains splashed into pools that opened one into another and finally spilled out through the doorway, echoing loudly in the ceiling, where mist hung. Through the passageways more water swirled, ankle deep, cool and pale. He crossed his hall, passing under the waterfall that sprinkled down through the balustrades of balconies high above, mounted stairs, and came out at last in a room with one wall open entirely to the roof of the forest and the ocean beyond. The river that ran down the hill on which the palace was built had been diverted in order that it might fill the great square pool that formed most of the floor of the room. It poured down the wall, troubling the otherwise placid surface of the pool, and spilled out on the other side to cascade through the gap in the floor to the hall below. Ixelion paused. There was no sound in all his vast house but the voice of water, dripping, splashing, running, dancing with itself, singing to itself as it moved from spire to floor and so out to meander through the forest. He walked around the pool and stood at the window, so wide that many spans of his arms could not measure it. The sky met the forest, mingled with it, and filtered to the earth as fog. The air was still. No wind ever trembled in the marshes or riffled the oceans of Ixel, and the sun had never shone full on the crystal domes the people lived in or heated their white skins.

"I am back, my brother, I am home," he said softly to his sun, and for a moment a faint gleam of diffused gold bathed him, pushing down through the gentle rain that had begun to fall, but then the mist closed in again, and Ixelion left the window.

In one corner of the room was a chest made from the pastelled pink, blue, and mauve shells that littered Ixel's beaches. He went to it and raised the lid, placing the box that Falia had forced upon him carefully inside. Tonight I will turn the pages of Fallan's history, he promised himself, caressing the warm, dry haeli wood, his finger tracing its gold veins. Tonight I will go to Falia. And will you also look upon the thing that is forbidden? some other voice in his mind prompted gently. He closed the chest quickly. Going to the pool, he plunged in, swimming from one end to the other and back again, letting the cool, slippery greenness fill his mouth and slide like a loving hand over his skin. He could not forget how Fallan's soil had cringed away from him, the alien, the one who was whole and did not belong in a place of dying and fracture. Falia's touch had sullied him, and he wanted to wash the decay from his body, but Ixel's clear water could not flush the pictures from his mind. At last he left the pool, descended to his hall, and went out under the rain.

He made his way into the forest, his feet sinking into the sopping undergrowth. He shook back his heavy wet hair and raised his face so that the broad, drooping leaves could brush it. As he walked he plucked flowers for Sillix, stars and diamonds, ellipses and crescents and circles that spun from root to petal, spears and threads that wove in and out, flowers like eyes and flowers scaled like fish, all scentless and colorless yet possessing in their multiplicity of shape an unexcelled beauty. They grew everywhere: on the trunks of the trees, on the ground, in the bosoms of the rivers, where they clung, drowned, to the mud and stone of the beds. Ixelion knew that Sillix had no need of flowers, but it was a politeness, a gesture he would welcome.

He came out of the forest and walked along the ocean, its

beach the only place where nothing grew, stepping over crabs and streamers of black seaweed. Out of the translucent crystal domes lining the beach the people came, the children running to hold his hand, the adults waving and greeting him, their round, pupilless eyes bright.

"Sun-lord!" they called. "Ixel has no soul when you are gone. Welcome home! Did you see a Messenger while you traveled? One came for Grenix, and Lanix has also taken his last journey through the Gate. Has the Worldmaker made anything new?" They were as avid for news as ever, and though he called answers to them as he passed their doors, the last question he ignored. The Worldmaker would never again make anything new. He now raged and roared through the universe, bellowing his hatred for all that he had made, flinging his malevolence against the worlds still shining with his first light, and sucking strength from those he had gathered under his fiery black wings. But he will not take Ixel! Ixelion thought fervently as he left the beach and approached Sillix's doorway. Never! Not my gentle, curious people. Only by my death. He stopped on the threshold, stunned. My death? How can I have come to consider such a thing? I cannot die until my sun and I burn away together at the end of time. Suddenly he felt the box of haeli wood in his hands again and with a cry dropped it, but then he looked down and saw that the flowers he had picked lay scattered over his feet. Bending, he gathered them up, and Sillix appeared, bowing gravely.

"So you have returned, sun-lord." He smiled. "That is very good. Enter."

Ixelion preceded him and then turned, laying the flowers in his arms. "I did not bring you a gift from another world this time, Sillix," he said. "I have not been in places where there is happiness."

Sillix's brow furrowed. "Are there places without laughter, Ixelion? How strange that the Worldmaker should have made beings that do not laugh. I thank you for the flowers. The gift of your presence would have been enough. Please sit."

Sillix's home was one room made of green-tinted crystal that had been hewn out of the rock on Lix and polished to the smoothness of glass. Just outside the doorway was a small fire pit where Sillix cooked his fish and seaweed. A row of windows ran around the dome close to the ground, and within, under the windows, a circular seat, so that the occupant of the house could sit wherever he would and always be able to look out upon ocean, river, or forest. Mist blurred the upper reaches of the dome. There was no bed, for the people of Ixel slept under the surface of ocean or river, where they were born and where they spent the first ten years of their long lives.

Ixelion sat on the window seat, but Sillix folded his long legs and sank to the floor, tucking his webbed feet beneath him, his eyes on his lord. There was something different about Ixelion. The sea-green hair dewed with moisture still lay waving on the thin shoulders. The long, delicate body still filled the room with a faint golden light. The eyes still brimmed with the essences of sun, water, and living things. Sillix could not put a name to what he felt emanating from Ixelion, and in the end he mentally shrugged. It has been three years, he thought. I have not seen him in all that time, and of course there has been some change in myself. He can never change. He has sat in this house with all my elders, every one of them since the Worldmaker caused the people of Ixel to be, and he was here alone even before that, master of the waters. Ixelion sensed the quick scrutiny and smiled.

"Are the fish plentiful, Sillix? Do the rivers stay clean and the forests grow?"

"All is well, lord. Why should it not be? New homes have been built, for there are many children, and last year a group of the river-dwellers set out on the journey to the other side."

"On the other side there is less water, smaller trees, more grass, and stronger sunlight. Did you tell them this?"

"I did, but they still wanted to go. They are young, Ixelion, and full of adventure, and the lands on the other side lie virgin, waiting for us to spread over them."

"I am very glad, Sillix," Ixelion said with a smile. "In the beginning, when the Worldmaker and I walked here together, he told me how there would be a slow maturing on this world, and much time would pass before the people would multiply. They are ready now to explore and change."

"It is very good," Sillix replied, and Ixelion repeated sadly, "Yes. It is very good."

After a silence during which Sillix again studied his lord, he dropped his gaze and asked in a low voice, "Where is the Worldmaker, Ixelion? Is he still making? Has he left the All? Why does he not come to Ixel anymore?"

Ixelion glanced swiftly at the graceful, bent head, the supple webbed hands pressed against each other. Once he would have told the truth to Sillix. Once he would not have known the difference between truth and untruth, as Sillix still did not know it, but that had been in the times when the Worldmaker still took his place as head of the council, before he became the Unmaker, when there had never been any lies, not in the whole of the All. Even now, Ixelion knew, after so much breaking and disfigurement, the greatest weakness of the sun-people was their difficulty in separating truth from lie. It was becoming clearer to them, but that clarity was itself a small beginning on the path to the black fire. To discern a lie, he thought, we must have some knowledge of what it means to be a liar.

"The Worldmaker is not making anymore," he replied finally. "He has not left the universe. He may return to Ixel someday." And all those things are true, Ixelion thought, rising. True and unimaginably terrible. "I will welcome you whenever you wish to speak with me," he finished. "My halls are not sealed from you." He lifted the sun-disc from his breast and held it out, and Sillix kissed it. Ixelion embraced him and left, walking back along the beach in the increasing dimness of evening. The rain still fell. He held up his arms to it as he went, and by the time he reached his palace, it was full dark.

The water flowed on through his lofty rooms, now lit by great shafts of yellow light that his sun had left for him. It mingled with the mists gathered high above him, making rainbows in the frothing falls, turning the fountains into jewels that sprayed out like crystal haeli flowers and fell to the floor like dying stars. Ixelion walked beneath them slowly, thinking of his mortals diving deep beneath the warmer ocean on the other side, sitting under the benison of a sun no longer shrouded in fog, placing their feet on dry land. He mounted the stair, circled his pool, and stood for a long while gazing out onto the night. Though he could not see beyond the soft darkness, he knew that forest, marsh, and beach were deserted and his people lay under the water, rocked by the almost imperceptible swells, dreaming the hours away. A kind Time he gave us, Ixelion thought. A sweet, friendly Time. He allowed his mind to range near and far as his eyes gazed unseeingly into the night, but beneath the reveries was the chest, and the box that lay within it. At last he turned his back on the window and went to the corner. Lifting the lid, he drew out the box and carried it into an inner room where sunlight flooded the crystal walls and the only water present trickled in tiny rivulets across the doorway. He sat in his chair, conscious as never before of the busy voice of the palace. The box was fastened with a copper hasp, but it was not locked, and he parted it and lifted the lid. For a second the light in the room dimmed. Ixelion glanced up, startled, his heart all at once thudding against his breast, but soon the warm glow wrapped itself around him again. What makes you think that you are strong enough? something whispered in him. What madness has taken hold of you? He looked down into the box.

Within lay a thick volume, bound in leather and lettered in gold. Ixelion lifted it out and quickly closed the lid, for beneath the book he had glimpsed a dull, metallic glint, and his heart had leaped into his mouth. Not yet, he thought. Not yet? Not ever! I will live on Fallan for a while, and then I will take the thing, untouched, to Janthis. The book was heavy. He ran his hands lovingly and wistfully over the supple binding, the gleaming letters. *The Annals of Fallan*, he read, *Being a History of Fallan and Her Worlds from the Time of Making*. Ixelion opened it, and a wave of vanished laughter and lost innocence, broken dreams and wasted hope rose to him as Falia's spiked red handwriting sprang out at him. She had written in the common tongue as the Law demanded. *Before the beginning was the Lawmaker*, he read. *And the Lawmaker made the Worldmaker and commanded him to make according to his nature. And the Worldmaker made the worlds. . . .* Ixelion could not go on. He riffled through the pages, aching with sadness. The first chapter was well known to him. The Annals of every system began with the same words, and he did not want to see them again, in Falia's hand, red against the yellow vellum. He sighed and leaned back, closing his eyes and grasping his sun-disc. I will go back, back to the pain of my last visit, he thought dimly, already tranced, the Annals under one limp hand and the box at his feet.

*

On Ixel the sun rose and set, the people swam and fished, and the endless rain fell. But Ixelion was now once again on Fallan, walking toward the deserted sweep of stone stairs that lifted to Falia's palace, high above. It was noon, but the sun's rays lay red and ominous over the treeless, rolling country, sliding stealthily through the bending silver grasses and changing to a dull ocher where they touched the blackened crops rotting in the fields. Furtive shadows moved on the periphery of his vision, and he forced himself to turn his head. A procession of vaguely human shapes was disappearing over the brow of the nearest hill. In their arms and slung over their shoulders, severed limbs gleamed dully like the fat stems of obscene flowers. They did not notice Ixelion, and he averted his gaze and quickened his pace.

As he began to mount the stair he heard a muted roar behind him and turned unwillingly. Fire flicked orange on the unbroken line of the horizon; silhouetted against it horsemen rode to and fro with lances raised, black men on black horses, crying out like hunting animals. Wails and shrieks came faintly on the wind, mixing with the acrid odor of burning, all imbued with the same cold essence of death. He turned back abruptly, stepping carefully where the steps had crumbled or split and grass now tufted, one hand going to the colorless gem hanging on his breast. A sense of oppression came burgeoning out from the palace's great twin arches lost in dimness above him. "I am not a judge, I am a guardian," he whispered as he passed under them. "I am not a lawmaker but an interpreter." The hall was deathly silent. Ixelion crossed it, still whispering, fingers tight about the crystal, and by the time he had come to the far end and had passed Falia's stone chair, he knew that he was himself again, armored against the decay around him, invulnerable to any lurking seed of dissolution. He climbed the black-sunk steps behind the chair, and above the first level the halls grew smaller and somehow lighter, as though some vestige of Falia's quicksilver integrity still clung to the walls and lingered in the musty air. He went from room to room, climbing more stairs, searching quickly and methodically. He did not stop and seek an echo of her in his mind. He knew that she would no longer be capable of calling to him.

He finally found her, in the small, octagonal chamber that

crowned the myriad tiers of her palace. He stepped through the archway and saw her facing him, sitting motionless in a high-backed wooden chair, her outline black and silver against her sun, which seemed to leer in through the wide stone aperture of the window. Wind stirred her hair and sighed gently in the corners of the naked room. Ixelion looked about him, but there was nothing else to see. A stone floor glimmering gray, stone walls bare of any adornment, the curved vault of the ceiling now rivered in cracks from which dust floated, and Falia in her chair. He went closer. Her hands were folded in her lap, and under them Ixelion could make out a container. Slowly he bent, as from it there rose a perfume, a faint sweetness. It was a large box made of pale-blue wood grained in tiny channels of gold, and under his fingers it was warm. Haeli wood. He remembered then that he had admired it once, long, long ago, and she had told him that Danarion had given it to her after some council meeting on Danar, when he and she had walked together under the blossoming haeli trees. Ixelion squatted before her, lifting one of her limp hands and brushing the cold fingertips with his own.

"Falia," he ordered quietly, "come here." She did not move, and he repeated the words slowly, emphatically, still holding her hand. Her feet were covered with a thin film of dust, and dust lay also on her shoulders and her head. "Come," he said a third time. "Ixelion is here. He wishes to speak with you." After a long time her hand trembled, and she withdrew it from his grasp. Then she took a deep, uneven breath and blinked. Her head rolled back against the carved support of the chair, her shoulders slumped, and the hand that he had held fluttered anxiously over the box in her lap as though she feared it would no longer be there. Ixelion rose and stood looking down on her, giving her time to take the last steps into the present, and then he spoke. "Falia, get up. Come to the window."

She gathered the box to her breast and rose stiffly, turning to face him, and even in the brooding dimness he could see the glow of a happier, more innocent time dying slowly behind her green eyes, struggling against this day, this hour.

"Ixelion," she said, "how dark it is! Is it night?" As she looked at him the gentle fire went out of her face, and her eyes widened.

"No, no," she whispered. "Not yet. I must rest a little more. I am weary."

He took her arm and drew her to the window. "Look down," he commanded harshly, "and see what you have done." His grip tightened, and reluctantly she put one hand upon the stone casing and leaned out, the other hand still clutching the fragrant box. Far below, down on the floor of the world, the dreary land stretched away into an infinity of cold dimness. The sky was so dark that the stars shone faintly, their light stronger than the frail rays of the exhausted sun. Ixelion knew that if he had led her to the opposite window, he could have shown her the devastation of her warring mortals: fire devouring the pastures and murder, suspicion, and despair stalking unchallenged among the armies. But here there was peace of a kind, unquestioning, accepting, the peace of defeat. For a long time she looked and then she drew back. "I did not do this," she said. "How can you accuse me of such a thing? I am not like Kallar or Mallan. I did not surrender to black fire, I did not bow."

"But neither did you fight. You went away, Falia, you retreated into your mind. You did not even send us word, and we did not suspect. Where have you been?"

She put a hand over her eyes. "I have been walking alone on the hills, under my sun, in the time before the Worldmaker shaped mortal men." The hand passed over her face and fell once more to the box. "Ah, Ixelion! How much simpler existence was then, when the worlds were whole, when he loved what he had made. . . ."

"Hush!" he said sharply. "Not here."

She smiled painfully, and Ixelion noticed that in the short time they had been speaking tiny lines had begun to inch through the skin that since the beginning had been smooth and beautiful. The silver hair now had a metallic dullness, the long neck held a hint of slackness about the jaw, and around the grass-green eyes and the soft mouth the flesh had begun to pouch. He resisted the urge to step away from her and glanced out at her sun. She followed his gaze and then abruptly sat again in the chair, cradling the box.

"Tell me, Ixelion," she said haltingly, "what year is it?"

He was glad that he stood behind her. "I do not know," he replied steadily. "How did you allow this to happen to you? How long has it been since you looked out?"

She answered him in a low, hurried voice, her eyes on the stone wall in front of her. "I don't know. Perhaps two hundred years of mortal time have passed since the Trader came through the Gate and sought audience with me. He said he dealt in woods and fruits and had brought tree seeds for us, but also that he had run from Tran with a great and dangerous treasure to place in my keeping."

"Tran!" Ixelion exclaimed. "But the Gate on Tran was closed a millennium ago!"

She nodded. "I know. I was there, we all were, when Tranin went down into black fire. I should have been suspicious of the Trader. I should have ordered him to carry the treasure to the council. But I was proud, and secure in the knowledge of my safety. Let the others fall, I told myself. I, Falia, am incorruptible! I took it from his hands and was seized with the desire to keep it for my own. That overwhelming greed should have warned me that the Unmaker was breathing through my Gate, but I was oblivious to all save the feel of the thing under my fingers. The Trader laughed at me and went away, leaving me with it. I took one look and knew what it was. I was afraid for the first time in my life, and my sun felt my fear and quivered in the sky." She rose suddenly and cast the box to the floor. "Cursed be the Unmaker and his selfishness and his hatred! Cursed be the Trader, whose heart was as black as his scarf!" She wrestled with herself, both hands now tight about her necklet. "I should have carried the thing to Danar and given it to Janthis as soon as I recognized it, but instead I came up here and looked at it. The more I looked, the more afraid I became. I fled often into the times when the suns and we were new, and though each time I came back, I was tainted, and Fallan began to slide away from me. The people from my other planets began to complain of the riders, saying that I favored them and gave them everything and that they would not share because I did not order it. There was thieving and murder, but because I have no authority, I could not judge. They demanded new laws, but what right do we have to make laws? I did not fight. I did not seek help from the council, because I knew that Janthis would order the closing of my Gate. I sealed my hall and came up here and went away. That is all!"

Ixelion wanted to ask her what the treasure was, and suddenly his mind was inflamed with a desire to see it for himself, but he recognized the desire as a foreign emotion, imposed on him by the dark power that now flooded Fallan and wished to drown him also. He had no difficulty in extinguishing it. I am whole, he said to himself. Ixel is whole. We will stay that way forever. He walked around to face her and offered her his hand, but she looked up at him, pleading.

"Once more, Ixelion, I beg you. Come back with me to the days when you and I would sit together before my hall while the riders wheeled below us and the wind smelled of new growth." He would have liked to visit her again in those times, unchanged and beautiful, but he shook his head, reaching down and pulling her to her feet.

"No, Falia," he said roughly. "Time on Fallan is in the hands of the Unmaker now. It has become a trap, an invitation to illusion, as you well know. The members of the council are waiting for you by the Gate, and you have a decision to make. We must go now."

She did not protest again but picked up the box, rose without another word, and led the way out of the icy chamber. Down the stairs, through a hall which opened out into another wide chamber, she glided before him, cleaving the darkness with her silver hair, still faintly burnished by her sun's waning light. He caught up with her as she crossed the last cavernous hall, where her riders used to prance, where in the nights she used to borrow light and heat from her sun and fill the airy space with joy, and together they came at last to the pair of arches, and the gray stairs, and the long plain beyond. She went out under the arches, turned, and touched the ground beneath them three times. "The seal is broken," she said softly under her breath. "Let mortals walk here again without fear. The chambers are empty."

Ixelion saw that when she rose, she could not straighten. He was swallowed in pity mingled with horror at the inexorable rush of aging taking place in her, as though all the splendor that should have been hers forever had lost substance and become nothing more than a moment of dream.

Halfway down the stair she sank onto the stone. "I must rest for a while, Ixelion," she begged. "There is a weight within me. I cannot carry it." Wordlessly he sat also, putting his arms around her, closing his eyes so that he might not see, shutting out the hostility around him, which grew more tangible with every passing second. He felt them also, the seconds, falling delicately against him like blown feathers, drifting around him, seeking a way to enter him and change him. His immortality seemed fragile here, a thin ice-cup ready to shatter. He sensed the eyes of the Unmaker fixed on him and him alone, jealous eyes, cold as the touch of black fire, seeking the flaw in him with which to pry him apart, and Ixel with him. You loved us once! he cried out in his mind. We flew on the solar winds with you, the one who made us, and we worshiped you. Why do you hate us now? You have broken our hearts, all of us.

"Get up, Falia," he said, helping her to rise, urgency in his voice. "I can stay here no longer."

The golden veins of her hands stood out through her transparent old-woman's skin, and her mouth was a wrinkled black fruit. "Please, Ixelion," she said, pushing the box toward him, "take this and give it to Janthis for me. I cannot face the shame of placing it in his hands myself. In it are the records of my worlds from the beginning. See that they are written into the Book of What Was. Also . . ." Her voice became a sibilant thread of air. "Also it contains the thing that must be guarded by the council. Tell Janthis that on no account must he open it."

They went on, and at the foot of the stair she stopped him once more, sticklike arms and swollen fingers plucking at him, brittle white hair tufting from her balding scalp.

"I did not tell you all," she whispered. "The Trader returned and demanded the treasure from me. He said I was not a fit keeper, that he had changed his mind and wanted it back, and all the time he was laughing." She lifted her head with difficulty and gazed past him into the depths of her failing sun. "I broke the Law. I murdered him. I told myself that I was right to do so, that the treasure was safer with me than in his perfidious hands, but I know now that I killed him because I wanted it for myself."

There was nothing he could say, and he turned from her toward the tunnel, crossing the fan of roads that swept from the entrance to run over her silent plains, knowing that she followed him but no longer wanting to walk beside her or speak with her. He moved from the half-light of Fallan into the full darkness of the tunnel without a tremor. Moments later Falia slipped after him. The Gate on this world was not approached through massive, ornately carved arches and brilliantly lit passages. The tunnel was of earth, supported by plain wood brought in the beginning from Shol, and floor and walls were free of decoration. The torches that had once lit the traveler's way had long since gone out, for the guards who had tended them and had watched the comings and goings of the people were dead, slain unprepared as the invaders from sister planets had poured through the Gate. Ixelion walked on. The floor was level and the air was very still. There were no bends, and long before he came up to the company, he could see the faint halo of sunlight that surrounded them, flowing in their veins and pulsing through their skin just as it had once lived in Falia. He turned. She was close behind him, her hands flat on her necklet, her head and shoulders bowed, her white hair only a smudge above the shadow that she was. Turning back, he could see the tall arch, and through it a black sky blazing with constellations. His eyes found his own sun, white and glittering, Ixel and Lix two pinpoints of light dancing beside it. Farther away was Ghakazian's sun with its crown of satellites, and Sholia's twins set in the net of their planets like many-faceted crystals. Danarion's sun was only a mist, so far out into space that Ixelion could hardly see it. At the foot of the arch and just beyond it, on a spur of Fallan that seemed to jut out over an abyss of fearsome nothingness, the members of the council had gathered. They did not move as he stepped through the arch and came up to them. A Messenger was there also, a little apart, wrapped in its constantly shifting spectrum of rainbowed light which flickered and coiled as it fought to maintain itself within Fallan's atmosphere. A drift of perfumed heat came from it to tickle Ixelion's nostrils as he bowed to it profoundly, and then he spoke to Janthis.

"I found her in her chamber, walking in the past. She did not surrender. She ran away because she was afraid."

The company's eyes slipped from him to the tunnel. Falia stood now with one withered hand against the wall, straining to be upright. Pride shone suddenly out of the ravaged face, and she looked from one to the other with a deliberate slowness, searching their eyes. Ghakazian stared back without expression, his braceleted arms folded across his brown chest, his long dark-brown hair stirring in the draught that blew from some air vent high in the roof of the tunnel. Only his wings betrayed his unease, fluttering spasmodically, opening to brush the archway and close again. Sholia had her hands behind her back, her fingers nervously twisted in the cascade of deep golden hair that fell almost to the ground, and her fear was a palpable thing. Danarion was watching Falia, with undisguised pity, as though she were one with her mortals, all now prisoners, all condemned. Falia stood a little straighter and faced Janthis, but before she could speak, he held up a hand.

"You have a choice, Falia, and though you know it, I am bound to remind you. You may either remain here with your people and make what reparation you can, or you may return to Danar and go from there to be judged by the Messengers. What will you do?"

"I have betrayed my people," she answered immediately, "not out of corruption but out of cowardice. I did not bow to the Unmaker, but neither did I resist him. I ran away. I am as guilty as Mallan and Kallar, and the Messengers will not spare me. They are just, but they have no mercy in them. They will condemn me to death." The word filled her with such horror that she swayed against the wall. "I cannot put right what I have done," she went on shakily, "but I can go down with those who worshiped and trusted me. I will stay."

Janthis nodded. "Very well. Your necklet."

With trembling fingers she drew it over her head, kissed it, and passed it to him, and as it left her grasp the lingering spark of fire deep within the polished disc flared once to a blinding brilliance and then died away. A pinpoint of redness remained glowing in its heart, but it too quickly went dark. The necklet now weighed in Janthis's hand like a cold, damp stone, and he handed it to Danarion.

"Will you close your Gate yourself, Falia?" Janthis enquired gently. She nodded dumbly, her face as white as her hair. "Then farewell. We will not forget you. We will walk with you in the past, where there is no grief."

No one else spoke. After a moment Falia pushed herself away from the wall and raised her arms, holding them out straight, palms down. With a slow force she turned her wrists upward. The company felt the pressure of the power still within her, and the stone archway began to groan.

"I close the Gate of Fallan," she called. "Henceforth neither mortal nor immortal, Maker nor Messenger nor any created thing may enter here. The stars are forbidden to the people of Fallan, and Fallan is forbidden to the people of the stars." Her arms grew more rigid. The stone framing her creaked and began to tremble, and cracks ran lightly through it. It seemed to protest with many voices, and a milky gray fog began to gather from roof to floor. Those watching saw a horse come galloping toward them, its neck straining, its eyes rimmed in white and nostrils flared. Fog dewed the rippling flanks and shredded back from a streaming mane. It thundered between the lintels yet drew no nearer. Its mighty shoulders quivered with the effort of its flight, but under it the earth had dissolved and left only thick cloud so that it could make no progress. Falia's courage faltered, but only for a second. "Close!" she shouted. "I, Falia, command you! Your service is at an end!" The horse's frenetic pounding slowed, and its head came up and froze. One hoof remained raised. The mist darkened, thickened, and became at last a wall of Fallan's earth imprisoning the sleek, grained lines of a carved wooden horse, which looked red, as though it had been there forever. Falia was gone.

The others waited silently, hardly daring to move. Soon two hands began to appear, etched ever more deeply into the impenetrable wall, palms facing outward in a gesture of warning. Burned into each palm was a rayed sun; between them were the delicate outlines of Fallan's sun, Fallan itself, and its sister planets. "It was too late," Sholia said flatly. "It is always too late. Each time I hope will be the last, and each time another sun-lord is forced to stand in agony and pronounce sentence upon himself."

"Where is the Lawmaker?" Ghakazian muttered angrily. "Why does he do nothing?" He turned to face the invisible corridors, leaning outward, his wings slowly unfurling. "I am going home to Ghaka," he snapped, and without bidding them farewell launched himself down with a rustle of dark feathers and a rush of warm air. They heard him call once to his sun, and then he vanished. The Messenger, its duty as witness to a Gate-closing discharged, had gone as quietly as it had come, leaving a sense of relief behind it.

Janthis turned to Ixelion. "The records," he said. "Did she give them to you?"

Suddenly Ixelion remembered the box that he still held. The records, and something else. A treasure. A thing of destruction. He wanted to hand the box to Janthis, but unaccountably his fingers tightened on it. I will take it home for one night and sit with it on my lap as she did, in memory of her, he thought to himself. I will cradle it and look out upon Fallan in the star-studded sky. I will go back to that day when we sat together on her stone stair and talked so happily of nothing. He nodded reluctantly to Janthis.

"I have them. I would like to read them before I bring them to the council. Is it permitted?"

Janthis looked long at the box now wrapped in Ixelion's long arms but finally gave his consent. "Do not neglect your people while you mourn, Ixelion," he warned. "Do not forget that though a night passes slowly in your palace, the years flow swiftly on your world."

Ixelion glanced at him sharply. "I learned this long ago," he answered. "Why do you speak to me as though I were a mortal?"

For a moment despair passed behind Janthis's dark eyes. "I am afraid," he replied simply as he recovered and smiled at Ixelion in apology. "Go home, all of you," he said. "The danger has been held at bay yet again."

Ixelion opened his eyes. Fleetingly Janthis's face hung before him in the dim room, the lips still parted in speech, and then there was nothing but the endless gush and roil of water and his own hands caressing the Annals. She should have taken the treasure from the Trader and run with it to Janthis, he thought. Why that sudden need to look at it, the selfishness, and then the greatest of transgressions? But that same need was curdling in him again as it had done for the one warped moment when she had spoken of the thing that now lay quiescent at his feet, and he knew that he must never speak with her on that last day again. Feeling thin and somehow drained he lifted the book from his lap and held it against his cheek. Falia. The monotonous chatter of his waterfalls and streams wove with the sick vestiges of longing still tugging at him, and suddenly he wanted to stand and shout "Stop! No more water! Give me silence!" as though he might slay the desire to bend and pick up the box if he could only end the sound of water. A council meeting was due soon, he knew. He would be called, and until then he had only to place the Annals and the other thing in his chest and firmly close the lid. I must take the Annals in the wooden box, he thought suddenly. Someone must have seen it in my hands by Fallan's Gate. I would like to keep it. It is so beautiful, so warm and dry. But to keep the box I must first remove the treasure. His spine seemed to bend of its own accord, and his hands reached down, trembling. Then he realized what he was doing and sprang up, dropping the Annals into the box with head averted and shutting the lid and fastening the hasp. I am playing with death, he thought, horrified. Walking into his three-walled room, he flung the box into the chest and dove into the rocking coolness of the pool. I will spend more time with Sillix, he vowed. I will not be alone. He swam determinedly, refusing to bring forward the other thought that hovered behind the image of Sillix.

Sillix will keep me from myself.

Sillix will prevent me from being alone.

# 2

Danarion paced slowly under the spreading haeli trees, their golden leaves whispering sleepily above him, their red, sticky buds exuding a fragrance that would linger on his body and in his nostrils for the rest of the day. Ten dark and sullen years had passed on Fallan since its Gate was closed, but only one winter on Danar, and now spring had come. The endless forests glowed yellow and flame, the corions dozed, drugged by the scent of the birthing blossoms, and the people sat far into each mild, sweet night, unwilling to pass into unconsciousness and miss a moment of the unfolding of the season. Green and blue birds followed him, singing wantonly around his head, swooping recklessly to brush his shoulders. Once in a while he sang with them absently, his eyes on his feet. Falia's cold necklet was in his hand, a weight of preoccupation, the only token of fear and failure on Danar, and though it offended his fingers and filled him with distaste, he carried it with conscious care. The necklet itself was not repugnant. The finest craftsmen on Shol had made it as they had made all the others, with every skill and vision they had possessed, and it was as consummately wrought as the World-maker's weaving of the stars' glory. Thin gold links hung with pearls and fastened with Lix crystal went around the neck, and hanging on two gossamer-thin filaments of golden webbing was the sun-disc, rayed also in the pale, glittering stone that was Ixel's only wealth. Each necklet was distinct, for the craftsmen had put something of each wearer's world into it. Falia's had links shaped like tiny horses, the eye of each animal a splinter of green emerald, each flaring tail streaked in silver. The Worldmaker had finished each necklet with benevolent spells of power. Power for preserving, for interpreting and upholding, power for peace and order. But no power to heal, Danarion thought grimly. Why should he have given us that? In those days there were no hurts. The necklet hurt him now, wreathed as it was in invisible coils of deceit and corruption, and he quickened his pace. At a word from him the teasing birds drew away, hovering for a moment before they flitted to be lost in the foliage, and he rounded the last bend, which would take him to the edge of the forest and the city beyond.

Halfway along he stopped. A corion lay across the path, blocking his way, its golden fur dappled in sunlight. It was spread-eagled luxuriously, its long-clawed limbs loose in the grass, its tressed tail curved along its back, the crest of green feathers on its head now lying like a shimmering cap to curl beneath its pointed ears and under its chin. Danarion hesitated, smiling, his heart suddenly lightened at the sight of the great beast so indolently at ease, so free from necessity or any care. The corion sighed, its huge ribs rising and falling, and opened one azure eye lazily. It sighed again ostentatiously, and the black tongue came out to explore the furred and feathered nose, revealing sharp white teeth. It yawned with a show of mild annoyance, and raised its head.

"So it is you, Danarion," it said in a voice as rich and dark as the roots of the trees that dug deep beneath it. "I suppose that you want me to move so that you can get past me."

Danarion stepped up to it and bowed slightly. One did not fear a corion, but one did accord it respect and regard it with awe, speaking to it politely, for its dignity and self-possession demanded a certain manner of approach. Danarion had always wanted to put his arms around one and bury his face in its warm fur, but he had never been invited to do so and probably never would be.

"I would not dream of disturbing you, Storn," he replied. "I can go around you if you do not feel like rising."

"Of course I do not feel like rising," Storn retorted, with a rumble of laughter. "But for you, sun-lord, I will rouse myself from this pleasant torpor. What a day it is!" The corion rippled easily onto its haunches and flexed its crumpled green wings. "I can never decide whether I like better the days of buds and smells or the time of the seed-fires. Are you going to council today?"

"I am."

"I feel sorry for you. It is much too lovely a morning to do any thinking. I myself have just returned from Yantar, where I visited the high thorn groves. They are in bloom, and the hills are covered in white. Very pretty. The Gate was busy. Many people are coming to Danar to see the haeli trees in bud." The corion suddenly cocked a knowing eye at Danarion, and the feathers on its head flared out. "You were away for a long time last autumn, and Janthis too. Can it be that there is a new world in the making?"

Danarion shook his head, sadness once more filling him, his throat swelling with remorse. He answered as steadily as he could. "Unfortunately there is no new world about to burst forth in the All, Storn. Janthis and I were on Fallan."

"Oh," said Storn with disappointment. "Then I have no further interest in the matter." The beast stifled another yawn. "No doubt Fallan is wondrous to the people who inhabit it, but I am content with Danar. What do you have in your hand?"

Danarion rebuked Storn gently. "It is business for the council," he said in a tone that clearly forbade another question.

"Ah," Storn remarked. "I only mentioned it because it smells . . ." The feathers flattened and rose again and the tail curled tighter as the creature tried to select the right word to describe what its nostrils told it about the thing Danarion held so tightly.

"It smells . . . foreign."

"It is indeed foreign," Danarion finished, bowing once again. "I apologize for disturbing your rest, Storn. My house is open to you always."

The corion watched him go for a moment, but once more the warmth of the sun and the thick fragrance of the haeli buds insinuated themselves behind its eyes, and it closed them, slipping into the long grass and its dreams simultaneously. The next traveler along the path had to detour in under the trees, for Storn would move for no one else that day.

Danarion climbed the steep streets of the city, answering all greetings with a word and a smile, but he did not stop to finger cloth or run his eye over the jewelers' wares as he usually did. He moved briskly between the lofty wooden buildings, their carved walls glowing soft blue in the sun, the veins and knots sparking gold. He glanced neither to right nor left at the doorways that invited passersby into courtyards full of fruit trees and children running in the shade or murmurous with the splash and tinkle of fountains. He stopped once to let a cart laden with fat purple vegetables go by. It was drawn by four youths clad in the short blue tunics of summer who saluted him, laughing, as they went. A young corion rode atop the load, its tail resting against its paws, the intermingling gold fur and green feathers gleaming, and it inclined its head to him gravely. He walked on, crossed a square drowned in sleepy sunlight and empty of people, stepped quietly by a group of two men and a woman sitting on the ground, their eyes tightly closed, their fingertips meeting together, and came at last to the belt of trees that separated the mortal people from the domain of the sun-lords.

He entered the Time-forest's golden shade where nothing lived but the trees themselves, feeling time swirl for a moment around him like a gust of wind, the swift passage of mortal time tugging at his heels and the majestic, slow movement of his own powerful time surging to meet him. The wood was not forbidden to mortals, nor the mighty crenellated towers of the city within a city that rose beyond it, but few mortals chose to take this route to the Gate. It was too silent, too fraught with an unfamiliar mystery that spoke to them of things they were not created to understand.

Now he could see the foot of the stair between the bluish trunks and fluttering leaves, and his eye traveled upward. Tower piled on tower, walls enfolding walls, wings flung out to more towers and more walls, the palace on Danar was a city carved out of gray stone, designed in the beginning to be the hub of the universe. Shol sat in the center, but Danar had been the council's meeting place since the Worldmaker had spoken Danarion and his sun into life.

Danarion began to climb the stairs leading up to Danar's Gate, five hundred here, five hundred on the other side of the palace, one step for each sun-lord in the universe, a name carved deep into each step. Once these stairs had never been free of the weight of immortal feet, and when night fell, the sun-people passing up and down them had lit the darkness with a vision of stars that had fallen to earth. Now those brilliant beings were only names stamped into rock. Only five remained. The rest served black fire behind closed Gates, or had fought until their suns exploded, or had vanished in the place of the Messengers. Those names glided under Danarion's feet, each conjuring a face, a world, something unique that would never be replaced, time that had passed and could not be wound back. Mallan, Kallar, Firor, Nagerix, Sigrandor, Falia . . .

Danarion came to the first break in the stair. Here two corions

sat on watch, one at either side of the silver-patterned stone, their
eyes sternly facing out over the treetops, their mouths firmly shut,
their crests rising, their wings unfurled. If it had not been for the
gentle rise and fall of their chests, they might have been taken for
stone themselves. Danarion did not disturb their vigilance. He went
on climbing and at last reached the terrace, also guarded by a row
of corions. He went straight in under the arch, through the empty
entrance hall beyond which threw back to him his mournful tread,
across a courtyard, up steps, and along a passage whose gilt-traced
walls and floor tiled in crystal spoke of solemnity and power. A
thousand sun-people had strolled laughing through the palace's high
passages, filling its echoing stone vastness with vitality and light,
bright jewels and drifting hair, a kaleidoscope of beauty and color
flowing in and out of the halls and under the banner-hung arches.
In the center was the enormous, clerestoried copper dome to which,
in the end, each passage led. Under its ceiling the black marble
table stretched, bounded by a thousand stone chairs. On a dais at
the head was the raised seat that would never be filled again and
behind it, like a solid halo, a giant gold sun that measured the wall
in a great circular sweep. To right and left, at the base of the sun,
were doors. One led into Janthis's chamber. The other would never
open again. Danarion caught up with Sholia, and hearing him
come, she slowed and turned with a smile, the two discs hanging
from her necklet sparkling gaily.

'Danarion! I went down into the city this morning. It has grown
since I was last here, and the horses brought from Fallan all those
years ago have multiplied beyond all expectations. The foals are
being born with golden eyes, though, like your people. Have you
noticed?"

He laughed. "Of course I noticed. How are things on Shol?"

"Untouched," she replied simply, and they both sobered, pacing out of the passage and onto the gleaming black floor of the
council hall. The great circular room was empty. Sunlight lay in
long falls of gold poured through the clerestory windows ringing the
dome, was reflected back by the smooth, glassy surface of the floor,
and slid palely over the jeweled ceiling. Before them stretched the
stone table, the expectant, empty seats. They walked slowly behind
the rows. On the table, fronting each chair, were the necklets of

those who had fallen, casting their own reflections on the polished surface so that each one seemed sunk deep into the blackness. Danarion did not need to count them, for he had been present at the closing of all these Gates, as had Sholia. Though he sometimes stood in a trance in the halls and corridors of the palace, walking again on worlds that had long ago become inaccessible, forbidden to his body, he never relived their last days.

It took a long time to reach the head of the table, passing under shadow and out again, drawn into the aura of dominance that still surrounded the massive raised chair, but at last they reached their seats and settled themselves, looking back down the acres of shining black marble, the silent further caverns of the room. Sholia sighed, one hand on her throat, and sat still, her eyes closed, her golden hair resting softly around her. Danarion laid Falia's necklet on the table before him, glad to relinquish it, and waited. Presently Ixelion arrived, walking quickly. He did not greet them, and they did not look at him. He slid into his chair, put his elbows on the table, and slipped his pointed chin into his webbed hands. The great, empty chair enveloped them in its brooding atmosphere. More than once, out of his own longing, Danarion had thought that he caught a glimpse of a presence sitting there, the nebulous outlines of the form he loved, but if he turned his head, he saw nothing but dark stars and trees, faces and beasts, carved in mute profusion on the solid stone.

He knew that he should discipline his mind in that moment, throw off the heaviness of melancholy insinuating itself beneath his control, but he did not. He allowed himself to slip into the past, to a time of peace long gone, not reliving it as he was capable of doing, but hovering outside the scene, as the mortals did when they wanted to retrieve a memory. He was standing behind his own chair, looking at himself seated, talking to Sigrandor opposite him. Sigrandor's ruby eyes were glittering with mirth, and his red-gold flames fluttered and danced across the table like lively children. Chatter and laughter filled the dome. Tranin was leaning close to Falia, whose silver hair hid her silken green shoulders, and over them all Ghakazian circled, the beat of his brown wings fanning them, his necklet hanging, his naked limbs spread wide, unwilling to remain still. Janthis had his face turned to the being in the great chair, his sun-ball blazing in his hands. And in the great chair the Worldmaker sat, his arms folded, smiling as he surveyed the full table. I must look long, something whispered at the back of Danarion's mind. This is a memory, this is the last day he took his place with us, the last day a thousand sun-lords met together. Ah, so beautiful you are, so full of light and goodness! I will never love any as I worship you! His heart full, he saw the Worldmaker rise. Immediately all talking ceased, and Ghakazian glided down to stand at his place at the table.

"Well!" said the Worldmaker, and his voice quivered in their veins like wild music.

"Is it good, all that I have made? You, my first ones, are you satisfied?"

"It is good!" they called back to him.

"And are you content to know that you belong to me?"

Suddenly Danarion sensed something, a change in the gentle tones, subtle and minute. His heart bounded in his chest, but in those days he had had no words to describe the emotion now inching through him. He tore his gaze away from the Worldmaker and glanced at Janthis. The smile had left his face, and in his hands the sun-ball shrank to a red glow. Danarion looked back at the Worldmaker, who still smiled, but something had grown in his eyes, a coolness, a hint of mockery. Of course we belong to him, Danarion thought, puzzled. What does he mean? Then a desolation swept over him. He wanted to reach out his arms and wail, but he did not know why. The Worldmaker raised his arms, and it seemed to Danarion that the light that blazed from his fingers flickered with black tongues for a moment.

"You belong to me. You and your worlds are mine!" the Worldmaker said again, and Danarion realized that he was no longer speaking to them at all. Janthis had not moved. His eyes were on his sun-ball, where the light struggled to burst out. I do not understand, Danarion thought, love and bewilderment churning in him. I do not understand . . .

A door opened, and Janthis came to them, sun-ball in hand, gliding quickly over the floor. Danarion returned to his present with a jerk. I still do not understand, he thought. I wish that I had not allowed that memory. Sometimes I fancy that I am becoming resigned to the loss of him, but it is not true. I ache for him.

Janthis reached the foot of the Worldmaker's chair and sat

down, placing the dead sun-ball on the table before him, smiling at the three of them.

"Where is Ghakazian?" he asked.

"Up here!" Ghakazian's voice floated to them, and they looked up. He was perched on the sill of one of the windows high under the dome, and as they watched, he jumped lightly, spread his wings, and came to rest behind his chair. "I have been watching you all," he remarked. "Not a word said, and the silence and stillness so deep. If we must council, then let us do so quickly. Danar in the spring is a wonder none should miss."

"We are so few now," Sholia said quietly. "Only five of us left. We have not been watchful enough."

"He hates us more than he did the others," Janthis said abruptly. "We are the products of his first delight in making. Our devotion to him was absolute, and we knew him well. He has glutted himself quickly on the rest of the universe despite our efforts to impede him but has saved us until the last to be savored at leisure. Firor was less of a prize to him than Falia." He held out a hand, and Danarion lifted the necklet and gave it to him. For a moment he fondled it, sighing, then rose and, walking to Falia's empty seat, reached over and placed the necklet gently on the table. A long silence followed. Ghakazian moved his weight from one foot to the other impatiently.

"Falia should have chosen to go with the Messenger," he said. "Surely it is better to face a final judgment, take a last chance, than to be immured forever behind a closed Gate."

"Perhaps," Janthis answered. "Others have chosen that way. But great courage is needed to face the emissaries of the Law-maker."

"The Lawmaker!" Ghakazian scoffed. "I am beginning to wonder if he exists at all. None of us has ever seen him. We have only the Worldmaker's word that the Law has sentience and unlimited powers, and I for one am not prepared to take the Worldmaker's word on anything anymore."

"He told us so before his fall," Janthis reminded him, "and the first chapters of all the Annals were written in the dawning, when mortal life was still only in his mind. He made me first. I am the firstborn of all the sun-people, and I believe him when he spoke of the Law as personality."

"Then why does the Lawmaker not help us?" Ghakazian pressed. "Why doesn't he reverse his laws?"

"He cannot reverse a law without changing his own nature," Janthis answered patiently. "You know that, Ghakazian."

"What really happened between Lawmaker and Worldmaker, Janthis?" Sholia asked. "What was it that caused the Worldmaker to turn against us? How can a Maker cease to love what he has made?"

"He still loves us"—Janthis was smiling wryly—"but with the blind, selfish love that demands an eating up, a complete possession of the made. He knows that he was told to make, and that though he could love what he made, he could never own it, and it was this that festered in him. To make without ownership, to weave, blend, intricately create only for the Lawmaker drove him in the end to stand apart, to claim all the worlds of making as his property. He wishes to deform it all because no matter what he says or does, no matter what power he displays, it will never belong to him. He disfigures so that the inheritance of the Lawmaker may be worthless."

"And also because of the pain his love has brought to him," Danarion added quietly.

For a moment they all sat in silence; then Janthis straightened. He resumed his seat, and as always his hands went out to enfold his lifeless sun-ball.

"Once again we have had a loss," he went on. "What are we to do? It seems that each Gate-closing comes too late, but I am loath to order you and the other sun-people to close all your Gates. Such a brutal ending is not, I think, permitted, unless we are so hard pressed as to be faced with the final dissolution of the All as we knew it."

"He knows all our weaknesses," Danarion said. "Falia was kindly, and knew only good. How did she fall? What was it that crept through her Gate unchallenged? I do not see . . ."

With one accord they turned to look at Ixelion. He still sat with chin cupped in his hands, eyes fixed on the table, unseeing.

"Ixelion," Janthis prodded him gently. "What did Falia say to you? Did you bring the records?"

Ixelion blinked, then sat back heavily and brought up from his lap the haeli wood box. His hands shook as he laid it before Janthis, and Danarion gave him a sharp glance. Something was worrying Ixelion.

"They are here," Ixelion said. "I have read them. It seems that a Trader brought something precious to Falia to give to the council, but instead of bringing it to Danar, she kept it for herself. So she fell."

"What precious thing?" Sholia asked loudly. "Did she tell you what it was?"

Ixelion shook his head. "No. I do not know what it was." And that is the truth, he thought. I lifted it out of the wooden box, and it was a plain iron casket, small and without adornment. I did not open it. I put it into my chest, and there it lies.

Sholia appealed to Janthis. "What could it be? What treasure is there that can bring destruction to a world such as Fallan?"

She fears, Ghakazian thought, leaving his place and walking up to where Janthis sat. Always she fears and watches. As he passed behind her his hand rested on her head and then stroked her hair gently.

"The seeds of corruption may enter a world and yet lie barren forever," Janthis said. "Nothing is evil of itself. But these seeds can take root and grow in soil too simple and ignorant to recognize them for what they are. The Gates were not made to keep out evil, for in that time evil had not come into the All. It was the unthinkable, the totally unknowable." He opened the box and took out the Annals of Fallan. "I will study what Falia has written, but if you, Ixelion, have read the records and yet have no answer, then I doubt if I will divine anything either."

"Where is this treasure now?" Danarion asked. "Did it remain in Fallan, Ixelion? What did Falia do with it?"

They swung intent, earnest eyes upon Ixelion, for this was a new threat, a subtle thing not encountered by any of them, a new ploy of the Unmaker's. Ixelion looked from one to the other, his hands rising to clench his sun-disc. Help me, he begged silently, help me, but he felt as though a strange wall had risen between him and his kin. Now was the time to tell all, to put words against that wall and be whole and at one with them again, but his pale face became even whiter and his eyes clouded. I have done nothing yet, part of him insisted. I will tell them, and Janthis will come with me to Ixel and take the thing away, and I will be saved. But he also felt the greed, coiling inside him like mist off his ocean, the need to know, to feel, to see. Danarion watched him carefully, unable to decide whether Ixelion mourned for Falia or was distressed by something else. The hands with the sheen of pearls trembled on the thin breast. Then Ixelion swallowed and answered.

"I do not know where this treasure is," he whispered. "I believe it to be still on Fallan."

Immediately he changed. He felt it deep inside him, the first true change that had ever occurred to him, and he looked at his fellows and saw them in a way he had never seen them before. The first lie, he thought to himself, sick with self-loathing. Take it back! Take it away! I do not want this change! What have I done?

Peace, Ixelion, another voice inside him soothed. The treasure is safe on Ixel. You need never look at it, just leave it in your chest. Have you not saved the council from evil? What if Janthis had taken it from your hands this day, and opened it? Then only darkness would lie ahead, forever. You are strong, stronger perhaps than Janthis, who does not have the responsibility of a world laid on his shoulders. Be at peace.

Yes, he agreed fervently with himself. Yes. Such a little lie, and so necessary. He released his sun-disc and sat straighter.

"She did not tell you?" Ghakazian exclaimed incredulously. "You, Ixelion?"

"That is not good," Janthis said heavily. "I wish that you had pressed her for its whereabouts, Ixelion, for now we must go forward not knowing whether it has been rendered harmless on Fallan or is already at work somewhere else." His black eyes slid across Ixelion's face, a musing glance, but he did not see the torment. His thoughts raced over the news Ixelion had brought. Finally he sighed, his fingers stroking his sun-ball. "Perhaps Falia, in her greed for this thing, would have hidden it from you in any case," he concluded. "It is beyond our power now to find it, so we must hope that it rests on Fallan."

Ixelion was moving, distressed, swaying back and forth on his seat, his hands combing his long green hair. Danarion still watched him, anxiety dim within him.

"Is there something left to say, Ixelion?" he asked gently, and

Ixelion abruptly stopped his movements, willing his body to be still. Everything inside him quivered, poised for violent action, demanding that he rise, run from the hall, go anywhere, but escape from Danarion's quizzical eyes and the presence of the others which had become suddenly an overwhelming unease containing him when he wanted to leap free. He put his hands one over the other, on top of the table, and lowered his gaze to them.

"No," he replied sharply. "I did not dare to question Falia about the precious thing. At the mention of it a dread fell on me and I doubted my strength." Only part of a lie this time, he thought to himself, and so much easier to push up my throat and over my tongue. You will live to thank me, all of you, for keeping the thing from your eyes and minds. Danarion looked at the lowered head for a moment longer, then sat back mystified.

Suddenly Sholia spoke. "Could the treasure be . . . be him? The Unmaker himself? Could this be a way for him to enter the worlds?"

Her question stunned them. They looked from one to the other, and all at once fear sat at the table with them, a black fog that curled silently from the shadows of the room and flowed between them, waiting for them to take it into their nostrils, their mouths. Even here we are no longer completely safe, Janthis thought. A word, a gesture can invite an attempt, no matter how subtle, on our invulnerability. Here in this hallowed place we know that we are safe, yet no longer feel so. He looked steadily into Sholia's face. "No," he said. "No matter how vast his deviousness, he can no longer himself pass through the Gate of any world in any form unless we knowingly or unwillingly invite him. He cannot face an unfallen world directly, for it would cause him too much pain. He cannot twist and murder us unless we will it, unless we allow his power to influence us. You spend too much time brooding on the meaning of fear," he ended kindly. "Fill yourself with the ecstasy of the dawning of time, not the setting." She accepted the discipline without smiling, her face white, knowing that if she had not voiced the doubt, it would be borne by all of them.

"Why can we not do battle against him?" Ghakazian demanded, his brown eyes fired, and Danarion slapped a hand on the table.

"What weapons will you use?" he snapped loudly. "The power of your sun? It would take every ounce of your sun's strength simply to drive the Unmaker from your Gate, Ghakazian, and your worlds would be left in darkness. You and your sun would die. Or would you somehow arm your people with spells and words of casting away? Your innocent people, who have never heard a lie, who do not know the meaning of the word *murder*? Can you not see their bewilderment? 'Why must we try to harm our Maker?' they will ask you, and will you explain it all to them? If you do, you will have already opened your Gate to him. Such knowledge given to the mortals of your systems"—here he swiftly scanned them all—"would mean an immediate and irrevocable fall. Their strength is in their ignorance. You do not help by entertaining thoughts of battle. We are the Worldmaker's creatures, the products of a mind of unimaginable wisdom and ingenuity, and even the frail defenses we could use against him were made by him."

"We are not his playthings!" Ghakazian roared back, his wings suddenly unfurling like a dark cloud above and around him. "The Lawmaker ordered him to make with wholeness, make with beauty! The Lawmaker commanded him! We are flawless. We will fight him with truth, with wholeness and goodness!"

Danarion had risen, his hands flat on the sun-disc flaming on his breast, his golden eyes large with the intensity of his words. "Truth has no arms!" he shouted. "Think, Ghakazian! Beauty cannot fight! The things that we are, that our mortals are, can only be a wall, a defense against what he is. To take up his weapons is to put on his evil!"

"Stop!" Sholia cried out, her eyes squeezed shut, her hands pressed over her ears. "Oh, stop! I cannot fight. I do not want to fight! I only want to see all as it was. I want him seated with us in his chair, I want Falia back, and Firor. I want the past to be the present once again!"

Danarion heavily resumed his seat. Ixelion had buried his face in his hands. Ghakazian folded his wings and his arms, muttering to himself. "The Lawmaker has forbidden the closing of any Gate unless those within it have become a danger to the rest," Janthis said emphatically, rising. "He has chosen not to unmake the Worldmaker, and if you think about it, you will see that had he done so, he would have become like the Unmaker, but infinitely more terrible. He has not forgotten us, but his time is not our time, just as our time is not the mortal's time. This council is over. Go home, all of you. I will summon you when I need you." Quickly he turned, climbed the three steps leading up to the dais, and disappeared behind his door. Ixelion stood up immediately, his limbs clumsy, his head averted, and fled the chamber. Sholia reached up a hand to Ghakazian.

"Come with me to Shol for a little while," she begged him softly. "We will walk on the docks and watch the ships unload their cargoes."

He nodded briefly, and arm in arm they traversed the black, smooth floor, their feet covering stars, their shadows drowning the worlds sunk deep beneath the surface. Only five systems lit their way, glowing in a soft, muted pattern of steady light. The rest of the floor was in darkness.

Danarion remained for a while, leaning back in his chair, watching the beams of Danar's sun turn from white to pale pink as the sun crept along the table toward its setting. Birds flew in and out the clerestory windows high above. The enormous sun hanging on the wall to his right, beyond the Worldmaker's chair and the dais, gradually gathered the gloom to itself, fading from bright gold to a sullen, dark copper. Impatiently, almost angrily, he turned to it and spoke a word, and the surface burst into life, flooding the upper end of the hall with brilliant rays of light. Ixelion, he thought. Ixelion. I do not really know. I do not have the Unmaker's cynical ease of divination, I cannot feel for the seeds of something I have only seen at its blind conclusion. He wanted to talk to Janthis, but the door was tightly closed, and no sound came from within the small room. He did not dare to knock. What if a Messenger were there? He got up and left the hall, brow furrowed, and when he found himself outside the palace, on the wide terrace where his sun had laid its myriad scarlet fingers, he paused. "May I sit here on the step, beside you?" he enquired politely of one of the long row of corions fronting each pillar, and when the beast inclined its head, not looking at him, he sank down beside it, his gaze traveling the tops of the haeli trees beyond, the gold of their leaves now slashed with red. Deliberately and consciously he repeated to himself the bounds of his responsibilities, savoring the comfort and gladness of each word, and when they had all been laid out in his mind, coherent and sane, and the image of Ixelion's face had faded, he closed his eyes and withdrew into the welcoming heart of his sun, resting without anxiety, wrapped in its warmth and its uncomplaining obedience.

# 3

Ixelion ran out of the hall along the lofty passages that wound unhurriedly toward the terrace, burst out between the pillars and the unmoving corions, and bounded down the steps. When he reached the stone plateau that broke the long flight of stairs, he veered left, slowing to cross the wide stone causeway that arched from the steps, over the gardens below, and brought him to the far end of the terrace. Here a stone door twice his height stood open, sunset reaching into the shadow beyond. Two fantastically elongated corions reared their wings at each side of the door, their slim muscles carved in the stone, their outlines limned in gold, while a stone sun rayed out above. Ixelion plunged into the corridor. I must get away, he thought. I must go home, I must guard what I have in my chest, beside my pool. What if Sillix entered my room while I was absent, and found it? The thought, irrational and impossible, drew a muffled cry from him. He forced himself to walk now, for people passed him, bowing, the citizens of Danar on their way home from Yantar or Brintar. They greeted him respectfully, and with a supreme effort he answered their words and smiles.

A Trader came toward him, the light, transparent body allowing him a milky glimpse of distorted torchlight and undulating fretwork on the tunnel wall before he shied away. The Trader raised his eyebrows and smiled. On his back he carried a bundle and around his hairless head wound a scarf of many colors. Ixelion kept his eyes averted, his hand brushing the tumultuous carvings that blanketed the passage. Reliefs of mortals from Danar and Shol, winged lords from Ghaka, his own round-eyed, graceful fish-people crowded the walls, mingled on the ceiling, reached out to one another and the great suns scattered between their hands. The riders from Fallan also stalked there, frozen in stone, but now their hands seemed to convey a terrible longing, and their eyes and fixed smiles told of the things that were lost to them and would never come again.

Now the Gate was visible, two corions facing each other across its width, and through it Ixelion could see the darkness frosted by cold starlight, as though he stood on Lix and saw the ice and crystals rearing glittering and exotically beautiful against deep space. He crossed the threshold, and the corions did not move. For one moment he paused, looking over the whole vast sweep of the All, the rock of Danar beneath his feet; then he leaped outward, calling to his sun. Bear me, carry me, bring me! he mouthed. I am wounded, I want to come home. He felt its response, a gentle, enquiring tug which became a grasp that tightened, a fierce clutch of protection that gathered him ever faster into its blazing light. For one moment he saw it, a conflagration, a rolling ball of searing whiteness. He thought that he flung out his arms to it and shouted, but in the weird, timeless confines of the invisible corridor he knew that he had no arms, no mouth, no body. I hurt! he told it. Heal me! But he knew also that healing was not in the suns, as it was not in him.

Then he came to rest before his Gate. With a regret that he had never known he thought of the mists of Ixel, which shrouded his sun and kept its full glory veiled from him. He stepped under the arch, and the murmur of the water rose to enfold him again.

At the mouth of the tunnel Sillix was waiting for him, sitting in the river where it poured in a smooth gush over the stone lip. Rain pattered on his head and dripped from his shoulders. When he saw Ixelion emerge, he rose, scattering droplets like sprayed flowers, shaking back his hair. Ixelion barely noticed him, and Sillix padded quickly to take his arm.

"Sun-lord," he said breathlessly. "Oh, thanks be to the World-maker! I have been waiting here at the Gate for two long months."

Ixelion stopped and turned, fighting irritability. "What is it, Sillix? I am in haste, I must go at once to my halls. Have you been there in my absence?" he finished roughly and Sillix drew back a little, astonished.

"No, lord, of course not! You know that I cannot enter when you are away at council."

"Well, what is it, then?"

Sillix's webbed fingers touched his arm again, a brush of reassurance, a tentative, soft caress. "The fish are not right, Ixelion. I cannot say exactly what I mean, but they are washed up on the sands and do not move. We cannot eat them. They do not taste right."

Ixelion felt as though a cool, foreign hand had curved itself around his heart. Swiftly he scanned the divided, meandering river, the fog-clothed, flower-heavy forest, the tips of his towers, and the odd dull glint of diffused light on the half-hidden houses of the people. His eyes encountered nothing strange, nothing new. But he was conscious of change as his glance returned to Sillix's trusting, relieved face. It was in the air, in the water, dissolving with the mist, unfolding with the colorless, complex blooms, a dullness, a tinge of weariness. It was within himself. Terror filled him, became one with the change, became another new emotion, despair. He did not as yet savor it slowly, in self-pity. He stalked warily around it in his mind, suspicious, afraid, winds of past and future tugging drearily at him. I have done nothing! he protested silently. I have protected the council, I have saved Janthis and the others from the danger of destruction! I, Ixelion, have done this great, this noble thing!

Suddenly he became aware that he was glaring deep into Sillix's eyes. "Very well," he said with effort. "I will come and see the fish. They are sick, Sillix."

"Sick, sun-lord?"

Ixelion tore his gaze from the uncomprehending, dumb beauty of Sillix's rain-drenched face. "Show me," he ordered, and followed Sillix toward the forest and the ocean beyond.

The fish were lying on the broad sweep of the beach, cast up by the tide among the untidy streamers of dark seaweed. There were not many, a scattering of still, glinting shapes, but Ixelion could smell them long before he bent, and out where the ocean rocked toward the sand he saw more of them floating quietly, unresisting, waiting to be thrown up in their turn. Sillix stood by as Ixelion lifted one of them. The pale eye flicked once, the fish flapped in his hand and then lay motionless, dying. Ixelion placed it gently back on the sand and straightened.

"What of the rivers?" he asked brusquely.

Sillix stepped to him, and Ixelion again felt his need to touch, to be comforted. "The fish of the rivers are as they were, also the fish out in the depths where my son dives. It is only these, close in to the shore. The small ones. What shall we do?"

"Bury them in the sand, and keep burying until no more are left by the tide. It is nothing, Sillix, a moment of imbalance, that is all. Have you eaten any?"

"We tried, but they tasted sour. Is the seaweed good?"

Suddenly Ixelion was overwhelmed by an urge to shout into the innocent face, to see shock in the bland, trusting eyes, but he struggled with his panic, his teeth clenched, his eyes on the fish at his feet.

"Yes, the seaweed is good," he answered. "Do what I tell you now, and don't eat any more of them. I must go."

Sillix reached out for the sun-disc lying on Ixelion's breast, but Ixelion had already swung away. Sillix's webbed hand dropped to his side, and he watched Ixelion disappear under the forest's dripping eaves, dragging yellow shreds of sunlight behind him.

The water flowing out the doors of the palace was silky-cold and dark, and the hall was filled with green gloom. Ixelion stood on the threshold and shivered, listening to the voice of Ixel as he had never listened before. Even the fogs murmur, he said to himself. The flowers creak open, displaying their limp, pallid petals. The trees and vines suck at the sloppy soil with wet, greedy words. My hair squeaks under my hands, damp, limp, cold. As he stood there a picture came into his mind. He saw Sholia walking along the wide paved road that ran down through her city's tall buildings to the harbor, her escort fell in behind and before her, carrying flags embroidered with Shol's two suns, the gold thread and blue background shining as the wind pulled them taut. Her people came running, and they bowed before her, worshiping. She waved, pacing lightly and slowly down to where her ocean sparkled, sapphire and white. Sapphire and white, Ixelion thought, coming to himself. Her people honor her, pile gifts before her, fete her in great ceremonies, yet she is no more powerful than I, her brother. The water swirling about his ankles suddenly filled him with distaste, and he strode forward shouting, "Light! Give me light and warmth!" Immediately the sun responded. He ran quickly through the hall, along his passages, up his stairs, until he found himself beside the deep pool high above Ixel. Out beyond the rim of the huge window his world lay clasped in an embrace of rain and dimness. Is it still there? he asked himself breathlessly. Is it still safe? Walking softly, as though not to disturb something dreadful and unnamed, he went to his chest and, dropping on one knee, raised the lid. It was still there, resting innocently in shadow, a small gray metal box with a hinged, rimless lid. For a long time he gazed at it, many thoughts flitting through his mind, behind them all a growing desire to hold it, cradle it, that same desire that had flared new and hot when Falia spoke of it. A treasure of death. Did the secret of death, then, lie under his gaze?

Finally he lifted a hand, and the lid of the chest banged shut. Sighing, he rose and stepped into his pool. The water closed over his head like a waiting caress. He sank to the bottom and lay on his back, his breath stilled, his eyes open, his hands moving with the minute swells caused by the river that fell down the wall and splashed into the pool. He did not direct his mind, did not know what thoughts to command. He saw Sillix, and the dying fish. He saw Danarion's face, watching him at the council table. He saw himself, walking up the steps of Falia's palace, whole and free, unfettered by despair, greed, or anger, and he saw himself walking down again, Falia behind him, his mind already sown with the Unmaker's will. Then, all at once, he was on Shol, standing at the foot of the mountains, green fields stretching away before him, rippling in wind and sunlight. His hair was warm and flowing free, his feet were sunk in warm earth. He smelled the dryness, the heat, the strong twin suns pouring over him undiluted. "Oh," he breathed, lifting face and arms to the burning blue sky. "Oh, what delight, what unutterable pleasure." Blue and white, not gray, not gray . . . Ixel was a wet, cold dream, dissolving in his mind like its own mists. Sholia should share this world with me. She has two suns, after all. I do not belong on Ixel, a poor world where my sun and I can never meet face to face.

Light as a bubble, he drew his feet out of the soil's grip and glided forward, scented wind filling him with intoxication, sun glittering in his pale eyes. He floated over the fields toward the lip of the cliff he somehow knew was there, and suddenly the ocean was below him, a rich carpet of blue and green, whitecaps dazzling to his unaccustomed gaze. A ship was passing the headland, whitewash gleaming as its prow split the water, its golden sails billowing. Singing rose to him faintly, calling up a vast longing within him, an unformed sadness. Just as he was poised to drift down closer to the ship, he found himself looking up through cool greenness, surrounded by the quiet words of the water in his pool.

He rose in one clumsy, anguished movement, jealousy curdling inside him, his nostrils still quivering with Shol's sweet, hot air. I did not command that vision, he thought, standing trembling on the edge of the pool. Where did it come from? But he knew, he knew.

"Enough!" he called aloud. "I will take the treasure to Danar, and so be myself once more. Then the fish will not die, and change will once more wheel about me, not inside me." He stumbled to the chest, wrenched it open, and lifted out the casket with fingers that shook. It weighed heavy in his hands, heavier than it ever had before, the steady sunlight in the room making no gleam on its dull surface, and it seemed to Ixelion that he held in his grasp something entirely Other, something outside and beyond the universe. It was aloof, lying there quietly waiting for him to make his choice.

But if I take it now, he thought, then I will never know what it is. May I not just look at it, just once? No! something in him shrieked, wild with fear. No, no! But other voices clamored, voices of envy and lust. They hold you light, Ixelion, the rest of them. You are the sun-lord of a worthless world full of simple people, far from the wonders of Danar, the riches of Shol. What is the crystal of Lix compared to the fragrant woods of Danar, the breathtaking stones and metals of Shol? You are worthless to all but your simpering, stupid people, who worship you because they know no better. Do you not deserve a little dignity? A brighter sun? A drier world? Does Janthis give your words as grave a consideration as Ghakazian's? He writhed in the grip of the words that came whispering, pouring into his mind, trying to catch the screaming denial behind them all and hold on to it, and so gain the strength to say with his mouth what he knew he should say, but all he could see was the vision of Sholia, encompassed by all the pomp of Shol, and himself gliding over verdure in full, hot light.

Staggering, head down, he went to the window and collapsed onto the sill, the casket tight in his grip. Raising his head, he looked out. Evening was falling. It seemed to him as though evening was always falling on Ixel, the sun always divorced from the earth, the rain always pattering, the mists always hanging in the trees, the rooms of his palace, his hair; he even fancied that it seeped into his body, making it thick and cold.

He tried once more to save himself. I was made for this world, he said to himself. My body is thin and supple as a fish. My feet and hands cleave the water as cleanly as those of my people. My lungs recognize both air and water. I *am* Ixel, its soul, its life. I was fashioned out of the water and the soil. Yet your blood is the royal blood of the sun, the insidious voice whispered back, and though the earth of Ixel is your mother and the Worldmaker your father, the sun is your other self. You long for it, you desire its heat, you thirst for dry land beneath your feet. "Yes," Ixelion whispered back. "Now I do. Once I was content, but no longer. Why should I, out of all my kin, be so deprived?"

He shut his eyes, and his hand moved to grasp the lid, lifted it, laid it back gently. Blindly he explored the thing that lay exposed in the casket. He felt a coolness and indentations of many shapes. He did not know what he had expected. A circlet of power, perhaps, or a vial full of some strange, magical elixir. Something potent that would burn his hand or explode knowledge in his face. But not this puzzling labyrinth of tiny hills and valleys. With a last shudder he opened his eyes and looked down.

At first he could not understand what he was seeing, it was so simple, so ordinary, and he let out his breath in relief, feeling an urge to laugh. Falia, for some reason of her own, had tricked him, lied to him yet again. Then, like a wave of fresh terror, the indentations suddenly came together to form a pattern. Dread shivered over him, prickling in his hair, drying his mouth, and he slammed the lid shut and rose. Throwing back his head, he screamed and screamed again, the sound echoing out to fill his chambers with agony. The sun dimmed and struggled to rekindle, but Ixelion did not notice. He pounded his fist on the closed lid, crying. "Not this!" he wept. "No! No! Ah, not this!" The words came back to him softly, sibilantly, mingled with the fountains, slid down the walls and curved with the water that fell between the balustrades to flow over the floor of the hall and out into the river.

He stumbled to his feet and ran, the casket held out before him in both hands. Down to his hall, out the vaulting door, into the darkness, still weeping. Straight to the Gate he sped, slipping on wet undergrowth, pushing aside the flower-ridden tree branches with his slim shoulders, splashing up the river to where it became imprisoned in the torchlit tunnel that led to the Gate. The guards saw him come and stood upright, the light flooding from him catching fire on their capes of scale, and he went by them like a wind, eyes wide with panic. Then, on the rocky lip of Ixel, out beyond the Gate, teetering on the edge of the universe, he stopped. If I take it to Danar, it will torment Janthis until he is impelled to open it, and then the Gate on Danar will have to be closed and the halls of the sun-lords will be inaccessible to the rest of us forever, he thought. The risk is too great. I will keep it here on poor, wet Ixel, least of the Unmaker's concerns, where his malevolent eye seldom turns. All at once Ixelion's feverish horror left him, and he felt as though a weight had rolled from his back to go tumbling out into space. His spine straightened. Slowly he turned back through his Gate and walked home smiling in relief, the treasure tucked under one arm. He was not aware that his world had grown darker, a steady dark like a soft twilight.

As soon as he stepped under the portals of his doors, he knew that he was not alone. He stopped dead, fingers tightening around the treasure, eyes darting about the hall, but the water poured on gently, the mist hung very still high above. Was Sillix above in the high chamber, with more calamitous news? Angrily Ixelion waded through the hall and up the broad, water-filled ways to his topmost room, wanting only to deal with Sillix and his whines so he could be alone. He was so preoccupied with the certainty that Sillix stood beside his pool, that meek smile on his face, that he strode under the dripping stone without caution. Then he came to an abrupt halt.

A man stood beside his pool. No, it was not a man but a Trader. Ixelion could see the outline of the window and the drizzle-drowned forest roof blurring through the semitransparent body, the long arms and legs. Around the opalescent head went a voluminous scarf, the mark of a Trader, and with a queer convulsion of his heart Ixelion saw that it was black, the ends slashed in brilliant orange. He could not move. He felt as though he had suddenly become one with the water that swirled and trickled around them both; he was melting, oozing into the endless, restless flow.

"Who are you?" he croaked. "How did you get in here? My halls are sealed."

The Trader inclined his head, and the lipless mouth smiled briefly. "I greet you, Ixelion, sun-lord. As you can see, I am but a Trader, and in answer to your second question, which you ought to be able to answer for yourself, I am not hindered by any seal. I am not mortal and I am not immortal."

"Well, what do you want?" Ixelion rejoined sharply, the awful cloud of fear lifting a little. "If you seek crystal to take to other worlds, you must see the miners on Lix."

The Trader's smile grew broader. "I do not seek goods for trade, sun-lord. I have come for something that does not belong to you, that is forbidden to all those of the suns. I gave it to Falia to take to the council, but she did not take it to Danar, did she, Ixelion? She gave it to you, wicked Falia. Now I will take it to Janthis myself."

Ixelion drew in a deep, shaking breath, his mind racing, the treasure in his grasp suddenly heavy and bitter cold, as it had been once before this day. He did not speak; he could not. But she slew you, he thought. She killed, she destroyed you. The Trader from Tran.

"Come," the Trader said more briskly, his strange, slitted eyes glittering. "Give it to me and I will be on my way. I serve neither black fire nor the council. I serve only the Law, and the Law states that what you have in your hands is forbidden to you until the end of the ages."

Ixelion swallowed, his fingers tightening about the casket protectively. "Tran," he whispered. The Trader nodded, smiling again, and rounded the pool to stand close to Ixelion, his body shimmering like a waterfall. "I carried it from the ruin of Tran," he said. "I was in haste and did not know whether the Unmaker had knowledge of the thing I found in the smoke and fire. I took it to Falia, believing that in her hands it would be safe, for Fallan's Gate was still open. I did not relish being consumed by black fire." His smile split his face, and Ixelion suddenly hated that smile. "I was consumed by white fire instead"—he chuckled—"but I am many, Ixelion. I am like the Messengers, not understood by the worlds, a creature of deep space, tolerated because of the work I do, but I am less respected than the Messengers. And rightly so. I do not die easily, even as the sun-lords do not, for I can make my body thin, so thin that fire passes through me, or thick as a tree to withstand time. I died on Fallan," he sneered. "Oh, yes. I am not as strong as a sun-lord, or as powerful, but I have many lives. Enough talk. Give me the precious thing, and I will be gone."

Coldness crept into Ixelion's mind, and he knew at once that never, never would he give up the thing. The time of excuses, arguments, lies to himself was over. He wanted it, and he would keep it on Ixel, no matter what.

"I do not believe that you will take it to the council," he said. "How do I know that you are not from the Unmaker, and he will take it for himself?"

The Trader shrugged. "Even if I were to give it to him, what of it? It is not forbidden to him. He has a right to it, just as he has a right to you and every other sun-lord. Every created thing. All of us, his."

"No. We belong to the Lawmaker."

"Pah!" The Trader's smile had gone, and peevishness marred his face. "Where is he, then, in all your distress? He is a myth, nothing more. Has it ever occurred to you, sun-lord," he sneered, "that for a thousand thousand ages Janthis may have been lying to you? That the Worldmaker has never ceased to be what he was, and it was really Janthis who changed and hid his change from you? Why do you follow him like an adoring mortal, eh? He lies to you all, he manipulates you to his own ends. How can the Worldmaker, more powerful than all of you, be changed, without yourselves changing in turn? Faugh! You sun-lords with your arrogance and your petty little games of sun power. You make me disgusted."

Ixelion tried to battle the doubt seeping into his mind at every word the Trader said, but he knew his weakness, and every word spat at him found an answering chord in him. It really is too late, he thought in anguish, looking into the twisted face before him. I can never go back, for to go back implies that I am not as I once was. My wholeness has therefore become hollow like a shell. I know now what I have done. Be silent, you tool of black fire. You have done your work. Even without you, I was condemned by my own hand.

"Let me tell you something, Ixelion," the Trader went on softly.

"I did not come here for the treasure. I knew before I passed your Gate that you would refuse to give it to me. I serve the Law, as I told you before. It is dear to me as nothing else is dear. Listen to me. The treasure will tell you what you should do, and it can help you if you will let it. It is forbidden to you, but why? Because the one who possesses it possesses more power than any other. What I say is true. Falia opened and saw and knew, but Falia did not have the courage to use it, so it destroyed Fallan. *You* have the strength. *You* can use it to outwit the Unmaker. The Law is above dark and light, and so must you be if you want to save the universe. Defeat the Unmaker with it, Ixelion. Restore the balance of the Law!"

The Law is not above dark and light, Ixelion thought, forcing his mind to reject the Trader's smooth argument, though the effort was like pushing his way through mud. The Law divides dark from light. The Worldmaker placed himself outside the light, and thus outside the Law. "Surely the treasure can tell me what I will do, not what I should do," he managed huskily. His head swam, and the Trader nodded mockingly.

"Time divides here, now, in this room," he said. "You must choose the path of the future. Destruction, Ixelion, or the help of your treasure?"

"I will take it to Janthis," Ixelion replied stubbornly, faintly, and the Trader laughed.

"Do you trust him that much? Or yourself? Give it to me, and I will deliver it. To Ghakazian, perhaps, or the beautiful Sholia. She, indeed, has the power to use it."

Ixelion was galvanized. He leaped back. "Go away!" he snarled. "Ghakazian, Sholia, we are all equal."

"Oh? Really?" And the Trader was gone, walking on the surface of the water, out of the room, out of Ixel, laughing. "Hurry, Ixelion," his voice floated back. "The ocean is beginning to die."

Heart pounding, Ixelion walked unsteadily into the room, where his chair invited him to slump onto it. Very well, he thought. Very well. I think I knew that it would come to this, from the time Falia thrust the haeli wood box into my innocent hands. Mine. Not Ghakazian's, or Sholia's. It came to *me*. Jealousy needled him, a stab of sudden hate in his mind. I will open it and I will learn, and then I will fight.

He swung back the metal lid of the casket and lifted out what lay within. It was a book, its covers hard and smooth except for where its title had been impressed into the ivory-colored substance, horn or bone, Ixelion surmised, or some matter created by the Worldmaker especially to confine such a precious thing. He looked down at the curling silver letters sunk deep into the cover, written in the common tongue, and only the tips of his fingers tingled. He was calm and cold. *The Book of What Will Be in the All,* he read. That was all, and that was enough. The Book that had been forbidden to them from the beginning, whose whereabouts none knew or cared to know. But now . . . Was it really found on Tran? Ixel wondered reverently, stroking it. Was it cast up from the bowels of the earth when the volcanoes vomited fire and the rocks split open to swallow Tranin and his sun? Or did the Unmaker give it to the Trader in order to bring chaos upon us all? It did not matter. It was here, under his loving, questing hands, it was indestructible, it was his very own. Now he would know what was to come, and that power would be his forever. He opened the Book. The pages were white and thin as silk, the words tiny and silver, and at once his own name leaped out at him two, three, four times. Eagerly he began to read.

He read through many days and nights of Ixel time, moving only to turn the whispering, feather-light pages, oblivious to the slow passing of his own time or the rush of weeks outside, where Sillix and the people crouched in the sand and no longer buried any fish, for the few had become mounds, walls, towers of stench and disease. He would occasionally draw in his breath and exclaim in amazement or anger, but he did not pause. He began the last page and was all at once aware that Sillix stood before him, hands twined together, eyes big and full of fear.

"What do you want?" Ixelion snapped, not looking up, and Sillix ran to him, falling to his knees and putting his hands on Ixelion's arm.

"Forgive me for coming here," Sillix said in his high treble. "I would not have done so, but, sun-lord, you must help us! It is all wrong, all terrible. We can no longer rest in the ocean for it is thick and murky and hurts us. There are no fish that we may eat. Help us, Ixelion!"

Rage overcame Ixelion instantly. "Get up, Sillix!" he shouted, pushing him away and rising himself. "Can't you see that I am engaged in important matters? Get away from here. Eat the flowers. Sleep in the rivers. But do not come to me again!"

Sillix recovered his balance and rose, shocked and bewildered. "But I love you, sun-lord," he faltered, the response of a hurt child, and Ixelion went rigid. Light blazed from him, and Sillix saw that the flames dancing around him were tipped in black.

"I do not want your love, mortal!" Ixelion screamed. "I only want your obedience! I am the master here!" He shook the Book at Sillix. "I will outwit her! She shall not come here and take Ixel from me. It is mine. You are mine! You poor, craven little creatures. Don't you know that your Maker is evil, evil, and he will come with Sholia, and they will try to enslave you? Get out of my sight. I want to be alone."

Blinded and stunned, Sillix half-stumbled, half-ran out of the room, scorched by the fires that coiled after him. Ixelion slumped and with a last scream flung the Book into a corner, where it lay open, the pages trembling in the breath of the running waters. He began to weep, great sobs that Sillix could hear as he sped horrified through the hall and out into the forest. Ixelion staggered under the arch into his chamber and fell into the pool, still crying. The water hissed as he sank, and a steam boiled up to fill the room.

# 4

Sholia, Danarion, Ghakazian, and Janthis sat at the council table,
waiting. Three summers of Danar-time had come and gone since
Danarion had talked with Storn the corion under the spring-sweet
haeli trees, but to the lords who sat quietly staring into the smooth
blackness on which their hands rested, the time had been as nothing. Now winter visited Danar. The haeli trees stood blue and leafless, their knees hidden in the golden flurry of the autumn's
accolade. The corions had withdrawn from the presence of men,
back into their tunnels at the foot of the hills that rose behind forests
and city, where they slept curled together and dreamed of sunshine
and summer stars. The mortals kindled fires on their small hearths,
for this was the season of companionship and sociability. It was not
a cold season but a season of rest for the natural world, when the
trees' sap ran slow and thin, the grass stopped growing, and the birds
flew into the city to rain brilliantly hued feathers on the populace.

Within the council hall the late-afternoon shadows lay long
and dim across the starred floor, and none had called the sun to
dismiss them. Wind wove in and out of the high windows, found a
voice within the stone, and called softly down to the four clustered
at the end of the table, but it was not heeded. Ghakazian ruffled
his wings.

"Call him again, Janthis," he said quietly, and Janthis rose, a
small silver hammer in his hand, and went to the sun-disc that
swept from wall to wall behind him. He walked slowly, knowing in
his heart that this call too would go unheeded. He struck the disc
with the hammer, and immediately a low swell of sound began,
throbbing in their ears, echoing above them in the copper dome,
spreading out to seek the Gate, and when it ceased, they knew that
far away on Ixel it resounded to Ixelion's hearing. Over the hum of
its dying Janthis regained his chair. For a while longer they waited,
not looking at one another; then Sholia stirred.

"He does not come," she said. "Why? The call would reach him anywhere. On Lix, in his pool . . . Anywhere."

Danarion watched his fingers interlock with tension. Ixelion was troubled when I saw him last, he thought. Sitting here, his eyes running from us like a hunted animal on a dying world. I should have gone with him to Ixel, talked to him. But about what? His own gaze met Janthis's in resignation, and Janthis passed his hands over his face, a curious gesture of mortal fatigue.

"Danarion, Ghakazian," he said. "Go to Ixel and find him. I think . . ."

"What?" Sholia cried out. "You think what? Not Ixelion. It cannot be."

"It can," Ghakazian replied harshly, and Sholia went very white.

"He would have been doubly on his guard after walking the ruins of Fallan," she said stubbornly. "You know how close he and Falia were. Surely he went back to Ixel with the vision of her fall painful in his mind, his resolve to stay free hardened!"

"Perhaps he could not bear the thought of the long years ahead without her," Ghakazian said more gently. "He was too lonely, and the loneliness bred despair."

"And perhaps he may simply be in his sun," Janthis remarked dryly. "We cannot know until you go to him. Sholia and I will wait for you here."

Danarion rose unwillingly, knowing that he had failed Ixelion, that he must reproach himself.

"Stand behind me," Ghakazian said to him. "Place your hands on my shoulders."

Danarion did so as Ghakazian spread his wings, and without another word they lifted from the floor of the chamber, Danarion's hands gripping Ghakazian's wide, naked shoulders, the dark brown hair taking the wind and blowing back into his face. Out of the palace they swept, the wings beating slowly, lazily. Ghakazian swung to the left, glided over the stone arch that leaped to Danar's Gate, and came to rest at the mouth of the passage. Danarion released his grip, and together they passed under the stone sun, between the two carved corions, walking swiftly to the Gate. They stepped off the rim of Danar into the star-pierced blackness, calling to Ixel's sun as they fell. It heard them and answered, sweeping them toward itself, but long before they flashed past it, they felt the wavering of its power, and dread enfolded them as they were jerked toward the Gate. The sun released them, and they tumbled through. Glancing at each other in consternation, they ran, speeding along the causeway beside the muttering canal. There had been no guards at the entrance. They came out suddenly under Ixel's gray sky and stopped as though an invisible hand had been raised against them.

"Can you feel it?" Ghakazian whispered. "The disintegration? What has he done, Danarion?"

"He lied to us," Danarion answered grimly, his flesh cringing away from the dank, hostile growth under his feet, the dead, stinking fog that seemed to billow hungrily toward him. "He has fallen. Carry me, Ghakazian. I cannot bear to walk this world."

Obediently Ghakazian turned his back, and together they rose into the heavy air. Ghakazian's wings were soon drenched in the mist which clung to their hair and dribbled down their spines, and the feathers spewed back a shower of cold as they made a circuit of the dense forest. Then Ghakazian turned and sped toward Ixelion's ice-pinnacled palace. As they drew near it they saw that the protective seals quivered at the doors and the windows showed no light. A bitter, angry feeling of defeat stole over Danarion, so familiar, so very familiar. Ghakazian folded back his wings and alighted on the topmost, water-drowned step, and Danarion put down his feet unwillingly. The stair bit back at him with the cold teeth of suspicion.

"You go in, Ghakazian," he said quickly. "I want to find Sillix while there is still time. Hurry!" He ran back down the stair, fighting the suffocation of twisted mortal time he knew was all around him, already an enemy of mortal and immortal, already laden with death. He did not ask himself how. He knew how, and he also knew that he had left Ixelion to carry some insupportable load on his own.

He reached the forest and plunged in under the dripping trees, and immediately was surrounded by a hostile watchfulness. His hands went to his sun-disc. I cannot be touched unless I choose to be, he said to himself, and I do not choose. Leave me be! Light beamed from him, and the vast eye of the forest drooped shut. He ran on, all at once aware that he was not alone. Shadows flitted from tree to tree, keeping pace with him. "Sillix!" he called. "Come out! It is I, sun-lord of Danar! Come out!" But no voice answered him, and the shades went on breasting him under the black protection of the forest.

At length he broke from the trees' grip and found himself on the beach, a thin, sullen line of grayness that bent away from him in a vast arc. The cold steams from the still ocean wafted an engulfing rot to his nostrils. Up and down the shore he ran, the only light the streamers that flowed from his body, but the little green crystal domes were empty. He swung away upriver, urgency brimming in him and ready to spill out in panic, and then Sillix was there, his people running after him. He threw himself into Danarion's arms and clung to him, panting.

"Danarion, help us, save us! Ixelion is not with us anymore, there is a new, strange Ixelion beneath the waters of the magic pool. The ocean is dead, and the river disturbs our sleep with a new voice of dread. Help us!"

Danarion held the slim, wet body for a moment and then stood away, taking Sillix's hand and drawing him toward the beach, away from the silent, watching crowd. "Listen to me well," he said. "What I must say to you is pain on pain, for me as well as for you. A great horror has come upon the All, Sillix. Your lord has fought it for many eons, but now it has taken him as it has taken many of his kin. Your Gate must be closed, so that Ixel's fate may not become Danar's, or Ghaka's, or Shol's. I do not know yet whether Ixelion will stay here with you or go with the Messengers, but whatever he may do, you and your people must leave this part of Ixel. Go to the other side."

Sillix's round, pale eyes met Danarion's golden ones, mystified, afraid, struggling to understand. "The Gate will be closed? Our Gate? No more crystal from Lix?"

Danarion sighed inwardly, not in exasperation but in sorrow. "No more crystal. Take the people and go, Sillix. Learn to sleep on the land, to gather food in the forests. The rivers will not die, but no longer will they flow clean and fresh forever. You must fight to keep them running."

"What of the Worldmaker?" Sillix retorted, a gleam of hope brightening his face. "Go to him, Danarion, and he will come and make Ixel beautiful again."

Danarion shook his head. "No, he will not. And if you hope, Sillix, then hope that he may never again set foot inside your Gate."

"So it is true, the terrible thing Ixelion told me," Sillix said softly. Danarion looked at him sharply, a question in his eyes. "He said that the Worldmaker had become evil and he would come here with Sholia and make us all slaves. What is a slave, Danarion?"

Danarion stepped to Sillix, and pressed the cold, webbed fingers to his cheek. "Just do as I beg," he said, his voice breaking. "Farewell, waterman."

Sillix spoke no more. His eyes glazed over, so deep was his pondering, and he bent, kissed Danarion's sun-disc, and was lost to view under the dimness of the trees beside the gurgling river.

Danarion began the long walk back to the palace, scarcely able to move for the sudden flood of malevolence that poured over him. "You cannot touch me!" he shouted aloud. "You may grind Ixel under your black feet, but I am still inviolate. Leave me alone!" The weight of malice lifted a little, and he pushed through the forest, heart pounding. Ahead lay the palace. Close to panic, he ran up Ixelion's water-slick ramp and through the hallway.

Ghakazian bent and, speaking a sharp word of command, struck the crystal floor beneath the entrance three times with his outstretched palm. The seal wavered and parted, and he walked through it, pausing a moment in the hall, senses alert. The dreary sound of water filled his ears. The sight of it filled him with disquiet. Although it ran or splashed or trickled everywhere, gushing from the heights above, cleaving around his ankles to seek the stair behind him, it was no longer clear as glass but green-tinged, carrying with it some minute growth that he had never seen before on his infrequent visits to Ixel. He loved Ixelion as a brother, but a world where mortals lived submerged and moved contented through endless rain had always awed and mystified him a little. Now the water was more of an enigma than ever. Now it was imbued with an alien flavor whose aftertaste was fear, and Ghakazian rose and hovered, shaking it from his feet before circling the hall.

Ixelion was in his high chamber. Ghakazian, his instincts honed by wind and speed, knew. Cautiously he left the hall and flew slowly along a passage that ended in stairs, and another, smaller hall, and more stairs, all quivering under the flow of water. He stayed close to the misty ceiling, ducking under the cornices, and then there was a dry floor, and Ixelion's chair. Ghakazian came to rest, his eyes on the room that opened through the small archway. "Ixelion," he called softly, "are you there?" But only the endless pattering of water on water answered him with foreign, unintelligible words. A faint glow of light sluiced through the doorway. Ghakazian walked in.

At first he believed that his instincts had played him false and he was astonished, for the room was empty. Shreds of fog fluttered through the wide, unprotected window, bringing with them a darkness that shivered against the soft yellow light. But apart from the water that poured down the wall and entered the pool, there was no movement. The pool. Ghakazian stepped to the edge and looked down. Ixelion lay deep, deep down, his eyes open, his hair floating out around his head, his hands crossed on his breast. Above him the water rocked, making him seem to sway gently, and in the light that emanated from him Ghakazian could see those strange flecks of disease all around him. But here, in his pool, the flecks were black. Ixelion! Ghakazian commanded in his mind. Awake! Ghakazian is here. He wishes to speak with you.

The hands seemed to stir on the thin, pearled breast, but the eyes did not flicker. Ghakazian stepped back. There was nothing to do but wait for Danarion, and together they would raise Ixelion.

His glance wandered over the room, and he spotted a book flung down in the far corner by the window, its pale leaves fluttering. Idly Ghakazian walked to it and picked it up, riffling the pages. It must be Ixel's Annals, he thought. Has Ixelion written in it lately, and will it tell us how he fell? Then he felt the book jump in his hands, and the pages suddenly folded back, gossamer thin, as white as ice on Lix. *Ghakazian stood before his Gate,* he read, *with his armies ranked behind him. "Sholia has betrayed us!" he cried, and winged and wingless alike answered him with a shout. "We will go to Shol and make war on Sholia and the Unmaker, and take Shol for our own!"* What nonsense is this? Ghakazian frowned to himself. Winged and wingless form an army? Go to Shol? No mortal can travel the corridors from world to world except within its own system. He lowered his eyes to the text once more, intrigued, but then heard footsteps coming rapidly across the inside chamber. On an impulse he wedged the book under his belt, beneath the shadow of his wing.

Danarion came into the light, and Ghakazian went to him, pointing to the pool. "He is down there," he said, "deeply tranced. I do not know where he walks, and I did not try to follow him. We must call him back, Danarion."

Danarion strode to the edge and looked down, nodding. "Ixel is becoming a waste," he said. "I spoke with Sillix. He told me that Ixelion related to him some tale about the Unmaker's coming here with Sholia and subjugating everyone. How did the first fuel for the black fire get in here? Take my hand and join your will to mine. If he has not gone into his sun, we should be able to raise him."

Ghakazian reached out, and the light fingers he touched to Danarion's own were cold. Danarion glanced at him, but his mind was full of Ixelion, and he did not wonder. Quietly the two of them strained after Ixelion, following him back down Ixel's long years, and at last they found him sitting beneath a tree and watching the ocean, flowers in his lap, his chin resting in his palm. Thus he had sat long ago, on some morning in the dawning of his world, the only sentient being on Ixel, whole and at peace. They called to him, but that time had not been their time, and they could not stay. The vision thinned, lost color and definition, and they loosed hands and gazed down at him. He had not stirred.

"His Gate must be closed at once," Ghakazian said, "before he wakes and decides to leave Ixel forever. He must not be allowed a place with us."

Already I am lonely for him, Danarion thought, and that loneliness I will add to the loss of all the others, my friends, my companions in power. Instantly he saw himself as the last sun-lord, pacing the empty passages on Danar alone while the years fell and lay around his feet, not touching him because he would live on and on, hearing nothing but the sound of his own feet, seeing nothing but the vast hall, its floor now dead of stars save where Danar's sun twinkled alone in all that black eternity, the table glittering with necklets that would lie thus until the universe ended. The cold from Ghakazian's fingers seemed to spread up his arm and into his heart, and desolation wrapped him round. Without answering he placed his hands on Ghakazian's shoulders, smooth and hot, glowing golden as the sun's blood pulsed beneath the surface of the skin, and the feeling of inevitable defeat was gone. Ghakazian lifted him gently, and they turned their backs on the pool with its shadowy burden, flying with a rustle of brown feathers and a rush of warm air out of the chamber, out of the hall, out of doomed Ixel.

Ixelion lay in the pool looking up, aware of the two forms that bent over the water, their outlines distorted and blurred, but he did not rise. It was not Sholia and the Unmaker, and that was all that mattered. He watched them, knowing them, carefully closing his mind to them, and when they had gone, he left his body again and went to Lix. He stood on a jagged peak, the glittering deep cold of ice and crystal beneath and behind him, the immeasurable lost fields of black space all around him. He saw Fallan's purple, tired sun, ringed in tongues of black fire. He saw dark flames leaping from Kallar's sun, and Mallan's. For as far as his eye pierced, the suns hung captive, wounded, dying, consumed. Turning without emotion he saw Ghaka's sun, fair and full, and the twins of Shol beaming out like white gems, and far, so far, the shining mist that was Danar's sun and the center of all power.

No, he thought coldly. Not all power. Not even a portion of power. Again he deliberately faced the harsh, triumphant song of black fire. Sholia will come here with the Unmaker, the Book said so and the Book is true. But the Trader lied. I cannot fight them. It is impossible. Better for me had I given the Book to him and gone down in ignorance. The Gates are a joke, frail as paper, useless as a puff of air, and Janthis is wrong. They do not keep corruption out and never have. Each lord must do that for himself, and I did not do that, and I am now on the verge of surrender. The fuel lies dormant on Ixel, waiting for the spark that I or Sillix or any one of the mortals must inevitably put to it.

Lix spread out under his feet, mile upon mile of sharp tumbled rocks, only their tips catching sunlight. The rest of the little planet was sunk in night. Ixelion left it and drifted toward home. By now Danarion and Ghakazian would have gone back to Danar to recommend the closing of his Gate. Well, it meant nothing. He had the Book, and it would stay with him, safe, and would torment no one else.

He slipped easily into his body, flexing his limbs in the water's lightness, and was suddenly aware that another form leaned over the pool, long and white, with hair that brushed the surface of the pool. Fear for the safety of his treasure brought him roaring from the depths. Sillix ran back but did not cower away from Ixelion, stopping just inside the door and standing straight and proud. Ixelion ignored him. He flew to the corner, but the Book was no longer there. He ran around the room, swept the windowsill with frantic hands, leaned out into the dimness, but it was gone. Raging, he turned on Sillix.

"Where is it?" he shouted, tall and menacing. "What have you done with it, thief?"

Sillix trembled but stood his ground. Light streamed from his lord, hot and powerful, but when Sillix raised a hand to shield his eyes, he saw that the light was fringed in blackness. Tiny snakes of black flame darted from Ixelion's mouth and played about his stiff, accusing fingers.

"I have nothing, sun-lord," Sillix managed to say, covering his eyes completely with both hands. "I came to say farewell. Danarion told me to take the people to the other side, but I could not go without a word of blessing from you."

"Blessing?" Ixelion went rigid. "You should have asked it from Danarion, your new lord. Or have you crept to me ashamed because you forgot your allegiance to me?"

"I do not think that the allegiance of this world belongs to you anymore, Ixelion," Sillix replied steadily. "I do not understand it all, but it seems that *you* have betrayed *us*. Ixel's soul has put on fetters, and that is why the ocean is sick. Farewell, sun-lord. We will survive."

But Ixelion had ceased to listen. The little water snake has the Book, he hissed to himself. He has been sneaking about while I lay tranced in the pool, and he found it and looked into it, and that is why his eyes no longer speak to me of innocence and trust but pierce me through with accusation and new knowledge. He knows now that I can do nothing for Ixel anymore. Guilt came upon him, creeping like a ghost out of Fallan. He met it, embraced it; he did not run, and it turned into a need to destroy that flared within him. Sillix had turned away and was walking through the inner room, and with a snarl Ixelion sprang.

"The Book!" he yelled. "The Book!" Forbidden words streamed

from his mouth, words of destruction, words of command, and Sillix halted. The light left Ixelion and streaked across the floor like a black-tipped, golden spear. It bent, coiled about Sillix's legs, rose to his waist, his shoulders, wrapped itself about his neck, white-hot, sending out a hum of barely harnessed power, and Sillix screamed once. The spear became a cloud of dazzling brilliance. Ixelion spoke again, and Sillix lay at his feet, a clumsy muddle of limbs, a bundle of bones on which the skin hung loose.

For a long time Ixelion looked down at it, and then he bent. Roughly his webbed hands moved, tossed aside, pulled apart, but the Book was not there. Anger fled as loss overtook him. Grasping the body by one arm, he dragged it back into the other room and heaved it into the pool with one savage movement. Sillix did not sink. He lay light and empty, on the surface, his green hair spread wide, rocking as though he were asleep, but he was not asleep. He was ugly, misshapen, he was dead.

A cold wind rose from the darkness of the forest, blowing wetly into Ixelion's face. The trees began to snicker, a low whisper of derision that wafted through the window and swelled to a crescendo of scorn. Hahahaha, they tittered, and the mist joined in, sighing its mirth. The water laughed, deep and constant, a mocking, low-pitched gurgle of sound. One of them has it, Ixel thought with a chuckle. One of them stole it, stole it, hahahaha. Ixelion put his hands over his ears and ran to where his chair waited. Let them keep it. Let them come to the brink, even as he had done, let them topple over, and let the Unmaker laugh, let him come. I have lost it. It is gone. He sat in the chair, head sunk on his breast, his sun-disc black now, gleaming dully. At least I shall not run into the past as Falia did, he thought. But he had the unpleasant feeling that even if he had tried to leave his body, it would now be impossible, that he had lost more than the Book. He was trapped in an endless present, he echoed in it like a man in a lofty, locked room, un-changing, a prisoner with his disfigurement. He could no longer even weep.

They came to close the Gate, and this time it was Sholia who trod the paths of suspicion and enmity that led to the palace, her hair glimmering bright and clean, her aura cleaving a passage of light through the envious forest. She stepped through the shimmering seal, endured the alien touch of the myriad waters, and so came at last to the room where Ixelion sat. She called him, she touched his hands, she used a word of entreaty that was also a word of compulsion, but he did not respond. Then she saw Sillix, his face twisted toward her, the sockets of his eyes gaping dark and terrible, but she did not scream. Slowly she went to the pool.

"No power on Ixel can harm me," she said clearly, "nor can it hold me. It cannot hold you either, whoever you once were. Go to the Messengers. Go!" She raised her arms. Far away her sun heard as she bound it to her aid, and it responded. The surface of the pool heaved, then subsided and gave back to her nothing but her own fractured image. Walking back to Ixelion, she lifted the necklet from around his neck, gasping at the coldness of its touch, kissed him, and left him, head sunken on his breast, flowers growing in his hair, and the green watermold clinging to his body like a dripping winding-sheet, making her way back to the Gate with the same courageous deliberation.

"He cannot come," she told them simply. "Perhaps in times to come he will wake, but not yet."

"Then I must close the Gate and leave him," Janthis said unwillingly. He turned to the Messenger which quivered silently nearby, a perfumed smoke rising above the column of shifting colors. "Do I wait?" he asked it, but it did not reply, and after a moment he sighed and turned back, facing the archway and the faintly glimpsed water running down the canal beyond. He raised both arms, palms out and forward. "By the power vested in me as the firstborn of all the worlds," he said quietly, "I command the sun of Ixel and Lix to obey me."

He did not need to raise his voice. A rumble of deep sound came to him out of the passage, and light flickered around him, docile and eager.

"I am sorry," he whispered to it. "Give me your strength now, so that the end may be staved off yet again. Patience I ask of you, and a lonely watch until he that sleeps will wake again, and perhaps stand with his people once more."

The light rioted around him and then suddenly steadied, forming a blaze that filled the Gate. Janthis flung back his head and breathed full and deep, gathering together his power. "I close the Gate of Ixel!" he called, and it seemed as though his voice went rolling and echoing backward into the listening cavities of space. "Henceforth neither mortal nor immortal, Maker nor Messenger nor any created thing may enter here. The stars are forbidden to the people of Ixel, and Ixel is forbidden to the people of the stars. Close, now, close! I, Janthis, command you! Your service is at an end!" The light began to shrink until it had fitted itself into the arch, filling the Gate with blinding whiteness.

Almost imperceptibly it changed. The tingling glow faded, took on substance and movement, became a waterfall, pounding from the keystone of the arch to join the river in the tunnel with a sound like a continuous thunder. For a moment it flowed, ponderous and powerful, and then a greenish hue began to steal through it, and where the color threaded, the water became solid with a great crackling. Those watching found that they were looking at a wall of green Lix crystal, massive and impenetrable, coldly, sharply beautiful. In silence they waited. Finally, on the one smooth portion in all that many-faceted glitter, two hands appeared, silver-etched in the green, palms outward. Between them Ixel's sun took shape, and Ixel itself, Ixel of the fair waters, and tiny Lix with its cold and its glory.

"He was not given the choice," Ghakazian protested loudly. "It was taken from him because he could not be raised. That is a merciless thing." He half-turned to the Messenger, mild defiance in his stance, but the Messenger ignored him. "I suppose it is not my affair," he muttered. "It must be between Ixelion and the Lawmaker."

"I tried," Sholia said. "No spell or calling would bring him as he brought Falia. I do not think that he is wandering in the times that have been."

Suddenly the Messenger spoke, and as it did so its colors quivered violently and merged into a uniform, soft violet. "You are right, child," it said. "No spell of yours could move him, as it moved the waterman from the thinking pool. That was well and kindly done."

So you took him, Sholia thought, the reflection of the Messenger glazing her eyes with foreign color. You bore him away. And will you come for me one day, strange one?

With an explosion of brightness the Messenger sprang away

from Ixel, and they watched it flash and burn on its journey among the stars, bound on some new errand. The four of them together turned their backs on the Gate for the last time, stepping out into the corridor and vanishing, leaving Ixel to its loneliness and its fate.

# 5

Ghakazian swept through his Gate, singing, scattering the daily traffic of his people who came from and went to his other planets, making them laugh. He launched himself from the dizzying height of the ledge, somersaulted three times, then challenged the wind as he sped down the green valley that snaked between the peaks. The mountains rose like granite needles, each tip carved into the huge likeness of a winged one, stern, sightless eyes draped in cloud. Ghaka seems almost inhabited by giants, Ghakazian reflected, grinning to himself at the sight of hundreds of massive faces turned to him, wingtips rising above waving hair and set mouths. Filka, with the slight droop to his eyelid that Ghakazian remembered so well. Nenka, his forehead broad-furrowed. Hiranka, the only Elder carved with wings fully extended, because he had raced Ghakazian himself up the wide valleys for fifty days and had almost won. His descendants still won the winged ones' races, but there would never again be a Hiranka to challenge the sun-lord himself.

Still singing, his wings making tumbling eddies in the warm air, Ghakazian wheeled and flashed like brown lightning over the white-timbered villages, where his wingless ones came running out to wave at him. He swooped low, raining soft down-feathers and music upon them, his naked body almost as brown as his tangled hair but glowing with a shine like new honey. He called them by name, the dark-skinned men and women, the giggling children, and then he was gone, bolting into the sky, hovering outside a cave that angled back into one of the fanged mountains. Just above him Hiranka stared proudly above the clouds, the ever-present wind soughing past his outflung stone wings.

"Mirak!" he shouted. "Come out! It is I, Ghakazian."

A young man emerged from the cave and stood at its mouth, grinning and blinking in the sunlight, one hand on his small hip. His body was brown also, his hair long and black and snared haphazardly on the black wings that reared over his shoulders. His eyes were clear amber, flecked with green when the full sun caught them.

"Sun-lord, I am tired." He smiled. "I have been chasing Hira all over the sky. I think he is going to be another Hiranka, and already he spends much time looking into the past, watching his ancestor glide among the mountains."

"With dreams of challenging his lord one day, I suppose." Ghakazian laughed. "I am glad, Mirak. I would like nothing better than a race around the world. Has the sun shone while I have been away?"

"Unremittingly," Mirak answered gravely. "But if it pleases you, let it withdraw for a time. The grass pleads for rain, and so do I. A little rain will keep my son at home for a while and allow me a few hours of thought in peace." Mirak spoke lightly, but at his words a shadow passed over his lord's face. The eyes darkened, the wings missed a beat, and Ghakazian fumbled to hover again just beyond the lip of rock.

"Rain," Ghakazian muttered. "Rain. Ah, Ixelion!" Then the moment was gone. "So be it." He smiled. "Let us have an afternoon of rain." He raised an arm and shouted a friendly command. The sun flared for a second and dimmed, and Mirak saw large clouds hurrying to cover it.

"Thank you, Ghakazian," he said, and he called over his shoulder, "Hira, Maram! It is going to rain."

Ghakazian had time to see Mirak's wife and son come running before he left the cliff, beating his way leisurely downwind. By the time he reached his own domain, the land beneath him had opened under a swift pattering of gray water that was swelling to a steady squall, and before he could rise above the level of the clouds, his feathers and his hair streamed with moisture. Lightning forked suddenly and thunder reverberated. The rain shushed down faster. He broke through the gloom and came out into full sunlight. He amused himself by walking on the clouds until he was dry, his wings trembling like those of a hummingbird; then he turned to his hall and, parting the seal, went inside.

The entrance was a tall, thin arch that began near the middle of the mountain peak and rose to a point of almost painful clarity and sharpness just under the summit. No stone effigy of a winged ancestor frowned over it, as over every other peak on Ghaka, and as Ghakazian dove to it, it seemed to him that the sill of the arch gave the cloud that foamed right up to it an illusory solidarity, made it a false earth. Only the first hall was floored or roofed, and it was here that he received his wingless ones, who sometimes climbed the steep stair cut in the mountain and stood dwarfed within, craning their heads backward to try to glimpse the unadorned roof. Ghakazian would fill the lofty hall with light, so that they would feel less lost, and would stand on his wide gray dais and joke with them, his wings discreetly folded behind him. It was not that they were envious of their winged brothers, or conscious of any inferiority to them. But the hall of the sun-lord awed winged and wingless alike, and the wingless preferred soil under their feet and the sky above, not all around them.

Behind the dais was another, smaller arch, hewn from rough rock, and walking under it, Ghakazian paused, his entrance chamber behind him, an abyss before. Below him a funnel fell sheer to the roots of the mountains, an infinity of dark, silent space; above, it ended in open sky. The crag was hollow. Ghakazian could enter it between the teeth of the summit or through his hall.

Above and below the arch wide rims of stone ran around the circular rock wall. It was here that Ghakazian lived, received Mirak and his other winged mortals, and floated with them on the flavorless airs that blew from the depths in a never-ending draught. If he wanted to stand and think without disturbance, he flew to the high rock rim and perched there. Now he stepped into the nothingness and drifted upward, coming to rest on the ledge, where his sun never failed to drench him in its benison. With a sigh of satisfaction he lifted the sun-disc which sparkled on his breast and, clasping it in both hands, began to recite his responsibilities. I am not a Maker, I am the made. The words were engraved in his mind like flaming suns, and he saw them clearly as he called them to pass before his inner eye. I am not a lawmaker, I am an interpreter. I am not a healer—here he hesitated before going on firmly, a vision of Ixel's Gate flicking between the eternal words of power—I am a maintainer. I am not a king, I am a guide. Slowly and deliberately he spoke, strength growing in him, and then he let the disc fall and shook out his wings.

As he did so he felt his feathers catch in something at his waist, and with a shock he remembered the book he had picked up so casually from Ixelion's floor and tucked under his belt. It was still there, and he drew it forth, warm from its contact with his skin, gleaming in the rays of the sun. I read something in it. He frowned to himself. Now why can I not remember what it was? Why did I bring the thing with me anyway? As he fingered it the book jerked in his grasp. The covers fell open, the pages riffled past his startled gaze, and there it was, the passage he had been trying to bring to mind. Magic beat up from it—he could almost see the force of the spell—but he knew that it probed him in vain. He could not discern whether it was a spell of protection or warning and shrugged impatiently. Begone, he spoke in his mind to the shimmering charm, and he dropped his eyes to the tiny silver writing picked out by the sun. *Ghakazian stood before his Gate,* he read as before, *with his armies ranked behind him. "Sholia and the Unmaker rule the universe now!" he cried, and winged and wingless groaned in answer. "There is none left to guard the light but us! We must go to Shol, beautiful, rich Shol, and make war, and take it for ourselves, and the light."*

What madness is this? Ghakazian thought, irritated. It does not read the same as it did on Ixel, I am sure of that, but what it said then I cannot recall. Sholia and the Unmaker? Ixelion, what poisoned nonsense wreathed about your mind as you penned these words? Truly, you fell. I suppose I must take the book to Danar, but it cannot be incorporated into the Book of What Was in the All. It is the rambling of a mind being frozen slowly by black fire. Later I will read more, to see if the knowledge Janthis seeks is somehow wrapped among the madness. He will not rest until he knows how Ixelion fell. Ghakazian tossed the book carelessly onto the ledge and, spreading his wings, flew out into the sunshine.

Tagar was sitting in front of his house, his hands clasped about a wooden cup, as Ghakazian glided down out of the new-washed blue sky and came to rest before him, scattering raindrops. The rain had stopped, and beyond the low stone building the valley meandered back and up toward the mountains, gleaming clean and drenched. Far away, misted in the humid air, a winged one wheeled high above the arms of the valley where they narrowed to a point and vanished into rock and shadow, but here in the shelter of gentle hills and Tagar's gray stone wall the sun warmed them, and there was no wind. Tagar smiled, and his red-clad arm came out to touch Ghakazian.

"Sun-lord," he said. "Welcome home."

Ghakazian smiled a greeting and sat on the wall, sun beating into his face, his wings draped behind him to droop over the grass. "Is all well with you, Tagar, and with my wingless ones?" he enquired politely. The man inclined his head slowly with a natural dignity. The hands that laid the cup aside were large, big-knuckled, and thickly lined. The face was lined also, creased around eyes that had spent uncounted years squinting into bright sunlight and far distances, taking the measure of time and seasons, meditating upon the intrinsic mysteries of night and day, rain and shine, cold and heat. He was a large man, slow with the slowness of the clouds that drifted shadow over the valley, with the pace of quiet contentment of his flocks as they ambled over the fields. Before long his time on Ghaka would be over and a Messenger would come for him, but until then he cared for himself and those who acknowledged him as their elder with a quiet pride. The sky was not his concern. It was the earth that had formed him, and it called him still with its deep, sane voice. Now he answered with calm deliberation.

"All is well. Nothing has changed, and nothing ever will. Why should it, Ghakazian? I walk the hills with my sheep and wait to feel within me the signs that will bring me to the Gate for the last time, but I do not think that my time is coming for a little while yet." He smiled at the tumble of wind-strewn brown hair and fluttering feathers. "Have you been far afield in the All?"

"Yes, I have been far," Ghakazian replied shortly. "I have been to Danar and then to Ixel."

Tagar drank reflectively and then set his cup on the stone path that ran from the gate in his wall to the open door of his house, just beside him. "Is the lord of Ixel content?" He folded his arms and leaned his red-clad shoulders against the warm stone of his house. "I saw him once when he came to visit you."

You are a strange mortal, Ghakazian thought, his eyes leaving Tagar's weathered face and fixing themselves on the dot that still circled lazily far above, black against the deep blue sky. I feel that if I told you what has happened to Ixelion and all the others, you would simply nod and understand perfectly. But though I would wish sometimes to share it with you here, in the freshness and quiet of your valley, it is forbidden. Wise you may be, but innocent also, and innocent you must remain, your simplicity the only thing in your life that does not change but grows deeper and sweeter.

"I do not know whether he is content or not," Ghakazian answered frankly, for contentment meant many things. Then he suddenly left the wall and stood over Tagar. "Tell me," he said abruptly. "Has any mortal gone through the Gate to other worlds, not just to Linla or Roita, but out through the deeps of space, at any time since the ancestors were made?"

Tagar looked up at him, surprised. "Surely you ask me something you must know yourself, seeing that you were here when the mountains themselves burst through the soil. Not in my memory, nor in the memories of any of my line before me, has such a thing been possible. The Worldmaker forbade the realms of deep space to all mortals. Why do you ask?"

Ghakazian shook his head. "Idiocy," he muttered. "The fantasy of a crippled mind."

A cry made them both look up to see Mirak swooping low over their heads. They called back a greeting, watching him together until he dwindled to a speck and vanished, leaving the airs that eddied between the peaks behind them empty. Ghakazian flexed his wings. Tagar, still sitting on the ground, saw them rustle open between himself and the sun, an unfolding of shadow, a far-flung, sweeping double fan that arced dark and powerful against the white brilliance of light behind them. He shivered suddenly, a breath of cold contracting his muscles, and his gaze dropped to the sun-lord's brown feet, where the end feathers trailed the ground.

"Well," Ghakazian finished, "I think I will go to see how Brengar's crops enjoyed the rain."

Tagar struggled to his feet and, bending, kissed the sun-disc. When he withdrew his mouth, it tingled with cold. Slowly he rubbed it, and Ghakazian rose in one mighty rush of hair, limbs, and thrashing wings and was gone.

Ghakazian spent the rest of the afternoon going from valley to valley, talking with those who tended grain fields and beasts far below the eyries of their airborne brothers. As he moved among them, chased the children, smiled upon the women, conversed with the tall, straight-spined men, he found himself once more filling with pride for this, his charge, his boundless, beautiful land. The mountains were his, the green, fruitful valleys were upheld by his breath, the people's well-being and his own immortality fed upon each other.

When the sun began to sink and the light changed to a soft, warm red which slanted over the fields and gave the peaks long shadows, he flew pensively back to his hall, and the echoing rock funnel beyond. Tomorrow, he thought, I will go through the Gate to Linla and glide above the desert and visit those who live in the caves beneath the orange cliffs. I will even go to Roita and lie on my wings in the snow. He came to the lip of the funnel, swayed for a moment on the sharp rock, then plummeted down, calling to his sun as he did. Outside, on Ghaka, the sun slipped away serenely, but inside Ghakazian's mountain it blazed true and bright, making the shadows that limned the cracks and crannies withdraw. He went to his stone perch and rested there, listening to the wind sough through the hall and up toward him from the dark honeycomb of the mountain's roots.

He knew that the book was there, for as he had poised above the funnel he had remembered it with sudden clarity. He stood now for a moment looking down, brow furrowed, its presence a palpable thing there on the ledge behind him. Finally he turned and picked it up. Mortals from Ghaka on Shol! He chuckled to himself. Poor Ixelion. But I am Ghakazian the strong, Ghakazian the mighty. This time the book did not quiver in his hands as he thumbed through the pages, still frowning. Paragraphs leaped out at him instead. He saw his name again and again, and other names that he knew. Mirak, several times. Tagar, four times in one short passage. Where are the words of Ixelion and his people? he thought, still skimming. Where the rain, the ocean, the fog-hung forests and the rivers? If these are Ixel's Annals, then Ixelion has been toppling into black fire for a very long time. It reads like the Annals of Ghaka, and yet it cannot be, for I myself write in that book. Unless . . . Unless it is . . .

For the first time he closed the book and looked at the cover, his thin-boned hands relishing the cool smoothness of the ivory-colored binding, silver letters spidering under his eyes. At first he could make nothing of them, but then suddenly they seemed to come together, six innocuous, simple words. *The Book of What Will Be,* he read. He swayed, and only the reflex swiftness of his wings' immediate response saved him from falling. "Ahhh," he breathed. "Ah, no, it cannot be." The Book slipped from his fingers into the chasm. With a howl he plunged after it, catching it before it could disappear into the underground streams and lightless holes of the mountain's feet. Then he bore it gently through the small arch and into his hall, the fear of loss still beating erratically in his chest. He stood on the dais and read the title once more. "So this is how Ixelion fell," he whispered, and his voice traveled the long walls and returned to him. "And was this also Falia's doom? Was this the treasure?"

He closed his mouth, but his thoughts sped on. There is no word of Fallan in the Book, nor of Ixel. It is all of Ghaka and Shol. He opened it again slowly, gingerly, and the passage that had first intrigued him spoke to him. *Ghakazian stood before his Gate . . . Sholia and the Unmaker rule the universe now . . . make war . . .* No, it lied, this magical, this priceless relic of the dawning of time. Sholia, like himself, would never fall. War was the last resort of the fallen. Mortals could not travel through the Gates to other worlds. "You lie," he whispered. But in a creeping fear, in a certitude that came dark and edged with despair into his mind, he knew that the Book of What Will Be could never lie. It was a part of the Beginning, when there had been no lies. Sholia would indeed fall and make a bargain with her master, the Unmaker, and he, Ghakazian, would have to fight. How would it end? Frantically he scrabbled to open the Book near the end, but the leaves were gummed together, and he tore at them in vain. "No wonder you were hidden," he said to it softly, urgently, through his teeth. "No wonder you were forbidden to the sun-lords. Right from the beginning you held between your covers the story of the gathering tragedy that has come upon the universe, and the Lawmaker knew." Ghakazian's head came up. The Lawmaker knew. Of course. He must have known, even before he spoke the Worldmaker into life and commanded him to make. How can the Lawmaker not know everything? And so . . . And so the Lawmaker is not as we believe him to be.

Ghakazian felt as though something had lifted him and flung

him bodily far out into space, as though all his joints were broken, all his golden blood were crystallizing into ice and lumping, painful and cold, in his veins. That is why he will not help us. That is why he does nothing. He knows it all. "Sholia!" he choked, holding the Book high over his head, but it was not for Sholia that he sank to the cold stone and lay with his wings curled around him, weeping. It was for his own disillusionment.

He did not know that he could weep. He had believed that tears were a part of the Unmaker's work, coming from the planting of bitterness and sorrow in the fallen, and he clutched the Book to his breast and cried until he was spent. I will not weep again, he thought, opening his eyes, still lying on the dais, and looking down the vast sweep of the empty hall. I will not allow such pain again. If I am to fight to save Ghaka as the Book foretells, then I will read the Book from the beginning to the end and so discover what I must do and how I must do it, and whether all my effort will be in vain. But even if the Book tells me that I shall be defeated, I shall still fight. For Ghaka, for Shol, the jewel of the universe, for Danar and the council. The thought of Danar brought him to his feet. But I cannot keep the Book, he said to himself. I must take it to Janthis when I have read it. I will explain to him that he must close the Gate of Shol without delay. Not that any Gate-closing so far has done any good. Always too late. They should have listened to me when I spoke to them of fighting, for surely it is better to smash the innocence of the mortals in order to save the worlds than to protect them with falsities and put all our hopes in the closing of the Gates. Janthis is a fool.

Strength came to him, a surge of cool resolution, a throb of assent that seemed to flow from the Book and through his hands. He strode back to the arch, intending to read the Book on the seclusion of his ledge, but all at once he paused. For the first time he was aware of the depth of the abyss that yawned open below him, and for a moment, for just a fleeting second, he imagined himself falling, falling, his wings shredded and useless, his skin burning with the speed of his destruction. Then it was gone, unremembered. He floated upward, reached the ledge, and in the steady aura of borrowed sunlight turned to the Book's first page.

He did not know whether he read for one day or a thousand.

He stood on the ledge, the Book held in both hands, lost in the time that would be. The words seemed to change into visions as his eyes passed over them, so that one scene followed another, in his mind and yet too real to be only in his mind, a succession of colors, odors, emotions that enveloped him completely for as long as it took him to read on. He saw himself perched in the rock funnel, reading. He saw himself take the Book to the council on Danar and while he spoke to his kin he smelled Danar's hot sun and saw it catch the gems on Sholia's bracelet, a thick gold band studded with bright red stones that he had not seen her wear before. He felt the frustration and anger as Janthis ordered him to give the Book into his keeping. He argued for war, and war was once again denied him. He saw himself standing inside his Gate, looking out over the star-sick sky, but between himself and the stars the sun-lords gathered, accusing, pitying. He shouted words of defiance at them, knowing something that they did not know, something that filled him with a secret triumph, but though the Ghakazian that read tried eagerly to probe the mind of Ghakazian the vision at the Gate, he could not discover what the secret was. His kin would come to close his Gate. Though the Book did not say so in words, he knew it. But he was not troubled at all, for the Book showed him that long before they came, he would stand in the same place, facing back into Ghaka, addressing an army. He could not see it—and while Ghakazian the vision spoke to it, Ghakazian on the ledge asked breathlessly, Why? Why?—but he knew it was there, and though the mile upon mile of valleys lay patchworked under his gaze, the grass green and long, the houses low and white and ringed by stone walls, the jumbled whispers of a thousand thousand of his subjects pressed against his own thoughts.

He turned a page, and suddenly he was on Shol, kneeling behind one of the orange ornamental shrubs that flanked the foot of the sweep of marble stair that rose to Sholia's palace. He crouched low and held his breath, for on the top step, tall and beautiful in his arrogant nobility, immortal and invincible, stood the Unmaker. Sholia was there also, clothed in white and gold, her face the color of her gown, her hair like her suns, rich and pure. They spoke together, but Ghakazian could not hear. Then the Unmaker raised a hand. Ghakazian felt the whole of Shol draw in a breath and wait.

He waited also, but for something else, a thing hidden deep in his mind, but before it surfaced, he found himself back on the ledge, and the last page rustled under his hand.

Disappointment flooded him, as though he had dreamed as the mortals did and had woken from the sheen of magical wonders to a drab sky and the four gray walls of a rough-hewn hut. What do I do after that? he asked the Book angrily. Do I fight? Or did I fight and lose and was I imprisoned on Shol? How did I get to Shol when my Gate had been closed? How was it that the valleys were empty, and yet an army, my army, thronged the fields invisibly? Puzzled and shaken, he laid the Book down and began to pace slowly around the ledge, both palms laid against his cheeks. I will raise an army of mortals, he thought. The Book said so, and the Book cannot lie. But neither can it tell me how I will achieve this thing. I take my army through the Gate, to Shol. How?

Dawn came to Ghaka. The sun stepped over the horizon and spread itself out behind the mountains, expanding to flow pink and new down the valleys. The mortals woke from their dreams and long memories, but Ghakazian, for the first time since he and his sun had dawned together, did not leap out of the funnel and soar to greet his brother. An urgency burned in him, a feeling that he must find the key that would unlock the events to come. Things must change on Ghaka, he vowed. The people must be taught to kill, Shol must be saved from Sholia and the Unmaker, I must take over its rule myself. Perhaps it will be my doom to fight them, perhaps it was that that tugged at my mind as I hid behind the shrub. His hands fell away from his face, and he began to smile at the picture. "It will be," he said aloud. "I will conquer. Then the council will honor me and reopen Ghaka's Gate." He came to the little arch and passed under it and so to his hall, walking bemused, wrapped in his reveries. He crossed the hall and came out, and so deeply thralled was he that he did not fly but walked down the steep, winding stair that took him to the foot of the mountain. My mortals must be given the power to leave Ghaka, he thought finally. Somehow a way must be found. We cannot wait for destruction to finally come upon us.

Then suddenly his mind was clear of all thoughts. It was as though someone had reached in and brushed them away, and he felt his head hollow and dark, a cavity that waited obediently to be filled. He stood still and closed his eyes, everything in him poised on the brink of the knowledge he knew must come, everything terrified that the moment would pass him by and never return. His fists clenched. His wings drew in tight to his body. But when it came, it was gentle and sweet, voiceless, wordless, a sudden flowering. His mind showed him a small, dimly lit room, full of dust and age. Around the walls were shelves lined with books of every size and description. In the middle of the floor stood a reading desk, its pedestal of blue haeli wood carved into the likeness of a rearing corion, its smooth, tilted reading surface upheld by the beast's front paws. Ghakazian loosened. Energy pulsed through him, and leaping into the air, he turned and swooped across the sky to the cave and the entrance to his Gate. Of course, his heart sang. Of course, the wind answered to the cry of his wings. He dived into the cave, glided along the tunnel, and then was through the Gate and falling into the corridor, shouting for Danar's sun to recognize and bring him. He had not found the key, but he knew where it must be sought.

# 6

It was an early spring evening on Danar. The air was cool and still. Stars were beginning to blossom, white against the deep blue of the sky, and in the west a ribbon of purple streaked against the horizon. Ghakazian returned the nods of the corions who sat before the pillars of the entrance to the council hall, and after one glance back down the deserted flow of steps that would have taken him into the strange haeli forest where the two time-streams on Danar intermingled, he bounded inside. The lofty rooms and silent corridors were full of a soft, diffused light. No sound but the shush of his wings greeted him as he rose and flew to the central hall. It too was empty, the table reflecting mutely the splash and slide of light on the jewels that encrusted the dome, and he closed his wings and came to rest before the large sun-disc hanging on the wall. Without pause he strode to the door on the left and knocked. After a moment it opened to him, and Janthis greeted him warmly.

"Ghakazian! What brings you to Danar? Come in."

Ghakazian stepped inside, and Janthis closed the door behind them. Ghakazian glanced swiftly around. The room was small and seemingly bare. Opposite him three stone-rimmed windows gave out onto darkening sky, and Ghakazian knew that if he stepped to them and looked down, he would see the tips of the haeli forest and beyond that the torchlit city, lying on the slope of the hill that lazily became the vast high cliff where the corions wintered, deep within the stone. One of the walls was gray and blank, but that was an illusion. At a word from Janthis the gray would fade to the dark brilliance of black glass, and the universe would glow back at him, each system clear and true. At another word Janthis could call to him one sun, one group of worlds, and their images would rush to fill the wall.

The wall opposite the mirror wall was also gray and blank. Ghakazian had never seen it change, nor Janthis approach it. He had often wondered if it showed the leader of the council the Un-maker himself, or perhaps the realms of the Messengers, or even the place beyond everything that was, where the Lawmaker lived outside time and space. Now Janthis spoke, and twilight became the full benison of noon. He turned to Ghakazian.

"No council will be called for a long time yet, and the yearly rush of mortals from Danar's other planets to see the budding haelis has not yet begun. What is on your mind?"

Ghakazian found unaccountably that he could not meet the steady, dark eyes of the other. Janthis was smiling at him, and Ghakazian crushed the urge to challenge, to foment argument over something, anything. He fixed his eyes on the dead sun-ball which lay on the sill of one of the windows, seeing himself and Janthis reflected in it but curiously distorted, their shapes elongated and curved, his own wings black around him.

"I am seeking an answer to an important question, Janthis," he answered evenly. "I want to study the Books of Lore."

"Of course. Usually only Traders passing through Danar re-quest a day in their dust. Perhaps I can help you?"

Ghakazian tore his gaze away from the ball and looked at Jan-this. You cannot help, he thought, the words almost a sneer. You are pale, Janthis, you are polite, you are incapable of dealing with our common fear and giving real aid.

"No, I need no help," he said, already turning away. "I ask only light from Danar's sun. I will read, and then I will leave all as I find it."

Ghakazian alighted at the foot of the narrow, winding stair and walked along the dim passage. Presently he came to a plain wooden door, and pushing it open, he stepped inside, blinking at the sudden glow that met him. Janthis had filled the room with Danar's oblig-ing sun, and for a moment Ghakazian stood still, looking about. He had been here only once before, long ago, but everything was as it had been then, and as he had seen it in his vision. The row upon row of books, the low ceiling, the pale blue pedestal with the corion's claws curling up over the edge of the reading surface. The room was very quiet, with a self-contained, ageless silence that he was all at once unwilling to disturb. Somehow the atmosphere was filled with the mute wisdom of the ages and did not invite intrusion.

He held his wings tightly against his back and walked forward, his heart sinking. So many books, hundreds of them of every size and shape, each asking a mind of great capability to unravel their mysteries. Well, he thought. I have the time. I have all the time there is, and if the Book spoke true, then I am bound to find what I seek.

He approached the shelf nearest to him and saw to his relief that the books had not been piled haphazardly. On a small gold plaque set into the shelf he read, *The Law Pertaining to the First-born.* In an orderly succession the books marched away, rounded the corner, and were lost on the other side of the room. Ghakazian raised his eyes. The plaque on the next shelf read, *The Law Pertaining to the Messengers.* His fingers itched. He doubted that he would learn anything about the Messengers that he did not know already, but he had the curiosity of the rest of his kin when it came to the denizens of deep space. He passed on, each plaque giving him only a fast-growing sense of the weight of power of the Lawmaker, and the complexity of the All. There were Laws pertaining to the inanimate suns, to the suns without worlds, to the living and insentient, to the Traders. He exhausted one wall and stepped over to the far side of the room. Here were the Laws pertaining to the sun-lords and their suns. Here, too, was the Book of What Was in the All, volumes garnered from each world and growing all the time, the collected histories of the immortals and their charges. At the top, lying on its side, was a single slim book, bound in white leather and lettered in silver. Ghakazian took it down, turned it over and read, *The Law Pertaining to the Book of What Will Be.* He almost opened it but then shook his head and put it back. He would not be diverted. Perhaps he might return one day and turn its pages, but not now. He went on searching until finally he found the books of Laws pertaining to mortal men. One by one he wrenched them from the shelf and skimmed them eagerly, but they did not hold what he wanted. The volumes dealt with the laws governing birth and dying, memory, limited powers, and even mortals in the realms of the Messengers, but nothing revealed a command that would send them unharmed through a Gate onto another world. He tossed each book back onto the shelf, disappointment becoming an irritated anxiety. I am on a foolish errand, he told himself. What am I doing here? I shall go back to Ghaka and get the Book, and bring it and its nonsense to Janthis.

He was about to turn away when his eye caught the last plaque, low down, almost at his feet. Sighing, he bent and read, *The Law Pertaining to the Gates*. With a quick intake of breath he squatted, his wings scouring the dust from the floor behind and beside him. "Immortals and Gates, Messengers and Gates, Traders and Gates," he murmured, his forefinger trailing along the volumes. Then he had it. He drew forth the book with a short laugh and placed it carefully on the reading desk. *The Law Pertaining to Mortals and the Gates*, it said. Eagerly he turned to the first page.

At first, as he perused slowly, he was convinced that the book could tell him only those things he knew already, but in a more orderly way. On the day when the Worldmaker had come to Ghaka to complete his Making, he had talked long with Ghakazian, explaining to him the position the yet uncreated mortals would hold, and the mortals on Ghaka and its satellites had been Ghakazian's study and his love for many centuries. He knew it all. But he read on, committing every word to memory so that he could bring them out for further thought when he was home. The sunlight illumined the pages steadily. The silence remained whole and dumb. He passed from chapter to chapter, his concentration complete, only his eyes and his long, feather-light hands moving.

When he had gone through three quarters of the book, he stiffened and exclaimed softly. It was not that he had read something he was not aware of, but the piece of information he had just consigned to memory came back and reformed, was changed, and sparked with new meaning. *A mortal cannot use a Gate to travel the invisible corridors from world to world*, he had read, *for its body is incapable of the rapid transformation from blood and bone to pure essence and back again. Permanent division of body from essence would be the result. Only at death can a mortal travel beyond time and space, because it is then that body and essence assume a new form together.* Ghakazian read it again, with close attention. *Only at death can a mortal travel . . .* And death released new powers in a mortal essence, powers for the metamorphosis of the body. But without that body a mortal could go through a Gate unencumbered, a pure essence, deathless, and no mortal on any other world would be able to withstand its strength for possession or command.

"Ah," Ghakazian hissed through his teeth as he slammed the book shut and ran to replace it on the shelf. "I knew! All the time

I knew, and yet I did not know. I will tell them, I will explain to them what they must do, and they will do it for love of me."

He hurried out of the room, banging the door shut behind him and running up the curving stair. Once he had gained the upper chambers, he took to the air, racing for the pillared terrace and the Gate beyond.

He sped through his own Gate, burst out of the mouth of the cave, and plummeted like a stone, dropping until he had reached the level of Mirak's home. "Mirak!" he shouted. "Come out! Hurry! I have something urgent to discuss with you!" Mirak emerged almost at once, and with a jerk of his head Ghakazian darted away. Together they skirted the peaks and came at last to Ghakazian's crag. Ghakazian did not pause but swooped up and over the top, disappearing into the rock funnel, and Mirak rushed after him. Only when they both perched on the ledge, warmed by sunshine, and Ghakazian had made certain that his hall was empty of wingless ones, did he speak. It was necessary to choose words that Mirak would understand, that fitted his experience, and Ghakazian tried to shrink his own weight of knowledge to match.

"Mirak," he said, leaning back against the rough wall of the mountain, his arms folded, "when are you to die?"

Mirak frowned in confusion over the odd question. "Not for another four hundred and twelve Ghaka-years," he answered.

"If I asked you to die tomorrow, would you do it?"

Mirak's eyebrows shot up in astonishment. "I do not understand, Ghakazian. How could I die tomorrow, even if I wanted to? I must live until it is my time to leave Ghaka forever."

The brown eyes of his master suddenly swiveled to him and fixed him with a penetrating stare. "Tell me," Ghakazian went on evenly, "how would you kill a man, Mirak?"

Mirak's puzzled smile faded. It seemed to him that the draught from the depths below had ceased to blow around him and had been replaced by a brooding cloud. He lifted his shoulders to dispel it, but his wings felt heavy and difficult to control, as though he had been flying through a rainstorm.

"I do not know," he answered, and his voice sounded weak and thin to his ears. "And even if I did know such a terrible thing, I would not do it."

"Even for me, your life, your soul?"

Mirak swallowed. "Sun-lord," he blurted, "I have never asked a reason from you for the things you bid me do, for all things in your mind are pure and good, and it is our duty and our pleasure to obey you. But for this, I would ask why. And after asking why I would consider well."

Ghakazian unfolded his arms and, jumping the abyss, came up to Mirak. His hands stroked the brown skin, ruffled the long feathers, played about the high forehead.

"Mirak," he whispered, "I must tell you a story, but this story is not like the stories you tell to Hira, it is not about the ancestors in the dawning of the world. I would ask nothing of you that would mean your harm. A blackness is eating up the worlds one by one, slowly but surely. If it comes to Ghaka, the people will change. They will learn how to hate and kill. But I, Ghakazian, know how to defeat this blackness, if only you and all my mortals will help me. Together we can keep it from Ghaka's Gate, but that can only be accomplished if the people do exactly as I say, without question."

Mirak had listened, his face impassive. Now he asked, "What is the nature of this blackness?" The query was sharp, and Ghakazian removed his hands and clasped them behind his back, under his wings. If I tell him, if I say the words, then innocence will flee from Ghaka forever, he thought. Yet they must be said. The people must know. His eye caught sight of the Book lying just where he had laid it, and he stepped away from Mirak. I could bend you to my will by the raising of my smallest finger, he thought. I have the power. Yet I will not do so unless there is no other way. You are my treasure. You will understand.

"The blackness spreads," he said deliberately, "and at the heart of this blackness is the Worldmaker. He is not as he once was, Mirak. He fought with the Lawmaker, and he has become the Unmaker. The sun-lords have done what they can, but it is not enough. Now I propose to give battle to the Unmaker, for I know that he will go to Shol and be admitted, and Shol will fall. But he shall not come to Ghaka!" The brown eyes had become hard as the granite that entombed the pair of them, and Mirak was swept with an urge to cower down onto the ledge. His sun-lord had always been laughing and kindly, and this being with the first glimmerings of a real and awesome power that Mirak had not been aware of before filled him with terror. Light flaring from his outflung arms and crackling in his streaming dark hair, Ghakazian shouted, "I will go to Shol, and there I will force him back, and Shol will belong to the people of Ghaka, in peace and plenty!"

"Can it be true?" Mirak whispered, and all at once the fire left Ghakazian, and he slumped, giving Mirak a tired smile.

"I am forbidden to lie," he said gently. "In the ages before the darkness came, I did not lie to your ancestors because I knew only truth, and now, even when it has become possible for me to deceive you, I do not. If I lied, I would cease to be what and who I am. You have never heard an untruth, Mirak, and if you trust in me, you never will."

"I have always trusted you," Mirak said haltingly, still trembling at what he had seen. "Give me time to ponder what you have told me, sun-lord, and then I wish to hear more."

Ghakazian bent and, reaching behind him, lifted the Book from the rock and handed it to Mirak.

"Read this," he ordered. "Stay here and learn. This is the Book of What Will Be. It will tell you all you need to know. I will go and speak with Tagar."

Mirak took it gingerly and almost dropped it. He had never held such a heavy thing, nor one so cold. Yet its beauty drew his eyes, and a longing stole over him to hug it, kiss it, cradle it. Reverently he turned to the first page. For a moment Ghakazian watched him, a slight, smug smile coming and going on his mouth, and then he swooped through the arch, across the hall, and out over Ghaka.

Tagar leaned on his low stone wall and looked out over the lush peace of the valley to the mountains beyond. He was uneasy. He had gone about his small duties in the morning, taken his midday meal, walked onto the slopes to see to his flocks, still wrapped in the same mood of grim waiting that had not gone away. The night before he had commanded a dream of water, and he remembered that he had lain on his bed and in his sleep listened contentedly to the drowsy patter of rain on his roof. His dream had taken him outside, where he had found a river flowing around his house, and he had knelt on its mossy bank and trailed both hands in it, reaching for the smooth multicolored stones on the bottom.

But then the dream had changed. He had risen to survey the valley but had found himself looking at a weird forest of trees with black, twisted trunks covered with some kind of fungus, which assumed shapes of such marvelous complexity that they took his breath away. Fog shrouded the roof of this forest and ribboned toward him, white and cold. Suddenly he was afraid. He had never known fear before, but there it was, sliding to fit the interior contours of his mind as though it had been made to find them. He turned. Beyond the forest, where it thinned to become pale grass as tall as a man, there was a house. He told himself it must be a house, for he had no other word to describe it to himself. It was neither farming cottage nor caved peak but was made of spires that glittered green even in that dim place, and its windows were closed eyes. The fear intensified. There was something in that magical building, something or someone in agony, but before he could will his dream-feet to move, he had opened his eyes to find himself on his bed in darkness, the room full of the coolness of the coming dawn. The dream had fled, and with it the fear. Only the foreboding remained.

But that had been last night. Now he considered the tallest peak, where his sun-lord lived. A cloying breathlessness seemed to flow from it and spread toward him, and he wondered if there was to be a storm. I should call the sheep, he thought, but he did not move. The air was sluggish, and the arms of the mountains seemed to reach out to squeeze the valley. They are like arms, he said to himself. Today they feel greedy. A lizard darted along the wall, stumbled over his hands, and disappeared. Tagar jumped and then laughed, but the laugh died in his throat, for he sensed some dark presence. A shadow fell across his back, tall and menacing, and he whirled, his heart in his mouth. But it was only his lord. He bowed clumsily, his heart still throbbing, and Ghakazian came closer to him in a rustle of folding wings.

"You startled me," he said awkwardly, and Ghakazian chuckled.

"Were you far away, Tagar? I saw you leaning on the wall, dreaming. Very small you look, from up there." His arm swept the sky. "I have a serious matter to discuss with you."

"I am ready to hear." Tagar had regained his composure.

"Good!" Ghakazian made as if to sit on the wall but then changed his mind and began to pace before Tagar, up and down, his hands by his sides. "Tagar, you are the oldest of my wingless ones, and the wisest. You know the earth of Ghaka as Mirak knows the sky. You have my respect as well as my love. If I told you that between the going down of the sun yesterday and its rising this morning the world had changed, what would you say?"

The dream came back to Tagar, exotic and frightening. "I would want to know the nature of the change, and how it came about."

Ghakazian stopped pacing for a moment and looked at him. "You and I understand one another," he said brusquely. "For hundreds of years we have explored Ghaka and each other, shared dreams and talked through many happy days. There is a closeness between us. Listen to me as a friend." He ended his scrutiny and began walking again. Tagar, waiting for an explanation, watched him uneasily, for his protestations of friendship rang suddenly hollow.

"The Worldmaker no longer behaves according to his nature," Ghakazian went on, avoiding Tagar's startled glance. "He stopped making and began destroying many eons ago. Suns and worlds have fallen to him one by one, and most of the universe is in agony. It need not concern you why this happened. The important thing for you to remember is that until now there was only defense. But a means of attack has come into my hands." He came to a halt in a flourish of feathers and a flash of necklet. "I know I can defeat him, but not without your help. If I asked it of you, Tagar, would you kill a man for me?"

"I can only barely imagine what it would be like to take life from a man," he answered softly, "and it is horrible, a tear in the wholeness of my essence. Greater, perhaps, than the sorrow that must be crying out in the universe if what you have told me is true."

"You cannot believe? I have seen it, Tagar. I have stood at the Gate of Fallan when it was closed against the Unmaker, I have been present at countless council meetings when Janthis seeks an answer and sits and looks at his empty hands. I have trod the stinking wet soil of Ixel in pursuit of a word from Ixelion, and I saw him defeated."

Tagar flinched. Ixel. He had never been curious about the other worlds, but at the mention of Ixel he knew that he had been there last night in his sleep. He heard his spirit begin to weep, long echoing sobs of desolation and loss, and he was certain that from this moment on he would never be the same again. His sun-lord had betrayed him.

"It is not that I doubt you," he said amicably, though he wanted to go into his house and shut the door and never come out again. "I have loved you, but not even for you would I risk such a wrenching within myself."

Ghakazian came closer. "We have a chance to return the All to what it once was," he said quietly, but under the gentle tones was a new thing, the faintest hint of a threat. "I am not truly immortal as you are, Tagar, and this you know well. When Ghaka's sun burns out and its life is ended, then I also will be annihilated, as though I had never been. This is the Law of the sun-lords, under which I and my kin live. But for you it is different. Your essence goes on and on in a changed body, on a new world. But not here." He sidled up to Tagar, and his breath was as cold as ice. "Not on Ghaka, not on the earth you have felt beneath your feet for five hundred years. Yet can any mortal truly desire eternity in a realm about which he knows nothing, where the beloved things he has grown up with all his life may not even exist? I offer you instead a small reprieve, on a world where, as I have told you before, there are houses, beasts, green growing things. I offer you more mortal time, a longer life, on Shol."

"As what, sun-lord? As a prisoner of the knowledge that I killed? And what would I be on Shol, wrongly changed? Of what use is a mortal's essence without flesh?"

"You may be wise," Ghakazian snarled, "but you do not have the wisdom of the sun-people. I will give you a body on Shol, and you will fight. Afterward you may enjoy the fruits of your obedience by staying on Shol, or perhaps I shall return you to Ghaka. I do not know. I shall not—." He stopped abruptly and bit his lip, and then Tagar stepped back and turned away.

"You shall not what, sun-lord? You shall not care anymore? What has happened to you? Oh, can you not see that whatever sickness ails the universe is now beating through your own golden blood? Bring Janthis to Ghaka! Let him tell me that I may murder and destroy other men, and then perhaps I will obey you!"

Ghakazian shrugged, and his wings unfurled, a dark cloud of warning. "Think about it," he said. "You have influence with my wingless ones, your words to them would carry great weight. But make no mistake, Tagar. With you or without you I will take an army to Shol, and if it is to be without you, then beware!"

Tagar shuddered, but Ghakazian pressed him no further. He lifted lightly from the ground and drifted with a deliberate impudence over Tagar's head; then with a crack like the breaking of a dry branch he was gone. Tagar felt something settle on his shoulder and reached up. It was a feather, and in the muted sunlight it gleamed gold, deep green, and rich amber, a thing of perfection, of strong, matchless beauty. He laid it against his cheek, and it rested there, warm and soft. Presently he slipped it into the pocket of his thick shirt, and opening his gate and passing through it, he set off down the valley.

# 7

The sun was sinking, peaceable and calm. Birds twittered spasmod-ically as they gathered to return to their nests for the night. Deep-ening scarlet light lay like the folds of some royal garment over the fields, but with each step he took an anxiety grew in Tagar until his feet quickened and began to run and his breath came short and painful. He turned aside onto the white path that wound beside the stream and under the willows, then curved along the base of the green slope that became barren rock rising to cliff. Every now and then he glanced at the cliff face, already drowned in shadow, but he saw nothing of the winged ones. The path began to dip, and there below him lay a farm. Lights gleamed in the windows, and Tagar could hear the sudden delighted laughter of one of his many descendants ring out, clear and full of mirth. He slowed his step, came to the gate, and leaned on it for a while to get his breath. Then he went through and hurried to the door, his hand reaching out to knock before he came up. The door swung back, and his grandson smiled and waved him inside. He stepped into the little whitewashed room and heard the door close behind him with a relief that set his knees shaking. He leaned against the wall, and the younger man touched his elbow.

"Tagar, what is it? Come and sit. Have you set a date for your death?"

Tagar did not acknowledge the joke. The matter of his death was no longer a thing of jest. He opened his eyes. Natil's wife sat smiling a greeting at him, and the child came up to him and touched him reverently on the leg. Briefly he rested his hand on the blond head, but Tagin pulled away.

"Tagar, your hand is cold," he complained. Tagar knew it. He was cold all over. He drew Natil away from the family, back toward the door.

"I have no time to sit," he said quickly. "And neither have

you. Listen to me, Natil, and ask no questions. You must take Rintar and the child and go through the Gate immediately to Roita. Something terrible is happening to Ghakazian. No!" he snapped emphatically as Natil, astounded, opened his mouth. "Let me talk! Waste no time, and do not stop to gather any belongings. If you meet friends on the way, urge them to do the same. If you do not, you all may die."

"Die? Tagar, that is impossible. What has happened to you?"

Tagar gripped him by both arms. "If I can, I will come to Roita and explain," he said, "but now I must go and warn as many wingless ones as I can. Do you trust me?"

"Always," Natil said, bewilderment in his face.

"Then hide from the winged ones. Leave the path to the Gate if you see any circling above. Oh, do this, Natil!" He shook Natil's captive arms. "Ghaka faces destruction!" A sudden thought burst upon him, and his eyes blazed at Natil. "Traders . . . have you seen any Traders?"

Natil frowned. "One came a little while ago and took a pile of Rintar's weaving. I think he is still on Ghaka, somewhere."

Somewhere. Ah, Maker, I cannot walk all the roads of Ghaka, it would take another fifty years. But I must try. "Did he say where he was going?"

"Yes. He wanted wool from Inak."

"Then I will go to Inak and call at all the farms on the way. Hurry, Natil! Go now!"

He opened the door and was gone, and Natil walked dazedly back into the room. Two faces were turned to him, two motionless figures waited on his word. He blinked, and then something of Tagar's own fierce urgency was born in him. "Put on your jackets, both of you," he said quietly. "Pick up a loaf of bread, Rintar, and I will carry blankets. We are going to Roita."

Half the night had gone, and by now Tagar had walked many miles through a darkness which lay thick and blinding around him. Stars blazed high above, but they lit only the tips of the mountains. Tagar kept his eyes fixed on the gray road that unwound beneath him. He had visited six families, twenty-five people who had left their homes out of respect for him and even now trudged toward the Gate, but he had not found the Trader. The Trader had taken wool from Inak. He had stopped at the farm of Pandil the carver to deliver a small piece of haeli wood from Danar, but he had not tarried.

Tagar stopped for a moment to rest, squatting on the road, breathing deeply. I am far from my home now, he thought. If I turned back, I would still not reach it before the dawn. For a few more seconds he gathered his strength, and then he rose and walked on. He saw no lights. There was only the solid black bulk of the mountain's thigh on his left and the descending sweep of an opening valley drowned in darkness on his right. Before him the road vanished, diving to find the lowland, and he knew that around the next bend the friendly lights of a farm would twinkle up at him. He came to the corner, paused, then firmly walked on.

Ahead of him was the Trader, a wavering, formless sliver of pale transparency that glided swiftly and noiselessly over the rock-strewn ground. After a moment of weak relief that buckled his knees, Tagar broke into a run, calling frantically, but the Trader did not slacken his pace. He was humming. Tagar, his own breath ragged in his throat, the blood singing in his ears, could still hear the undulating, tuneless whine. "Trader!" he screamed. "I have words for you to carry!" The Trader did not hear him. He skimmed forward, his scarf a flutter of colorless froth in the night. With a sudden despair Tagar knew that he could not reach him before he vanished out of sight. He spurted forward, a last cry gathering in his lungs, but it never rose to flay his tongue. There was a rustling of wings above him, the keening of wind in outflung feathers, and Ghakazian landed on the road in front of him.

Restlessness had sent Ghakazian swinging out under the motionless stars. He had cruised the mountaintops and flailed above the scanty forest that straggled between cliff and valley sides, and finally he had dropped down to where the rough road wound between the farms. He had followed it slowly, not knowing quite why. He would rather have been streaming high in the night sky, his dark gold skin turned to silver by the stars which flickered like the tails of quiet fish in a dark pond, but he had kept to the road, a tiny ribbon below him. Mirak, already webbed tight in the spell of the

Book, did not concern him. It was Tagar who troubled the sun-lord's thoughts, Tagar who had dared to say no. I will scorch him, Ghakazian thought grimly. I will cause the sun to wrap him in its fiery arms, and then we shall see who dares to refuse aid to his lord. One lick from the sun's long tongue and Tagar will lead his people under my command. So he smoldered, his mind turning slowly around his coming victory on Shol, the road reeling out under him.

Then he saw Tagar, and at the same moment he glimpsed the Trader. Tagar had begun to run. He was shouting something to the Trader, but Ghakazian was too high to hear the words. He hovered, watching, and suddenly he recognized his danger. Tagar would repeat his threat to the Trader. The Trader would go to Danar, and Danarion and the others would come to Ghaka. The plans would be ended. Wretch! he thought, a fume of wrath rising in him. Ungrateful mortal! I offer you Shol, I offer you an end to the danger that sits, unwinking, at the Gate, and this is how you serve me. His knees rose to his chest, then his legs shot out behind him. His arms and his wings spread wide. Like a falling star he plunged toward the road, coming to rest in a shower of golden sparks before Tagar. The man fell, scrabbling at the stones like an ungainly beast, then came awkwardly to his feet. Ghakazian folded his arms.

"Oh, Tagar," he said softly, sorrowfully, though his great anger pulsed through the light flaring from him. "I know your every thought. Where is the trust between us? Where your obedience, your love? The Trader has gone upon his way." He shook his head in mock sadness, and Tagar looked beyond him. The road was empty and silent. With a muffled cry he hung his head. Ghakazian watched the trembling of the blunt hands, the effort to quiet the still-heaving lungs. "You would betray me, Tagar?" the deep, sweet voice went on. "Me, the only hope of the universe? Shame! Shame!"

Tagar said nothing. He had closed his eyes, thrusting his hands deep into his pockets. One of them found the feather he had placed there while the sun still shone and the grass was still green and fresh. Tears trickled down his cheeks, but pride forebade any sound.

Ghakazian damped down his fire and came closer. "I will ask you one last time, Tagar. Will you lead your mortals to Shol with me?"

Tagar shuddered. Then his head came up and he found his

voice. "The corridors are forbidden to mortal men. So is the taking of one's own life or that of another. The All will not be saved by the breaking of laws, Ghakazian. I love you. I have loved you since I was a child upon my mother's knee and you came to her house and amused me by making the sunlight into a ball and rolling it about the ceiling. That I can never forget. I will go on loving you no matter what my fate. But I can no longer obey you, for when you speak of obedience, you are already acknowledging that everything has changed." Finality, weak but definite, was in his tone.

For a long time they eyed each other, Tagar full of fear but upright, Ghakazian brooding sullenly, light pooling now from his feet, now trickling yellow from his hidden hands and welling up through his arms. Where it met the night, Tagar could have sworn that it acquired a darker blackness.

When Tagar could bear his scrutiny no more, Ghakazian loosened his arms. His actions were brisk, assured, his words crisp. "You must come with me," he said, and quickly he laid hands on Tagar, spinning him around as though he had been a feather himself. With a quiet word to his sun he lifted Tagar, bearing him lightly. Tagar bit his lip to stop himself from crying out as the road swayed dizzily and all at once the dim land fell away from his feet. Ghakazian's arms held him surely, effortlessly. Tagar felt their warmth, and the sun-lord's neckleted chest fed the same steady comfort into his back, but he shrank now from the power latent there, for Ghakazian's easy breath was icy.

For a time that seemed to Tagar to be the dreaming unreality of eternity, Ghakazian flew, straight and evenly. Tagar had no sensation of speed until he glanced down and saw how the clustered lights fled and the glittering of stars on the rivers was like a flash of white fire that snaked over the land and was gone. Then all at once Ghakazian muttered in surprise and checked his flight. Tagar's fingers clutched emptiness, and his heart gave a lurch. Slowly Ghakazian began to circle lower and lower, and Tagar strained to see what it was that had caught his attention. Ahead of them, looming dark and jagged, was the peak that held the Gate, while all around them the stone ancestors frowned at one another, motionless presences in the night. But below, on the road that wound from both mountain and valleys and ended at the foot of the stair, there was movement. Tagar could not discern what it was, but Ghakazian suddenly shook him and shouted, "What mischief have you fomented, faithless one? Where are they going? To Roita?"

Tagar looked down in despair, and all hope left him. People were moving slowly along the road, without light or laughter, a long, straggling column of uncomprehending tiny forms with faces turned to the Gate stair, obeying his frantic, half-hysterical command. But it was too late, he wept to himself, too late. They should have kept to the fields, crept along in the shelter of the rocks, anything but used the road. Ghakazian roared out a word, and sunlight flooded the road beneath. The people tumbled to a halt, shrieking, but suddenly a calm fell on them, and every face was upturned. "The sun-lord," they whispered, their eyes sparking in the circle of brightness that held them, their hair shining as though they stood under a noon sun. But there was no gladness in the shiver of sound, and Ghakazian noted its absence.

"Where are you going at this hour?" he demanded, and though they tried, they could not glimpse the form behind the voice, so painful was the light blazing down on them.

Natil stepped out from the crowd and, shading his eyes with a hand, answered boldly, "We go to Roita. The hour does not matter. Day or night, the Gate is open."

Run! Tagar tried to shout to his descendant. Run, run, run! But he realized that he had not opened his mouth, and he knew that Ghakazian had overridden his will for the first time in five hundred years.

Ghakazian laughed. "It matters now!" he called back roughly. "Henceforth the Gate is forbidden to you. I have work for you to do, and you will have no time for visiting."

A murmuring of astonishment rose, and while the people exclaimed to one another in voices that still betrayed no understanding, Ghakazian changed his grip on Tagar. At that moment Tagar knew that Ghakazian was going to kill him. Horrified and disbelieving, he struggled in his lord's arms, but Ghakazian only held him more tightly.

"Yes," he hissed. "I will destroy you, Tagar, and in doing so I will teach the people the price of disobedience. You will wait at the Gate, but no Messenger will come for your essence. You will wait for me, and when I come, you will follow me, for if you do not, you will be a prisoner of Ghaka forever."

"Sun-lord," Tagar croaked, wide eyes fixed on the road that glimmered far below him, his spine, his limbs, his very being cringing away from the fearsome nothingness between himself and the distant people, "do not do this terrible harm to yourself. If you murder me, then you also will be wounded beyond hope of recovery."

"What do you know of a sun-lord's soul, you worm of the earth?" Ghakazian retorted through clenched teeth. "Do not presume to be my teacher, wingless one, road-crawler. Die!"

He flung open his arms, and Tagar fell. Like a wounded bird he dropped, his limbs curling under him, his shirt flapping obscenely. Wind screamed at him, and its force made him close his eyes. He did not cry out. He had no thought. His last emotion was one of deep, agonized remorse. His body crunched against the stones of the road and lay there limply, arms and legs still crumpled beneath it, his gay red shirt spread like a flower blossoming under the weird bubble of daylight in the midnight calm of Ghaka. The people drew back, whispering in puzzlement. Several of them looked up, trying to see Ghakazian where he hovered hidden in white brilliance, and after a moment a woman went to Tagar and stirred him gently with her foot. "Tagar, Tagar, why do you not get up?" she asked. When she received no answer, she squatted, and then she saw the blood, pooling crimson under his head. She touched it gently, wonderingly, still caught in a more merciful time, but Natil, after one glance, understood. Ghaka herself had become an enemy.

Natil's head swam. All around him he saw the things he had always seen: dark sky, stars, the comfortable heights of the mountains, the farm-dotted valleys. He felt the breeze. He breathed in the odors of grass and stone, crops and animals. But a new and terrible awareness of these things came to him. He could not analyze it. It was as though all his life he had been sweetly asleep, dreaming of a Ghaka that had never existed. Now he had woken. Something had fallen from the sky, tearing apart the dream from the reality, and he would sleep no more. He tried to remember what that dream had been like, but memory had fled, leaving only shreds. Surely it was not all a mirage! he thought in panic. Such

freedom I knew in it, such happiness and security! He did not realize that he had never used those words before.

He moved forward and, kneeling beside Tagar, turned him upon
his back. A long sigh went up from the crowd, for Tagar's nose lay
along his cheek, and blood was congealing down his neck and in
his hair. This is death, Natil thought, calm and cold and very distant. The other was a pleasant piece of flimsy. This is how it ends.

Ghakazian fluttered lower. "Tagar refused to obey me," he said
levelly. "I punished Tagar. So will I punish any mortal who dares
to oppose my will. Go home now, all of you, until I decide how I
shall accomplish my great plan. Do as I say, and you will become
heroes throughout the All. Tagar's essence awaits my pleasure at
the Gate, and if I choose, it will stay there forever, but that is none
of your business. Do not attempt to use the Gate. I will order winged
ones to guard it."

All at once the light went out and night collapsed upon the
road. Natil, raising his eyes, saw the sun-lord dart away in a shower
of red sparks. He rose stiffly, standing with one arm around Rintar
as she cuddled their son and wept. The people were creeping away.
Many were sobbing, though some did not yet know why they cried.
The little family was soon alone with its ancestor under the soft
night sky, in the new silence.

"Natil," Rintar said, wiping her face on his sleeve and lifting
swollen eyes to meet his own, "I have the strange feeling that I have
never wept before. Isn't that foolish? I think . . . I have forgotten
something . . ." She began to cry again, and Natil shivered as he
felt the wind tug at Tagar's wet shirt and brush it against his ankle.

"I don't know what to do with him," he whispered. "Should I
carry him to the Gate for the Messengers? Or are Gates and Messengers a fantasy? Do I leave him on the road, lay him in the grass,
what?"

In the end he sent Rintar and the boy home alone. He walked
to the nearest farm and borrowed a cart. Dragging Tagar's heavy,
loose body onto it, he set out for the Gate. Little by little the thin
gray ribbon of stair loomed larger, winding precipitous and narrow
around the mountain, but by the time he had hauled the cart with
its pitiful burden to the foot, he realized he could do no more.
With his last ounce of strength he pulled Tagar from the cart and
propped him against the unyielding rock, then, groaning with ex-

haustion and misery, lay beside it himself. Is there a Gate? he thought in anguish. Are there worlds beyond worlds, where people still dream? He laid his face against his outstretched arm and sobbed.

When he was spent, he left the body of Tagar and went home. There was nothing else to do. He trudged back the way he had come, pulling the ridiculous cart behind him, unable to plan, to decide how to circumvent the coming day. He looked back once, afraid yet compelled to affirm the fact that he had indeed seen a terrible thing, hoping vainly that it was not so and that he had only been entangled in some fragmented vision, but Tagar still sat propped against the foot of the soaring rock wall, his head loose upon his chest, his legs splayed with his hands resting between them. The dark was lifting now as dawn breathed gray and soft upon the night, and the first steps leading to the Gate glimmered beside the body, still only blurs like strange, pale faces peering watchfully down the road. Natil whimpered, turned, and hurried on. The road unrolled slowly beneath his feet, a single curving ribbon of almost-light, bounded to left and right by darkness. A stifling silence went before him and filled the air behind. He found himself breathing quietly, with caution, and the merry rattle of the little cart's wheels sounded dangerously loud.

Why am I so afraid? he asked himself. He longed for new sunlight, the birds' morning songs, the safe, friendly sounds of slammed doors and voices. He did not dare to take his eyes off the road and fancied that its grayness was less dense, but he could not be sure. He reached the place where he had borrowed the cart and turned onto the path to the farmhouse, searching eagerly for light from the windows. When he saw that there was none and that the house squatted, watching him come with an impatient greed, he pushed the cart through the open gate and fled, racing back to the road, not slackening his pace now he was rid of his obligation. I did not imagine it, he thought. The sky is lighter. He glanced upward, his heart lightening for a moment, but then, far away, he saw the dawn limning the colossal effigies of the winged ancestors. They seemed to acquire definition with an appalling rapidity as the sun rose behind them, and although their mighty outlines shrank to harsh silhouettes and darkened momentarily, they did not lose the impression of power and malice they had given Natil in that second when he had sought the sun. They faced one another across the valleys, wings furled uneasily but for Hiranka, whose wide stone feathers boasted an exuberant, uncontrolled vitality. I have never seen them look like that before, Natil thought in despair. How can stone hold so much movement?

As the sun tipped the images Natil saw a small feathered form leave Hiranka's shoulder and swoop toward the neck of the valley, three others with it. They were still far away, four brown specks against the vast red semicircle of the rising sun, but Natil flung himself off the road and ran into the field that bordered it, curling himself into a ball, forehead rammed against knees, arms circling his trembling legs. Why am I doing these foolish things? he wondered. It was as though someone else were being born in him, someone with a long-dormant instinct for self-preservation suddenly awakened. It was as though when a part of him died, there on the road under the merciless glare of the sun-lord's light, another part had begun to bud and then blossom, garish blooms of action without thought, the purpose obscure but looming pregnant with disaster. They came toward him, gliding swiftly on the dawn wind, and he heard them calling to one another or to the sun, he could not tell. He closed his eyes. Now the rush of air under spread wings hummed to him, and he sensed that they had checked their flight, they had seen him.

"Natil, why are you lying in the wet grass?" one of them shouted down to him. "Do you think you are a sheep?" They laughed and though Natil strained to detect hostility or mockery in the merry voices, he could find none. The laughter was open and kind. He opened his eyes and struggled to his feet wonderingly, standing to watch them hurtle toward the Gate. I am not the Natil who met Tagar at my door, he thought, but you, my brothers, have not changed. Why? Ghakazian sent the essence from Tagar by force, and all my kin on the road were changed. Don't you know? At the thought of Ghakazian he shivered, and regaining the road, he walked on.

The morning had dawned fair. Sunlight glittered on the moist ground, slicing bright and new between the peaks and flashing over the valleys. The sky was cloudless and very blue. But Natil, turning at last onto the path that meandered to his own gate, heard no birds or lilt of human voice.

He closed his door quietly behind him, walked along the dim, narrow hall, and turned in to the fire room. The hearth was black-scorched and empty of new wood, and night still lingered in the corners where the sun did not probe. His wife sat on a stool, her loom a wooden skeleton against the wall beside her, her hands loose in her lap. She glanced up at him as he came to her, but she did not rise. Natil lowered himself to the floor, where a draught blew down the chimney to chill him, and brushed the sweat from his face with both palms of his blood-stained, grimy hands. Rintar looked away.

"My father," she said. "Did he come from Linla with his family? Did my grandmother build the loom for me and teach me how to weave? Tell me, Natil, is there a world called Linla at all? Where did we come from? There is nothing behind us that I can see, and ahead there is a darkness. You and I are here in this small, cold room, in a house set down between the feet of mountains, and though I know somehow that I have been here forever, yet it is all strange to me. Tagin and I came home and slept, and though I tried to command a dream, I did not dream at all."

"Hush!" he said, more sharply than he had intended. "I think that the times of dreaming are over, Rintar. A spell has been broken, and we must try to forget the peace and wonder of the dreams. Where is Tagin?"

"Still asleep." Her head was averted, and for a moment Natil studied her anxiously. A lethargy was on her. With her shoulders hunched under the green shawl and her spine bowed she looked suddenly old and tired, a woman hanging in the years between maturity and age, her true age impossible to guess. His hands found his own face once more. Hesitantly his fingers traced its delineations, and he was not reassured. So there is to be this also, he thought. In the dream, time moved with us. Now it roars behind us, herding us quickly to an end that can no longer be predicted. He wanted to reach out for Rintar, to hold tightly to himself the only security he had left, but his hands came away from his cheeks and he looked at them.

"I did not know what to do with Tagar," he whispered, and at that name Rintar cowered further.

"I do not want to think about him," she said harshly. "Who was he, anyway? An old man. Just an old man ready to die!"

Natil came to himself and stood, gripping her arms and drawing her unwillingly to her feet. "Then think about Ghakazian!" he said roughly. "There is not much time left, Rintar. I do not know why, but I feel hunted. Something hangs over the valley waiting for a word, a fullness of moment, oh, I don't know! We must make a plan. We cannot stay in the house."

"Nor can we go to Roita, if there really is such a place. Ghakazian forbade us to go to the Gate."

Natil remembered. He was astonished that he had ever forgotten. Ghakazian the Disposer, Ghakazian the Unhuman, the being who was appointed to order their lives, had told them to go home. Now he knew where the four winged ones had been going. So there was a Gate. That much was real. Now it would be guarded against them, because Ghakazian wanted it so. He looked into Rintar's brown eyes, not seeing them, frowning, holding back the terror that had no meaning so that he could think.

"There are two alternatives," he said at length. "We can leave the house tonight and try to slip through the Gate, or we can go in the opposite direction to the caves that lead under the mountains far in the north, and hide. I wonder what the others will do?"

"I don't care!" Rintar shouted, pushing him away. "I want to stay here with the sheep and my garden and the fish in the river. I will obey the sun-lord, and he will leave me in peace. Whatever he asks me to do, I will do it. You are not yourself, Natil, and neither was Tagar. We belong to Ghakazian. He is our good."

Natil swung to the window and, placing both hands on the sill, spoke to Rintar quietly. "What was he in the dream, Rintar, this Ghakazian, this sun-lord? Think carefully."

Rintar exclaimed in mingled exasperation and impatience but stood thinking as he had told her, and gradually the lines of pique in her face smoothed out. Desire for what had been, sorrow at the loss that she had been desperate not to confront, gentled in her eyes and her lips. She began to cry. "I want to understand," she said brokenly. "I want to dream again."

"Never again," he replied shortly, still with his face turned to the sky outside. "Do you remember Ghakazian in the days before he hovered above us and flung my ancestor to his death at my feet?"

She made as if to cover her ears, then straightened and answered levelly. "He was . . . well . . . he just *was*, Natil. The sun did his bidding and he loved the sun. He made rain come. When he was not on Ghaka, the soul somehow went out of all of us, and when he returned, the world was whole again." She fell silent, and at last he dropped his arms and folded them, turning into the room, leaning against the window.

"That is all?"

"He owned Ghaka . . ." she concluded lamely, and Natil raised an eyebrow bitterly.

"Owned? What word is that? He was Ghaka's good, but he did not own Ghaka. Ghaka belongs to us, to you and me, the winged and wingless, the people of this earth." He stamped his foot. "These mountains. We were born here. Where was he born? Where did he come from? What is he? Is he a child of the sun?"

"He is immortal." She struggled with the words. "He was here on Ghaka before any of us. The W—" Her mouth fought to catch the memory before it passed through her mind and was lost forever. "The Worldmaker made him and the sun together."

"How do you know that?"

"The ancestors . . ."

"Have you seen the Worldmaker? Where is the long memory that let you see him talking to the ancestors? Rintar!" He was in haste to make her see, and his urgency made him cruel. "Wherever he is from, whatever he used to be, we can no longer walk in dreams where he was good and beautiful. There may or may not be a Worldmaker. That is not our affair. But there is a being on Ghaka who wishes us evil, who will use us, who is very powerful, who is not one of us. We call Ghakazian 'he' and 'him' because we have no word to describe what he really is, but one thing I know. He is out to destroy us. Perhaps he was once the soul of Ghaka and demanded nothing of us but that we should exist, but now, today, he is our herdsman, our slaughterer."

"Why do you talk this way?" Rintar was beside herself with fear. "You do not know these things any more than you know why we have lost our true memories. Yes, Natil! Lost them! I do not believe the past was a dream. I believe in yesterday as it really was!"

"I believe nothing," he ended, with such ferocity that she lost all desire to argue and slumped back onto the stool. "All I know is that we must run."

"There is a Gate," she went on slowly. "There must be, for Ghakazian spoke of it. If we must leave our home, then let us try to pass through the Gate. It does not matter whether Roita exists or not. Better to go through a Gate into the unknown than to stay on Ghaka. If Ghakazian is as you say he is, then to stand against him is futile. I wish," she finished bitterly, "that I had never been born."

Silence followed her words. The room seemed to grow colder and gradually, as their eyes roamed it, to be smaller, uglier, than ever before. Across the tiny hall they heard Tagin cry out, but Rintar did not stir. Presently he came to them, hair tousled, feet bare. He saw his father and rushed to him, and like a stiff, unwilling tree branch Natil was forced to bend and lift him up.

"In my sleep Tagar came to me," the child murmured, "with gray hair and skin as pale as a Trader's. I do not like him anymore."

Rintar rose at once, with purpose. "Set a fire, Natil," she said. "We will eat hot food and drink a little, and then we will go. Night will cover our path to the Gate." She did not look at him. She went into the hall, and Natil, about to set his son beside the hearth, glanced out the window. Winged ones were circling the valley, thirty, forty of them, wheeling silently and ominously over the fields. He withdrew quickly, knowing he and his family could do nothing until the sun went away and darkness came to hide them from the eyes as keen as a winter wind. When he ventured another look, the sky was empty, but he thought he saw a swiftly moving cloud angle in the direction of the sun-lord's crag.

# 8

The four winged ones whom Ghakazian had sent to guard the Gate against those who might try to leave had cheerfully done as they were asked for only Mirak knew his lord's mind. Mirak himself went home to his cave, pondered what he had read in the Book, and brooded, but Ghakazian left his peak and flapped uneasily to and fro over his peaceful-seeming land. The Trader was still on Ghaka. He could do nothing until the Trader left, for no word of his plans must reach the council, and all that day he wheeled slowly up and down, back and forth, his shadow streaming with him over the sheep-dotted hills and silver-specked streams. Tagar clouded his immortal mind, Tagar who had refused him, Tagar whose essence waited somewhere in the cold damp crannies of rock near the Gate. Tagar had diminished him somehow, but his murder had been necessary. So much that he did not like would be necessary in order to save Shol from certain destruction. The sun beamed down, flowing over him, diffusing through his floating hair, heating his light body, but there was no longer any room for sunlight in his mind.

In the evening he descended his rock flue, dropped to his arched doorway, and walked his dark hall, wings towering above him, chin outflung, fingers absently stroking his hair. All of them, he thought. I must not miss one. I must send winged ones to cover the whole of Ghaka, and even the caves in the north must be searched. I will speak to them and they will understand.

The Trader moved through the deepening twilight, his purchases slung over one narrow shoulder, his eyes contentedly watching the slow passage of rock and hedge that seemed to glide past. Avenues for trade were shrinking in the universe, he reflected, but on Ghaka it was still good to wander from farm to farm exchanging goods and news without anxiety. Steadily, negligently, he watched the mountain loom, thinking of the hot sun of Danar that awaited it, and its imagination was still entangled in the blue shadows of the haeli forests when it came to the foot of the stairs and saw Tagar. For a moment he simply stood and looked, but then he went up to the body and spoke.

"Are you sleeping, mortal?"

There was no answer. Wind stirred the gray-brown hair that curtained the invisible face and fluttered on the still, red-clad breast. After another moment of observation the Trader bent.

"Are you tranced?" he enquired politely, but puzzlement was growing under the reluctance to disturb. He put out one delicate hand, drawing back the thick hair. He could not comprehend what he saw, but a chill sent his body shaking, milky and tremulous, against the rock. Withdrawing his hand, he tightened his scarf, whistled as he turned to scan the twilight, then swiftly squatted, feeling under the hair for the chin. Tagar's head lolled suddenly back. The hair fell away from the face, and the Trader cried out as he recognized Tagar, but he did not take his fingers away. He looked for a long time at the crushed nose splayed against the cheek, the vacant, sightless eyes, the dry, black blood crusted over the bruises.

"On Ghaka?" he whispered to himself, his thoughts racing. He knew what form of horror he was seeing, and bringing his other hand to rest on the back of the head, he lowered it carefully to lie once more against the chest. "What did you do, Tagar?" he muttered, standing irresolute, while around him night deepened. "Ghakazian must be told of this." But even as he turned back along the road a shadow came between himself and the strengthening brightness of the stars, moving lazily yet filling the Trader with such foreboding that he stopped and remained still until the sky was clear again. "I must consider," he told himself, standing in the middle of the deserted road like a thin shaft of moonlight.

Gradually certain things came together in his mind; the emptiness and silence of the countryside throughout the day, the feeling of oppression which had caused him to avoid conversation with the few wingless ones he had seen scurrying north beneath the shade of the sparse trees, and most of all, the sudden need he had felt to blend with grass and stone when he had heard the steady beat of wings disturbing the hot afternoon. A group of winged ones had rushed by him overhead, and he had felt weak. Why? He had decided that it was because he had suffered Ghaka's uncurtained sun and overrich air for long enough and needed the balance of a drift through deep space, but now he knew better. Ghaka had begun its long, inevitable plunge to the waiting feet of the Unmaker. The Trader shivered. "Unmaker, Unmaker," he hissed, thinking of the things he had seen on his journeys between the worlds, and then he turned and ran to the Gate stair, veering past Tagar's indifferent remains.

He began to climb, thinning his body so that he almost floated from step to step, counting them to himself as he went so that he would not think of how Janthis's face would look when he stood before him to give him his news. Ghakazian does not know that Tagar lies at the foot of the mountain, he thought suddenly. If he knew he would not let me go. He paused and looked out and down. Nothing could be seen of Tagar's body. The earth below was lapped in darkness. The Trader began to run lightly to the last spur of rock and the entrance to the Gate. With relief he at last breasted the short tunnel cave, bracing himself against the constant wind that blew through the opening where the winged ones alighted to approach the Gate. The Gate loomed ahead, a thin arch whose sides were two vast wings sweeping upward to meet over the keystone, and beyond, the Trader could see black space and the steady pricks of white stars.

Hearing voices, he halted. Four winged ones waited between himself and his freedom, talking quietly together, lit dimly by such sunlight as Ghakazian had given them to illumine the cave. But it was not their presence that caused the Trader to quiver like strung pearls. Another consciousness permeated the shadows, and the Trader felt the wash of a terrible rage and an impotent power tug at him. For a moment he was afraid; then he turned to quest the darkness. "Who is there?" he called softly. "Who angers?" The rage disappeared, and then little flurries of sadness, pleas for help probed him. The winged ones chattered on, oblivious, but because the Trader was not a mortal, it was in his power to divine partially the hearts of essence and star, immortal and the Law, and he suddenly knew what waited, trapped, before the Gate. Tagar. The name echoed in his mind as though the man himself had spoken it, the voice anguished and full of betrayal. "I know," the Trader whispered back. "I will go to Danar. I will tell them, Tagar." Something moved in the black stillness, a flick of gray instantly gone, and the Trader shrugged his load of wool higher on his shoulders and walked boldly forward. The winged ones' conversation ceased, and they sprang to block the Gate as he emerged into the light, but when they saw the transparent body, the voluminous blue scarf wrapping the bald head, they relaxed.

"What do you take from Ghaka?" one of them asked him curiously, and he glanced from one to the other, seeing the smiles, the warm, friendly eyes. These young men were still whole. "I have wool for Shol, just a little, and a woven carpet for Storn of Danar to sleep on in the winter," he answered politely. "Now let me pass."

"Ghakazian said that none might pass," another said anxiously in a low voice, and the smiles left their faces to be replaced by an embarrassed indecision. The Trader took a firm step and spoke loudly, aware of the time it had taken him to look at Tagar and climb the stair, aware also that other eyes must find the body and tell the sun-lord where it lay.

"I am a Trader," he said firmly, pointing to his scarf with one twig-thin, shimmering arm. "I am not bound to obey any sun-lord as long as I obey the Law. Ghakazian's pronouncements have nothing to do with me."

They consulted together, their whispers rising sibilant to feather out against the rough rock ceiling, and the Trader waited calmly, humming one of his tuneless songs. He knew that he could slip through their hands without effort if they chose to detain him, but he also knew that he was forbidden to do so. Presently they turned to him.

"We are sure that the sun-lord would not want us to detain a Trader," one of them said, a twinkle in his eye, "and in any case you could never be held by such as us. Go to the Gate."

The Trader bobbed his head and strode past them, passing under the arch and out to where floor and ceiling suddenly fled and his world waited to claim him. Lightly he stepped away from Ghaka. He knew that he would never set foot on it again.

With a curt word to his wife Mirak left his cave and dropped into Ghaka's night, unfurling his wings and swinging west to where

Ghakazian's slim peak reared black and sharp against the lighter dimness of the sky. He flew steadily, roads meeting and parting like spiders' webs far below, until at last, allowing the uprush of air near the crag to pull him over the crest, he folded his wings and came to rest with supple grace on the inner ledge. Ghakazian was not there. Mirak leaned into the chill breath of the mountain, glided down to the archway, and passing through, walked across the dais. At the far end of the hall there was a glimmer of pale light, feeble as starlight on a moth's wing, and in it Ghakazian stood, one elbow in the palm of a hand, the other hand curved about his chin. His wings were unfurled and draped loosely around him, an untidy huddle of trailing feathers, and he was muttering quietly to himself. He did not hear Mirak approach until the other came into the fitful glow of light around him; then he started and whirled. Caught off guard, made anxious for the first time by the dark corners of his own domain, he shouted at Mirak, "What do you want?" Immediately he recovered himself and walked forward smiling warmly, reaching for Mirak's shoulders. "I did not mean to raise my voice to you," he said. "I was deep in thought, and I was expecting no one. Perhaps I should seal my funnel as well as my door."

Mirak drew away, hurt. "Would you close yourself off from me, sun-lord?" he said. "The Book states . . ."

"I know what the Book states!" Ghakazian snapped. "Do not forget just who you are, Mirak. I have deigned to take you into my confidence, but that does not mean you may regard yourself as my equal. I have no equal."

Warily Mirak's eyes traveled Ghakazian. There was peevishness in the set of the wide mouth, a sullen caprice evident in the shrug of a brown shoulder and the way the eyes slid sharply to meet his own.

Ghakazian shook back his hair. "Why did you come, Mirak? I would have sent for you if I had needed you."

"I could stay in the cave no longer," Mirak confessed. "My mind was too full of all that I had read and heard. Why do we wait?"

Ghakazian opened his mouth, then checked himself. No. To tell Mirak about the Trader who still wandered somewhere over Ghaka's night-dusted roads would be to admit to him that he was afraid of the judgment of the council. Pah! he thought derisively. The council can council from now until the end of the universe and still do nothing but waste breath. Only I dare to perform, to do. He said gently, "Mirak, I want you to fly to the Gate and ask your brothers there whether any traveler has attempted to leave. Traveler, mind you," he emphasized, holding up an admonitory finger. "Bring me word as soon as you know. Watch the roads as you go, and tell me also who moves along them and why."

"But lord, I thought perhaps . . ."

"Do not argue!" Ghakazian felt his temples swell with the effort to remain reasonable and calm, and he looked at Mirak feeling a faint contempt not visible on his face. "Time is growing short. You must learn to do as you are told." Ghakazian turned his back and began to pace again, head down, feathers trailing the smooth floor of the stone hall with a swish.

Miserably Mirak left him, leaping into the darkness. He has much to occupy his mind, he thought determinedly to himself as he left the high black sky and sought the lower, more turbulent air so that he could watch the roads. Time is growing short. How is it that time can now move faster? I do not understand these things, I can only obey him, trust him. There is a great work for us to do together.

Effortlessly he adjusted his flight to the constant eddies of night wind which played over fields and rushed through the clefts in the broken, serried feet of the mountains, soon turning toward the Gate crag far ahead, a spear of blackness. His eyes scanned the ground below him. Nothing stirred. No lights blinked up at him, no snatches of night song came to his ears. The wingless are silent tonight, he thought. Sulking perhaps, because of the once-wise Tagar and the closing of the Gate against them. I pity them, the mud-walkers, the sheep-herders. A rush of intoxication flushed warm through his limbs, and he smiled to himself, turning his head for a moment to watch the rhythmic rise and fall of his wings. When he looked back, he thought he saw a bulky shadow move on the crossroad below, where the road that snaked up into the widest valley met the larger thoroughfare that ran straight to the Gate stair. He darted low, veered, then came around again more slowly, almost grazing the earth. With head turned to scan the hedge he saw a shadow with more solidity than the streamers of darkness that tangled in the undergrowth. His feet found the road as he folded his wings, and he stood gleefully with arms outflung.

"I see you," he called. "Come onto the road."

Natil grimaced in bitterness. Rintar grasped his arm with a sudden convulsion of fear.

But Tagin crawled out immediately and sprang to his feet.

"Oh, it is you, Mirak!" he said. "Were you looking for us? We . . ." But he did not finish, for Natil scrambled after him and swept him into his arms.

"Why were you hiding in the hedge," Mirak demanded disdainfully, "in the middle of the night? Where were you going?"

Mirak saw fear on Natil's face and a fleeting indecision. Then Natil pointed down the road.

"We are going to my brother's house, there beside the Gate mountain. Not that it is any of your business, Mirak. We mourn for Tagar. We are lonely."

"Indeed," Mirak sneered, but doubt clouded his features. "The Gate is closed to you, Natil."

"But my brother's door is open, and you know perfectly well where he lives," Natil replied patiently. "I must take the Gate road to reach his farm. Or would you have me drag my family across the fields just so that I may not be thought to be traveling to the Gate? This is all foolishness, Mirak. Why may we not go through to Roita in any case if we choose? Ghakazian can find us just as easily there as on Ghaka."

Mirak's newfound compulsion to mock and bully swiftly ebbed. "He is not to be questioned," he said lamely. "I know where your brother lives, of course I know. I took him into the sky once so that he could see his fields laid out before him, and he was grateful." His smile came back, but this time it was rueful and engaging. "It is not my business to detain anyone," he went on. "Oh, go on your way, Natil! I was curious, that is all."

Natil set Tagin on his feet, took his hand, and walked away, Rintar following. Mirak watched them go until he saw them as he had first seen them, a patch of bulky shadow against the grayness of the road. Then he soared up, flashed over them, and was lost to sight.

Though he stayed close to the road, he glimpsed no other travelers. Soon the Gate stair was before him, a spiral of paleness interspersed with darkness that seemed to hold the mountain tightly in upon itself. He was about to twist himself vertically in order to skim the side of the mountain when again something caught his eye, and he dropped gently back onto the road and stood peering ahead to where the first step beckoned. There was a feeling of dank unapproachability between himself and the rock, an invisible stream of something that he could not interpret. A whiff of some distasteful odor came with it. He strained to see, but the mountain's star-shadow was deep, and for all his keen sight he could make out nothing. Summoning up his courage, he went closer. The smell intensified, and the feeling was like a barrier against him. If it had not been for Ghakazian's order to investigate the road, he would have taken wing, for a fear flowed into him also, but he squared his shoulders and stepped across the almost touchable line of shadow. His foot met resistance, something heavy and soft, but cold. He bent.

It took a long time for the reality of what he was seeing to gather into one perception, but as his eyes became accustomed to the gloom he knew. Tagar was a lonely thing, the first fruit of a new and ugly seed. He said it would not be pleasant, Mirak thought incoherently, frozen with horror. I must accept this, I must not be less than he is. But the accepting was still buried under his new visions of pomp and power, and he could not see the bloating form of Tagar as a consequence.

He rose slowly, hardly daring to breathe, and backed carefully into starlight. He could no longer see it, but that did not matter; he knew it was huddled there. Softly, afraid to make the slightest sound, he took to the air, hovering for a moment to brush the soles of his feet where they had pressed Tagar's leg, and then with a shudder he careened upward, away, to where the air was fresh and clean.

He spent longer with his kin than he had intended, standing uneasily against the Gate cave wall and listening while they laughed and chattered, answering briefly when they spoke to him but otherwise gazing out through the Gate to the forbidding reaches of space. He was afraid to leave them and venture out into the night, where that thing crouched, but he felt almost as exposed and vulnerable where he was. There are shadows all over Ghaka, he thought, appalled, and when the sun-lord takes the essences, those shadows will become as full of terror as the foot of this mountain. He edged closer to the Gate, but no comfort was to be had out where the stars burned away. He will take my essence also, Mirak thought. I can only go with him to Shol if I agree to become like . . . Tagar. Agree? Do I have any choice? He cried out with pain as all at once, for the first time, the full import of what it would all mean came clear in his head. His companions had stopped talking and were looking at him, and like a drunken man he pushed himself away from the wall. "I must return to Ghakazian," he said thickly. "I am expected." He did not want to walk back into those shadows, but to reach free air he had to. Without another word he ran down the tunnel, to where the cave mouth glimmered faintly, a window on escape. Where is the essence of Tagar? his mind whispered to him. It lurks somewhere, watching you, Mirak, watching all of you. He imagined that he felt lips brush his ear, a hand impress itself against his back. With a scream he flung himself out of the mountain. Sweating, pouring fear, he spun, his wings stiff and heavy, then regained control and strained for more height. He would fly upward forever, he would arrow to the sun and burn rather than touch Ghaka again. Before he overcame his blind panic, the Gate mountain had half-sunk below the dark horizon, and he had returned to the sun-lord's funnel. "He will let me read the Book again," Mirak gasped out loud as he felt rock graze his stomach, and he put his arms around the crag and closed his eyes. "I will read how it will be, and then I will be comforted." He launched himself down, falling into faint sunlight and the rustle of Ghakazian as he hovered above his ledge.

The sun-lord seemed to have overcome his uncertain temper. As Mirak stumbled clumsily to find his footing on the ledge he came and stood beside him, smiling. "Well, Mirak?" he enquired, but before he could go on, Mirak clutched at him, his breath still ragged, sweat still glistening on his face.

"Oh, Ghakazian!" he blurted. "I found Tagar! You told me how it would be, but I did not realize, I did not understand! Tagar, he . . . he stinks."

Ghakazian coolly shook himself free of Mirak's trembling fingers. "What do you mean, you found Tagar? I left him lying on the road. I presumed that you had seen him many times as you passed back and forth."

"No, no! He has been moved. Someone has . . . put him by the Gate stair."

Ghakazian rounded on him. "The Gate stair! Who? How long?" A thought smote him, and he whirled to grip Mirak violently by the wrists. Muddy orange light suddenly flared from him, and he shook Mirak. "What did the guards say?" he roared. "Has anyone been to the Gate?"

Mirak turned his head away, straining against the heat and turbulence that rippled under the skin of the golden body.

"A Trader went through," he managed.

"When?"

"At twilight, I think. Please, lord, I cannot bear this!"

But Ghakazian did not release him. Shafts of red light ran giddily around the rock walls, and under Ghakazian's fingers Mirak felt his flesh cringe and cry out against the fire.

"Did the guards see Tagar on their way to the Gate?"

"I do not know. I do not think so. They said nothing of it. Lord!" The plea echoed and at last came to Ghakazian's ears. He let go, and Mirak slumped against the wall.

"Did the Trader see Tagar, then?" Ghakazian murmured to himself. "If he did . . ."

"Tagar was horrible," Mirak said brokenly. "Will I be like Tagar, sun-lord? Is that how it will be?"

"It does not *matter*, Mirak, can't you see?" Ghakazian retorted. "Your essence will not care how your body rots away!"

"Rots away?" The words were hardly more than a movement of Mirak's lips.

Ghakazian considered him briefly, then dimmed his fire and spoke kindly. "Come, Mirak. Have you forgotten so soon the exalted position I have called you to? The Book knows."

A pathetic eagerness lightened Mirak's face, and he left the wall. "May I read it now?"

"In a moment. Were there any abroad on the road?"

Mirak remembered. "Yes," he replied. "I saw Natil and his family. They were on the Gate road. They said they were going to visit Natil's brother."

It did not really matter, Ghakazian knew, whether Natil tried to hide on Roita. He could talk his way past the guards and purchase a little time for himself. It was not Natil's flight that sent Ghakazian into a spasm of haste and fear but the stubborn disobedience behind Natil's action. I will not have him defy me, Ghakazian thought. I will take him, and I must hurry. Even now the Trader may be walking through Danar's Gate. He swung to Mirak.

"Go out and gather all the winged ones. Send them to the wingless with this message. They are to gather above their valleys, on the cliffs, on the peaks. Tell them . . ." His face suddenly lit with sly humor. "Tell them that I have a message for them from the Worldmaker."

"You will lie to them?" Mirak's eyes grew round, and Ghakazian hung grimly to his last shred of patience.

"There is no time to try and make them understand," he said slowly and deliberately. "Go and do what you are told, Mirak, and then you may read in the Book if you wish."

Unhappily Mirak hesitated, nodded, then flew slowly up to where black sky capped the ragged circle of the funnel's mouth. Longing for what had been filled him, and for just a moment he did not want to share in his sun-lord's exalted destiny. He only wanted to go home in peace.

Ghakazian watched Mirak until the darkness engulfed him, and then he went through his hall to the windy slit in the mountain that was its front entrance. He stood looking out over a floor of puffed, solid cloud hanging motionless in the night quiet. He had hoped to sway Natil, to persuade him to stand beside him and show the other wingless ones that they had nothing to fear, but Natil had spoken to him without shrinking even while Tagar's body lay at his feet, and now he crawled toward the Gate in impudent disobedience. Ghakazian knew he could do nothing against such stubbornness. Shall I speak to him at all? the sun-lord wondered. Or shall I find and kill him and be done with him? For the present he had forgotten Shol and Sholia's imminent alliance with the Unmaker and all his fine words concerning the preservation of Shol and Ghaka against black fire. His mind was full of spite toward Natil, and that spite began to encompass all the wingless ones. He saw himself killing Natil, and with the picture came a red tide of satisfaction, a greed to flaunt his ownership of all of them. Blindly he gazed into his shadow, which spread thin and menacing over the clouds, cast by the feeble sunlight left in the hall. When he had sucked all the sweet juices from his visions, he stepped into the darkness, spread his wings, and began his search for Natil.

When they could discern the foot of the Gate mountain, Natil, Rintar, and Tagin rested for a while, sitting with hands clasped. Tagin fell asleep, his head in Rintar's lap. Natil watched the clouds hang over him and the twinkle of far stars. I do not need the universe, he said to himself. I ask only Rintar, Tagin, and Ghaka. I have a right to these. But I am only a mortal, and Ghakazian is my disposer. "Come," he said to Rintar, who was nodding with tiredness over Tagin's heavy form. "It's not much farther now." He picked up Tagin, who woke with a protest, and set off again, Rintar trailing behind. He did not know what he would do when they had climbed the stair, what he would say to the guardians. Deep within himself he did not believe that they would reach the Gate, but he was doing all that he could, and he would not give up until the end.

In another hour they stood before the stair, looking up its steep, unlighted height. Rintar groaned. "I cannot face it," she whispered. "Let's sleep for a little while here at the foot, and go up just before dawn."

"It is already just before dawn," Natil whispered back, his eyes drawn to where he knew Tagar still sat. Dread stole over him, prickling up his spine, and he did not need to see into the blackness to trace the outlines of what filled the shadow. A stench lingered here, but Rintar was too distrait to notice it. He turned his back on it.

"Courage!" he said. "When we reach Roita, we can rest, and there are many places where we may hide." He did not even convince himself.

"It is not courage I lack," Rintar hissed back, "but new feet and a chance to warm myself. How cold the night is! Anyone would think it was winter."

Natil felt as though the presence behind him was sliding nearer. He swung Tagin onto his back and placed a foot upon the first step, not waiting to see if Rintar would follow. He began to climb.

Rintar was glad of the darkness, which hid the terror of the nothingness that fell away on her right. With one hand against the sheer wall of the mountain to steady herself she mounted, her eyes on the step in front, her attention fixed on the Gate far above. Fear of falling grew in her. She, too, had passed lightly and thoughtlessly up this stair many times, but that had been in the dream years. She brought to mind the comforting cave tunnel. Determinedly she saw herself walking along it behind Natil, safe rock at either hand, and as the minutes went by she pictured the Gate itself, but somehow it no longer beckoned her to places she had once known and loved. Its invitation was curt, almost violent, and she stood before it trembling, compelled to go forward, afraid to go back, yet not knowing what now lay beyond its arrogant carved wings. Natil paused, and she found herself with face pressed to stone, palms flat beside her cheeks, her knees weak.

"Dawn is not far off," he said. "The sky is lighter, I'm sure. We have passed the halfway point, Rintar."

She lifted her head to look at him, but he had started forward again. She thought that she could see him more clearly now, the slim back bowed under Tagin's drowsy weight, the confidence in the well-placed feet. Greatly daring, she turned and looked out over Ghaka. Clouds drifted just below her gaze, grayish now, and though she could not see the earth, the horizon had begun to divide once more into sky and world. Dizziness swept over her, and quickly she averted her face, summoning up her courage, and lifted herself onto the next step. She knew that whatever happened she could never make the journey back down to the floor of Ghaka. She was close to collapse.

In the hour before the rising of the sun, after he had searched the road and every farmhouse that lay along it, Ghakazian returned to the Gate mountain, hovering above it. Time was being wasted. Natil was causing him to expend himself in foolishness, and Ghakazian's maliciousness grew with his impatience. He had been about to alight at the cave and talk to the guardians when out of the corner of his eye he caught slow, dogged movement. He considered commanding the sun to pull itself free more quickly, to pin them to the side of the mountain with a sudden gush of heat, but the dragging, painful rhythm of their climb had already claimed his attention, and he watched them with curiosity. He drew back a little, under the edge of a cloud, and when they rounded a corner and were lost to sight, he followed. Even had he not attempted to conceal himself, he did not believe that they would have seen him. Everything in them was focused on the Gate, and he could almost hear the breath wheeze ragged in their lungs as they labored on. For a long time he surveyed them coldly. There was no pity in his gaze, only a callous interest that caused him to calculate their degree of endurance. They paused for a moment. Ghakazian could see Natil half-turn to speak to his wife, and then they went on. Not until they were at the last circuit of the mountain which would bring them to the Gate did he close in, fluttering down to the stair above them, just out of sight, and waiting.

The stair bent up and around, and with a sigh Natil carefully hitched his son into a more comfortable position and prepared to take the last corner. Beyond that was the heart, and a rock floor for his feet, and the short, easy walk to the Gate itself. He heard Rintar panting behind him. "Natil, my leg is pinched," Tagin whispered in his ear, a tickle of warm child-breath that stirred his hair and made him smile. He aimed a kiss at the straight little nose. "You can get down soon," he replied and took the next few steps with a lighter heart. The stair fanned out, the stone steps became imperceptibly broader, and Natil quenched an urge to run at them. The corner was there, now he was around it. As a sudden premonition of failure gripped him he glanced up, then cried out and let Tagin slip from his arms to teeter on the step behind. Rintar shrieked and grabbed for the boy, and all three of them swayed over the abyss.

Sitting on a step just above Natil was Ghakazian, elbows resting negligently on naked knees, his wings pulled to either side of him like a cape that gleamed sullenly in the strengthening, heatless light of dawn. The soft brown hair lifted spasmodically from the neck, stirred by the breeze that had sprung up. The dark eyebrows were raised in mock surprise, and the mouth greeted a shocked and bitterly angry Natil with a smile of mild disapproval.

"Well, Natil," Ghakazian said in tones of loving but injured reproof. "Have my wingless ones suddenly lost their hearing? Did I not forbid the Gate to all of them? And does the Gate not lie there"—waving behind him but never letting his eyes leave Natil's white face—"behind me, so close, oh, far closer to you now than your dear brother's farm? Why did I forbid the Gate to you, I wonder?" He paused and gave Natil an enquiring tilt of the head. "I see that you have forgotten, so I will remind you. I have work for you to do. I told you so when we met on the road. Do you remember that? How selfish you are, the three of you! Since you were born I have asked nothing of you, and now that I require your help, you behave as though I had become a monster, a tyrant, a thing to be evaded and despised. You return my love with suspicion, and my warnings and admonitions with disregard."

"I tried to tell you, Natil," Rintar screamed from behind him, "but you would not listen!"

Ghakazian's smile widened. "Women are often wise in their intuitions, aren't they, Natil? Why should you suppose that just because Ghaka has lain peaceful and sunny all these years, there would be no changes? The universe is changing, ah, yes, so quickly, and Ghaka must bend to take the load upon herself. Look at me, Natil!" The last words were sharp and commanding, and Natil had no choice but to raise his eyes to the glittering dark ones above him. As he gazed a last tide of love for Ghakazian, a helpless, hopeless welling of worship and the desperate need to trust filled his heart, and tears came hurtfully to trickle down his face. "A sun-lord's business is his own. It does not concern a mortal, nor should it. A mortal is born to obey in silence. You have not obeyed me."

"No, Ghakazian," Natil whispered, emotion strangling him, "but I have loved you, just as Tagar loved you."

That name seemed to act on Ghakazian like acid. He rose and shook out his wings, towering over Natil, and the sad, indulgent smile hardened into a cruel line.

"The universe will not be saved by love!" he spat. "Love is a luxury for the times of peace! I will not be insulted by the offering of your little love. Tagin, come here."

Fearless and uncomprehending, the boy wriggled from his mother's clutch, squeezed past a frozen Natil, and scrambled to the sun-lord's feet. Ghakazian bent and lifted him easily, and Tagin's fingers went at once to the smoldering sun-disc on the broad, hollow chest. Rintar moaned. Natil tried to speak again. Words of argument and denial, of things not reasoned but perceived, churned within him, but under the spell of Ghakazian's gaze he could do nothing but fix his eyes on the disc his son was fondling with such absorption. Two amber wings flared proud and shining at either side of it, and the chain was a range of golden mountains running around Ghakazian's shoulders, tiny yet perfectly etched. Wings and mountains, Natil thought. But that is only half of Ghaka. Perhaps we wingless ones with our green valleys and our white flocks have never meant as much to him as the sky men and the wind howling through the high, barren passes of the crags.

The words he had wanted to say dissolved away. He felt calm. Stepping back, he put both arms about his wife, and Ghakazian saw that he knew what was to come.

"This is necessary," he said loudly. "I need you, the cause needs you, but not as you are."

Tagin seemed oblivious to his surroundings. He continued to play with the disc, smiling and talking quietly to himself, but Rintar shook in a final panic. "Have pity, lord," she pleaded. "We will stay in our house, we will not be troublesome anymore," but Natil silenced her with a short word, holding her tightly.

Dawn had come. The clouds were imbued with a creeping glow of pink light. The sky was paling to a gentle grayness tinged with color, and the shadows on the Gate stair had retreated, taking with them all traces of the hours of sweat and stubborn painful progress that had led to this end. The air was damp and fresh, and far below birds could be faintly heard, singing to the rising sun. Natil looked at Ghakazian with a patient dignity that irritated the sun-lord into haste.

"You will understand before long," he said curtly. Then he raised an arm, and closing his eyes for a moment, he called out a word unknown to Natil and Rintar. Ghakazian did not shout it but rather sang it on a long, ululating note, strong and fiercely beautiful. The note grew until it throbbed in their ears, reverberating like a rolling drumbeat. Rintar began to cry and put her hands to her head, and Natil felt himself swaying, but Tagin gave no sign of having heard it. Ghakazian closed his mouth, but the music went on, and now it was mingled with something else, a mighty rush of sound, as though the sun had opened its mouth and was roaring across the land. The morning breeze began to tug more insistently at their bodies, whipping their hair into their eyes, and their coats flapped like ungainly flags. The breeze became a stiff wind that whistled as it stung them with cold, and they lurched against the rock wall, relinquishing their hold on one another to scrabble with iced fingers, seeking a spur to cling to.

Ghakazian watched impassively, his own hair lying soft and untroubled, his wings unruffled. Tagin prattled on. The voice bellowed now, a deafening, tossing cacophony of power, and the wind became a gale that fastened blind, greedy fingers on them and began to drag them from the stair. They fought it, their eyes forced shut, breath snatched from their mouths, small stones and rock dust stinging their faces, their ears full of the deep, insane screaming, but though they fell to lie against the steps, feeling frantically for any crack, a place to dig in bleeding fingers and scraping feet, the wind plucked them off. It jerked them over the lip of the stair and whirled them about like two streaming, multicolored leaves, and then Ghakazian spoke. Calmly he pointed at them, and after a short and definite word of command the noise and wind ceased, as though a giant hand had been clapped over the gale's mouth. The birds sang again, the clouds hung motionless, their pink fading now to white, and Natil and Rintar plunged without a sound to the rock-strewn foot of the mountain far beneath. "You also, Tagin," Ghakazian said. The child looked up at him, smiling. Ghakazian passed a hand over the round brown eyes, and Tagin went limp; then he tossed him away. Ghakazian did not watch him fall. He glanced up at the blue, delicate sky, spread his wings, and circling the mountain, sped toward his own hall. He had been diverted from his purpose for long enough.

# 9

The winged ones alighted one by one at the farmhouses. In every valley they repeated their message, knocking on doors, standing proudly in the sunlight, and speaking the words Mirak had given to them: *You must climb the sides of your valley and wait. The sun-lord will give you words from the Worldmaker. Take nothing with you. Go now.* Bewildered but obedient, they did so. Some went with great gladness, for the Worldmaker had sent them no message in many generations. Others, the people who had stood on the road when Tagar brought them the message of death, went with fear and a vague foreboding. But most of them toiled up the steep goat paths with an uncomplaining stoicism. By late afternoon they sat looking down over their own quiet fields, watching the smoke from their hearth fires thin and eventually die, noting placidly the erratic migration of flocks from one part of a valley to another and back again, waiting.

The winged ones also waited, but in a tense restlessness. Unwilling to return home, they wheeled in ragged clouds between the crags as the afternoon slipped toward evening, and at last Mirak went to tell Ghakazian that the valleys were empty. Ghakazian spoke to Mirak from the wide sweep of his dais. "Send the winged ones forth once more, Mirak. They must say this to the people. 'The Worldmaker has ordained a great change for Ghaka. No longer will the wingless ones be chained to the earth. In his wisdom and kindness he wishes them to enjoy the freedom of the skies also, but their bodies must change. He will change them if they display their trust in him by stepping from the peaks. He will hold them up, he will not let them fall, and he will teach them how to fly.' That is what they must say."

Mirak felt the trembling begin in his legs. His wings shuddered against one another. "But Ghakazian," he said huskily, "that is not true. There has been no message. He will not hold the people up, he will let them fall, they will all fall . . ." He swallowed, and his voice died away. He looked long at Ghakazian standing in the ominous, dying light of approaching sunset, and it seemed to him that the sun-lord had already taken on the shadows of the coming night. His wings were a black serrated cloud. Darkness misted in his hair and shrouded his body in a garment of mystery, and his face was a pale, sickly oval striated with bands of blackness. Only the sun-disc still sparked light, but it was not the light of a healthy and joyous sun. Its rays pierced the dimness with slow, sulky reds and oranges, and its heart glowed a somber silver.

"Stop whining and think for a moment, Mirak," Ghakazian said, his voice echoing forlornly to the high rock ceiling. He did not need to say more. Mirak, after his first horrified protest, understood very well, although he did not want to. He had been abroad all day. He had seen the wingless ones close their doors and walk the valleys, scramble over the teeth of the mountains, strain and weep to reach the top to be at the appointed places with such transparent humbleness, such simple eagerness, that he was ashamed. He had lost sight of the goal. Ghakazian knew that he had forgotten the visions of the Book under the glaring reality of Ghaka's day. He spoke to Mirak musingly, putting all charm and affection into his voice. Not that it mattered. He could destroy Mirak as easily and ruthlessly as he had done Natil and his family. But the other winged ones were more gullible than Mirak. They would listen to Mirak because they respected him, and they would believe.

"On Shol there is a palace of such magnificence," he said, "that it is beyond your imagination. When the Unmaker is driven back and Sholia is in the hands of a grateful council, I think I shall take it for my own. If you wish, Mirak, you may come back to Ghaka with the essences and rule here." Mirak still stood with head sunk on his breast, and Ghakazian, after a quick glance at him, went on craftily. "The council will reward you for your loyalty and devotion to me. Janthis will give their bodies back to the essences, and Ghaka will be full of laughter and gaiety once more. Your world will be a good one to rule."

He knew that such a thing was beyond the power of Janthis, but Mirak did not. He also knew that no sun-lord was allowed to call himself ruler. It was in the responsibilities. At the thought of them a blinding pain shot through Ghakazian's head, leaving him sick and shaking. He quickly put away all contemplation of the duties he had kept in the forefront of his life. He had not recited them in a long time. He knew that he would never do so again.

"Yes," Mirak responded at last, reflectively. "I love Ghaka. I would be a good ruler for her. I would harm no one. Very well, Ghakazian, but I am tired. I will go and pass the words." He turned and walked toward the arch, a froth of sickness in his mind that dragged his feet and wings. Ghakazian let him reach the opening and then called, "Mirak!"

Mirak turned back heavily. "Lord?"

"Tell the winged ones that if any of the wingless refuse to jump off the cliffs, they must be thrown down."

Mirak was too far away to see Ghakazian's face. "Very well," he choked, fleeing the chamber.

He rose gasping from the crag as though it might suffocate him and flew clumsily upward to the crowds of his waiting kinsmen, calling Ghakazian's message to them as he went. They listened to Mirak and did not dare to question. Most of them knew nothing of the events of the past days apart from the fact that the sun-lord had for some reason of his own decided to forbid the Gate to all mortals for a while. They accepted Mirak's command to them because he had always been close to the sun-lord. Shells of ignorance and innocence still wombed them, and if the Worldmaker now willed that they should share their sky with the wingless ones, they would acquiesce without grumbling.

Neither did they balk at Ghakazian's last order to Mirak. They could not imagine why any wingless one would want to defy the Worldmaker and not launch himself forth, but if some refused to do so, the Worldmaker's wishes were clear. Word passed from mouth to mouth. In their rustling thousands they beat their way swiftly down the valleys, and soon their honeycombed peaks stood silent in the rays of the setting sun.

The wingless saw them coming, great clouds that jostled the air, drew nearer, became flocks of giant birds bearing down on them. Each valley felt the shadows flicker and pass, each crowd lining jagged cliffs and crags drew back in momentary uneasiness. The winged slowed, hovered above the people who peered upward wondering, then came to rest behind them. Spokesmen stepped forward, and in the calm of a red sunset began to recite.

Mirak had led his own flock of winged ones to the valley that had once sheltered Tagar and his numerous descendants. These were the mortals who had listened to Tagar's breathless warnings. These had obeyed him and tried to reach the Gate and had been turned back by a blaze of light on the road and the incomprehensible sight of Tagar plummeting from the sky, never to move again. They faced Mirak with silent suspicion, the precipitous drop to the valley floor behind them, and when he had finished speaking, the feeling of wariness had deepened. There was no Natil to step forward and question, but a whisper sighed through the crowd, and it swayed. The Worldmaker? . . . Jump off the cliff? . . . Why does he want to give us wings? . . . A chance to fly! I cannot believe it! . . . A chance to tread the clouds . . .

"The Worldmaker's mind is not our mind!" Mirak shouted. "It is not for us to ask why. He deigns to give you the power of flight. Who will trust him and go?"

The muttering died away. All eyes were fixed on him, and he strove to stand tall and proud, willing his gaze to travel the bewildered faces that thronged him with confidence and assurance.

"Where is the sun-lord?" someone shouted, the voice high and tense. "Let Ghakazian himself come and tell us what the Worldmaker wants of us!"

Wants of us, Mirak thought. If the wingless had no doubts about the message, they would have said "wants for us." He looked at all of them as he answered with words that came from a mind already darkening with a multiplicity of alternatives, all of them lies.

"If he came and stood before you, your decision would be influenced by your love for him," he said loudly. "A sun-lord is forbidden to coerce his subjects, even by his presence. When you meet him in the sky, he will express his approval of your trust in him and in your Maker. He believes and hopes that you can obey without relying on his advice. He bids me tell you to accept this change with dignity. Ghaka has matured."

For a long time they simply faced him unmoving, their faces and the very stiffness of their stance betraying the agony of their thoughts. Mirak felt the mellow warmth of the descending sun on his back. He saw his shadow and the shadows of the winged ones beside him lengthen to lie across the trampled grass and climb the grim crowd. Wind from the valley below came to insinuate itself among them, leaving the smell of sheep and wet flowers on their rough-woven clothes, in their nostrils, speaking dumbly to them of fire new-kindled on their hearths, of the evening meal eaten around the friendly flames in cheerfulness, of their own beds, where they would lie content and drowsy and listen to the night sounds while starlight filtered through the open windows. They did not want the change the Worldmaker had offered them so suddenly and capriciously. They wanted to go home.

Then a young man elbowed his way to the front and faced Mirak, his blue tunic covering broad shoulders and the well-muscled thighs of a shepherd, his face comely and brown and framed in short flaxen hair.

"I am content to live without wings," he said clearly, his words distinct in the evening air. "All my life I have walked the valleys, watched my sheep, and felt good earth beneath my feet. But the Worldmaker speaks. For the first time in many generations he concerns himself once more with the affairs of Ghaka, and we greet his gift to us with grumbling and suspicion. I love the soil, but who am I to say that I will not learn to love the sky? The Worldmaker made us. He knows what is good for us, even if we do not. I will accept his desire for me. I will step from the cliff."

All at once the rows of stiff figures unfroze, drawing closer together and talking in hushed, excited whispers. Mirak caught his breath and did not dare to blink as the young man turned from him and began to walk toward the edge of the cliff. The crowd parted for him. He reached the brink and paused, looking up into the reddening sky. He smiled. Slowly his eyes slid down, surveying the dizzy fall of sheer rock that dropped from his feet to be lost in the evening dimness already spreading over the peaceful valley. Then he raised his arms.

"I believe!" he shouted. "I trust!"

Proudly he stepped forward, leaned outward, and with a cry he launched himself into the abyss. The people rushed to the edge, fists clenched, bodies straining. "Fly, Crenan, fly!" someone shouted.

But Crenan plunged down, turning over slowly as though a giant wheel had impaled him on its axis, and though the people could not hear him strike the ground, they saw the jagged rocks leap to shatter his spread-eagled body.

For a second there was profound silence again, a silence filled with shock and disbelief. Then the people turned, and a woman began to scream, falling to the grass. "You lied!" someone yelled at Mirak. "Liar! Liar!" They surged toward him, rage in the groping hands, the incoherent words, but at a signal from Mirak the winged ones rose gently into the sky, and those below could only shake their fists. Some had already begun to move away weeping, seeking the goat track that they had toiled up, their stricken minds already running to their own doors.

"Cast them down," Mirak ordered. Swiftly the winged ones obeyed, gripping hair, placing strong, relentless arms beneath thrashing shoulders, catching at a fleeing cloak. Like a storm gale howling out of the mountains panic rushed across the exposed hilltop, spreading a madness of terror. The youngest children, seeing their elders run here and there demented, thought that it was a game and shrieked with laughter, but the older ones knelt screaming in the grass and covered their faces.

Like the dregs left after an autumn wind, like deadwood to be disposed of, the people were plucked from the cliff. On the fringes of the melee winged ones hovered, darting to gather those who stumbled inland. All the latent disdain that had slept uneasily within the sky people, all the mute hints of their own superiority that had lain buried deep with their pride suddenly burst into flames of contempt and maliciousness. With an increasing eagerness they went about their task, hands gripping shrinking flesh without pity, power surging new and unchecked, a tumult of exultation. "Die!" they screamed. "Die, mud-diggers. Die, sheep-herders."

Mirak watched it all from high above. So this is authority, he thought. This is real power. I speak, and I am obeyed. I deploy, I dispose. He felt nothing as the cliff top emptied. When nothing stirred there but the grass bending in the wind, and the sun had gone to leave night drowning the valley, he alighted with the others and walked to the edge. He glanced over. Only glimmers of paleness told him where the mounds of his broken kinsmen lay. The winged ones gathered round him panting and laughing, their eyes gleaming. "Crawlers!" they exclaimed. "That will teach them to do as they are told. What made them think that the Worldmaker would give wings to such as them in any case?" But as they regained their breath and the sweat began to cool on their slippery bodies, their laughter died away to be replaced by an awkward silence. None dared to look at another. What, then, was the meaning of the Worldmaker's orders? None asked aloud why they stood there in the gathering darkness while others piled the feet of the mountains with blood and smashed bones and death.

Mirak, his moment of aloofness gone, began to shiver. He remembered the horror of Tagar by the Gate, and his own panic. Now, as he had feared, the shadows were again brimming with a hostile force that longed to clutch at him. His nervousness was communicated to the others. Silently they lifted and flew, circling far inland so that they did not have to feel the caress of the death-laden wind rising from the valley, and then turned toward their caves. Only Mirak did not glide to perch, relieved and spent, at his entrance. Alone he winged his way to the sun-lord's spire. Ghakazian would be waiting.

Through the dragging, creeping hours of late afternoon Ghakazian paced his hall, the Book of What Will Be in his hands. Occasionally he stopped and looked at it, running his fingers reflectively over the smooth cover, but he did not open it and read. He knew his destiny. He was no longer anxious at the passing of time. No matter what words the Trader spoke to Janthis, no matter what decision the council took, it would avail them nothing. The Book had told him so, and the Book was true. Soon, he thought with a quiver of anticipation, I will be on Shol. Even now the essences of my people are gathering. He fancied that he heard their cries, faint and far away as the light in the hall slowly faded. So will the fallen people of Shol cry out, he told himself, when the avenging arms of my subjects smite them. Is the Unmaker nearing Shol? Is Sholia even now sitting by her window, toying with the fascination of black fire? How strangely, how smoothly all things are drawing to a point. I am the hinge of the universe. I have the power to pivot it this way or that.

Outside on Ghaka the sun sank, and as the last of its light left the hall, Mirak dropped through the funnel and came to stand warily before him. They eyed each other in the soft twilight.

"It is done," Mirak said. "They listened, but they did not believe. We had to throw them over as you commanded."

"It is done," Ghakazian echoed, and Mirak heard weariness, even boredom in the deep tones. The body of the sun-lord seemed heavier somehow, and the graceful limbs worked sluggishly, as though the sun-fired blood that used to race through his veins had begun to cool and lose its potency. "So the valleys are empty, but the roads . . ." He stopped and licked his lips with a dry tongue. "The roads are full, and the Gate stair is crowded. Now we come to the final moment. I and I alone will make the skies as empty as the earth. Will you die here, Mirak, or will you go home to Maram?"

Mirak began to back away. "I had thought . . ." he croaked, but Ghakazian cut him short.

"I do not ask you to think," he sneered. "Did you *think* that you would pass the Gate in your handsome body, with your glorious black wings? No, you did not, and yet you hoped to, didn't you? It is your choice, Mirak. Because of my regard for you I will allow the fire to pass you by, and if you wish, you may remain alone on Ghaka, and all the sky will be yours forever. Have you lost the courage to stand by me on Shol? Did you *think* that I was playing a little game?"

The sneer had twisted Ghakazian's full lips into a grimace, but Mirak did not see. Nor had he heard but one word which had stamped itself on his consciousness and was eating deeper into his brain.

*Fire.*

*Fire*, the sun-lord had said.

He tried to answer, choked on the sudden fear that rose to engorge his throat, then turned and ran, tripping as he fell out under the arch, plummeting through the clouds like a flung stone before he found his balance and clumsily opened his wings. Only the reflexes of his muscles kept him flying. He was numb with fear. He tumbled onto the little lip of rock before his cave, fell to his knees, and with wings drooping crawled to find a corner to fit his back against. I knew, he thought desperately to himself. Of course I knew. But I was blind and stupid then. I do not want to give up my body. I do not want to die.

Ghakazian walked to his arch and looked out. Clouds moved quickly under him, as though hurrying to some unknown meeting, and as the sky cleared he saw the vague humps of the peaks crowned with the ancestors, their tips silvered in starlight while below, the mountains shivered down into blackness. Nothing moved under his piercing eye. The air smelled stale and used up.

He shook out his feathers, steadied himself on the edge of nothingness, and held both arms before him, rigid from fingertips to shoulders. Before he spoke, he found his mind wandering to the day when he had returned to Ghaka from the closing of Ixel's Gate and had hovered by Mirak's cave entrance. He had called gaily, and Mirak had come out to stand before him, tall and brown, healthy and smiling, hair straggling black over gleaming wings, amber eyes alight with pleasure. He had asked for rain. At that memory Ghakazian's arms loosened for a moment. He heard Mirak's voice again, young and strong and full of an innocent excitement: *Hira, Maram! It is going to rain.*

Mirak has changed since then, he thought. He cowers when I look at him, he whines when I speak. We have all changed. Annoyance shot through him as he saw Mirak run once more from the hall, bent over like a craven beast, and his arms stiffened again. His chin rose.

"It is going to rain," he hissed aloud. "Oh, yes, Mirak, it is going to rain. But this time you will not welcome it, and then . . . Then for the Gate."

He called to his sun. He did not address it as a brother but commanded sharply as a master, clearing his mind of all save the link that joined them. He felt its enquiring, glad quiver, and greeted it silently. Then he spoke again with a slow, deliberate emphasis, putting together words of antagonism and destruction never heard before on Ghaka. The drifting clouds suddenly raced away from him. Even the night darkness seemed to let go its hold of his feet and slip farther down the mountain. The sun hesitated, its doubt a mushroom burgeoning in him, and it probed his command shyly.

He repeated the order abruptly, pushing away the little flurries of affection, and then he heard its voice. Like a liquid tongue of flame drawn from a fire, like hot yellow syrup pouring slowly, it oozed over him.

No, it breathed, a scalding sigh. No, Ghakazian.

For a moment he was numb with shock. In all the eons since he and the sun had burst into life, it had never spoken to him, and he had not known, or had forgotten, that the suns could form words. He had loved it as a lamb, a puppy, a young and playful being brimming with an eagerness to please and to be loved by him, though the Worldmaker had in fact taken from its own energies to create him.

He became angry. "You must obey me!" he snarled. "You are unable to refuse. I have power over you, and you dare not deny me!"

He stood still, and its anxious turbulence made him close his eyes. It whimpered softly, it sighed, and he felt its presence leave him. Its last impression on him was one of hurt, of wounding, but he brushed aside its sorrow.

There was a pause. He waited patiently. Then out of the darkness a rain began to fall. Slowly and lazily at first, then faster it came, a hail of orange balls sizzling and leaping around him. Briefly he was reminded of the bursting of the haeli pods on Danar when in fragrant red fire the seeds were showered into the autumn air. The calm night broke into dancing, brilliant light which caused the shadows to gyrate as though the mountains themselves were tugging free of the earth and the valleys were heaving up and down like an ocean. A wind came too, a searing, humming blast that scorched the grass and shriveled the leaves on the tossing trees. Still Ghakazian waited. Night was dismissed. Wherever his glance traveled, there was light, not the bright sunlight of a summer day but the harsh, unreal glow of naked fire. He spoke again, and with a hiss the balls rolled away from him, crackling through the smoking air, seeking something to devour. One by one they found the caves that honeycombed the crags and peaks, and with a crash and a hungry hot roar they entered. Ghakazian folded his arms and leaned against his archway.

Then the screaming began. Not the constant, sullen whine of friction but the spasmodic outcry of flesh in agony. All at once the cave mouths were candle-lit, the sides of the mountains flickered in reflection. The winged ones staggered over their thresholds. One by one they toppled, wings streaming fire, flames sparking in brittle hair, skin blackening. Rain fell again from crag to scorched earth, now a shower of jerking, red-wrapped bodies. The tiny bonfires that littered the floors of the valleys burned fiercely for a while, and one by one died away. Darkness crept back, laden now with the stench of bubbling flesh and a curling, oily smoke. "Sun," Ghakazian whispered. "Sun?" But the sun did not respond. There was a rumble like thunder very far away, and then silence.

Ghakazian spread his wings and, taking to the sky, circled the crags slowly. The cave mouths gaped at him, dark and empty, and the sides of the mountains were smeared in wet soot that dribbled downward like black tears. Satisfied, he beat his way toward the Gate, arrowing swiftly over road and river, knowing that though Ghaka seemed to lie vacant and exhausted beneath him, he was not alone. He flew steadily until the Gate mountain loomed ahead. He slackened his pace, fluttered carefully up the face of the peak, and when he found a small ledge that jutted halfway up it, he alighted, standing easily and looking out over the approach road and the wide vista of valley that opened to each side of it.

The night was waning. He had not been aware of the passage of time, but now a grayness was spreading slowly like a pool over the sky and would soon seep down to the land also. He rested for a while, reviewing the night and the afternoon before it, and as he pondered a feeling of impending climax grew in him, a slow tide of creeping doom that he welcomed. I have come far, he said to himself, since I first took the Book from Ixelion's damp floor. It was fate that moved my hand that day. He did not ask himself just what he meant by fate, and though he had never used the word before, it gave him a quick flash of security, an assurance that he had taken the right path. Now, he thought. They are there below me. They wait without volition of their own, without substance, and before my sulky sun rises on Ghaka, my people will have conquered the Gates. They will be on Shol. I have done more in the cause of light and truth in one month than the council has been able to do in a hundred thousand. Now it is time.

He glanced out at the horizon. The soft light had strengthened, pushing through the thinning smoke, and the accompanying breeze wafted the foul odors away from the Gate mountain. Ghakazian looked down and laughed out loud. Now the riddle in the Book is solved, he thought. I am about to address an army though the valley before me and the road winding through it is deserted and still. Oh, wise Book! Oh, mighty Ghakazian, that I should have put my faith in it, and in my intellect. "Mirak!" he shouted, the name echoing mournful and thin against the rocks. "Come up to me! Now you may stand beside me and receive your destiny from my hands!"

No voice answered him. No bustle of eager wings cut the hush of early morning. But Ghakazian felt the ledge suddenly fill with a cold presence, and the shadow in which he stood acquired a sentience. He was not afraid. He had done this thing. He was the master.

"Tagar!" he called again. "Old one skulking by the Gate! I adjure you now to come!" For a fleeting second he believed that he felt ice brush his face, and then the shadow glowered around him with an unmistakable hostility that prickled his spine. "You can do nothing, Tagar," he remarked cheerfully. "Where are your hands, your strong legs? You and Mirak must lead the people to Shol. Find bodies in the palace. I will come later."

A whisper threaded the air behind him, but he ignored it, full of contempt for them both. He planted his feet firmly on the edge of the perch and his hands on his hips and spoke, his voice rising melodious and rich to ring out over the countryside.

"People of Ghaka, I salute you!" he said. "Now I will tell you why I have torn you from your bodies. Tragedy and evil are swallowing up the universe. The one who made you now hates you and tries with all his power to unmake you, to turn the good to corruption, to make you slaves instead of free. The end is coming. The destiny of the universe lies in the balance. Shol is the battleground, you are the warriors. I call on you to fight for truth, for goodness, for all that is right." He paused, feeling for more words, and the breeze seemed to bring him a soft moaning, a low, murmurous wailing that troubled the air and entered him to fill him with unease. But I own them, I control them, he whispered to himself. The edge of warning in the sound of their misery cannot touch me. Oh?

something else in him queried mockingly. You have unleashed a power on the universe unknown before now, an untimely birth, a monster. You manipulate things you do not understand. Have you more skill than the Messengers to transform?

Forcefully he shoved away the niggle of doubt. The Book spoke to me, he reminded himself. The treasure is my guide. I am doing right. It has shown me how. He spoke again, but behind his thoughts he saw the Messengers, and he knew that he feared them.

"Sholia and the Unmaker will rule the universe if we do nothing!" he shouted. "We must go to Shol and make war and save Shol . . ."

Suddenly his words choked him. He felt a tunnel enclose him. He thrashed, panic-stricken, to loose his mind from the suffocating weight pressing on it. At the end of the tunnel was light, and in that light he saw himself standing on the ledge addressing the invisible throng below, his arms gesticulating, his body pale in the dawn. Fighting for breath, he groped toward the vision, but it flickered out. Darkness filled his eyes. Then the light was back, presenting to him the same vision. He saw himself go through the same motions, vanish, come back to repeat it all three, then four times. Sweat sprang out on his forehead, for with the vision came a consciousness of time stretching, spiraling into the darkness of the future only to snap back and begin again the long, slow reach to the same beginning.

Trapped! he screamed soundlessly. Doomed to gather them in pain and horror, speak to them like this, gather and speak, gather and speak, forever? How many times in the past have I stood here, Mirak and Tagar beside me? Lived through the terror of their deaths? In a moment of insight rising from some part of him still untouched by what he had become, he knew that the Book was doing this thing to him, showing him its true purpose, the peculiar remorse and disillusionment that came hand in hand with the knowledge it bestowed. I did not ask to know! He writhed. You chose me, forced yourself upon me. I did not choose!

You chose, the clear beam of self-revelation rustled back. But you can choose no longer. You are a prisoner of the Book. The Future is fixed for you, and you cannot turn aside into another path. You have seen, and in seeing you have fastened the chains of an irreversible time around your neck. Now you know why the Book was forbidden to the people of the suns.

Ghakazian tried to close his eyes against the tiny figure of himself on the ledge but could not. Mercy! he begged, but even that cry was directed only at himself. For an age he crouched, tossed relentlessly, and then the tunnel was gone. The sun had risen. In awe, with a weakness sobbing in him, he struggled to his feet and looked at it. It had not sailed hot and yellow into the sky. It had crept unwillingly, its light muted now to an angry purple, and the dawn's light rippled purple also, giving to mountain and valley alike the hue of an everlasting sunset. Like Fallan's sun, Ghakazian thought, appalled. I remember the color of its sickness. But what have I done that my sun should be stricken so? Is it a punishment for looking in the Book? He backed away from the lip of the ledge, the devastation of sun and planet above and below him, the haunted shadow behind and beside him. He felt as though he alone was whole, caught at the center of a radiating disintegration.

"Go through the Gate!" he shouted. "Call to the suns of Shol, and they will carry you! I, Ghakazian your ruler, command you to obey!"

Then the invisible presences that had shared the ledge with him were gone. Shivering, he slumped upon it, while beside him on the Gate stair he heard a shuffle begin. Road and valley drained of their last life. The drift of menace wound slowly around the mountain, and while Ghakazian trembled and averted his eyes it poured through the Gate and was gone.

# 10

The Trader passed through Danar's Gate and paused for a moment, stepping out of the stream of travelers coming and going. He looked toward the entrance to the tunnel, where hot summer sun beamed out of a cloudless blue sky and warmed the stone flags of the tunnel for as far as its rays could reach. Delicately he inhaled the season, dust and the pungent, lingering odor of haeli flowers in full bloom, crushed grass, sun-licked mortal skin. He ought to have been able to calculate in an instant how many days had passed while he flashed down the corridor between the Gates of both worlds. He frowned. It cannot be more than four days, he thought. Probably only three. Surely it does not matter, surely three days will make little difference in the long run. He reached inside himself, thickening his body for the onslaught of Danar's atmosphere, and felt his bundle grow heavy on his shoulders. Shrugging it off, he spoke to one of the corions, who yawned under the sun-crowned arch.

"I would like to leave this here," he said politely. "Would it trouble you to see that it is not moved or trodden upon?"

The corion explored its teeth with a long tongue. "It would not trouble me, Trader," it replied. "Did you bring Storn's sleeping mat?"

"I did, but Storn will not be in any hurry for it. Winter is far off. I thank you."

He lowered his load behind the beast, nodded, made his way to the sun-crowned tunnel, and set off across the soaring parapet that met the long stair to the palace. Below him and to the right the Time-forest murmured languorously in the noon drowsiness, its shelter a deep blue, inviting shade where one or two corions stretched lazily. Because of the thickness of the leaves the Trader could catch no glimpse of the city beyond. He turned away and mounted the steps, finding himself suddenly alone. The crowds, which had no business with immortals, had come out from the Gate, turned away from the slim parapet, and descended the stair that skirted the forest and brought them to a road that led to the heart of the city. Gradually their laughter and conversation died away, and he walked across the terrace of the palace, under the short noon shadow of the frontal pillars, and across the cool gloom of the empty entrance hall.

It took him a long time to come to the place where the two immortals of Danar met with the citizens of their world, but at last he stood under the blue gold-etched ceiling. He did not sit but moved to the small table, picked up a bell, and rang it once. Sweetly the tone tinkled out and dispersed, leaving silence. He continued to stand by the table, a column of paleness, his luminosity so quenched in the fierce sunshine that a casual glance into the room would not have revealed him. Only his blue scarf and the round glitter of his eyes shone iridescent and visible.

Presently a door at the far end opened and closed, and Janthis strode toward him, a smile lighting the stern lips. He came up and bowed, and the Trader answered the courtesy with a fluid bending of his own.

Trader, you are welcome here, Janthis said, his mouth not moving. The words had come straight from his mind, and the Trader heard them clear and true in his head. He spoke again, still smiling. Have you come to open the Books of Lore?

The Trader suddenly quivered, and when he was still again, he turned away from Janthis, answering without sound, the ends of the voluminous scarf stirring over his back. The smile faded from Janthis's face. Tell me, he said quietly.

There is an evil on Ghaka. A Law has been broken.

The old familiar feeling of inadequacy and hopelessness settled around Janthis like a garment that he thought he had thrown away but found he had not. The Trader felt it curling into his own mind, transmitted whole and dreary from the other.

What Law?

The Law pertaining to the mortals, which states that a mortal shall go whole to the Gate when his time has come, and that a Messenger shall see to the transmuting of flesh and essence together.

I do not understand.

Still the Trader would not turn around. I saw flesh without essence on Ghaka, he said, his thin lips pressed together. And by the Gate there was an essence that waited without flesh.

Janthis allowed himself the privacy of a moment of sheer despair. Oh, Ghakazian, not you! I do not accept this. Somewhere the Trader is in error.

Were flesh and essence the same?

Yes. I knew this mortal well. His name is Tagar, and he was the oldest and wisest of the wingless ones on Ghaka. His descendants are many, and he was greatly respected by all men, winged and wingless alike.

Too old and too wise to break a Law, Trader? You know how easily in these ages a Law may be broken. Perhaps you had been on Ghaka too long and were confused. Perhaps Tagar was asleep, and in the shadows by the Gate you mistook your own thoughts for the wavering call of an essence.

Now the Trader turned swiftly to face the immortal. Denial blazed suddenly from his eyes, but his answer was gentle. Do not delude yourself, Janthis. The thought dropped quietly into Janthis's agitated mind. I am not a fallen mortal led into error by every sense, not able to trust what I see or hear. If I say I saw Tagar propped against a mountain, swollen and stinking, then I saw him. And if I say I heard his essence entreat me in the darkness by the Gate, then I am not mistaken. Nor do I lie, because I worship only the Law, and the Law cannot lie. I have fled the creeping fringes of black fire before. I know. I know.

Did you see Ghakazian while you were there?

I did not. I traveled the valleys, trading. I heard a profound and strange silence. I felt a threat in the rustle of wings over my head, and a need to hide. Ghaka has fallen.

No! The word burst in the Trader's brain, and he winced. It has happened before that the Unmaker's will has seeped through a Gate, darkening the minds of mortals and causing them to falter without the knowledge or consent of the sun-lord. Such a falling can be cured. That at least is within our power.

The Trader mentally shrugged. Such a thing would never have happened to Tagar, he said aloud, his voice a timbreless whistle in the hot air of the room. He would never have embraced the subtle blandishments of the Unmaker's vanguard. He would have recognized their disguise and dismissed them without ever knowing the true importance of the step he took. He of all mortals on Ghaka was whole and innocent.

Then how do you explain to me what you saw? Janthis's voice was level.

You need no explanation, the Trader replied. Someone murdered Tagar.

Silence fell between them. They considered each other without seeing. Who? Janthis thought to himself. Ghakazian knows the dangers. At each Gate-closing they have been impressed more deeply into each one of us. Suddenly he remembered that Ghakazian had come and asked permission to read the Books of Lore, and with a chill he now wondered why. I am not equipped to lead the council, he thought sadly. I fear the fire, we all fear it, but my knowledge of it ought to be the greater because I lead, yet I do not trust myself. I knew the Worldmaker as the others did not. His mind was open to me. It would be open again, I know, if I wished, but I am not strong enough to read it and retreat unscathed. The Trader broke in on his thoughts.

I do not know what is happening on Ghaka, he said. That is your concern. I only know that I am affronted and diminished because a Law has been broken. I do not tell you your business, nor do I offer you anything but my words to be accepted or rejected as you choose.

Pride does not suit you, Janthis replied. It is not impossible to corrupt a Trader, though you and your kin would wish it were not so. Have you forgotten the Trader from Tran?

No, I have not. The Trader sighed, his body pulsing, floor and wall shivering through him. It must have been a powerful thing indeed, the cause of his fall. I am sorry. I have traveled the worlds for too long without a respite.

I will order Ghakazian here, Janthis went on reluctantly. Where will you go?

I have to deliver some goods on Danar, and then . . . I do not know. Perhaps I will walk on the oceans of Shol for a while, or go home to my own realm. Trading is no longer good. Only Danar and Shol remain.

There are other worlds.

Yes. Far out in the universe, far from the dark side. Worlds the Worldmaker left unfinished. Worlds of molten rock, worlds covered in water, worlds without mortals, worlds full of strange beasts. The ones out there have no sun-lords to sit in council. They are of no use for trade. If Shol and Danar fall, it means the end of everything and the beginning of nothing. I think I will go home.

Thank you.

They smiled at each other as equals, bowed, and then the Trader tightened his body and floated from the room. Janthis continued to stand in the quiet, sun-drenched room, but no thoughts would come. Presently he went through the door and down a passage and emerged into the vast stillness of the council chamber. He climbed to the dais and, picking up the silver hammer, struck the sun-disc once. Then he went and sat in his chair, his hands covering the cold sun-ball on the table, the sound of the gong throbbing in his ears. I am tired, he thought in surprise. I, who never grow old or change, am weary.

Danarion came first, walking lightly into the chamber, his golden eyes still glowing from the summer brilliance of the sun. He came up to Janthis and smiled, but his smile was not returned, and he took his seat at the other's left hand, settling easily into a patient stillness. Sholia entered next, her long, gossamer-thin gown shimmering many colors in her own bright aura. She greeted them and slipped quickly into her chair, and her eyes flitted around the high windows.

"Ghakazian isn't here yet?" she said, and Janthis stirred at last, his hands leaving the sun-ball to fold themselves crisply on the table.

"He may not come," he replied brusquely.

Danarion's head came up. Sholia's gaze swiveled to him in puzzlement.

"Why ever not?" she asked. "He may find the council meetings irksome—you know how restless he is—but he would not disobey you."

Janthis's eyes met Danarion's in a brief moment of understanding, and Danarion paled and looked away.

"A Trader has just visited me," Janthis went on. "He came here straight from Ghaka. He tells me that murder has been done there."

Still Sholia did not see. "He told you what? How odd the Traders are, with their preoccupation with the Law and their exotic stories! I have always meant to read the Books of Lore pertaining to them, for I often feel that I should know them better. Sometimes they surprise me . . ."

"Sholia." The word was a command to silence, and Sholia bit her lip, her hair curtaining her face as she bent toward the table. "I said murder," Janthis went on quietly. "All is not well on Ghaka, and I have called this meeting in order to put some questions to Ghakazian."

"He is a sun-lord!" Sholia burst out. "What is a Trader compared to him? A Trader can be mistaken!" Then her hands came up to cover her face.

"Don't be hasty," Danarion said to her gently. "Murder on Ghaka does not necessarily mean the corruption of the sun-lord, you know that. Let us wait and see what Ghakazian has to say. Even now he may be moving to cut away an isolated evil. You dwell too often on your fears."

The hands slid slowly downward, and Sholia smiled at him faintly. "You are right, of course. When he comes, he will refute the Trader."

Sharp words rose to Janthis's tongue, but he swallowed them, studying the smooth, light-filled face and emerald eyes with care. Sholia had once been full of a cool dignity. But Janthis, standing back from the eons behind her, saw that she had changed. She was no longer balanced. Even in the timeless space of the sun-lords' palace she projected a mortal diffidence that did not belong to her nature. Well, he thought, I suppose that some change in all of us was inevitable. When the Worldmaker's nature became twisted, when he chose to claim all that he had done for his own, change rocked the universe. Though we cannot be touched in any specific way unless we wish it, still the breath of Unmaking must affect us. To remain invulnerable is impossible. To stay as we are is a struggle.

Sholia felt his gaze on her and sat straighter, her smile broadening determinedly. "In a way we all lean on Ghakazian's loud strength," she said. "We take courage from his arguments. Let us wait and see."

They waited. As noon slipped into afternoon the sun left the hall to trickle down the stone walls outside, but the three at the table kept their light to illumine the dim room. Finally Danarion sighed. "Call him again," he said, and Janthis rose, picking up the silver hammer. But before he could strike the disc, there was a sudden flurry of busy sound, and Ghakazian himself dropped from a window high above, glided down, and alighted by the table. He did not take his place beside Sholia. Instead he swaggered to the foot of the dais, where Janthis had laid down the hammer and was turning. They all looked at him aghast. The golden light that had always welled through his brown skin and had cast a warm, red-gold pool around him now pushed feebly outward in dull orange, ragged streamers. The brittle hair was straggling down over his shoulders, framing a face whose breathtaking, pure aquilinity had thinned and hardened into the sharpness of incipient cruelty. Around the mouth went two distinct, deep lines like clefts in one of his own mountains.

The eyes had not changed. They still glittered with the alertness of a bird, but that watchfulness now had a quality of greed, the predatory gleam of a thing of prey. Only the wings still rose majestic and beautiful above and beside the proud head, the feathers folding sleek and warm into each other. Janthis's eyes flew to the sun-disc suspended on the chest. More orange flames whirled within it, tinged in black.

"Ghakazian . . ." Sholia whispered. He glanced at her contemptuously and then away. "Well," he said. "You called me and I have come. For more useless talk, more senseless sifting in the rubble of the worlds. But this time you will all be silent and listen to me."

"So the Trader was right," Danarion breathed, horrified, and Ghakazian rounded on him. For one moment fear flared in the sullen flicker of his fire.

"What Trader!" he snapped, but Danarion, eyes full of this terrible disintegration, could say no more. Janthis answered.

"A Trader came here straight from Ghaka," he said. "He told me of a murder. Ghakazian, what has happened to you, and how?"

Ghakazian laughed bitterly. "What? And how? I can tell you what will happen to you and how, and I think you ought to heed me. I have something precious in my possession. Falia did not have the strength to use it right, and neither did poor Ixelion, but I had the courage, I did not quail when I learned from it what is going to befall. You!" He rounded on Sholia, pointing a rigid finger, his lips curled in an angry sneer. "I loved you! You and I were like Ixelion and Falia, brother and sister and more than brother and sister. Yet I know you now as I never did before. Traitor! You and the Unmaker will council together, and he will come at last to Shol, as in his black heart he has always longed to do, and take it for his own!"

Sholia rose shakily from her chair and backed away, white to the lips. "Ghakazian, you rave," she whispered, and then the others shook off the spell of shock, and Janthis ran down the steps from the dais and raised a hand to Ghakazian. One quiet word of coercion left his lips, and Ghakazian's arm fell to his side.

"You are forbidden to do that!" Ghakazian snarled.

"It is not for you to question me," Janthis replied coolly. "Now, Ghakazian, we will listen to you. You are a threat to each of us here whether you believe it or not. Take your place at the table. Sholia, sit down." She did so, still shaking, tears not far away, and Ghakazian moved grudgingly to stand in his accustomed place. "Now where does this mad accusation against Sholia come from?"

"Mad? I will tell you who is mad!" Ghakazian exploded. "You, Janthis, you! I come to ask you for the last time. Will you waken the mortals to their true danger, and make armies, and stand against the Unmaker?"

Janthis's shoulders slumped. "I have told you before, we have no weapons with which to fight," he said tiredly. "It is forbidden to take their innocence away from the mortal people."

"But we do have a weapon," Ghakazian hissed softly as he reached behind him and drew something from his belt, "a most precious, most powerful weapon. Falia gave it to Ixelion, and I took it from Ixelion's floor when you and I, Danarion, went to Ixel to raise him and could not. I do not need it anymore. Here, Janthis. I give it to you."

Malice darkened the once-handsome face, and Janthis noticed that now tipping the fingers of the hand that extended to him were talons, long, curved nails that clicked against one another. Sickness washed over him. I cannot be invaded unless I will it to be, he reminded himself. I can take this thing without hurt. Slowly he reached out, and as he took the offering Ghakazian chuckled.

"I have read it," he said. "I know all, I can see all. I am now the master of fate." But as he spoke he caught the glint of sunlight on a bracelet Sholia was wearing. It was a band of thick gold studded with red gems. He knew that he had never seen it before, and yet he had, and for a second time he felt the suffocating tunnel begin to close around him, forcing his eyes and his mind to look in one direction only. He remembered then that the Book had shown him this moment also, his standing here addressing a shocked and aching council, and the sun sparkling on Sholia's wrist. Before he could scream, the moment had passed, and the room opened out again behind and beside him. Janthis was standing with the Book in his hands, feeling it reverently, his eyes wide.

"The Book of What Will Be," he said wonderingly. "Now I understand. Of course. Only this treasure could have brought about the fall of three worlds so swiftly. Where was it found? Who found it?"

"It came from Tranin, naturally," Danarion said thickly, his eyes riveted on the Book. "Don't you remember? It is all in Fallan's Annals."

Then Sholia leaped to her feet. "Throw it away, Janthis!" she shouted. "It is forbidden! Do not look at it, I beg you. Ghakazian tempts you, oh, surely you see it!" She crumpled, tears pouring down her cheeks. "It is all over, all finished," she sobbed, sinking back into her chair. "One by one the Unmaker has plucked us out. He has conquered."

"No," Janthis responded softly. "Be comforted, Sholia. He is not yet the victor. If Ghakazian had brought the Book to you on Shol, what would you have done? How long could you have resisted its call? But he did not bring it to you. It lies here in my hands, the treasure of the ages, and here it will stay. I know that the Lawmaker himself has decreed that though the past and present may lie open to us, the future must be forever dark. I will not disobey him."

Ghakazian was convulsed. Eagerly he pressed forward, leaning far over the table. "That was before the Worldmaker fell!" he shouted. "In his falling much was changed. The old order cannot stand. There are Laws that cannot now apply to us. We must use every means at our disposal to fight with. Why can't you see that this thing was delivered into our hands to serve us in our greatest need! Perhaps the Lawmaker himself caused it to be found!"

"In that case," Danarion replied acidly, "why did the finding of it bring horror and death to Fallan and Ixel? And," he finished deliberately, "to Ghaka?"

After a long silence Ghakazian stood up nonchalantly and folded his arms. "I have read it," he remarked. "I can tell you what it says. The Unmaker will enter Shol, and you, Sholia, will welcome him. Take my advice, Janthis. Guard Shol. That is what he is greedy for. Make armies to throng it. Meet the Unmaker once and for all. Let the struggle come to a climax."

With great respect Janthis laid the Book before him on the table, and whether it was because of the sheen and smoothness of the binding reflecting his own light or because the Book had light of its own to share, the sun-ball beside it glowed briefly yellow and warm, a moment of pale resurrection.

"You are blind, Ghakazian," he said with difficulty, close to tears himself. "You are deaf also, and sick. Can't you see that the Unmaker has seduced you? Whatever you have done to Ghaka cannot be undone. Your Gate must be closed."

Sholia expected a violent outburst of protest from Ghakazian, but he simply began to smile, a slow secretive smile. Looking at him, she felt a vague and new anxiety wake in her to stand beside the others in her mind and add its clamor to the fears already lodged there. He knows something that we do not, she thought. Something that he has done. She put her conjecture into Janthis's mind, and though he acknowledged it with a faint nod, he did not share her sudden certainty. He knew more about the Book of What Will Be and its powers than any of them, how Ghakazian's mind would be full of visions and strange dreams. All the same, Ghakazian's reaction puzzled him. He has fallen far indeed, he thought, if the closing of his own Gate can cause him so little pain.

"Very well," Ghakazian said airily. "Come and close my Gate. I do not care. It does not matter anymore. I will still have Ghaka."

"An imprisoned world!" Danarion snapped. "Have you no regard for the people in your care, Ghakazian?"

"But of course I do!" Ghakazian's smile beamed out, still full of hidden satisfaction. "Go ahead and close the Gate. They and I will survive together."

Janthis turned to Danarion. "We will go to Ghaka at once," he said. "Danarion, call Storn."

Danarion sent his thought ranging over Danar, seeking the great beast. At last he found it. Come, he asked gently. You are needed in the palace, Storn.

Has the Worldmaker returned? The query was eager.

No. Janthis has a task for you.

Storn's disappointment flooded Danarion. Oh, I will come.

As they waited Ghakazian began to pace. Then the corion came stalking into the room, green wings flat along its back, its paws falling with soft thuds on the black floor. When it reached the foot of the table, it halted, settled onto its haunches, and let its eyes quickly roam them all, resting a moment longer on Ghakazian.

"Well," it said. "You bid me come and here I am. What can I do?"

"We have a new task for you, Storn," Janthis said. "Ghakazian has brought a most precious and powerful treasure to Danar, and it must be guarded at all times. The Lawmaker made it, but not for the eyes of mortals or immortals. Will you accept the care of it?"

"I will, of course, perform gladly any task you give me, Janthis," Storn answered, whiskers quivering under the black nose. "Shall I take it to the mountain?"

"Only when you retire there for the winter. Then you must sleep with it beneath you. It will give you marvelous dreams. For the time being I will place it in a chamber by itself, down near the Books of Lore, I think, and you and your brethren must take turns to see that no one but myself enters the room where it is."

"What is this thing?"

"It is a book. Come and see."

Regally the corion padded to the head of the table. Its muzzle passed over the Book enquiringly, ears flattening and rising in concentration.

"Indeed, he made it," Storn commented at last. "How good and rich it smells, like a haeli forest after rain! But there are other odors here, Janthis. They are not so pleasant."

"The Book has been on a long journey," Janthis responded seriously, though his eyes twinkled at Storn. "Go now, Storn, and tomorrow you can begin your vigil. Choose other guardians well. This task is not simply a matter of custom, like the guarding of Gate or palace. The fate of Danar depends on your watchfulness."

"I understand," the beast replied, "though who should want to open this Book without the Lawmaker's permission I cannot imagine." Storn turned and left the hall with a slow, sinuous dignity, and they heard the emerald wings crack open beyond the entrance.

"What a fool you are, Janthis," Ghakazian said scornfully. "You would place the Book in the care of a vain and ignorant brute."

"Your own vanity and ignorance have made you more brutish than you can possibly imagine!" Janthis cut back angrily.

The other two did not hear the sharp exchange of words. Their eyes were fixed on the Book.

Suddenly Janthis was aware of the intense silence around him, and seeing the blank eyes fastened on the Book, he took it, rose, and walking to his own door, thrust the Book within. Coming back, he was about to speak when Sholia forestalled him.

"You could read it, couldn't you?" she faltered. "You used to stand between us and the Worldmaker. You have a place of your own in the scheme of things. Surely the Book is not forbidden to you? And then . . . when you had read it . . ."

"I could tell you what to do? No, Sholia. It has less power over me, but that does not change the Law. It will remain unopened forever, if that is to be."

She heard the undertone of rebuke and subsided into a chastened silence, but in her and in Danarion the desire to fondle and touch it had been lit and would smolder.

"We have wasted enough time," Janthis went on. "We will go now to Ghaka. You know your choice, Ghakazian. You can come with us and be immured behind your Gate, or you can go from here with a Messenger and be judged."

"So that the Messengers may annihilate me? No, I will not. They hate us, the strange ones. Their judgments are not fair. They want to be done with the trivialities of mortal and immortal alike and have the universe to themselves. I will return to Ghaka. It is my home." No sorrow for Ghaka colored his words, and there was no trace of remorse in the hard face.

They all rose and without further comment left the hall. Ghakazian went first. He knew that if he tried to catapult himself through Danar's Gate and escape, he would be quietly and firmly prevented. In any case, he thought, where can I go? I do not want to reach

Shol as I am. That is a new problem, but I can ponder it when this little move in the game is over.

One by one they passed under the massive stone sun raying out over their heads, paced the Gate tunnel, and vanished into the blackness of space, calling to Ghaka's sun. Long before their feet touched the spur hanging in the void, they saw and felt Ghaka's agony. The sun's pull was weak and erratic, jerking them violently, and its light did not grow and fill their vision with its roaring energy. It beat an angry purple, its perimeter bulging and sinking like the heaving of an ocean. Ghakazian was unconcerned, and he alighted smiling. The others followed, grim-lipped. They became aware of a Messenger's presence, its thin plume of fragrant smoke rising, its ribbons of iridescent color quickly weaving a tall, vibrating shape.

Uneasiness fell on all of them. They bowed low to it, but it did not speak. Only Ghakazian remained upright, regarding it impudently, his foot tapping.

"Well," he said. "Let us conclude this silly pretense. Why we bothered to close Gate after Gate down all the long ages is beyond my comprehension. It would have been better to leave them open and so spare ourselves all the anguish. One mighty flood through all the worlds, and a quick ending." In spite of his words he glanced at the Messenger and found his heart beating fast. He spun on his heel and strode in under the portals of the Gate, turning to face them when he was inside.

"I would like to speak to some of his mortals," Danarion said. Janthis nodded, and Danarion stepped past Ghakazian and was lost to sight. The others waited anxiously. Janthis turned his back on the Gate and gazed out into the stars, brooding. Sholia could not take her eyes off Ghakazian's shadowed face. His feeble and sickly light played fitfully on the rock above his head but could not pierce the deeper dimness of the tunnel. Unwillingly he found his own gaze meeting hers, and he felt great sadness for the last time. I wish that it did not have to be this way, he said to her in his mind, and she saw the tight face soften. I would give anything to be as I once was, but what is the use? I have done what I had to do. I have sacrificed myself. I have loved you, Sholia. I have been Ghaka's good, I have gloried in my charge, but in order to be the good of the universe I have diminished myself and Ghaka. Forgive me.

She did not argue with him. Her heart was too full of yearning for all that had been and would not come again. I have loved you also, she whispered back in her mind. Now who will take my hand and lead me from the mist of my own terror? Only in the past will we be together, and always the present will wait for me, beckoning me back to duty and my own battles. Nurse your sun back to health, Ghakazian. Do not let it die. I could not bear it if I knew that your fire had gone from the All.

But it was useless, as she was well aware. He could not heal his sun, and even if he had been able to, the link of love and trust between them had worn too thin. She walked through the Gate and put her arms around him, laying her head beneath his shoulder. For a moment he responded, both his arms and his great wings enfolding her. She fought the panic that mingled with her need to embrace him one last time, for his body was as chill as space itself and fed a breath of desolation into her veins. Then he pushed her away. I will survive, he said to her silently. I am immortal. I am a god. She turned and left him, and until Danarion returned, she stood beside Janthis, head hanging. When Danarion came back, he was pale and silent.

"Did you see them, did you speak to them?" Janthis asked him.

"I saw them. I did not speak to them," was all he said. They waited for more, but Danarion closed his mouth. For a while there was a silence, full of thoughts of the past, that all were reluctant to break. But finally Danarion held out a hand. Ghakazian knew what was required of him. Impatiently he pulled his necklet over his head and dropped it into Danarion's palm. The words of admonition and accusation would not come to Janthis's tongue. Danarion and Sholia drew close to him, a trio of light, and all three turned their faces for the last time to Ghakazian and the world of Ghaka beyond him.

"Close your Gate, Ghakazian," Janthis commanded sternly, and at the words all emotion left them. Ghakazian began to laugh, but they took no notice. They waited unrelenting, and finally he stopped snickering.

"I suppose there is enough power left in my sun to close the Gate," He choked, still shaking with mirth. "Oh, very well. I am not particularly sorry that I will never see any of you again. I have grown very tired of your never-changing company." Nonchalantly he raised his arms and stood straight. "Come to me, sun, and obey me this last time!" he shouted, and slowly the air around him began to fill with a sliding, glancing violet light that coiled about him, waiting for direction. He clapped his hands, then held them out toward the Gate. "I, Ghakazian, lord of Ghaka, close my Gate!" he shouted. "Henceforth neither mortal nor immortal, Maker nor Messenger nor any created thing may enter here. The stars are forbidden to the people of Ghaka"—here he paused and seemed about to burst into private laughter again, but he controlled himself and went on gaily—"and Ghaka is forbidden to the people of the stars. Close, my Gate, close! It does not matter. None of it matters in the least. I do not need you anymore."

For the briefest moment there was a cessation of all breath and movement. Then a wind came howling out of the cave tunnel, whipping at the light, swirling the purple color this way and that. Ghakazian folded his arms, fluffed out his wings, and began to laugh again quietly, watching. Light and wind seemed to find a center in the Gate arch and jostled and shrieked between keystone and rock floor before the sound of the wind died into a rustling and the violet light formed shapes. Suddenly the Gate was dense with birds that fluttered and flapped against one another, fighting to free themselves from the press of those struggling next to them. Wings thrashed helplessly. The whole space of the Gate itself seethed with violet feathers.

The rustling began to die away. The color faded to the gray of stone, and the birds hardened rapidly into carvings, each tiny head, each outflung wing etched delicately and brilliantly, filling the Gate. The sun-lords did not wait to see the final stamp of warning appear. They turned away, each of them carrying the indelible imprint of Ghakazian standing negligently just within the Gate, arms folded on his dark chest, a smile of secret satisfaction on his face, and his wings flung wide, to fill their vision with a remembrance of his beauty.

# 11

Melfidor rose from his desk, stretched until his bones cracked, and with a sigh of contentment turned to the window. In daylight, from his office high in Sholia's palace, he could see nothing of Shaban, only the changing shades of grass as wind, cloud, and sun passed over the level plain running from the terraces, but often at night the lights in the Towers of Peace glimmered fitfully. He watched them now as they pricked against the evening. Tomorrow I will take out my boat, since Sholia is still absent, he thought. I can get around the headland and fish for a while. Chantis won't mind. There's nothing much left to do, now that winter has come and everyone has stopped caring about feasting. When Sholia returns, I must show her my plans for the new ships. I might even ask her if I can captain one of them myself. After all, my ancestor sailed to the farther shore and brought back the first copper to be seen in Shaban. Now the mines send us copper every day. He smiled, wandering for a moment in his ancestor's memory, which showed him a weathered ship dipping beneath his feet and a thin line of land, gray against a wide, sun-washed horizon. He leaned against the stone sill and whistled softly. Or perhaps I will go through the Gate tomorrow instead and visit my family and bring back fruit for Rilla. My father will ask politely of the doings in Shaban and whether or not the plains people have tarried here on their way to their winter quarters, and my mother will tell me again how the first member of her family saw the sun-lord say farewell to the Worldmaker before the Hall of Waiting, but both of them will have eyes full of the ripeness of their orchards and noses full of the smell of fruit hanging heavy to be picked, and neither will really care how Shol is faring.

He heard the swift patter of feet approaching his door, and as he turned it opened, letting in a flood of lamplight and the figure of Yarne.

"Melfidor, are you finished here for the day?" the younger man called across the room. "I'm going home now. Come down to the house and eat with me."

Melfidor left the window and moved within the shaft of light. "Thank you, Yarne, but I don't think I will. My mind is too weary. Perhaps tomorrow night."

"Rilla is sure to be there. I know you haven't seen her in four days."

Melfidor smiled at the sheer breathtaking beauty of Yarne's gleaming white-gold hair, the smooth skin molded so perfectly over delicate bones, the clear blue eyes. "Your sister is busy embroidering another masterpiece. When she wants my company, she'll let me know."

"Well, at least take a day off tomorrow and come riding with me," Yarne urged. "A few hours away from all this"—he waved a graceful hand in the direction of the littered desk—"will do you good."

"I might, if Sholia hasn't returned by then."

"Where did she go?"

"To Danar, I think. Janthis called her."

An immediate reverence straightened the engaging smile. "I wish he would come to Shol sometimes."

"You can see him in your memory."

"Not very well. My ancestor stood behind the crowd, and all he caught of Janthis was a glimpse of half his head." Yarne grinned ruefully and went to the door. "I can't persuade you to come with me?"

"Good night, Yarne. Give Rilla my love."

"Of course. And don't forget that my father, Baltor, is giving his farewell feast in three days time. A Messenger is coming for him. I hope the sun-lord is back by then."

"She will be. Go and eat!"

Yarne nodded and left, and Melfidor slowly paced to his bed, turning to survey the room, dark now but for a thin spear of light on the desk and a faint glow of starlight outlining the window. So Baltor was leaving them. He could not remember a time when he had not been able to look up to the highest parapet and see him pacing, the sun-lord by his side. It would be odd to see her there alone, unchanged as always. The picture gave him a sudden spasm of unreality. Shaking his head, he lay down, folded his arms on his breast, and closed his eyes. A farewell feast, and half of Shaban will be there to watch Baltor withdraw into his last mortal thoughts. That will be good. How empty my mind feels, how scoured! I command a night without dream, a night of utter silence and knitting-together. He opened his eyes again but now did not see the warm shadows of his room. The silence he had called covered him like a blanket. He sank into a state of rest, withdrawing to the place where no thoughts or dreams were, leaving consciousness as though he had walked out of a room and deliberately shut a door behind him, but in that room his body repaired the damages of the day and his mind renewed itself.

The Gate on Shol was not guarded. The heavy copper doors stood open upon the universe, and through them a traveler could glimpse the first intimation of Shol's wealth and magnificence. The Gate had no passage but led directly from one dimension to another, so that one who alighted before it, his back to the panorama of white stars and deep black space, faced the busy, full-lighted opulence of the Hall of Waiting. There travelers said their farewells, gathered their bundles together, and shared one last cup, with laughter that echoed to the haeli-timbered roof. The Hall of Waiting had a smaller entry upon whose lintel and stoop the reliefs formed the same pictures as those on the larger ones framing the Gate. On either side of the door the dark-pink copper showed the rising tiers of the city of Shaban, while across the stoop ships sailed a copper ocean the color of hot bronze in a drowsy noon. Above the heads of those who came and went stars pricked a gleaming red sky, seeming to twinkle as lamplight and torchlight slid across the solid copper and were netted in the artist's careful grooves. Upon each Gate door were two overlapping suns with Sholia's face etched in the center, her hair spilling out to become the rays of the suns themselves. To the mortals who brushed against that giant face it was beautiful, not with the implied surrender of a feminine curve to the cheek or a frozen tremble of acquiescence in the parted lips but with the stern otherworldliness of a god. The doors could not be closed, and the giant square piece of the universe seen through it seemed to hang on the wall of the Hall of Waiting like an improbably cold and alien painting.

\*

The bodiless army from Ghaka came to Shol's Gate on a winter evening. The Hall of Waiting was deserted. Lamps flickered in the damp wind, their light skidding unimpeded across the gleaming reaches of the vast floor, and only the sound of their guttering disturbed the quiet of the hour past sunset. Like a whispering, invisible river the unseen host hesitated, flooding to fill the Gate. Eyeless, the essences saw into the Hall. Without skin they felt the eddying of air around them. The journey from Ghaka had been a nightmare that had carried them through the unimagined terror of deep space and so to the threshold of a world they had only heard of from the lips of the sun-people. They had seen their own sun hanging behind them, grim and dying. They had seen Shol's twins rush toward them, orbs of white fire, and though they knew that they existed without eyes to be blinded or flesh to scorch, yet they had screamed without mouths to see and feel the forbidden, the frontier of a reality into which they had not been made to plunge.

But the corridor had brought them to Shol. They hovered on the edge of a world brimming with new flesh, with grass to press beneath boned and sinewed feet, with odors of flower and food to draw into solid nostrils, and they were hungry. For a long moment they paused, sensing their surroundings, until with a common need to clothe themselves in sensibility they passed under the Gate, spread out to fill the Hall, and began to trickle through the farther doors.

Shol was peaceful under a winter sky of broken gray cloud. Beyond the Hall of Waiting, across the short, naked plain where the land ran level before it fell away into the serried ridges that held the mighty city of Shaban, the ocean gave back to the sky an oily reflection of ruffled stars. Beside the Hall, at a stone's throw from the doors, Sholia's vast palace, which had been hollowed out of the mountain itself, glowed with borrowed sunlight. The palace looked out in one slow sweep upon the plain, the uppermost towers of the city, the curving bay, and the sea.

The essences left the doors and began to spread and drift, a nebulous cloud that rolled without sound toward the city, reaching the bastions where the flags flew, curling to fill the steep, winding streets, and tentatively brushing against closed doors. A new wind went with them, a moan of seeking and purpose. Behind the doors the inhabitants looked up from their evening meals. Some went to windows and thought they saw the lights of the part of the city on the next tier below them mist gray for a moment. All remarked that the wind was rising, and perhaps it would rain. The city was soon murmurous with unease. The foreign breath blew upon the ships anchored at the docks and seeped inside them, and portions of the cloud skirted the city and were lost in the hinterland and the forests beyond, still seeking. The keepers of the trees, the tillers of the soil, the Sholans who wandered the no-man's-land with their tents and horses shivered and looked about them in a sudden, sourceless disquiet.

But the essences of Tagar, Natil, Rintar, and Tagin and those of Mirak, Maram, and Hira left the Hall of Waiting and moved to where Sholia's terraces cut a broad stepped way from her many-arched doors to the floor of the plateau before the mountain. Shrubs lined the terrace, bunches of tubbed shadow, and between them the forlorn shades floated upward, Ghakazian's command to find bodies driving them, their own pitiful need a whip flaying against the bitter formlessness of their minds. They did not know that Sholia was still on Danar, listening with the rest of the council to their sun-lord's degradation. They felt her in the beams of light that spilled down the steps to greet them, in the warm air of her many chambers. Her presence permeated the painted walls and rustled in the gay hangings. As they parted and glided on separate ways they knew themselves more thin and insubstantial against her rich wholeness than they had against the incomprehensible energies of space. But they also felt the presence of their own kind, solid and comforting, and the need to knit essence and body together again was like a cold knife slicing through them. One by one they were drawn away from Sholia's high chambers, down long passages that narrowed to mortal dimensions and were now lit with lamps bracketed on the walls. So they found at last the feast they had sought.

Mirak found himself at the end of a long, brightly lit passage. Muffled chatter and laughter came to him from behind the closed doors that lined it, intensifying his wretchedness, and he turned for the frail comfort of Maram's presence to find that he was alone. Indecision filled him. He wanted to enter the rooms, to be greeted with welcoming smiles, but he also wanted to cling to some dark corner, to hide. He had just decided to go back down the dark staircase behind him when a door opened and a young man came out and began to stride briskly along the passage. He wore a soft white tunic that swung loosely against his long legs, and the lamp-light glowed in his pale golden hair. Vitality surged in his every step, and Mirak was drawn to follow. The young man flung open another door, speaking gaily to someone within, and Mirak watched, jealousy and longing spurting through him. He drifted closer. The man turned and came back along the passage, but Mirak answered the invitation of the still open door that splashed such friendly light across the corridor. Another mortal, brown-haired, young, and full of warm life, was preparing to rest. Mirak went to hang in the black-patched corner by the bed, watching the man's slow, contented movements. Presently he lay down with a sigh, and Mirak trembled, seeing himself, Hira, and Maram standing in their cave on Ghaka, hands folded like this man's, eyes open but no longer seeing, minds resting in whatever pleasant visions they had chosen.

He drew nearer to the man on the bed. Star radiance glimmered pale on the rings he wore, as though he held a white spell in his limp fingers, and his breast rose and fell gently. Mirak looked at him for a long time, wondering, torn between desire for a place to regain power over the world surrounding him and a small, insistent voice in his mind that bade him turn and flee to the Gate and fling himself back into the clutches of the corridor. He shuddered. Not that! he vowed. Never again the mad terror of the unplace where mortals do not belong. Quickly he made up his mind and, drifting low, bent over the tranquil form. He whispered, though not with the mouth he no longer owned, and his words scratched against the door of the room where the man's mind rested.

In the whiteness of silence Melfidor felt a tremor, and his mind ceased its work of regeneration and listened. The tremor came again, and Melfidor's mind turned from the depths of his body, rose to the door, and demanded to see. The room where he lay was not disturbed. Night had deepened, strengthening the blue-white light of the stars. The lamp on the desk had gone out. Shadows splashed the walls in long streamers of blackness. He glanced at himself and saw that no one was in the room. His mind withdrew behind its door, puzzled, but his essence knew he was not alone. Something had formed itself by the bed, and it quested him. The sun-lord often called him without sound, but she always spoke directly into his conscious thoughts and did not send a part of herself to fetch him. This thing near him was not of the light. Its presence did not fill him with gladness and warmth; rather, the room seemed suddenly to chill him. The impression it gave was one of cold space— not the busy space between Shol and its sister worlds, but the empty dread of timelessness, and it put forth sadness shot with fear and danger. He felt he ought to shut all the doors of his interior being, but the thing conveyed also the raw misery of a need, and Melfidor, in his innocence, was troubled. "What? What?" he whispered back. As soon as he acknowledged its presence, he could see it more clearly. It had the form of a man, and because he had never known a kind of death other than the completeness of Sholan death, he did not recognize, indeed he was incapable of discerning the wretchedness of division.

But he knew that this was no ordinary man. The door of his office had not been opened, and the thing bending over him was insubstantial, like a Trader. But a Trader's body was a pale, iridescent beauty. This presence was transparently thin and dark, though dull light of a kind seemed to permeate it, and its contours were forever blurring, as though it fought for definition but could not gain it. Its eyes were hollows of darkness, its mouth a line of blackness, but it was the wings that convinced Melfidor that he was sharing his room with a being from beyond all worlds. They rose to fill the shadows, the color of night on the ocean, wavering high, their outlines continually shifting as though they sought to brush aside the ceiling and spread free. He was not afraid, but he was anxious. "What are you?" he asked.

The being bent lower until its visage seemed to fill the doorway behind which his mind watched it. I am a dream, Melfidor, it said.

"But I did not command such a magical dream. Indeed, I commanded no dream at all. Just silence and mending."

Call me a vision, then, sent to you to give you a dream such as you have never had before.

"I do not want to dream tonight. Who sent you?"

It is a gift from your sun-lord, the presence said. Have you never wondered how mortals from other worlds live? She sent me to give you a glimpse of the rest of the universe.

Melfidor was about to reply that he had never wondered any such thing, but suddenly it seemed to him that he had indeed spent much time gazing at the constellations in the short summer nights, and he was filled with what seemed to be painful and familiar emotions: yearning for the forbidden journeys through the stars; hours of waking dreams in which he strove to put together all he had heard from Sholia and the Traders about the marvels that lay beyond the Gate; and under it all a bitterness that these things should be denied him because he was mortal. No! he told himself, bewildered. I have never looked at the stars with anything but wonder at their beauty. I have listened to the Traders tell their stories and have been glad to be Sholan. Yet he could not deny the tumult of memories and saw himself clearly, lying in the warm grass at midsummer, eyes fixed on the crowded night sky and longing, wishing.

"Are you a mind-picture?"

Not altogether. I come to you from Ghaka, the being replied.

Melfidor shivered. Ghaka. A Trader had brought him a feather from Ghaka once. He still had it somewhere. A long, curved, soft thing, brown in shade but bursting into dark greens and many shades of deep gold under sunlight. He had never wondered then what it would be like to fly, but now . . .

See, the thing from Ghaka hissed, coming close again. I will show you myself.

Unwilling, yet already drawn into a web of curiosity, Melfidor's mind stepped back, surrendering the door, and he felt the other's mind come through. His consciousness woke, but not to the dark office. All at once he was standing in the middle of a field, one hand raised to shield his eyes from the brilliant sunshine, the other holding his hair in a bracing, steady wind that tried to fling it free. At his back were many strange mountains, not thick and heavy and mounting in great bulk like the mountains of Shol, but thin and sheer, sharp peaks piercing the blueness of the sky, separate crags honeycombed with caves and crowded close together. Before him a wide valley snaked, dotted with sheep and streaked in gray, winding roads that led to houses set behind low stone walls. The air smelled dry and light, and full of nameless herbs. His head was flung back, and there, dropping rapidly toward him, was a giant bird. As it came plummeting nearer he saw that it was not a bird but it was a winged man. His limbs were curled beneath him, knees to chest, arms folded, and the wings were tight and thin along the bent spine. Just as Melfidor was about to cry out in alarm, for it seemed to him that the man's speed would smash him into the ground, he heard a cry of triumph and delight, and the wings unfurled with a crack like canvas sails suddenly taking the wind. The limbs opened wide, legs trailing, arms flung out in a gesture of complete, exultant freedom, and the head rose. "Oh, Ghaka!" the winged man shouted. "Oh, freedom!" He turned and became vertical, eyes closed, face to the sun. His wings beat against the air, and he rose, soaring slowly and majestically, then glided down again. Melfidor could hear him singing, a high hum that mingled with the sound of his swishing feathers to make a wild, compelling music. Melfidor thought it the most beautiful sound he had ever heard, and his heart leaped in yearning to be up there also, held by the winds, caressed by the sun. Suddenly the singer swooped down and alighted before Melfidor, smiling and panting a little, his hair catching in the upswept wings, his eyes fiery with joy. "Would you like to ride up there with me?" the man asked, and with a gasp of pleasure Melfidor held out his arms.

Then the vision was gone. Color and youth drained quickly from the brown face, and Melfidor found himself again looking into the hollows of fleshless eyes, while impotent dark shadows moved where the wings had rustled in the wind. He was in his body, in his office, his conscious self now shared with the stranger, the rest of his mind trying to understand what was happening to him. But the question was not part of the dream. It was repeated softly: Would you like to ride with me? Or rather, would you like to *be* me, Melfidor, and ride the gliding winds for yourself?

At the back of Melfidor's mind, there by the second, farther door that sheltered his consciousness, a warning woke. This is not memory at work, for in memory there are no mysteries, though I encompass the thoughts and actions of my forebears. This is not dream, for dream is my servant and can be summoned and dismissed at will. This is something new. Is it a part of my growth, an opening up within myself? He was unable to determine whether it was a good or an evil without the help of the sun-lord. He considered dismissing the thing that was already so at ease in his consciousness, but at the thought he faced a terrible sense of loss. I will tell Baltor in the morning, he decided, not caring that the thing now shared his thoughts. But tonight . . . tonight I will fly.

"You have offered me a chance to ride the winds for myself," he said. "I accept with thanks."

The dream smiled. "That is good. Now open the rest of your inner self to me, Melfidor."

Melfidor hesitated, and the room enclosing his resting body seemed to become very still, as though for a moment night had ceased to move toward morning and the whole of Shol had taken a deep breath. "Why?" he whispered.

"How can you truly see the ground below or hear the sound of wind in your wings or sing my song or feel the exhilaration unless consciousness be joined to flesh essence, imagination? Open. Open!"

Melfidor was reluctant, and yet the desire to see, hear, and feel it all again was overpowering. He turned to the door that sheltered mind and essence behind his consciousness, and the unknown thing from Ghaka rushed after him. Obediently the door swung wide, and Melfidor blinked, coming to himself. The room was still dark, and the quiet of night still shrouded the outside world. He flexed his fingers and began to sit up, and then he felt the thing pounce. With lightning speed it forced its way past his mind, and at the last moment Melfidor screamed, knowing what he had done, the swiftly flowing alien thing within him suffocating him, forcing mind and consciousness back as it filled him. Frantically he strove to slam the door, but it was too late. Darkness deluged him.

Mirak slowly opened his eyes and smiled. He rose from the bed and stood, numb with relief and satisfaction, feeling the blood course through his legs. He lifted his hands and looked at them, admiring the rings on his slim fingers, and then put them to his face, exploring its contours. What color are my eyes? he wondered. He pulled his hair forward, and it shone dully, a dim brown that would take life from the sunlight of day. Then he laughed softly. I am Mirak. I am Melfidor. I am Mirak-Melfidor, Melfidor still, Melfidor also. I know that you lurk within me, Sholan, blind, deaf, and dumb, a barren seed. How good, how good it is to see and breathe, to hear and feel! Come quickly, dawn, so I can be warmed by sun once more! He wanted to run to the window, spring from the casement, and soar free over this unknown world. He flexed his wings but lost his balance, sitting back on the bed with a bump. *My wings. Of course they are gone, what else could I expect?* For the first time he truly faced the burden of that loss with all it would mean down the long years ahead. He forgot Ghakazian's light promise of power on Ghaka, forgot why he was here in another man's body on an alien world. He sat on the bed and grieved for his freedom, and Melfidor struggled once in his mind and was still.

Shol was a place of haunting and dread that night. In palace and home, out on the windy plains, in ships caught in the lull of windless hours, it changed, and in the morning an alien race greeted the sun with greed appeased. Not all Sholans had been lured into captivity, for the population of Shol was far greater than that of Ghaka. When the families of the city sat down together to eat the early meal, children chattered to parents who remained unusually silent. Lovers stirred drowsily and then drew away from each other, a sudden unfamiliarity rising between them. The nomads led their horses to water, doused the cooking fires, and packed away their gear, though some stood by the river or smoking ashes, heavy-eyed and sluggish, as though the morning had come too soon. On the docks the dawn bustle was strangely cheerless. Fishermen sat in their boats with nets in their hands and did not move. Captains shouted at crews who fumbled at their work in dull perplexity. And in the palace Melfidor, Veltim, Chantis, Fitrec, the men and women who under Sholia held the reins of Shol in their firm hands, slipped from their rooms and wandered the high chambers and sunny balconies, avoiding one another, rediscovering the feel of a crisp winter wind on their skin and the inexpressible comfort of firm floors beneath their feet.

Only Baltor rose with the dawn full of new vigor. He flung wide the windows of his room, singing absently to himself, and when he had eaten, he cloaked himself and went out of the palace, running easily down the terrace stair and crossing the plain to the Towers of Peace. When he reached it, he paused, looking out and down over Shaban, now bathed in warm sunlight. The winter breeze tickled the bells strung from every curling eave, and their music came to him, a constant, pleasing tinkle of tuneless delicacy.

Whitecaps raced for the beaches and slapped under the wooden piers of the docks. Up and down the steep, stepped roads the people moved, slow and unhurried, and Baltor saw nothing amiss in a scene he had witnessed thousands of times. He swung the gate wide and passed through.

Baltor was untouched. Tagar had drifted into his room and had hovered over him for a long time, watching the face whose lines so nearly resembled his own. The black and silver hair had been spread wide on the pillow; the open, unseeing eyes were blank. With a mounting sorrow that numbed his need for flesh, Tagar knew that he was looking at himself as he had been on Ghaka, old and full of good knowledge, wise in the ways of mortals, ready to face the Messenger without rancor or regrets. He thought of this man's children, and their children. He thought of Natil and the quiet loveliness of Rintar. The more he pondered, the more reluctant he became to tear apart this life, so rich in living. If I do not enter this man, I shall never again feel fire or sun or walk the valleys of Shol as I did on Ghaka. But he could not. He stayed beside Baltor for the rest of the night, his misery growing, and when dawn changed the darkness to paleness, he turned and fled. Down through the morning-drowsy, empty chambers, through the entrance hall, out upon the terrace he glided, a howl of agony, and before the sun rimmed the horizon, he had vanished into the lonely shadows of Shol's mountains.

I will do anything to keep this, Mirak thought, looking out from a balcony cut high in the side of the mountain, an empty room behind him and the eyes of Melfidor scanning the brown plain below. If there is to be war, then I will fight as Ghakazian wished, but I will never give up my body again. It did not disturb him, whose keen Ghaka-sight had been able to recognize the quick dart of a field mouse from far above the level of the crag peaks, that he could not discern what manner of animal ran through the brittle grass a mile below. Already his essence was fusing with Melfidor's body, each penetrating the other, each taking color and direction from the other. Mirak's unconscious self was at work in Melfidor's memory and thoughts, selecting for itself a personality and the invisible fleshing of a foreign past. I am a shipbuilder. I like to sail and fish. I am the sun-lord's confidant. Emotions came with this shaping of a new man, but many of them were so alien to Mirak's essence that he shied away from them. A vision of paper and black ink spread out under his hands brought a wave of satisfaction, a pleasure of the mind that Mirak could not understand. The flood of worship spilling over his whole being at the thought of Sholia was easier to comprehend, but Mirak could not separate it from his own fearful scrabbling at the feet of Ghakazian's manipulative power, and the pure glow of Melfidor's reverence became ringed with a groveling, sick humility. Mirak had no feeling at all for water, but while Melfidor's love of the ocean tired him, he was able to blend it with his similar delight in the equally vast sweep of his own element, the sky, though that, too, was reduced by the memory of his last flaming fall. He pulled faces out of Melfidor's thoughts, put names to them, but could not untangle the complex auras around each one. He fingered Melfidor's long memory, the thread of kin-thoughts, and found there a people whose very atmosphere, the dreams they had conjured, the things they had done were offensive in their otherness.

Finally he reached for the hour of Melfidor's death, but a new and terrible thought stopped him. What will happen to me when Melfidor goes to the Gate? When I must flee his body and leave both his essence and his body to the Messenger that will come for him? Must I find another host, a Sholan who is strange to me, and discover and knit all over again?

Suddenly he realized that in the blind intensity of his thoughts he had mounted the railing of the balcony and was standing on its frail rim, leaning against the stone side. Horrified, he jumped backward. I must never forget that I have no wings, he thought, his heart scudding. Perhaps it would be safer to close myself off from Melfidor, let him live again without knowledge of me. I can watch him and learn, I can nestle in his mind while his consciousness goes through the days and nights. Yes, I will do that. I will relinquish his senses until I become accustomed to the prison of the earth, for if I do not, I could kill him or make his sun-lord suspicious when she returns. Mirak's gaze turned inward. He opened the door to Melfidor's consciousness, knowing that, in letting him in, Melfidor had relinquished authority over himself and would withdraw again when ordered to do so.

Melfidor caught the balcony rail in both hands and looked about

him, bewildered. Why did I come up here? he thought. Is Sholia
back? I don't remember rising this morning. It's cold, being so high.
For a moment he stayed there, his head aching, feeling sad and
very tired for no reason he could find. His attention was distracted
by a flock of birds arrowing noisily up from the misty plain beneath.
Darting and whistling, they drew nearer. He shuddered and stepped
back from the rail, turning to the little door behind him.

# 12

Ghakazian watched the Gate until the violet birds had fluttered to
immobility and the stars had been blotted out, then turned and
made his way down the short Gate tunnel, now thick with a stygian
blackness. So it has happened to me, he thought. My Gate is closed.
I am immured on Ghaka, and I am alone. He was calm, almost
detached as he came to the mouth of the cave and stood slowly
surveying his world. But this time they were wrong. This time they
have closed a Gate against the only aid capable of halting the All's
descent into the bowels of black fire. The time draws in on me, and
I must swiftly learn how to shake myself free of Ghaka. It will come,
I know it will. I have been obedient to the Book, laying myself
beneath its discipline, and the last venture must follow.

Ghaka was silent below him. He judged it to be about noon,
but time meant nothing on the stricken planet. No eyes glanced to
the sun, no feet carried strong bodies to the white cottages to break
the fast of the morning. Even the flocks had scattered, leaving the
burned grass of the valleys and wandering toward the mountains,
driven by the stench of death hanging like an invisible miasma to
where the high winds could not reach. The sun bulged purple in a
black sky and cast dark shadows on the ground.

Ghakazian, about to launch himself forth, paused with one
hand on the rock arching low over him. For a long time he studied
the sun. How many years are left to you and thus to me also? he
wondered. Are you diseased with an illness that is eating you away,
or simply wounded, unable to recover yet not sliding into death?
He did not bother to probe it. My essence lives as long as you
survive he said to it but more to himself, and once my essence has
found another body on Shol I am safe until that time.

He pushed himself away from the rock wall, but as he did so
he heard his hand click and scrabble against the stone. Startled, he
brought his fingers up before his face. Curved dirty-yellow talons

fanned out under his gaze, and the skin of his hands was leathery to the touch. He turned the fingers this way and that, then bent to examine his feet. The same cruel claws gripped the lip of the cave mouth. Angrily he tried to wrench them off, but they would not come, and the first pain of his life shot up his leg. Slowly he twisted them again, exploring the sensation. I hurt, he thought, appalled. How can that be? My immortality lifts me far above all mortal hazard. Very well. I am diminished but not powerless. I will go on.

He fell out of the cave mouth, opened his wings, and began the long flight to his home, beating steadily and surely between the peaks, whose feet drowned in shadow. He could not see what lay in that shadow, but he knew. The updraughts from the valley floors were warm and stronger than he had ever known them to be, though he had flown this way countless times. As he went he glanced into each cave, thinking that they looked like sockets from which the eyes had been violently wrenched, and saw how the black blood that had trickled down the face of the crags had dried indelibly. He missed none of them, a ruthless pride sweet within him. He came at last to his funnel, dark now without the obliging obedience of his sun, and folding his wings, he dropped inside.

"I must begin at once," he said aloud. "I must have courage, I must not flinch. This night must find me on Shol." He settled himself on the ledge and brooded in the darkness. But what of the Gate? Now that it is closed, how can even my essence leave this place? He drew out from his memory every bright scene he had witnessed while reading the Book to assure himself that he had been proceeding correctly, and once more he saw himself crouching behind the shrubs that lined the terrace of Sholia's palace, watching as the Unmaker talked to her. I must trust and obey the Book, he concluded, and first I must shed my body. The rest will follow, providing I do not turn aside. He leaned out over the airs that stirred around him, rising from the silent depths below. He imagined the bottom of the funnel, far beneath the level of the earth outside. He saw it as a bed of pointed rocks never blunted by the passage of wind and weather, black with moisture that trickled in a thin stream to drip into caverns even deeper. He refused to feel fear, to place himself on a level with Mirak. He brought his wings forward and wrapped his arms around them, holding them tightly before him, and then he jumped.

He pulled his wings closer to his waist and closed his eyes. Down he fell, turning slowly, the wind of his passage screaming in his ears and buffeting hot against his body. He no longer knew where the ledge was, or where the mountain's teeth waited to bite into him. He brushed against rock. It grazed his arm, and he loosened his grip on his wings for just a moment, a reflex of preservation, but it was enough. Of their own accord the wings flapped back and spread, and he found himself hovering in tight darkness, rock enclosing him. Without thought, gasping and trembling, he shot upward, reached the ledge, and hurtled through the arch into the wide coolness of his hall. Not that way, he thought frantically. Out under the sky.

He skimmed through the hall and left the mountain, flying down to where the serried range of cliffs bounded the nearest valley. Coming to rest on top of a cliff, he launched himself forth once more, not caring that he should join the dead wingless ones whose bodies littered the foot, but again his wings played him false and refused to remain imprisoned.

For a long time Ghakazian tried to destroy his body. He jumped from a dozen heights. He made fire and plunged into it, but fire could not hurt him. He lay beneath the water of a river, gulping and breathing coldness and a taste of greenness, but he was Ghaka, earth, fire, and water, air and mountains, and Ghaka, sick though she was, knew him and would not harm him. Finally he crawled up onto the damp, soft moss of the bank and lay on his stomach, dripping and laughing. He laughed in desperation, laughed at his own mad antics, and when he had finished, he lay quietly, listening to the utter blankness of evening around him, defeated.

When the absence of sound began to oppress him, he flew to the Gate, night hurrying on his impatient heels. He knew that even he could not bear to spend the hours of darkness with the rotting reminders of his perfidy. Standing before the Gate, he thought of all the words of coercion and command that were his to use but could find none that did not depend on a sun's power to bring them to life, and he was afraid to wrench more life from his own sun. There is nothing more I can do, he thought, a panic rising in him.

I am trapped here, and I am full of terror. Shall I go back to my hall? But this would mean flying once more over the obscenity of the valleys, and he did not dare. Shall I take my mind into my sun and stay there, forgetful of Ghaka, forever?

He began to pace up and down before the Gate, tugging unconsciously at his wisping feathers. I must get out, I must. The words chased around and around in his mind, and he began to mutter them, the echo of his low voice whispering back down the cave tunnel. Then he stopped and faced the Gate, standing rigid and angry. He pushed against it with his hands, shouting at it, and pounded it with his fists. "Open! Open, open!" he screamed. "Help me, someone, something, anything, help me! Open my Gate!" But though his hands bruised black and his voice grew hoarse, the Gate stood solid and mute, resisting him. Finally he aimed a savage kick at it and flung himself to the ground, sitting hunched and glowering against the rock wall, wings curving around him like a dark cloak. •

Then his name was called.

*Ghakazian . . .*

He did not hear it with his ears, or only in his mind. It seemed to quiver gently in his hollow bones like the first caress of his sun when he used to rise from his funnel to greet the morning. He looked up as though he expected to see the source of that soft voice, its tones still trembling warm in his flesh and in his mind, and it came rippling over him again in shivers of comfort and pleasure.

*Ghakazian.*

"Yes, yes!" he answered dry-mouthed, scrambling to his feet.

*You want to leave Ghaka?*

"I do," he replied, scarcely able to speak for the flush of ecstasy now pulsing through him and gaining strength, "but the Gate is closed."

*So it is. Why is it closed, Ghakazian?*

He knew that the voice had no need of explanation, but he did not dare to say so.

"Because the sun-lords believe that I have betrayed the Law and ruined Ghaka."

*And have you?* the voice asked, amused.

"No. I am trying to save the remnants of the worlds from the Unmaker, but they do not understand."

*I see.* Anger flicked through the warm washing of pleasure and humor, and Ghakazian felt it, a prick of pain instantly submerged. *And what will you do if I release you from Ghaka?*

"But the Gate is shut." Ghakazian smiled, caught up in the exuberance of his body.

*What will you do?*

"I will go to Shol, where my people are, and when the Unmaker passes through Shol's Gate, we will rise up against him and destroy him."

*How will you do that?* The voice was humoring now, indulgent, and the rivers of sweetness coursing through Ghakazian's blood seemed to thicken to a syrup. He felt all at once surfeited with pleasure.

"I do not know. All I know is that I will go, and I will fight."

*Ah. What will you give me, sun-lord, for taking you to Shol?*

"I have nothing to give, and besides, the Law forbids . . ."

*The* Law, the voice said disparagingly, and Ghakazian was buffeted by its sharp annoyance, yet under the irritation the stream of intoxication went on. *The Law,* the voice repeated. *But I am above the Law, Ghakazian. The Law is my servant. I break it when I wish. As for your gift to me . . .* There was a pause, and when the voice came again to Ghakazian, it hurt him, filling his veins to the bursting point with its sweet magic, lapping in his bones, singing in his mind. *You have much to give that I will accept. Ghaka is yours to give away. I will take Ghaka. And when you have entered Shol, I will take it also.*

"Who are you?" Ghakazian whispered, doubt faltering in him, and the voice laughed.

*You know who I am, my son, my sun-lord, my loyal Ghakazian. See!*

Then memory returned. Ghakazian found himself in his body on Danar, in a time ages gone, circling the council hall while below him the table was full of a smiling, chattering assembly. In the great carved chair raised to fit the dais steps, the Worldmaker watched them all, smiling, hands resting on his knees, dark eyes softly glowing in his thin face. Ghakazian fled the memory, and the voice chuckled. *You still love me, Ghakazian,* it whispered. *Admit to me that you love and worship me. Perhaps I will take nothing more from you than that.*

Ghakazian bent his head, trying to battle the spell he now knew had been cast upon him, but he no longer had the strength of innocence. What does it matter? he thought dimly. I can use him to get to Shol. Perhaps I have flirted too deeply with his fire in order to empty Ghaka, perhaps I am seared after all, but I will right everything when I wrest power from Sholia and cast him back into deep space. The greater good overshadows the lesser evil. Languorously, slowly his head rose, and when he spoke, he knew that he was telling the truth. Sholia, Danarion, all of them admit their love for him, though they no longer obey him. What is the difference? "Yes, I love you," he managed drowsily. "I, we, all of us have never ceased to love you."

*Do you worship me, also?*

The distinction was beyond Ghakazian's diminished powers to apprehend. He nodded. "Of course I worship you, as my people worship me."

*Good. You are quite right. You do indeed worship me in the manner in which your people abase themselves before you.* With those words the tide of ecstasy receded and was gone, and Ghakazian found himself shaking with cold. *I cannot open the Gate,* the voice went on, now toneless and stern and curiously bereft of timbre, like the whispers of the Messengers, *but I can pull you from Ghaka and toss you into the corridor, providing you are willing. You must be willing, sun-lord.*

Ghakazian felt the voice present to his mind a vivid and grotesque picture of his valleys and what they held. He knew he was being coerced, but he had no strength to resist. "I am willing," he choked.

*Then stand straight, bid farewell to your wings, and leave yourself open to me.*

It has all gone too far, Ghakazian thought faintly, doing as he was told. Even if I wanted to turn away from all I have done, I could not bring the people back or heal my sun or myself. Farewell, Ghaka. I am sorry, for I have loved you. He opened his eyes wide and turned to face back toward the tunnel, hoping for a last glimpse of his world, but a light was growing in front of him, the strangest he had ever seen. He wanted to call it darkness, but it was more than that, as though he had passed through to darkness's other side, where its heart glowed, its source, far from the fringes seen by created being. The darkness burned with a snaking, slow black flame. It did not crackle and spit as a mortal's fire would, nor did it burst out gaily like the white brilliance of a sun-lord's aura. It oozed outward, hung heavy, and slid back to its source. Ghakazian could not see any form at its center. Fear tendriled with the slide of those black tongues, and an unimaginable power mingled with the fear. Ghakazian knew that his own immortal powers, even in the days of his changelessness, were like crude toys beside those of this being who had once spoken the All into existence and who now had pulled himself small to fit a cave on Ghaka.

The fire expanded, sizzled cold along the floor, and slid toward Ghakazian along the walls, in no hurry to encircle its prey, for nothing could escape it. There was nowhere in the whole of the universe to flee to. Slowly it began to envelop him, its cold stunning him, killing the golden warmth of his blood and instantly freezing his mind. Yet the cold burned. Ghakazian wanted to scream, but fire scoured his mouth, leaped from his eyes, seared his throat, and he knew himself to be a pillar of coiling blackness. His thoughts fled into the safety of his essence, burrowing deep, and together mind and essence began to loosen from his body, not silently and easily, as he had always imagined, but with a tearing that made him writhe in agony.

Then he was looking at himself. He hovered over his body, peeled and shivering, and his body sank to the floor of the cave tunnel and lay black and limp, the wings crushed beneath it, the limbs splayed dark across the empty chest. He had no time to assimilate the shock, for an invisible force lifted him. Rock was all around him, yet he did not feel it. Then Ghaka's night sky opened, a panorama of blazing stars that seemed to streak toward him, leaving streamers of white fire, before he realized that the stars were still and it was he who sped. The voice by the Gate roared behind him, "Shol! Shol!" and Ghakazian found himself in the corridor, Shol's twins rolling nearer, two blinding orbs that filled his vision, tugging him obediently toward themselves. Then Shol's Gate was there. Ghakazian clutched for the lintel, felt for the lip with feet he thought for a moment he still had, and propelled himself through into the Hall of Waiting.

It was jammed with people. Light filled the big room. The

farther door stood wide, and beyond it the crowd spilled out under a windy night sky, talking, singing, and laughing. Red haeli flowers were banked against the walls. So Sholia has returned, bringing flowers from Danar, Ghakazian thought. But why? Carpets had been flung haphazardly down, and on them people sat eating and drinking, calling to one another between the slow rivers of humanity meandering along where no carpets lay. Ghakazian's gaze flicked over the Hall, and he finally saw her sitting in her chair against a wall, bending toward a man who squatted at her feet. For a long time he fixed his attention on her. She was dressed in white, and Shol's copper glinted dark pink on her brow and her arms. The gold of her body's light bathed the wall behind her and those who stood or sat near her. She was speaking steadily, her eyes on the man, her hands sometimes raised in a gesture but more often lying on the arms of the chair, and every so often he would nod gravely. Mortal and immortal were so perfectly attuned, so drawn together under the circle of light that they seemed blended into a soft skein Ghakazian could almost feel. The man rose easily, sat in the low chair beside her, and turning to her, began to answer or expound. He is an old one, Ghakazian thought, now able to measure him better. He reminds me of Tagar. Yet Tagar never came to me to converse, merely to pay his respects once a year, and it was I who went among my people, traveling the farms and crags, seeking them out. I had a simple and ignorant race of mortals not worth governing, he thought hotly. Shol is the sophistication of long ages. How great will be its fall.

The thought of Tagar dragged his gaze from the two, and he searched the company. How many of these are mine? he wondered. How many winged and wingless look out through the bright, flashing eyes and speak through these smiling lips? Once more his attention was caught, by a woman walking swiftly across the floor. Her gown was red, its heavy silk embroidered in silver leaves. Soft gold slippers with toes turned back covered her feet. Rings smothered her fingers, crystal from Lix, blue and emerald gems from Danar, and a piece of curiously marbled white-and-black polished stone that could only have come from Ghaka. She held herself tall, deftly swaying through the throng, but the impression she gave was one of nobility rather than arrogance. Black hair was pulled tightly back and knotted, and some pale winter flower had been woven into it. Over her arm she carried a white cloth gleaming with silver thread. His mind snaked toward her, feeling gently, but no answering touch greeted his probing, and he withdrew. She is not one of us, he thought. Not yet. As she approached, Sholia stood and raised an arm. The musicians were laying down their bells and pipes. It is the full panoply of a death for a man of some importance, he thought. Of course. Sholia had taken the shroud and was draping it around the man, and one by one the people came to greet him for the last time. I should go, Ghakazian thought anxiously. Even now a Messenger is flashing toward this Gate. It will see me. He moved into the room but somehow could not leave the Hall, and he found a dimly lit corner and shrank back.

Before long the last person had bent to revere, and Sholia took the trailing edge of the shroud and deftly wound it tighter, hiding the brown hands, passing it up over the head so that only the face showed. The man stood and addressed them all for a long time, Sholia beside him, and when he had finished, she drew away with a smile and a word that spread laughter through the Hall. Ghakazian envied her then, and his envy made him lonely. The bells began to tinkle. Looking toward the Gate, Ghakazian saw a faint rainbow light just beyond it. The Messenger had come.

Sholia dimmed her fire, and the room grew dark, but around the man a new light grew slowly, colorless and pleasant to the eye, like shallow water pierced by the sun. The lines grooving his face began to melt away. The dark eyes lightened, began to burn golden. The shroud lit and glowed with the fire welling through it. All at once the figure cried out and crumpled backward, but the light went on intensifying until the Hall was almost as bright as it had been before. The tall woman in red left the crowd and came forward, five others with her, and they lifted him and placed him on a litter. The crowd parted to let them through. Slowly they carried it to the Gate and vanished beyond. Ghakazian waited until the Messenger's perfumed flame had gone and the bearers had come back empty-handed, and then he mingled with the people who were gathering up children and cloaks and moving to the door. Sholia had left, and Ghakazian had no desire to follow her. As the lady in red strode out into the night he drifted after her. If the old man had been of such importance and the black-haired woman was his daughter, then surely he had found a body that would suit his purposes.

Rilla went quickly out of the Hall and, drawing her cloak around her, descended the road. She had decided not to wait for Yarne, who would linger to chatter with his friends, and she had refused Melfidor's offer of companionship on the walk to her house. It had seemed to her that he had been glad when she said no, and she wondered whether he had pressing business tonight in the palace. The night was fine, though windy, and she paused to look up at the stars and feel the air gust in her face. I don't feel at all tired, she thought. I'll go home and embroider for a while or make some music. Later, perhaps, Yarne will want to eat, and we can talk about Baltor. In another three hundred years I'll be following him through the Gate. I wonder if by that time I will have accomplished much good, and if the people of Shaban will want to feast with me as they just did with him. Ghakazian, following the blown shadow of her cloak, saw her hesitate at a low metal gate and drum her fingers upon it, her smile hidden from him, yet sensed. Then she unlatched it and passed through, the Towers of Peace rearing sharp and brightly lit on her left, and went down the steep steps to the road below. From here she could see her roof, its level a little lower than the tops of the drooping, leafless willows, and the sound of her bells strung under the curling eaves came to her faintly, a tuneless jangle carried by the wind. The tang of the ocean far below came to her nostrils, and one or two tiny yellow lights winked up at her from the bows of fishing boats out after the night shoals.

She came to the beginning of the high wall that surrounded her home, turned in at her gate, then stopped. Someone was perched high in one of her burgeoning fruit trees, and her heart turned over as she saw that he was standing on a branch, his arms folded across his chest. Carefully she pushed the gate closed and left the little winding path, crossing over the brittle grass until she stood directly under the tree, looking up through the lacing of black, sturdy arms. "Who is up there?" she called quietly, afraid to shout for fear of disturbing the intruder's balance. She saw a dark head move and a face peer down at her. For a long time neither stirred, but then with a rustle the climber swung himself onto a lower branch and dropped easily in front of her. "Telami!" she said in amazement, and her neighbor's eldest son grinned at her, embarrassed. "What were you doing in my tree?"

"I don't really know," he answered. "I was in my room, and I went to close the shutters against the night. Your garden looked so inviting and the tree so . . . so . . ." Abashed still, he hunted for a word. "So high above everything. Next thing I knew I was climbing, and when I got to the top, I fancied that I might fly. I'm sorry."

"It doesn't matter. You only startled me, that's all. But you had better stay off the roofs!"

He smiled at her a little shamefacedly and then spun on his heel and was gone, running out through the gate and along to his own entrance. Rilla regained the path and walked thoughtfully to her door. Yesterday she had seen a woman sitting on the roof of a house down near the docks. She had greeted Rilla gaily, as though it were the most natural thing imaginable to be cross-legged on the coral-colored slates, but Rilla had been too astonished to do more than raise an arm. Now she acknowledged a faint uneasiness as she shut her door behind her. The murmur of the fountain in the wide hearth room rose to meet her as she crossed through into her workroom. Shaking out her hair, she lit a lamp, then sat and drew the embroidery frame toward her, picking the needle out of the cloth and threading it quickly. One leaf, and then I will rest, she thought. I hope Melfidor remembers that he and I are to sail with Veltim in the morning. The house wrapped her in its friendly embrace. The fountain tinkled on. The shrubs and vines surrounding it creaked and whispered and grew.

When half the leaf was completed, she thought she heard footsteps coming rapidly through from the entry passage, and absently she called, "Yarne, is that you? I'm still up." No answering shout came. Tucking the needle carefully back in the linen, she got up and glanced into the hearth room, but it was empty. "Yarne?" she called again, crossing to peer along the passage to the door, but nothing moved. The house was full of night silence.

Puzzled, she went back to the little circle of lamplight but did not sit, for a presence had slipped into the room before her, and she felt it as soon as she crossed the threshold. She stood quite still, eyes and mind questing the room, wishing that she could take the four steps that would bring her to the blessed brightness of the lamp-light, yet suddenly not daring to. Ridiculous, she told herself, angry at her own cowardice. This is Shol, where nothing can harm me. Taking up her courage, she strode to her chair and sat but was immediately assailed by the feeling that someone now stood behind her. Her spine prickled. Rising, she moved chair and frame so that her back was now to a wall. Regaining her seat, she let her hands rest immobile on the embroidery frame while her eyes slowly scanned the room. Outside the lamp's steady beam was mystery, an ocean of dark unknown. Wind rattled the shutters on the window, thickening the rim of fear around her where the light found its limit. She had wanted to step to the lamp, but now she longed to pick it up and flee the room.

Then, to her horror, she saw it begin to gutter. The flame dipped and jerked and turned from yellow to red to a sullen, starved blue, but Rilla was powerless to lift a hand and turn up the wick. A breath seemed to sigh over her, and the flame danced, flattened, and went out. The rim of darkness rushed in toward her, but after a moment of blindness her eyes became adjusted to the dimness, and she saw night light filtering in pale bands through the shutters and the faint gray glimmer of the tip of her fountain latticed by the copper gate in the next room. Yarne, come home, she begged silently. I don't know what this is. I am afraid to move. Heart pounding, she stayed frozen in her chair. Then, out of the corner of her eye, she saw a shadow stir. Her trembling breath caught in her throat, but she forced herself to turn her head. "Something is there, I know," she whispered. "What are you?"

Her reluctant acknowledgment of its presence gave the shadow the power to take shape. It left the corner where it had lurked, took on substance, and grew tall, and Rilla saw two black wings suddenly unfurl to brush the ceiling. A man stood before her, a slight, crooked smile on his pale face. Black hair, or simply a denser shadow waved on his forehead and spilled over his shoulders, a blackness that matched his eyes and the towering strength of his wings. His arms were spread wide in a gesture of apology or encompassing, Rilla did not know which, and long slender, naked legs ran down to feet hidden in more shadow, which seemed to roil like a heavy cloud about the floor. He stood high, far higher than she even if she had been on her feet, and Rilla found her fear evaporating under the sudden heat of wonder and a strange gladness. It was as though a thing she had sought beyond all dream and waking, behind every thought and word, had come to her at last. Rilla, her astounded gaze traveling him, was his immediate slave.

No breath of warning disturbed her trust and innocence. Though the being smiling at her was unclothed, the perfect sweep from shoulders to delicate feet in itself a throb of pleasure in the beholder, it was Rilla in her stiff red brocade who rose naked and defenseless.

She took a step toward him and then halted, already aching with love for him. This love went from her without reciprocation, and its very flow engendered pain and a larger outpouring, so that the wound in her grew instead of diminishing. She knew, as he endured her scrutiny, that she was not looking at a man, but still she longed to lay her cheek against him, feel his arms go around her, and stay within his shelter forever.

I am not a what, I am a who, he replied lightly. His mouth did not form words but went on smiling. I am Ghakazian.

"The sun-lord of Ghaka? What do you want of me?"

I came to you because I need you, he answered.

Quickly she protested, "But you are a sun-lord, above all need. You do not eat, drink, or sleep. The life and death of one mortal is like the passing of an hour to you. How can you speak of need?"

It is not true that the sun-lords have no needs, he answered, but they are needs beyond your comprehension. I need my sun, not because I am conscious of needing it but because my life rests on it. I need the Law, not because I must consciously conform to it at every moment but because without the Law the universe could not have been made or sustained. I need you, not because I have any lack that you can fill but because I have set myself a task. He came closer to her, and she wanted to drown in the darkness of his wings. I need to share your body for a time.

"I do not understand."

You do not need to. Rilla sensed a faint sneer in the words. I will come into you. You would like that, wouldn't you? I will be you, and you will be me. Sometimes I will be myself in your body, and sometimes you will be yourself in your body, and sometimes we will mingle and be someone new. Can any love be closer or more fulfilling? Can the urge that brings mortal men and women together compare with it?

Rilla thought of Melfidor, whom she believed she had loved, and suddenly he seemed small and ugly, and very ordinary. She considered him with distaste, then turned from contemplation of him to the vision of this sun-lord entering her in some marvelous, magical way, filling her body. The yearning for him intensified until she wanted to fall on the floor in front of him.

"No," she whispered. "Nothing can compare. I do not ask what this task is that you must attempt. I only thank you for coming to me."

I will not harm you, he said. Perhaps you will not even be aware that I am you. Now close your eyes.

Unwillingly she did so, not wanting to be cut off from the sight of his beautiful face, and as soon as she did, she felt herself become a vast cavity, her veins empty, her stomach, heart, and lungs empty, her head a forlorn hollow waiting for him to fire it with life. Then there was a curious hiatus. She was sure that she had indeed slipped to the floor, though the back of the chair was under her hand, and she felt as though she were being sucked out of herself, her essence held to her body by the thinnest, most elastic of threads. The woman on the roof, she suddenly remembered. Telami in the tree. A gush of panic roared through her essence. It began to struggle, but then she felt it wrapped in something she could not define as hot or cold, it was so definitely either the painful touch of ice or the agonizing blossom of fire. Essence and body fitted together again, but not smoothly, not with the comfortable familiarity of long intimacy, and Rilla felt as heavy as a stone. She opened her eyes. He told me something that was not the truth, she thought dully. It was not ecstasy to be possessed by him, nor the pain of pleasure. It was hurtful and demeaning.

Another voice moved in her mind, a peal of spiteful laughter. Rilla, you are Rilla, it chuckled. At last I am fixed on Shol, and I will know all that you are. She put a hand to her ear, her sore eyes slowly traveling the part of the ceiling where the great wings had spread wide, and suddenly the lamp crackled into life and began to send its little glowing pool of light toward her.

I will do one leaf, she thought, and then I will rest. She sat and pulled out her needle, frowning over the shimmering green thread, but before she had taken three stitches, she heard the door slam, and quick feet tapped along the passage. Sweat beaded on her forehead and trickled cool down her spine, and then the fear was gone. "Yarne, is that you?" she called. "I'm still up."

She heard him pause by the fountain, and when he swept into her workroom, he shook droplets of water in her face. "It is indeed I," he said cheerily. "What a wonderful dying, eh, Rilla? His life was very rich and full. Are you hungry?"

"Not particularly. Don't shake water over me, it will stain the cloth. Where have you been?"

"In the palace, talking to Veltim and Melfidor."

"I saw Telami as I came home. He was standing in the fruit tree."

"I saw him too, looking out his window. Why was he standing in the tree?"

Rilla broke her thread, skewered the needle into the cloth, and licked at the blood oozing slowly from her thumb. It had been many years since she had been clumsy enough to prick herself, but her hands felt stiff and useless tonight. I know why he was in the tree, she thought. I know . . . But the reason fled even as she grasped it. "Perhaps he was about to command a dream of flying."

"Flying!" Yarne laughed. "Veltim was saying tonight that he had a strange dream about flying three nights ago. Is Sholia having a little fun with us?"

"I don't know. I think I'll go and rest now. Put out the lamp, will you?"

He picked it up, and together they crossed through the hearth room. In the small front hallway they parted.

"Much dreaming to be done tonight," he remarked as she kissed him on his cheek. "It has been a busy day."

"Indeed, it has. I don't think I want to sail tomorrow after all. I'll go early to the palace. I want to talk to Melfidor before he and Veltim go down to the wharf. Rest well, Yarne."

"You also."

She lay on her bed, intending to command a dream of Baltor in his youth. She was tired, but not with the weariness of a day's work well done, and she could not clearly order the visions she wanted. Uneasiness and a sense of unreality wrapped her. She heard her brother singing softly to himself as he prepared to rest. He sang every night, but tonight the snatches of melody seemed full of something poignant and far away, the ship calling for safety to an indifferent ocean, the lost calling for time to stand still. Her essence demanded unconsciousness, but all that night she dreamed of black wings flapping frantically against her window, rustling small and soft in her curtains, beating wide and high across a star-strung evening sky, and she came to herself long before the suns rose to greet Sholia with a joyful, playful speed. The dreams had left her cold with dread and an alien, inexplicable yearning for the dizzy, wind-teased cliff tops behind Shaban.

# 13

She bathed and dressed, ate a little, and then took her cloak from its hook by the door and let herself out into the thin light of pre-dawn. She lifted her head as she walked and inhaled the morning. The wind still tugged at the city, ringing the thousands of bells, but Rilla was so accustomed to them that she hardly heard them. Occasionally she passed someone going to work early and greeted him with a smile. But most of the streets that ran to meet her own were deserted. The perfume of winter filled the air, dry, delicate, and faint, the odor of resting trees mingling with gusts of sweetness from clumps of white winter flowers. She climbed steadily, and once above the city, she set out past the Towers of Peace and across the plain. The suns were up now, shimmering new and red on the horizon. She strode rapidly along the well-worn path, head down, hands folded under her billowing green cloak. Up here above Shaban the wind blew with a steady, keening whine, pulling at her neatly tied hair and bringing a flush of red to her sallow cheeks, coaxing her blood to run faster and tingling in her ears. On any other morning she would have hummed as she went, matching a tune to the working of her long brown legs, and taken time to watch the steadily lifting suns rise above the city and splash the face of the rock-held palace, but now her mind was full of an odd sadness that made her wish she had stayed in bed or got up only to sit before the wide window in her workroom and think nothing. A flock of birds wheeled by overhead, circling the plateau and screeching to one another, and she flinched and hurried on.

Reaching the long, gleaming terrace of the palace she climbed the steps hurriedly and passed under the lofty arches of the entrance with relief. In a matter of moments she was knocking on Melfidor's door.

He opened, greeted her gaily, and kissed her, and she followed him into the room. Sunlight hung everywhere, blushing the walls, entangling in the rigging of the huge ship model resting along one wall, lying across his desk, and picking sparks from his pens.

"I would have come to your house in another hour," he said, "but Veltim is busy with Sholia, and I had to wait."

"I don't want to sail today in any case," she replied, moving to the desk. "I think the wind is too strong for little boats, and besides, I have work to do." Green leaves, she thought. I don't want to embroider any more green leaves. I feel ill just remembering how long it took me to do half of one last night.

"Will Yarne come?" he enquired.

She turned, troubled, unseeing eyes upon him, her hands passing absently and clumsily over the litter beneath them. "Perhaps. You can stop at the house on your way down to the bay and ask him."

He moved to her and ran a finger along her jaw very gently. "Why did you come up here to see me?" he said. "Has Baltor's death left a wound?"

Impatiently, almost savagely, she drew away from him, jerking her chin from his hand.

"No, why should it? I don't know why I came, Melfidor. I didn't really think about it. I just . . . came."

"I won't go out in the boat today if you want me to stay with you. We can take food into the plain and go and talk to the nomads for a while. They will be camped out beyond the edge of the mountain until this wind drops."

"No." There was almost panic in the sharp word. "There are birds. Birds out above the plain."

"Rilla." He moved to touch her again, but she flung around to face the desk.'

Pulling out his chair, he sat down. "Would you like to see the plan for my new trade ship?" he asked presently. "It's finished, and if Sholia likes it, I can take it down to Depor, and he will begin to build."

She smiled, an effort of agreeability. It was as though he were a stranger, and she were seeing him as such, with a critical, judging accusation. You are not perfect after all, she thought. Why did I imagine that you and I might share our lives? I am Rilla of Baltor, my father was the greatest Sholan who has ever lived, but your ancestors did nothing but design ships, and neither do you. Only a sun-lord is worthy of me. I was born to rule as my father did. "If you like," she said offhandedly.

He leaned forward and slid a paper out from under her hand. "Here it is. I have done the cross sections on other papers, but this is how she will look from the outside."

Rilla took the plan and looked at it, and then peered more closely. "Melfidor, why did you do that?" she snapped, her voice high and breathless as she pushed the paper toward him, one finger on the curving stern. "Wings do not belong on a Sholan vessel!"

He took it slowly. "I don't remember doing that," he said, bewildered. "I have used Sholia as a figurehead. I must have thought I would lace her hair about the stern, but it was foolish. It does look like wings, and they must come off. They will catch the wind and slow the ship down."

Rilla, close to tears, was about to reply when her eye was caught by dozens of other papers on the desk, all scrawled over with something that made her suddenly go cold. There were feathers, long and short, curved thin and fluffed out, and there were wings, tall and folded, flung wide, wings bare of covering, like those of a bat, wings of every description, all seeming to flutter with a captive menace under her gaze. "Melfidor!" she whispered terrified, wanting to scream and scream, to fill the palace with the sound of this nameless, causeless horror surging through her. "What is happening on Shol? To me? To you? Telami . . ."

He jumped up and began to shuffle the papers together, thrusting them out of sight behind the desk. "Well, I thought . . . that is . . . I want to build a ship that will sail through the air, Rilla, and I sat down last night and drew the wings. I must catch birds and study them, take off their feathers, look at their bones . . ." Cautiously he raised his eyes to find her standing straight, all signs of panic gone. Her gaze met his coldly and with a level command.

"I was not sure," she said, and her voice was deeper. "The Sholan faces tell me nothing yet, and I must be careful. Who are you?"

Melfidor slumped to the floor in relief. "It is I, Mirak," he said. "Is it time to fight?"

"Get up!" Ghakazian ordered. "Don't grovel before me. Where is Tagar?"

Mirak scrambled to his feet and faced the red-clad, graceful figure with its delicate oval face and its bundle of black hair piled high on the small head. It was not Rilla's steady, friendly glance that met his own but the blazing power of his master.

"I don't know," he answered. "I haven't found him. But Natil and Rintar are here, all of us spread out among the people of the city and the plains."

"Good. Then all has come to fruition, and now we must wait. This Melfidor, what is his station?"

"He is a planner of ships, an overseer of the docks, a very important man," Mirak answered proudly. "He spends much time with the sun-lord."

The thought of Sholia brought a shiver of sickness to Ghakazian. He passed a tongue over dry lips and felt her close, a short walk away. He was netted in her power, an unsuspecting victim. No, he corrected himself swiftly. The All is the victim. I must remember that. "Good!" he said again briskly. "I will go to her and ask if I may work here in the palace. Yarne, my brother, is not one of us, and I don't want to stay with him any longer. Although"— and the lip curled—"he is far too busy being cheerful to ponder any changes in his sister. Get rid of those wings, Mirak. A flying ship!"

"I long for my wings," Mirak said timidly. "I am chained to the soil of Shol. We have sacrificed much for you."

"And for yourselves," Ghakazian retorted. "Which would you rather lose, your wings or your freedom as mortals? Stop sniveling. I also have left my wings before the Gate of Ghaka. I cannot return. The Gate is closed."

Mirak stood staring at him, appalled. "Closed? Why? How can I go back there now? Sun-lord, tell Janthis the truth. He must open it again!"

"He may do so as a reward to you when the Unmaker is no longer a threat," Ghakazian answered mildly, lying easily, but Mirak was not comforted.

"Did you bring the Book?" he asked diffidently.

Ghakazian snorted in derision. "How could I do that without hands to hold it? Go back behind Melfidor's essence, Mirak. I will call you when I need you."

Mirak sighed, bowed, and put out a hand to touch the necklet that was no longer there. Melfidor laid a light arm across Rilla's shoulders. "I am a designer," he said kindly. "My head is full of ideas, some good, some coming from the world of dreams and not practical at all. But I consider each one because that is my life."

Some of the stiffness went out of her, and she laid her cheek against his arm. "I'm sorry, Melfidor. It's not my business to understand your work. But I wish you would throw away the wings. Somehow the whole of Shol seems swept by the desire for flight, but it is not a gay thing, not a new game. It frightens me."

"Me, also," he said, drawing her close. The picture of Telami perched high and dangerously in the darkness filled her mind, but neither one spoke, and at last she kissed him and walked back to her house, oblivious to the bright day or the busy streets.

Hanging up her cloak with a forced deliberateness, she tried to settle to her work but found herself more often brooding, the needle idle in her fingers, her eyes fixed on the tossing branches visible through her window. "I am lonely," she said for the first time in her life, feeling the meaning of the new word, not trying to define it. I do not want to live here anymore with Yarne gone from dawn until night, listening to the silence as I try to work. My father was a great man. Surely Sholia will grant me a room in the palace where people come and go and I am under her direct protection. I will let Yarne have this house.

The room enclosed her with uneasiness, as though it held a tragic memory that it was trying to communicate to her. In the end she left it and fled the house, spending the rest of the day visiting markets down on the flat, crowded land before the docks. When the suns went down, she returned but did no more than open her door. The shadows of the hall rushed to her greedily, ready to draw her inside, and no light shone from the hearth room. "Yarne, are you home?" she called, and when she received no reply, she shut the door and made her way up to the palace, running into its constant warmth as though she were being pursued.

Sholia found her standing in the entrance hall, running a hand over the ships bobbing endlessly across the sapphire ocean on the wall and frowning to herself. Rilla, feeling her come, lifted her head and looked up into the dazzle of the ageless face. She took her hand away from the wall and ran her fingers lightly over the smooth, golden head, allowing them to drift down into the warmth of the heavy tresses in a curiously proprietary gesture.

Sholia reached up and imprisoned the wandering hand. "Did you come to see me, or are you seeking Melfidor?" she asked. "Do you need me, Rilla?"

A spark of something odd flared in Rilla's eyes, but she smiled and it was gone. "I came to you," Rilla replied. "I can no longer work at home. I ask if you will grant me a place here."

"Why is it that you cannot work at home?"

Rilla hesitated. "Because of . . . because I saw Telami in a tree and a woman . . ." She would have continued, somehow organizing her thoughts into the coherence that the presence of Sholia always called up, but she heard something in her mind whisper sharply, "No!" and found that her thoughts had been cut off and she could not remember what it was that had sent her running from her own front door. "Baltor is gone," she finished lamely. "I want to take his place."

Sholia studied her. There was something different about Rilla, the tip of a mystery. Quietly Sholia probed her mind and found there a fear of the house, a confusion of images of wings and birds, and overshadowing these, a loneliness no mortal ought to have felt. Puzzled, Sholia pushed deeper, past the whirl of conscious thought intertwined with emotion to the steady, unchanged flow of essence, and found herself turned back with a jolt of firm denial. Again she quested. Again a shock of resistance met her. Yet Rilla's eyes did not evade hers with the telltale shame of a mortal caught in the first stages of a fall. Sholia had seen such fleeing eyes many times on worlds now forgotten. What, then? she thought. What power has come to Rilla's essence to turn me back? What power on Shol is greater than mine? With a nagging familiarity her own fears returned, and with an adroitness born of long practice she dismissed them. I will allow her to come here, she thought, and I will watch her as I do the others, loving and guarding but in these times watching more than either. "If you take Baltor's place, you will have little time for your embroidery," she pointed out gently.

"I do not want to embroider anymore," Rilla said slowly, repressing a shudder. "I ask only to serve you as Baltor did. If I begin to understand you in the next hundred years, I will be content." It will not take me a hundred years, a scornful, emphatic voice inside her said. I have known you from the beginning. Rilla had not come to the palace to say these things, and her own words to Sholia bewildered her. Now, her eyes fixed on the sun-lord's brilliantly lit, unlined face, she wondered why she had ever spent so much time with her needle and thread when all she really wanted was to be with Sholia.

The sun-lord inclined her head. "I may not forbid you to carry on the work of your ancestors," she said. "This is part of the Law pertaining to your kind, Rilla. You may come. Melfidor will be pleased."

Rilla shrugged and smiled. "I suppose so. May I go now?"

Sholia stood and watched the straight, red-draped back glide out of sight, and then she went slowly to her own long hall, walking it and turning to sit in her chair under the flag of Shol, which hung limp in the stillness, its blue field and cloth of gold suns hidden. She had gone to the agonizing council meeting on Danar, she had seen Ghakazian impudently close his Gate as though it did not matter at all, and when she returned, Shol was different. It was in the air, a sense of expectancy as solid as the chair she sat in. It was in the faces of the mortals she believed she knew better than they knew themselves, a strange new sense of strain. It was in their movements, no longer light and free but fluid and unconscious like a nation of dream-walkers. Something was wrong, yet no one had come to her with a warning. She had gone to the suns, but the suns poured their undiminished energy into her with no hint of diminution, and she knew that she and they were clean. What brooded over Shol? I must go to Danar and ask permission to search the people more deeply, she thought. Are they beginning to undergo a change planned for them by the Worldmaker? I remember no such plan mentioned when he came to Shol and talked with me, he and I alone but for the suns and the mountain and the ocean. Or has his power begun to seep in somehow?

She rose and began to pace the hall, calling quietly for more light to chase the shadows lurking in every corner. Janthis warned me not to dwell on the meaning of fear, but if I pretend that it is not there, I delude myself and cease to watch for the things that cause it. Am I falling prey to my own vigilance? Am I generating a cause for anxiety, creating in my mortals a ripeness for the Un-maker by the very intensity of my fear? Carefully she laid out in her mind the little knowledge of changes on Shol she had gleaned and attempted to laugh at herself, as she saw only the vaguest of threats. She shouted for more light, and more, until the whole long room blazed with a blinding torrent of sun, but she walked slowly at the center, cold and full of dread, and was not comforted.

It seemed to her that the mists of unease that had dogged her down all the long centuries were at last coalescing into an ominous shape that as yet she could not recognize. Coming to a halt by the open door of her chamber, she found her fingers closing on the sun-disc hanging lightly on her breast. The urge to run away took hold of her, as it so often did. She wanted to fling the necklet to the floor and race from the palace, from the bell-haunted city, and disappear into the mountains, leaving the endless, useless defense of Shol to someone else. For an age she struggled with a desire for flight that she knew came filtering through the Gate as a command to surrender, but the moment of testing passed, and she was able to walk through the door unscathed.

# 14

Sholia left the palace gladly, hoping that mere physical distance could free her from the silent, invisible monster that waited in every room. She felt totally vulnerable, as though, unnoticed, something had been stripping her of the shields of immortality and power until she was little better than the mortals around her, and they saw it and rushed to pull her down.

She drew her light around her and stepped from the terrace stair onto the brittle coldness of winter grass, walking quickly away. The high lamps on the Towers of Peace glinted far away on the edge of the plain, and she made her way toward them, looking over her shoulder now and then to the dark, rock-gripped facade of the palace, where windows like mouths spat light at her with spiteful contempt. I cannot go back there! she thought. I must go into the suns, I must think. She came to the nearest Tower, built below the level of the plain and joined to it by narrow stone walkways built to span the gulf between, and here she paused to greet the men who walked the parapets and had seen her light gliding to them over the plain. Then she made her way to the gate and stood by it, looking down upon the city.

Shaban was restless. Few lights showed, but a thousand mutterings and sighings rose to her, mingling with the bells, whose own music sounded harsh and hostile. It seemed to her that the streets were full of a stealthy, furtive coming and going that she could only glimpse out of the corner of her eye, for each time she turned her full attention to a steep, dark street, there was only emptiness and a drowsy moaning of night airs. She called to one of her suns, and briefly it illumined the upper tier of the city, but under its midday glow Shaban was innocent and secure, and she dismissed it curtly. She turned away, but now the same threat of something twisted was at her back and seemed to follow her as she set out across the plain once more. Shol has cast me out, she thought, appalled. Without a hint of impending change she has turned to stand against me instead of with me. How did he do it? She halted in the middle of the plain, a tiny candle of wavering light, and an overpowering impulse to close her Gate rushed through her. She wanted to have done with it all, to be finished so that no one could demand from her those things she was no longer able to fulfill. She began to run, skirting the palace steps, brushing by the potted shrubs at their foot, and came to the outer door of the Hall of Waiting. She sped through it, then halted. A woman stood opposite her by the Gate, head sunk on her breast, arms limp at her sides. Sholia did not recognize her, for her brown hair spilled over her face and hid it, but she could see that she was slim and wore blue gems on her fingers. Past her, framed cleanly by the Gate, the blackness of deep space swirled around the clusters of the constellations, and the eternal silence of the universe breathed a stillness into the empty Hall. The woman did not look up, and Sholia went to her.

"Who are you?" she asked firmly. "Are you going out to Shon or Sumel, or have you come from one of them?" There was no answer. The head remained drooped on the blue gown, and the hands did not stir. Finally Sholia spoke a word of command, and slowly, smoothly, the head rose and the hair fell back. It was a city dweller whose name Sholia did not know, but the face staring back at her bore little resemblance to the smiling mouth and darting eyes she had seen under the trees with her children. Now the mouth was slack and slightly parted, the lips dry from the breath passing evenly over them. The eyes gazed dully ahead, and the large pupils did not respond to the flow of light as Sholia passed a hand in front of them. She repeated her questions, but there was no response. Then she bent and lifted a hand that rested limply in hers. Taking the palm, she pressed the fingers of her own hand against the woman's pale fingertips.

As she began to feel for the roots of this odd trance she was surrounded by a dense white fog. Streamers of it touched her mind lightly and with a damp coolness. Then she realized that the fog was a dense cloud cover, and she was speeding down through it, for the streamers broke, the fog creamed back over her shoulders, and she found herself high over earth, looking down upon two valleys full of gray light, a serried range of crags between them. Above her the clouds formed a solid, low roof of rain-burdened heaviness untroubled by any breeze. But wind hissed in her ears and pressed steadily against her forehead, for she was flying. The rustle of her wings came to her clearly, and she could feel the ripple of movement under the skin of her back. With the rhythmic flexing of her muscles a sense of fulfillment and contentment warmed her, and she happily scanned the lush green, rolling panorama beneath, glimpsing through the woman's lazy thoughts a cave mouth set high on a crag, a fire within, and food to prepare. As the woman checked her flight and began to angle down toward the sharp teeth of the range the rain began, cool and gentle, pattering audibly on her wings and striking her face. Sholia watched the country below rise slowly to meet her, and as the horizon became sliced by rock half-hidden in misty cloud a nagging sense of familiarity started in her. She had been here before. She had seen these valleys, not from the air, yet from some high place. As the woman swerved to hover upright and the mountains also suddenly became perpendicular, she found her eyes drawn to one isolated, rough peak thrusting from the earth, slit from the tip to halfway down its broken, sheer slope by a thin, soaring arch now blurred by the quickening rainfall.

Then she knew. Ghaka! She had often stood on the lip of the arch, Ghakazian's hall behind her and he himself beside her, looking out over the awesome grandeur of Ghaka's landscape. She did not stay to see more. With heart thudding and the intimation of some terrible mystery churning through her thoughts, she pulled out of the woman, releasing her hand and stepping away from her. The fingers collapsed to swing briefly against the blue gown, and the eyes continued to stare ahead, unblinking. No Sholan has ever been on Ghaka, Sholia pondered furiously, not even in the beginning. There can be no memory of such a visit hidden in any mind under my suns. The Gate of Ghaka is now closed, and Ghaka is a dying world; therefore what I saw, the trance this Sholan is living, belongs to the past, and not to Shol's past, but to Ghaka's. She is an alien, a Ghakan on Shol.

Then the truth burst upon her. A Ghakan on Shol in a Sholan body. The mystery of Rilla, the unspoken breath of threat and complicity, resolved into a shape of horror with yet another, darker mystery behind it. Once more Sholia placed herself in the woman's mind and for a second was standing inside a cave, eyes on the warm flames of a fire while the mouth of the dwelling was obscured by a thrumming pall of water. Then she wrapped her own essence around the woman's and uttered a firm order. The woman quivered and cried out in pain, but Sholia spoke again, heedless of her outrage, and holding the Sholan's mind steadily under her control, she forced it back to the Hall of Waiting and faced the woman, whose face had gone suddenly very white and whose lip was now caught between strong teeth.

"Let me go!" she hissed, the eyes no longer blank but full of fear and hatred. "I hurt!"

"Who are you?" Sholia demanded, and the woman squirmed, the hands clenched into fists. "Answer me!"

"Release me," the other begged through gritted teeth. "I am in agony, sun-lord."

"I will burn away all memory unless you answer me," Sholia said levelly, the sun-discs blazing white and searing hot. "I will make a shell of you, an unfilled emptiness. How did you come to Shol?"

Sweat stood out on the woman's face, dampening her hair, but even as she tightened her grip on the foreign essence within this lissome body Sholia felt a tremor of craft and slyness ripple through it.

"If you torment me further," the voice grated back, "I will tear into *her* essence. You are forbidden to harm your mortals in any way, I know that, Sholia, so let me go!"

A fierce wrath fumed up in Sholia, driving out every hesitation, and she drew herself up in a burst of energy. "You dare to speak to me in that way!" she shouted, the deep, vibrant tones booming to the ceiling. "The Law gives me all power over you, for you are on Shol without leave." She flung out her arms, and light exploded from her fingertips and splintered with a roar against the far walls. "I will consume you, Ghakan, I will plant a fire of torture in you that will never go out!" Her body had thinned and now poured heat and sun fire into the room. Her face had lost the softness of a mortal woman's and had become all bright bones under a skin like a molded sheet of incandescence, all fiery eyes.

The woman screamed and fell back, scrabbling against the side of the Gate, one hand shielding her face, but the Ghakan who squirmed in the sun-lord's grip was desperate. "Harm her and you will fall! You will fall!" it wailed shrilly.

Sholia paused. *You will fall.* Yes, it is true, she thought, the anger giving place to an anguished defeat. And if I fall, Shol is finished. "I will rip you from her body," she yelled in frustration, but already her hold had loosened, and the Ghakan turned and leered at her.

"You cannot take me from this body without killing," it sneered. "Kill her, take me from her, destroy me, then what will you do with her naked essence? Tell it how sorry you are?"

Sholia released the brutal fingers of her mind, and she heard the Ghakan essence laughing as it ran back behind the Sholan's.

The woman put both hands to her face and turned confused eyes to Sholia. "Sun-lord?" she whispered. Her hands fell, and she smiled faintly. "Oh, I remember now. I was going to Sumel for a little while. Why was I going there?"

"Go back to the city, go home," Sholia answered wearily. "The night is almost spent, and you need rest."

The woman turned obediently to the outer door, but not without a wistful glance through the Gate where the stars wheeled and flamed. "I was going somewhere," she ended lamely. "I do not want to rest. I do not like to dream anymore." Then she was gone, head hanging.

Sholia did not wait. Stepping up onto the Gate's narrow floor, she ran three steps and fell into the corridor shouting to Danar's sun to carry her. She emerged from Danar's airy Gate tunnel and paused for a moment. Dusk was deepening into a warm twilight. The haeli forest lifted its branches under the weight of a calm gloom. Resolutely, stilling the fever of haste in her feet, she took the stone walkway which brought her to the middle of the stair and climbed quickly. She reached the marbled flagstones of the cloister and, nodding to the immobile corions, went inside.

The passages were quiet. She paced them steadily and came at last to the chamber where only two systems pricked in the black immensity of the polished floor, Shol and Danar, winking up at her with a gallant courage as she crossed under the high dome. She ran lightly up onto the dais, swept past the dull gleam of the sun hanging on the wall, and knocked on Janthis's small door.

He opened immediately and welcomed her courteously, yet behind the soft words she sensed surprise. She did not consider how her fire still rippled, agitated, beneath her skin, and the furious burning in her eyes that had been lit by anger was still not subdued by the hard quelling of it. Janthis followed her into the room.

"Well, Sholia," he said as she turned to face him. "Why have you come to Danar?"

She did not hesitate. "Shol is slipping from my grasp," she snapped. "I don't know how or why. You must help me quickly."

He looked at her reflectively for a time and then responded, "Tell me."

She did so rapidly, putting together all the hints that had curled just out of reach of her consciousness, and she did not falter until she spoke of the woman by the Gate. Then her hands touched each other in a gesture he had come to recognize as uniquely hers. "It was an essence from Ghaka, I know. I flew the valleys, I saw the slit darkness of Ghakazian's door!" Agitation caused her to turn and pace to the wide bay window, and she stood gazing down into the sun-ball where it lay black and inert on the sill. "I cannot take the thread of that essence and feel my way from Shol to Ghaka. How did it come to Shol, and why? I almost lost myself, Janthis, I almost forced the essence into oblivion because of my fear and anger."

Fear, Janthis thought. It is always Sholia who must be fed courage with stirring words. It has made her vulnerable, eaten away at her strength. Has it eaten into her mind, also? Is she slipping into the fire by her own eagerness to hold it at bay? He walked to her and, taking her shoulders, led her to one of the gray, unadorned walls.

"You say that some of your mortals, perhaps all of them, have become hosts for Ghakans torn from their bodies," he said. "Let us look at Shol."

Something in his tone caused her anger to flare anew, but now it was tinged with the confusions of doubt and self-distrust. "You do not believe me!" she said incredulously, but he only put a finger to his lips.

"Watch," he ordered and touched the wall. "Shol," he said, and immediately the gray began to soften and run into the center as though the wall were being drained of color, leaving a velvet blackness in its place so thick and real that Sholia felt she might step through it into a new and undiscovered corridor of space. The grayness spidered toward the center, shrank, and was gone, leaving the whole wall a yawning gap leading to nothingness. Then, at the center, a light grew, was flung outward, expanded until another was spawned behind it, and another. They hurtled toward the room, filling the wall with a sizzling fire that reflected white on the faces of the two immortals, then were cut apart on the edge of the wall and vanished. Sholia felt as though she were being catapulted down a long, star-lined tunnel, but as she began to lean into it Janthis gently pulled her back and kept his hand on her arm. "Do you recognize the constellations?" he murmured. "The wall is a mirror that hangs outside the universe." He began to name them as they raced toward him, flowered, and broke apart. The momentum began to slow. The stars rolled soberly toward Sholia until they stopped and hung shimmering, and after an astounded second she cried out, "My suns!"

He nodded. "And there is Shol, with Shon and Sumel, like three crystal beads strung on an invisible necklace. Have you ever seen anything so lovely, Sholia?"

"My suns," she said again, but this time the words were a fluted breath of air.

Janthis beckoned. "Closer," he commanded, and the twins and their planets grew until they filled all the wall and their light threatened to spill out into the room. For a long time he stood very still, gazing intently at what the mirror showed him, his hand leaving Sholia and tracing an absent pattern on his chin, but she did not notice, so absorbed was she in her worlds, which hung clean and beautiful, the gems of the universe. Then abruptly Janthis made a gesture as though flinging something at the mirror, and the picture snuffed out instantaneously to leave the plain gray wall and a light in the room that seemed dismal and thin to both of them.

Sholia exclaimed in dismay, and he came closer to her, forcing her to lift her eyes to his. "Now," he chided. "I saw no blemish on your suns, no fading of their light, no haze of entrapment around them. Did you?"

"No," she answered reluctantly.

"They shine out as steadily as ever. Shol is still whole."

"But that is because I am still whole!" she almost shouted, drawing away from him. "The suns will show nothing until I go down, and I am slipping, Janthis, I feel, I know it. My mortals have been conquered, and I cannot remain as I am!" His calm pity infuriated her, and in desperation she smote her hands together. "Ghakazian was right! You are helpless, you will do nothing!"

"I cannot force you to see clearly through your wandering imagination!" he snapped back, exasperated. "You say Ghakazian was right, yet where is he now? Mired in his delusions behind a closed Gate. I was given life long before any sun-lord, Sholia. I wandered the universe with the Worldmaker. I knew him. Why can't you listen, and trust me?"

Perhaps you love him too well," she swiftly came back at him, disappointment flooding in to damp down the fires of momentary rebellion and another shard of terror piercing her. "Perhaps you are not willing to throw everything you are able against him. I bring you evil news, and you turn me away!"

He sighed and went to her, taking both shaking hands in his own. "Your life is ruled by fear," he said soothingly. "It has been so for generations. Now consider. Is it possible that the Unmaker is attacking you with all his subtlety? Suppose that through your Gate he has sent a message to your imagination, stirring it further with a great illusion?"

The hands resting in his became suddenly still. "You think that he invites me to believe that my mortals are beyond saving? That I see and feel only the extensions of an idea I have conjured myself?"

"It is possible, isn't it?"

"Yes," she said after a while. "It is. But I do not believe it so."

"You must stand firm. He wants Shol more than anything else, and he will worm his way into your world by any means he can," Janthis said, and Sholia was shocked at the bitterness that crisped his words and cooled his fingers. "He is unable to breach a Gate himself until the forerunners of his power have done their work and broken a world, and too often you forget that those mind-swaying pinpricks of his can easily be repulsed if only you will say a simple no to them. Ah, Sholia," he went on, "you know all these things. Why do you keep running to Danar like a frightened child?"

"Because I am a frightened child," she responded in a low voice, withdrawing her fingers. "I am his child. I am lonely. I miss Ixelion and Falia, but Ghakazian most of all. You, me, and Danarion are the only ones left, but we find no comfort in one another anymore. Come to Shol, Janthis, I beg you! Judge these things for yourself, and then tell me that I dream on the edge of the abyss!"

"I will not come and so add fuel to the fire of defeat already burning in you, Sholia. Stop behaving like a cringing mortal woman in fear of her life. You are not mortal. Take up your immortality. Use the powers that are yours to maintain a world that even Ghakazian used to call the crown of the universe."

She drew herself up, words of pleading and abasement on her lips, the prospect of returning to Shol alone so devastating that she was tempted to kneel before Janthis and beg him to let her stay on Danar, but she did not. Instead she brushed by him and stalked to the door.

"You and he," she said contemptuously. "You complement each other. You are in league with him, aren't you, Janthis? The link forged between you in the beginning has never been broken. No one aided Falia. No one cared to wonder at Ixelion's distress until it was too late. Why is it always too late, Janthis? He has picked us off one by one, and when Danarion and I are destroyed, then you and he will be free to divide the universe between you."

"The sun-lords fell by their own choice," he answered mildly. "What would you have had me do? Close all the Gates in the beginning in the belief that none of you were worth trusting? Have you forgotten the Lawmaker, to whom the universe belongs?"

"I have not forgotten him," she ended with a wounded pride, "but he has forgotten me. I am sorry, Janthis. You are wrong and I am right, and Shol will be the price of your foolishness." She swung the door open with a crash that echoed to the jeweled roof of the dome and was gone.

Very well, she thought enraged as she strode the vacant, placid corridors. I will go home. I will tear apart every mortal and toss every Ghakan essence out through the Gate, and when I have purged Shol, I will close the Gate myself. I will put the Law aside and use every power I have to create a new Shol. It is not possible that on a world as thickly populated as mine there are not some Sholans left untainted. They and I will rebuild together, and the Unmaker will be shut out forever. So will Danarion, another thought rebuked, and you will never walk these halls again.

She groaned and came to a halt, the new determination evaporating with her despairing anger at Janthis. She could not think. I belong here, not on Shol. A world is for mortals. Let them make or break as they choose, I ought not to be responsible. I am a sister of the suns, I do not understand the earth. But of course Janthis would chase me away.

Wearily she approached the terrace and stopped once more, but this time her mind flew furiously. Janthis will not help me, but there is help of another kind here on Danar. How could I have forgotten? The Book. The Book will tell me whether or not I move through an illusion, it will chart a course for me to follow. She felt as though a door had swung open behind her, and beyond it some friendly, invisible hand beckoned. She turned and ran back through the hall and found the narrow winding stair. When she reached the foot, she paused and raised her head, listening, but the maze of halls layered high above was quiet, so she crept along the short, dark passage, holding her breath. The thick wooden door leading to the little room that sheltered the Books of Lore was shut tight, and no light showed under its rim. There the passage ended, so she retraced her steps and found another door set tightly into the dim wall. Without sound, diffusing no light, she turned the massive iron ring in both hands, and the door swung open, taking her with it. Then she stood and looked about, her heart fluttering.

There was light in the room, but not enough to filter out into the passage. The sun of Danar had apportioned a constant, low glow to shine here at Janthis's command. The chamber was bare, the walls a plain white, the floor of stone, the ceiling beamed in haeli wood, but in the center stood a reading pedestal like the one in the next room. At its foot a corion crouched, its green wings folded flat on either side of its furred spine, its whiskered and frilled head resting on its paws. Sholia stared at it, but it seemed asleep. Its mouth was slightly parted, showing a glint of polished teeth, and the long lashes of its closed eyes quivered as it breathed deeply and evenly.

She turned her attention to the pedestal itself, hardly daring to breathe for fear she would wake the beast that took its responsibility so lightly. The Book of What Will Be seemed to gaze back at her with a disinterested otherness that made her reluctant to disturb it. The faint, unvarying light in the room gathered strength where it met the hard, smooth cover of the Book, sliding over it as though it were a dark mirror.

Creeping slowly, she approached it, and with each carefully placed step she felt desire mount, so that by the time she was close enough to touch it, her whole mind throbbed with a need to slake all doubts, to kill them forever with the long and cooling draught the reading of the Book would be. I should not be here, she thought giddily, excitedly, but the other voice in her prompted her. Janthis has rejected you. You are guiltless in seeking aid from someone else. For it seemed to her that the Book was not a thing but an infinitely mysterious person who called her to explore the complexities of its mind.

With one hand clutching her sun-discs tightly, she reached out, touched the surface, which begged reverent fingers to glide gently over it, and carefully raised the cover.

Then she felt the corion stir at her feet, and she snatched her hand away, wanting to kick the beast. She looked down. One intent brown eye was fixed on her, and seeing that she was aware of its scrutiny, it rose onto sleek haunches.

"I am addressing the sun-lord of Shol, I believe," it said in its rich, earthy purr, the iridescent green feathers on its head rising. "I am Chilorn. Were you seeking me? Do you bring a message from Janthis?"

Yes, yes! Sholia wanted to shout, feverish with the need to turn a page. He wants to see you immediately. Go at once! But in another second she was very glad that she had not, for the liquid, round eyes of the corion held her with something more than a friendly twinkle. Behind the respectful warmth was a steady, solemn appraisal and the clarity of a mind used to judging the doings of mortal and immortal alike with swift wisdom. It knows, she thought. If Janthis had wanted it, he would have spoken into its mind, and it knows that also. She felt as though the corion were laughing kindly at her, willing her to lift her lust for the Book and her agonies over Shol into the healing realm of humor.

"Forgive me, sun-lord," the beast said, drawing its lips away from those needle-sharp teeth. "Winter is almost here, and my long sleep approaches. Already I am drowsy. I did not hear your reply."

"That is because I did not speak, Chilorn," she answered with asperity. "I think you know that Janthis has not sent for you, and that I did not come to this room seeking you."

The corion nodded once in confirmation. "Forgive me again, sun-lord," it went on gravely, "if I point out that there is nothing here for you. Would you be so kind as to close the cover of the Book? I would not like to scratch it with my clumsy paws." It lifted a paw, and suddenly six black, hooked claws fanned out. It looked at her enquiringly, but again she sensed sober, incorruptible purpose behind the wide eyes, and all at once she laughed harshly, reaching out to flip the Book shut.

"My dear Chilorn," she said caustically, "don't you know that with one word I could reduce you to a tiny pile of ashes? You see, I am not as polite as you. Your hidden threats mean nothing to me."

The feathers on the corion's head flattened and then rose again, and it withdrew its claws, licked its paw, and met her eye. "You will not harm me, just as you could not lie to me. My humblest apologies, Sholia, for having the temerity to speak disrespectfully. Soon the Book goes into the mountain with Storn. Do you want to stay and talk to me?"

She shook her head, numb with disappointment, and went to the door, but with one hand on the iron ring she turned back to Chilorn. The beast had sunk to the floor again with its black nose between its two big paws, and the eyes stared at her steadily. She answered its gaze, and out of the corner of her eye the Book called her with one last enticing whisper. Has Janthis read it? she wondered. A wave of sick craving for it shivered over her, and almost without thinking she murmured, "Please?"

The corion did not move, but a low rumble of sound erupted from its throat, whether a growl of warning or a purr of farewell she could not discern. After a moment she went out, closing the door quietly behind her. But she carried the ache of unfulfilled need with her, and when she set her feet on Shol, the burden had not been whirled from her by the soundless, tearing energies of the corridor.

# 15

During Danar's hushed winter Janthis took to wandering, skirting the murmurous city, meandering far under the endless haeli forests, where the wind sang in the bare blue branches. He stood and watched the corions pass overhead on their way to their sleeping tunnels in the mountains, hundreds of them beating the sky with the sun flashing on their emerald-green wings, and he thought he could make out Storn in the lead, the Book clasped firmly in its mouth. He climbed into the foothills and sat for hours in the long, bare meadows where in the summer the sheep and goats grazed, his eyes following the pleasing slow sweep of country that dropped to forest and lakes far below, all now softly hazed with the same winter mist that drifted often to diffuse the sunlight.

Winter felt different this year. He had never counted the seasons that he had seen come and go on Danar, for the passing of time meant nothing to him. But now he noted the journey of the sun across the sky from its dawning to its setting. He found himself sensitive to the cycle of wind bringing rain, the cooling of the earth, a frost or two, bright sun, and the warming to rain once more. He began to fancy that the years did not take Danar and the mortals from a beginning to an end but chained them to a wheel that rolled them round and round, crushing them beneath its weight. A vain and foolish fancy, he told himself with irritation. The mortals are born, live, and then die to be taken by the Messengers. It is Danar herself who turns, carrying us with her. Yet he could not shake off the feeling of a closed and sterile circle drawing in on him.

One day he stood at the edge of a lake, his feet submerged in dark water, watching a rainstorm drive into the surface with a furious blind force, and he realized that the mortals were somehow freer than he. It is Danarion and I who go round and round, he thought, imprisoned with Danar's tortuous circling, round and round forever. Everything in the universe turns back on itself but the mortal people. His immortality had never been a burden to him before, he had not thought about it, but now his own time stretched ahead of him and promised only an endless predictability. He is doing this to me, he thought as his untiring legs took him over Danar's winterbound landscape. He seeps in everywhere. As Sholia has gradually become all fear and mortal femininity, as Danarion has slowly come to spend more time with the people of the city, loving them, so I must acknowledge my own partiality for despair. I am older than any other living thing in the universe save the Lawmaker and the Unmaker himself. Surely I may grow weary from time to time.

When spring stirred and the haeli trees unfolded pale blue leaves, he returned to his room in the empty palace. Calling for Shol, he stood before the wall, lost in thoughtful contemplation while the twins burned without variation, and Shol and its companions hung shimmering around them.

The leaves spread full and lost their shine, casting deep, blue-tinged shade for the people who brought food into the forests and spent the days before summer rediscovering the well-known paths through the ocean of yesteryear's leaves. The corions returned, dispersing through city, palace, and forest, and Danar rang again with the music of laughter. But Janthis still stood with eyes and mind focused on Shol. In the end, when high summer hung hot and heavy and the blood-red haeli flowers had long since ceased to shower the earth with perfumed petals, he dismissed the vision and sent for Danarion, walking slowly through his maze of vacant hall until he came to the sun-splashed flags of the terrace and the dazzle of a bird-busy afternoon.

He lowered himself onto the top step and presently saw Danarion emerge from the Time-forest, a young corion perched on his shoulder. The beast was whispering something in his ear, and Janthis saw him smile as he began to mount the stair. He looked up and waved, pausing to set the small animal down. It scuttled to the edge and jumped, spreading its glinting wings and gliding from sight over the motionless fringes of the forest. Janthis felt all at once lonely, the gulf between himself and every other thing an unbridgeable sorrow. But the mood fled, for Danarion smiled a greeting and sank easily beside him.

"There are children and young corions swimming in the lake beyond the west wall of the city," he said. "So many that it is difficult to tell which is which, and both shriek enough to break a mortal's ear. The little corions look so funny when they are wet and their fur hangs slick and bedraggled. I'm not surprised that the adults stay away from water. They rapidly develop too much dignity."

Janthis felt a stab of annoyance at Danarion's pointless chatter and with a burst of wild anger suppressed it. "I called you because I want to talk about Ghaka," he said abruptly.

Danarion fell suddenly silent, linked his fingers, and looked at the lacery of carving in the step below him. Grelinador. One of the first to go, he thought, the excited screams of the children fading quickly from his mind, taking with them the happiness of the day. I remember you as a spurt of blue fire. Grelinador the rock-melter. "What about Ghaka?" he asked tersely.

"Tell me now, if you can, what you saw when you sought Ghaka's mortals before the Gate was closed."

The horror of it came back to Danarion instantly, every detail as clear and terrible as though he stood on the Gate stair once again. "I can if you order it," he said with difficulty. "But such things are not good to remember in Danar's fragile peace."

"I do order it. I will tell you why in a moment."

Again Danarion was silent, struggling to find words that would describe the indescribable for the first time, and there was no gentle way.

"His mortals were all dead, every one of them," he blurted. "I stood on the Gate stair, and even before I saw the carnage, I could smell it. I came to the foot of the crag and did not walk the road. I crossed the fields, and when I came to the cliffs that bordered the valley, I saw them. Piles, mounds, mountains of mortal flesh broken and jumbled together." He swallowed and forced himself to go on. "All along the escarpment it was the same. I left that valley and found another, and it too was littered with bodies. I ran to the crags, but the caves were empty, and winged ones lay in shriveled black heaps below. I do not know how he did this terrible thing. Even to speak of it reopens a wound in me that will never heal. So many times I have stood with him here above the stair. I have walked in the past with him many times since his Gate was closed, listening to him speak of Ghaka and her people with such loving pride. He was so strong."

"Perhaps he was too strong," Janthis said quietly, "and his

strength grew into a need to dominate all around him. The Unmaker fed his strength with power he was unable to refuse, and with the urge to dominate came a blind certainty that he was always in the right, whatever he did. He fell by the Book."

"We each have a certain goodness that makes us weak," Danarion replied, his voice steadier. "I can tell you no more, Janthis. Nothing lived on Ghaka but the carrion birds and a few flocks and herds."

"And Ghakazian."

Danarion looked up in surprise. "Yes, of course. What terror, to be the only living thing on Ghaka forever."

"What of the essences, Danarion?"

Danarion froze. Slowly his head came around, and his eyes met Janthis's. "I did not even think of them, I was so burdened," he said. "I should have felt for them, stood still and quested them."

"You sensed nothing? No whispers, no shadows, no presences?"

"Nothing at all. Only a vast emptiness, as though the planet herself had suddenly become hollow."

Only a vast emptiness. *It was an essence from Ghaka, I know!* Sholia had almost shouted at him. *It does not matter,* Ghakazian had said gaily, rudely in the moment before his Gate was closed. *None of it matters in the least. I do not need you anymore.*

Janthis felt the golden blood chill in his veins. "Danarion," he whispered, and the fingers on the sun-ball suddenly loosened and began to tremble. "You did not feel the essences because they were no longer on Ghaka. If they had been there, they would have seen you, come to you, tried to speak with you. But they did not. Before the Gate was closed, Ghakazian sent them out of Ghaka."

Danarion bit back the questions rising to his tongue and began to think, and before long he knew that Janthis was right. Mortal bodies could not pass the Gate and go into deep space, but essences could. Up until now they had never done so, but Ghakazian had wrenched Ghaka out of the rightness of things. "Why?" he choked, but Janthis was not listening.

"Sholia was right, and I did not listen," he muttered hoarsely. "I did not listen! They have gone to Shol." He leaped to his feet, and Danarion rose with him. "How long have I been dreaming, caught in the Unmaker's web of doubt and indecision?" He brought his clenched fists together. "A winter and a spring on Danar. Three years on Shol. Three years . . . And where is Ghakazian?"

He turned and ran, shouting for Danarion to follow, and together they raced through the entrance hall and along the passages and came at last to the chamber of council. Janthis did not hesitate. He sped across the smooth black floor but suddenly came to a halt. "No," he breathed, and Danarion glanced down. Two lights twinkled up at them, the last two constellations left unsullied in that long, silent floor, and as they watched one began to flicker. With a cry Janthis launched himself toward the dais, Danarion on his heels. He flung himself up the steps, tore open his door, and fell inside. "Shol!" he shouted to the wall. Obediently the grayness quivered and slid into the center to be replaced by the tunneling blackness of space. "Hurry," Danarion breathed, and then the suns of Shol were hurtling toward them. All at once they slowed and for just a second appeared as they had always been. But their light soon dimmed as a black-tinged fog swirled around them. It thickened and took on a vast, towering shape that suddenly shrank and vanished into Shol. Danarion found himself gripping Janthis's arm with both hands.

After several minutes had passed, one of the twin suns began to swell. Slowly its size increased, and as it grew the light seemed to fade so that they were looking at a dull white, round heart beating against the universe. Shol and its sisters had begun to acquire the black rims Janthis knew so despairingly well. The rings deepened, took on a malevolent substance, and licked out with black tongues to encompass the suns, but suddenly the swollen sun began to shudder. For one wild moment it shook, dragging Shol and the other planets with them, back and forth, and before Danarion could blink, the pale, huge sun exploded. Shards of brilliant light rushed toward the two of them, and Danarion screamed and covered his eyes.

The sun had vanished as though it had never been, and the other twin fought to regain its place, its light flaring, dying, and flaring again. With a cry of anguish Danarion pointed. Of the worlds only Shol was left, teetering but steadying rapidly, one tiny pinprick of reflected light, and Sumel and Shon were no more.

But something else galvanized Janthis. He stepped closer to the wall. The rim of black fire had gone. A mist of grayness hung about Shol and did not disperse, but the roiling, curling fingers of death were no longer there. "Bring the Gate to view," he commanded, his voice trembling, and Shol's remaining sun rolled toward them, filled the wall, and slid past to bring Shol into their vision. Although the mist obscured it as it seemed to come closer, they quickly passed through it, and the square outline of the Gate hung before them.

But it was not as they remembered it. Its blackened lintels were twisted as though they had been taken by a giant hand and wrenched. Beyond, in the Hall of Waiting, a fume of black smoke billowed. Danarion moved back, but Janthis, tall and intent, stood his ground. In the Hall Sholia was on her hands and knees, her face upraised, tears pouring down cheeks smeared in grime. In one bleeding hand, pressed to the cracked and heaving tiles, was her necklet, broken and seared by fire, one of its sun-discs dead. Her singed hair hung tattered on her shoulders. She was speaking, sobbing, her mouth making words they could not hear, and then they could not see her, for the maimed Gate began to fill with tiny silver bells that rocked to and fro as they burst into being. Before long there was nothing to look at but bells, ringing out over the universe, and then there was nothing to see at all, for the bells melted into one another, their voices stilled. The Gate of Shol was closed with a sheet of solid, glittering silver.

"Enough!" Janthis whispered, and instantly the wall was a solid gray blindness. "I have done this," he said. "It is my fault. Gone, all of them, and I did not do what I should have, I refused to recognize the truth."

Danarion left him. He walked slowly through the council chamber, scarcely knowing what he was doing or where he was going until he found himself out under the hot sun, standing high on the terrace, the row of regal corions at his back. His pained eyes swept the healthy, light-licked reaches of the forest. Above it the tips of the city spires could be seen, giving back a dazzle that played genially and eagerly around them, and the first faint breeze of late afternoon was a stirring of fragrant air in his nostrils. I am the only sun-lord left, was the sole thought in his mind, and he could not form another.

# 16

Dawn was a flush of warm pink against the rim of the world when Sholia stepped from the Hall of Waiting and lingered for a moment, the safety of the Gate behind her, Shol's hostile, withdrawn presence tempered by the stillness of sunrise. She stood and let all anger and disappointment die, thinking of Chilorn and the mystery of the Book, while first one sun and then the other, much farther away, lifted into the sky. When their light had turned from scarlet to gold and had merged into one sparkling bright nimbus, she left the path leading across the plain to the upper city and came to the foot of her own wide stair. She mounted slowly, hearing the morning bustle on the Towers of Peace come to her faintly as the night watchers left their posts to the guardians of the day, and by the time she walked in under the cold shadows that still hung about the entrance chamber, she had almost convinced herself that Janthis had been right. Nothing ailed in Shol but she herself.

With a quick word she sent the shadows fleeing, and the palace filled with her light. "Sholia's back!" she heard someone shout, the voice echoing in the high balconies and sweeping stairs. Smiling as she made her way to her own quarters, she passed the hall of audience and glanced in.

Rilla was sitting in Sholia's chair, her head resting on the clenched knuckles of one hand, the other arm draped negligently over the carved wood of the support. Although the chair was placed at the far end, the room glowed with sunlight, and Sholia could see the woman's face clearly. The brows were drawn together, the eyes stared darkly into space. Sholia paced under the arch and swiftly approached Rilla, who at last was aware that she was no longer alone. The eyes lost their intensity, swiveling to follow Sholia as she came, but it was not until Sholia halted before the chair that the strange tension of speculation went out of the face and Sholia felt as though she were being disdainfully, intimately weighed in some scale of which she knew nothing.

"Rilla, you should not sit in my chair," she said quietly. "It was made with many spells for the use of an immortal and could be dangerous to you. Please step down."

It seemed to her then that a cloud of confusion blurred the face, but after a moment Rilla slid to her feet and glided down the two broad steps.

"What were you doing here?"

Rilla turned and looked straight into her eyes. "Waiting for you," she said simply, yet the whole of Shol spoke to Sholia in those words with a smug threat. You are here alone, the world said to her. We have been waiting for your return. We are before you, behind you. The tall, red-clad woman smiling in apology hid a menace Sholia could feel, and though she forced herself to view the words sanely and objectively, stripped of all hidden meanings, the full load of uneasiness returned to segregate her from those around her.

"Leave me alone," she said curtly. "I do not desire your company."

Rilla showed neither hurt nor offense. She bowed and went away, her back straight, her head erect, the brocade of her gown stiff around her. Sholia turned to her chair, but a long black hair had been caught by the scrolling on its embossed back, glinting dark and filling her with a surge of distaste. She spoke and then stood watching as the hair curled into gray ash, but still she could not bring herself to sit.

She left the hall and climbed until she found a balcony that gave her a view of the whole plain and the topmost tier of the city. With sun-discs pressed to her cheek she watched the slow trickle of travelers moving along the path to the Gate and the flickers of activity on the Towers of Peace until her attention was caught by someone on the Tower closest to the palace. He had scrambled up onto one of the parapets that protectively ringed the building and was walking back and forth, hands behind his back, looking into the chasm of rock below. She could not see his face, but he moved with perfect confidence, swinging his legs. One or two people passed behind him but did not even glance his way, and their very indifference sent a chill through Sholia. She had raised a hand to command him backward to safety and was ready to speak into his mind when she saw him pause. His face came up, scanned the horizon, and was lifted to receive the blessing of sky and sun, his expression one of utter contentment and a dreamy satisfaction.

Sholia began to shake. I cannot fight this kind of madness, she thought, and as she hesitated the man spread his arms, bent his knees, and jumped, still smiling. For a second he seemed to hang suspended over the abyss, as though Shol itself did not yet understand what he was doing, but then in silence he dropped out of sight beyond the rim of the plain. Still the people came and went. Some of them stopped to peer over the edge of the parapet, then shrugged, made a comment, and passed on. Sholia, watching aghast, knew then that Shol was no longer within her control, nor was it Shol. It was Ghaka, distorted, twisted out of shape, still suffocating under the disguise of Shol but already beginning to extricate itself, burst free in order to become a caricature of the true Ghaka.

Sickened, she backed away from the balcony. If Shol is no longer Shol but the embryo of Ghaka, she thought, then I am no longer sun-lord here. My powers are diminishing, and somewhere out there, among the pretty houses and steep streets of Shaban, Ghaka's sun-lord bides his time, waiting to rule a counterfeit Ghaka when Shol has forgotten her identity.

She ran from the balcony and sped through the passages, and when she reached the hall of audience, she turned to face the archway, flinging wide her arms and shouting words that brought a seal to shimmer instantly and impenetrably from ceiling to floor. She walked unsteadily to her chair, sat down, and leaned back, closing her eyes. Into the suns, she thought incoherently. My only refuge. Easily she slipped away, leaving her body relaxed and inert. Her nearer sun knew that she was coming and sent eager arms of white flame to embrace her. She sank into its fiery maelstrom like a drop of rain absorbed into the mighty rushing of a river. Its simple, awesome mind wrapped her around, and its pleasure was like a soothing balm spread over her. She felt no questions. It was content to cradle her with docility, and for a long time she nestled within it, her own strength growing, fed from its original source, closing the eyes of her mind to everything but the deluge of life the sun poured into her. Then she uncurled and looked out upon the universe.

She watched as Shol, Shon, and Sumel revolved in obedient

submission around her, and with her fiery eyes she saw their colors flaming in the blackness, green, blue, and red. Far behind her she saw her other sun, distant and smaller. I do not belong on Shol, she told herself again. I am not of the earth, I am of the suns, the wheels of space, I was born to flame the flare out across the universe forever. The suns are the true lords, unchanging, unwanting. But there, in the purity of otherness unimpeded by the silent whispers of the mortals' agonies, she saw clearly that this was not so. Though she might find the peace of inaction in her suns and be content to lie in their embrace forever, they could not give her happiness. They were less than she. They had no destiny other than to passively illuminate the universe and give beauty to the worlds, but she had been created to participate in both. The suns were in her veins, but the mortals were in her heart, and her responsibility to them would not let her rest. Her planets rolled slowly past her while she quietly considered what to do, and as the years went by she rediscovered the purpose for which she had been made. There in the sun she was a guide without a people. She must go back.

Reluctantly she shook herself loose, leaving the hot womb from which the Worldmaker had called her into life and drifting back to Shol. Her moment of weakness had passed. She no longer wished to run away, for she had run and been comforted, and now returned to her responsibilities. Three Shol-years had gone by; she had seen them pass like a dream from the unhasting heart of the sun, and it was time to plunge back into the turbulence of life.

She opened her eyes onto her quiet hall, aware that well-being and harnessed power hummed through her body as it had not done for many ages. But the atmosphere on Shol had changed. There was now an edge to the formless anxiety she had felt seething slowly in Shol's air and in the movements of men, as though it had intensified in her absence and was being sharpened to a fineness that would cleave the world apart. She savored it carefully as she rose and walked to the arch. The first thing I must do is close the Gate, she said to herself. Then I must try to regain control of Shol. I must find Ghakazian, learn why he has done this, try to persuade him to work with me to salvage what I can. The people must accept what they have become. There will be compromise.

She reached the seal and saw that beyond it stood Rilla, her form shaking with quiet undulations. Calmly Sholia bent and touched the ground three times, and the seal vanished. She walked through, and Rilla stepped convulsively to her.

"You sealed the hall," she said almost reproachfully. "I could not come to you."

"That is my prerogative," Sholia answered levelly, "and any business you have with me, Rilla, will wait." She strode away, but Rilla followed.

"You have shut us out for three long years," she protested. "Are you angry with us, Sholia?"

Sholia stopped abruptly and swung around, taking the long fingers in both her hands and smiling gently. "No," she said, "not with you. There is much you do not understand."

At once a tiny glow of amusement flared behind Rilla's grave eyes, and Sholia let the fingers drop with an inward stab of impotence. I will not be turned aside, she thought obstinately. "Baltor your father did not question my doings. It was not his place to do so, and it is not yours, either. You must learn to be silent and not impede me. You are not my jailor or my judge, Rilla." Again a flicker of malicious humor stung her, but she ignored it. "I want to talk to you, but later. I am on my way to the Gate." She began to walk away, and Rilla followed.

"Are you leaving us again?" Rilla asked as together they passed through the entrance.

Without slackening her pace Sholia answered, "No, never again. I am going to close the Gate."

Ghakazian halted, stunned. It's a trick, he thought. She will not close the Gate and shut him out, not if the Book is true. Where has she been for the last three years while she sat tranced in her empty hall? Did she go into the past, or into one of her suns? Or was she wandering in the corridors of space, seeking him? Did she find him, and does she go to the Gate to welcome him? What shall I do?

He ran down the stair and caught up with her as she reached the foot and started toward the Hall of Waiting. He grasped her arm and she glanced at him, seeing Rilla's troubled eyes and pale, trembling lips.

"You cannot!" Rilla burst out. "Would you refuse Shon and

Sumel to the people? Why, Sholia? Are you prepared to deny yourself the company of your kin? You will never see Danar again if you continue this madness!"

Sholia fed heat into the hand that gripped her, and immediately was released. "What do you know of Danar?" she said softly, her eyes suddenly narrowing. "I speak to you now, Ghakan whoever you may be, and not to Rilla. I know you are there. I know that your sun-lord walks somewhere on Shol, free and watchful. Danar is the only untouched world left, and it is too precious to leave threatened by my open Gate. Tell Ghakazian that I will not relinquish power on Shol to him. I will settle with him soon."

"Will you?" Rilla replied with a deepening of her voice. The large eyes had gone hard, and the mouth had thinned to a line. "The sun-lord of Ghaka is mighty. Only he dared to do the unthinkable. He knows your perfidy, the darkness in you that you hide so cleverly."

Sholia made no retort, though the voice tingled in her mind on the verge of a memory, and behind Rilla's eyes was the hint of long familiarity. She turned and strode on.

Ghakazian watched her go. *I will settle with him soon.* She is going to the Gate to greet the Unmaker, I know it. This is the time, the moment I saw in the Book.

He spun on his heel and ran back up the steps shouting, "Mirak! Quickly!" He sped through the entrance, and Melfidor met him as he raced toward the mortals' quarters. "The time is almost upon us," he panted. "Hurry down into the city, alert every Ghakan, send others also. Sholia waits for the Unmaker by the Gate. She has threatened to keep power and destroy me, and she will call her mortals to arms against us if we do not move first and slay them before they can answer her. Hurry!" Mirak nodded and left him, and he began to go from room to room of the palace, knocking on doors. One by one they acknowledged him as he called them, the black hair coming astray from its tight knot on the smooth head and tendriling around Rilla's face, the tense, beringed hands gesturing, the small, soft-slippered feet rushing like a wind through the corridors with the red and silver brocade gown whispering after them. "It is time!" he shouted into every room, and Rintar emerged past Chantis's mind and smiled at Ghakazian, Natil looked at him through Fitrec's mild gaze, and Maram felt fear squeeze tight about Veltim's heart.

When Ghakazian had completed the alarm, he went outside and slowly descended the stair. What of the nomads, he thought, the fishermen, the miners on the far shore of the ocean? Will they know? Yes, they will. The whole of Shol will know when the Unmaker sets foot before the Gate, and the Ghakans will understand.

He came to the foot and stood for a moment, looking out over the empty plain. No sound rose from the city, no swiftly rising murmur as Melfidor and the others sped from house to house. The wind that had soughed over the grasses of the plain for days, dreary and biting, had suddenly ceased, taking with it the dry rustle of the dark-green shrubs, the faint rumble of Shaban, the even fainter sound of the ocean foaming onto the shore of the bay. The stillness deepened, locking the sky into a uniform, heavy gray through which no sunlight could penetrate, and with it came an oppression that bowed Rilla's slender shoulders and sent the birds that wheeled high above the plain flapping awkwardly to settle on the ground.

Standing before the Gate, struggling with herself, Sholia felt her mind go dim and her own warm fire flicker in her veins. Why do I wait? she thought in anguish. It must be done. Yet as she hesitated a thousand pictures welled up in her, sweet and happy. She saw Danarion and herself walking beneath the haeli trees, and the Hall of Waiting seemed to fill with the scent of the drifting red blossom. She saw herself in the corridor in the days that had gone, free and unconquerable, every world open to her. She stared out through the square of the Gate, and saw the stars burning like white candles, calling to her, singing their music, which brought forth an answering yearning in her blood. But Danar's fate hung heavy in her hands, and beneath the swiftly growing weight of an alien oppression the determination to do what she must was hardening.

She pulled herself upright, moving as though a rock had been strung about her neck. Her arms came out and felt as heavy as Shol itself. Her mouth opened, the formal words of closing on her tongue, but then she stopped. Far out in space she saw a thin mist, darker than the blackness between the stars, writhing toward Shol, and with it came a dread and confusion that froze all thought and chilled her limbs. Slowly it snaked to the Gate, began to curl through it and past her, filling the Hall and drifting out onto the plain. She heard something shout in her head, Close the Gate! Close it now! and fought to form the words, knowing what she was seeing, but her tongue would only stutter, and her fire thickened and cracked from her fingers like a cold, dead tree branch. The voice went on shouting at her in a rapid, shrill tone of panic, but beneath it a whisper came. Don't you want to see him again after so many ages? He is coming to you. Will you shut him out?

One last time she tried, drawing herself erect, but the words had now formed a mad dance in her head, and she could not catch them. With a cry she turned and fled through the murky Hall, out onto the dour, gray-laden plain, and across to the foot of the palace stair, now glimmering pale under the low, threatening sky.

Stumbling up it, she caught a flash of red out of the corner of her eye as she saw Rilla crouch down behind one of the shrubs now resting motionless in its dull orange tub, but she did not stop. Sobbing, she raced to her chamber and flung herself across her chair, covering her head in both quivering arms. "No," she wept, "no, no," and her newfound strength melted away, leaving the dregs of terror and failure bitter in her mouth.

The fog found her and roiled slowly into the room, smelling of ice and timelessness. Though it sifted despair into her consciousness, it could not penetrate her essence, and presently she rose and stood facing the door, which was now scarcely visible. I should have closed the Gate the minute I returned from Danar, she thought dully and wearily. But it is too late now. The time of Shol's falling has come at last, and I have failed.

The stifling atmosphere seemed to intensify suddenly, an equally crushing silence woven into it. The people of Shol looked at one another, the solid sky, the sullen earth with mounting horror, a panic surging through limbs that could only tremble with the need to flee, for the suffocating weight bearing down on mind and body prevented movement or coherent thought. Sholia felt it as a great fatigue that pressed against her eyelids, and for the first time she was overwhelmed with a desire to let them close, to lose herself in the state of half-rest, half-dream that was the mortals' domain.

Then a rumble began as though the drums of the earth were rolling far beneath city and palace, and Shaban began to shake on its deep-sunk foundations. Sholia stood pale and still, feeling the throbbing in her feet, watching her walls shudder. The sound grew fainter, rolling away to trouble the ocean and stir under the far valleys, but the fear that had come with it remained to tingle in her blood like some dark poison, thinning her fire and dispersing her power like blown mist. Awkwardly she turned to face the door, both hands clasping the sun-discs, which hung heavy and rapidly cooling on her breast, as though they also cowered before the one who was coming. He had placed a foot over the edge of the Gate and even now was walking out of the Hall of Waiting; she knew it. He was striding the shrinking soil of Shol, he was coming.

She wanted to die then. She wanted to throw herself to the floor and let her life ebb away so that she need not see him. Run to the suns, her mind hissed desperately at her, leap back into the past. But even in the midst of her terror she was aware that he could easily call her back from both. In her imagination she saw him begin to climb the stair, tall and beautiful as she had seen him last at council so many eons ago. As he came she felt the ache of longing for him begin.

A rush of chill air that began to blow through the door found her and snatched the last of her warmth, so that her fire died to a dim pulse. She began to shiver, fumbling to release the sun-discs, which stuck, frozen, to her fingers. A voice moaned in that wind, whispering her name with all the hopeless loneliness of the Unmaker's dominion, and it filled her with a new, quiet sorrow. Footsteps sounded in the corridor outside, firm and confident, each one matched to her heartbeat, and she brushed aside the tears and strove to stand straighter. He did not come to Falia, she thought dimly, or to Ixelion. But he comes to me in person, as I have always known, deep inside me, that he would. Will he torment me? She tried to bring the bright gaiety of Danar to mind and the faces of Danarion and Janthis, but they hovered momentarily behind her eyes like pale, insubstantial essences and then were gone.

A shadow fell across the threshold, long, black, and menacing, reaching almost to her feet as she stood at the far end of the vast hall. This is the final power in the universe, she thought. This rules and has always ruled. Light or dark, good or evil, it is the ultimate reality. Then the shadow retreated, and he himself filled the archway. He paused, then crossed the floor. He was exactly as she had remembered him, tall and graceful and perfectly made, his long brown hair waving back from a face so exquisite in the contours of its flowing bones that it sent a stab of painful delight through her. The arms were held out in greeting to her. The mouth was parted in a smile of joy, and the wide-set eyes mirrored back to her, as freshly and gloriously as though it had happened a second ago, the burst of wonder that had been her first emotion at the time of her making. Slowly, regally he came on, the smooth, naked body flexing with an easy power that glimmered silver and rose-pink around him, and Sholia fell to her knees. "Maker," she sobbed, the fear, the agonies of panic and terror gone, so that only an adoring and repentant child remained. "Maker, Worldmaker." He came to a halt before her, and she could no longer look up at him, so dazzling was the beauty of his face. She dropped her gaze and, putting out a hand, touched the thin foot resting so close to her. "Oh, Maker," she whispered, "I have needed you for so long, all of us, trying to live without you, and you deserted us and went away. What did we do that made you angry with us?"

# 17

He bent and placed both hands on her head, letting them slide soothingly down until they rested on her shoulders, and then he took her arms and raised her gently to her feet. "Sun-child," he said, and to Sholia his voice was like the stir of a million first breaths on the dawn of the first day of his making. "I am not angry with you. Am I not here with you again on Shol? I have come to take all anxiety and all need from you. Put yourself in my hands, dear Sholia. Take your rightful place as my subject, the fruit of my thought, and I will remove from you all responsibility. I have come to rule on Shol. If you obey me, you shall never be separated from me. We will feed on each other. Can anything be more glorious?"

She wanted to fall down before him again, to cling to him forever. She wanted to do anything he asked, for she knew that if he left her again, the anguish of his absence would be a drug of death in her veins until her suns grew old. But she could not answer him, for her eyes had fallen on the collar around his neck, half-hidden by the shining hair. It was not like that when I used to sit at the council table and look up at him, she thought, bewildered. She felt a soft blanket of balm, murmuring of the unimportance of small things, of inconsequentials, try to wrap the thought, but she fought against it. His collar of authority, which had been made of white starlight and the energies of the Lawmaker, was now black and twisted like the dross that falls from metal as it is purified. He saw where her eyes had been drawn and laid a finger lightly on her cheek, and from somewhere deep within her a voice began to cry and wail in the agony of betrayal and loss. Ah, no, no! Let them all be liars, let the sun-lords down all the ages be deceived, let Janthis be a guide into illusion, but let the Worldmaker be true! She could not lift her gaze from the thing around his neck to the mild rebuke in his eyes, but with an effort that cost her everything she had, an effort like that of ripping her essence from her body, she took one step backward, away from him.

"You are the Unmaker," she choked. "More than anything in the universe I wanted to believe that you had not changed, that somehow the past had been wiped out, and when I saw you coming to me, the one who made me, the one who was my only good, when I saw that you were as beautiful as I remembered, I was full of joy. But you caused my eyes to lie to me." She stopped speaking to gather what little strength she had left, the voice of wounding keening in her. "You come to Shol in maliciousness and hatred, seeking to break and blacken what you have made."

As she spoke she saw the pure glimmer of his body thicken to a sullen gray shot through with dark red, and the light went out of his face, leaving it harsh and full of a poorly veiled hostility. Sometimes she had wondered what he would look like if the moment should ever come when they stood face to face. The moment had come, and she was conscious of relief. Although he had changed, he was the same. The edge of awesome purity and joy had gone from him, but he had not lost his unmatched loveliness. A little confidence returned to her. Hope fluttered in her, and her eyes still showed him to her as the Worldmaker. For a long time he measured her, and once more that strange wind out of the depths of his darkness came to whine about her, chilling her heart and stultifying her mind. Then he spoke.

"Come outside, Sholia," he said, and his voice now was grating and flecked through with the ice of his turbulent, servile wind. "I want to show you something."

The words were a command. He took her arm, and now his fingers flooded pain through her flesh. She went clumsily, his closeness an overwhelming confusion of joy and revulsion, and like a dream-walker she followed him, her arm numb, her mind blank. He halted her at the top of the steps and let her go. "Tell me what you see," he ordered, and immediately the gray fogs lifted, shredded, and were gone. Weak sunlight filtered over the plain, ran down the sides of the Towers of Peace, and pricked on the ocean, and Sholia scanned it all slowly. It did not seem real to her, a flimsy paper world without a third dimension, a vulgar slipshod imitation, and she answered brokenly, "I see Shol."

"And what is Shol to you?"

Distaste for her world seeped into her. Shol was a heavy, thick place, earthy, odorous, and she saw herself streaking toward one of her suns, light and free. But she knew that the Unmaker was again giving her a lie to see, and somehow it was easier now to shrug off his subtle message. "Shol is my responsibility," she replied, her arm still numb, her lips feeling twice their proper size. "I am the guardian of Shol."

"Yes, guardian," he sneered. "Lord without power to rule, immortal without permission to intervene. That was how I wanted it in the beginning, but that is not my desire for the sun-lords any longer. Look well upon Shol, child. I am ready to put real power into your hands. Power to rule, to control every living thing under the suns, to order Shol, Shon, and Sumel exactly as you wish. You will no longer be custodian. You will be monarch. Real power, Sholia, to break or bind, to create or annihilate. No Law will touch you. You will be above and beyond the Law, even as I am. The last four Shol-years have brought doubt and misery to you. With what I offer, you could have smashed the Ghakans and reshaped Shol as you wished. No more doubts, Sholia, no more hesitation, no more Law. Be ruler of Shol. Receive the homage of your people, which is your right. You are an immortal, and what are they compared to you? You are a god. Take up the power of a god."

At his words Sholia's mind was suddenly full of swirling, bright images. She saw herself seated in her chair, but it was now a throne. Her mortals came to her on hands and knees to receive a touch from her fire-filled hand. They spoke to her in reverent whispers, not daring to raise their eyes to her, for the power the Unmaker had given her had bestowed upon her also a terrible beauty, and her mortals loved her with the anguished, unslaked passion of slaves. Yes, she thought. It is my right. I deserve it all.

"What of Ixelion, Falia, Ghakazian?" she managed.

The Unmaker laughed, a sound without mirth. "I offered them nothing. Why should I have? You and Shol are the center of my universe. I offer this only to you, my beloved."

"And what must I give you, Unmaker, in return?"

He swung to her, and in his eyes there blazed such greed, such spite, that she felt as though he wanted to devour her. "I ask only that you acknowledge me as your overlord," he said, his voice shaking with the intensity of his lust. "You need not kneel before me.

Just say the words. You have said them before, many times. They will cost you nothing, Sholia, and bring you everything."

Yes, I have said them before, she thought, shrinking from his convulsed face. But in those days they were always followed by other words. *Over us both is the Law.* She opened her mouth to say so, but the Unmaker had crouched away as though her very thought had wounded him.

"Not the last words!" he hissed. "Not them. Just the first. You have nothing to lose. When the suns burn out, you will cease to be. Then it will not matter anymore, any of it. Say the words!"

It was then that Sholia knew he no longer loved her, or anything that he had made. Janthis had told her so often enough, but with a seed of hope nestling in her she had not believed. How, she had thought then, could a Maker ever hate that which he had created? Surely some love would linger in him, no matter how deeply change had been wrought in him. But now she saw that the pain of his own terrible fall was with him still and had not diminished with the passing of the ages. It gnawed at him with teeth unblunted, and in his agony he reached out to revenge himself on the Lawmaker by maiming all that he had made. He would not suffer alone. He would take the worlds down with him.

She tore her gaze from the panorama spread out below her and saw that he had recovered. Hard and bitter eyes bored into her own, and he seemed to lower over her like a storm cloud, black and threatening, but she drew herself up and found courage. "No," she faltered. "I will not say the words. It is against the Law to place you at the pinnacle of worship, Unmaker, and if I acknowledge you as my lord, I place myself beyond hope of a favorable judging from the Messengers, for I will then be outside the Law, even as you are. It breaks my heart," she finished in a whisper, "but I must refuse you."

"You poor, deluded little fool," he snapped back, his voice shaking with the intensity of his rage. "Playing at purity and loyalty so blindly while the rest of the universe bows its head to me! I have offered you unlimited might, an omnipotence undreamed of, and I will not do so again. A moment of magnanimity stayed my hand, but I need not have paused to speak kindly to you. Think of the chance you have let go by in the years to come. I will shut you up in the mountain. I will slow time and make you feel it as the mortals do, so that every second passing is like eternity itself, and I will fill the minutes with such yearning for me that neither peace nor sanity will come to you again. I will cause this moment to be relived by you, over and over, so that you may fully taste the consequences of your arrogant error."

He surged toward her as he spoke, and she cried out, pulling her hair to hide her eyes, for the turgid gray and red light swirling around him had turned to rivers of blackness flowing around his knees, curling about his waist, licking from the gaunt, sickly paleness of his face. His mouth became a yawning cavern, and forked tongues of black fire slipped between his teeth as he croaked at her. His eyes had vanished, and in the sockets churned more fire, orange and black flames leaping. He was all the more horrible because the charred and ruined remnant of his beauty mingled with the thing he had become, and it was of Ghakazian that Sholia thought as she shrank away, Ghakazian at his Gate-closing, speaking silently to her of the ravished trance of death, the wooing compulsion to submission singing madly and unrestrainedly through his polluted glory.

She fell to her knees, her eyes squeezed tightly shut, groveling before him on the pavement, which had cracked and blackened under his feet, and he bent over her and screamed, "I will stay on Shol! I made it and it is mine! For ages beyond ages I have craved to feel it under my thumb, and I will prowl the fringes of the universe no longer! But you I will grind under my heel, Sholia, and surely you will wish that I had never formed you!" He turned and strode to the top of the stair, pulling his oily wreath of unfire with him. Raising his arms, he seemed to grow, a tower of menace that dwarfed the pillars, vaster than the mountain, more arid and desolate than the plain across which his shadow spread. "Shol!" he roared, and his voice boomed out. Once more the Towers of Peace shook on their deep foundations, and the city trembled.

Then a madness came upon the inhabitants of Shol, who woke from their trance of death to find death rushing to meet them. The Ghakan essences had thrust the weaker Sholan minds behind them and rose up to slay, the voice of the Unmaker boiling and bursting within them, a red goad of destruction. Mothers turned on children, kitchen knives in their hands; wives saw their husbands lurch toward them, hands curving for their necks. In the boats, out where the nomads rode, in the mines, beside the ocean death struck with a frenzied arm. The city began to scream. Blood streamered pink in the water. The Unmaker shouted to Sholia without turning, "You see? You hear? You dared to refuse me?" Then he laughed, and Sholia turned her head away and covered her ears.

At the moment of stillness Ghakazian stood on the plain, his heart racing with excitement. Sholia had disappeared into the Hall of Waiting, but he was certain that in spite of her words she would not close the Gate. His time of testing had come. Watching the birds wheel and settle unsteadily on the grass, he wondered whether he should follow his people into the city, go back into the palace, or simply wait and see what Sholia would do. He decided to wait. The path crossing the plain was too vulnerable. He lifted his shoulders uneasily, trying to free them of the same weight that kept the birds silent. He found it difficult to breathe. Apprehensively he glanced toward the entrance to the Gate. Plumes of gray mist trickled from the Hall of Waiting, and through them Sholia came running. Seized with a momentary panic, Ghakazian rushed to hide behind the frail cover of the shrubs before the palace. He knew that Sholia saw him as she fled up the palace stair, but she no longer concerned him, for out of the Hall a thicker smoke began to pour, clouding the being who followed her.

Time stood still. Ghakazian berated himself for his weakness, knowing that he must soon be vindicated, but his will had deserted him. Then he heard footsteps above, and with all the strength he possessed, he looked up.

Sholia and the Unmaker emerged from the dimness of the entrance hall, he with his hand on her arm, and behind Ghakazian's undeniable throb of joy at the sight of the one who had made him was a swift-rising wave of exultation. The Book spoke true! he thought feverishly. I remember! I saw myself thus, hiding behind the shrub, hiding behind Rilla's slender form, while the two of them welcomed each other. Through Rilla's dark eyes he watched them talking together while behind him he felt Shol tensed on the edge of its doom. The Ghakans are ready, he told himself. At any moment now they will begin to kill, and I must mount the stair and face the Unmaker. A thrill of anticipation mixed with fear went through him but quickly died, leaving puzzlement, for the Unmaker had suddenly rushed at Sholia, who stumbled back and fell before him, her face ashen. Then the Unmaker changed before Ghakazian's eyes. Black he became, and very terrible, and he leaned over Sholia like a hungry predator that pauses in its moment of triumph to relish every throe of its victim.

All at once Ghakazian felt something move in his mind, shift from its place, and as it jerked it rearranged his thoughts, dropping them into new positions, giving them new colors. He felt as though he had been lifted and taken apart, then settled gently in his former place, but he was not the same. He understood. The truth burst upon him, and he gripped the coarse branches of the shrub with both strong, feminine hands to keep himself from howling aloud. No! he thought aghast. It cannot be! I have done all as the Book commanded, and the Book is under the Law. It cannot lie. No, Ghakazian, it did not lie, something sane and cool whispered inside him. It showed you here, behind the bush. It showed them there, talking together before the palace. These things have come to pass. But you shaped the naked visions in the Book with your own imagination. You were the liar, not the Book. The future has become the present, and you have been led to your own destruction.

He tore his hands from the shrub and put them over his mouth, rocking to and fro, moaning to himself in shock and horror, and at that moment the Unmaker turned and spoke to Shol. A knife twisted in Ghakazian's heart, but before he could fully appreciate what he knew would happen next, the city erupted. Screams rent the air, voices thin with panic filled the streets with pleas for mercy, and the sighs of death were drowned in the tumult. Ghakazian cast himself full length on the ground, but he could not weep. I have been duped, he said to himself, but it is too late to redeem myself. Very well. I am lost, and nothing I do matters anymore. I will wait, and perhaps I may still find vindication and a measure of peace here on Shol. I must not care anymore. Bitterness and self-loathing darkened his mind. He dragged himself from the ground and began to shamble across the plain.

Sholia lay faint and exhausted, her cheek pressed to the tiling, which filled her nostrils with the stench of burnt stone. Shudders had gripped her body as he bent over her, but now he had left her to go to the lip of the steps, and the sound of his great voice bellowing out over the plain was somehow more terrible than the nakedness she had felt under the glare of his eyes. Shol woke to chaos, but she hardly heard it. What shall I do? she moaned under her breath. Oh, what shall I do? Painfully she dragged herself up again onto hands and knees, the black-streaked, icy sun-discs swinging from her neck, and began to crawl toward him. Fear was like chains around her ankles, holding her back, and mists of terror caused the sweat to run, golden and wet, down her spine, but she struggled to cover the short distance between herself and his black-clouded legs as he looked out over Shol and laughed. He spoke to her, but his words made no sense, thickening the curtain of dread in her heart. She did not know what she would do when she reached him, but she must not lie on the smoking stone in cowardly surrender.

Then, when if she had managed to raise a hand, she could have touched him, something spoke to her. A small, level voice came clear and sweet into her mind, bringing with it a breath of sunshine and warm laughter, and she came to a halt in amazement. You have two suns, it said. You have two suns. She felt a little strength return to her. Of course, she thought as she fought to stand upright, the pain of his fire all around her now. But, oh, my beautiful suns. He heard her rise and swung to face her, and she placed one hand on her sun-discs and steadied herself against the balustrade of the stair with the other. "I will give you one opportunity to leave Shol of your own volition," she said to him levelly. "If you refuse, I will throw you out."

For one moment the wheels of orange and black in his sockets became the eyes that she remembered, two hard orbs that reflected his momentary astonishment. "Can the created command the creator?" he sneered. "You are pitiful, Sholia. Bow before me!"

"I have two suns," she whispered faintly, clutching the sun-discs as though she would crush them, and it seemed to her that with the frantic tightening of her fingers a tiny glow of new heat was born within them. "Two suns, Unmaker," she said again, and all at once doubt clouded the ravaged face. For a long time she met his gaze, and he poured into her all the dread and fear he could muster, but one of the sun-disc's golden fire was growing under her hand, and she stood her ground. Below them on the plain the people of Shol toppled through the gate beside the Towers and ran aimlessly, some falling, some staggering in the direction of the cave-hollowed mountain, but sun-lord and Unmaker faced one another oblivious.

Finally he stirred and smiled at her slowly. "I made the suns also," he said, but she took no notice of the hint of supreme power behind the words, for the voice had left a seed of courage in her, and she knew that come what may, he would fill her mind with unspoken lies and doubt-filled dreams no longer.

"Will you go?" she asked quietly, though her heart pounded as though it would burst, and he shook his head.

"Shol is mine, and here I stay."

She closed her eyes and, feeling outward for the sun she had so lately fled to for comfort and renewal, spoke to it softly. Oh, my sun, listen to me. I ask for all your power, all your light, though it may mean the end of both for you. I hold out my hands to you now. Place yourself in them and obey me, I beg, for the saving of Shol and the continued preservation of Danar. If it is to be so, will you accept your death from me? She lifted her hands, palms upward, and again the Unmaker laughed, but she ignored his scorn, for a gentle, willing presence feathered out into her mind, and she felt her fingers spark and tremble. Then she heard the voice of her sun for the first and last time, thick and hot. *I know it all*, it breathed. *I give.*

"How much you have broken!" she said aloud to the Unmaker. "How many long partings you have caused, in pain and sorrow!" Gaining her full height, she spoke one quiet word. Light burst from her, kindling in her hair, shooting white from her fingers, shining with a dazzling suddenness on her face.

The Unmaker stepped back, still smiling, as though he would humor her for a moment, but the smile left his face when she spoke again, for a sheet of flames leaped up around her, stretching from balustrade to pillar, crackling hot and new between them. "So you wish to play with your pretty toy!" he shouted. "But the game does not beguile me, Sholia. You are like a mortal who tries to hold back the wind with his naked palms."

She saw him draw in a deep breath, and when he exhaled, a gush of blackness vomited from his mouth and turned back on him, and through the wavering shimmer of her own fire she saw it burst into spears of dark flame. He had not walled himself off as she had done. His very body seemed to erupt. He grew taller, a living tongue of writhing heat that was more bitterly cold than space itself. Only his face remained visibly the same, a livid, haggard oval staring at her from its heart. He moved his arms, sending waves of ice toward her, and her own fire turned from yellow to red and began to sink. The fire that would have seared all life from a mortal man was powerless to beat down the source of all fire, and Sholia cast about desperately in her mind to bring forth every word of power once taught to her but never used. The Unmaker shivered toward her, and she felt her skin go numb as he approached, but she held firm, and her tongue found another command. Hold for me, my sun, she begged. Give me not only your fire but your being also.

High above Shol the sun began to swell. It grew and began to throb, filling the sky with a pulsing whiteness, and though the wall of flame sank into nothing and vanished, the palace began to heat. The stone beneath her feet grew warm, and behind her she heard the cracking of pillars, the startled settling of walls and ceilings. He knew what she was about to do. "You will destroy yourself!" he screamed, but she, feeling her blood flow faster and hotter and her mind begin to hum, answered calmly, "So be it." She would have spoken further, but the humming grew, taking into itself the power to form speech. She could no longer hear, and the blood driving through her body was like molten metal, flooding into every organ, changing, transmuting. He saw her gasping, and the breath that left her mouth flickered blue, but she did not halt the sun that poured its sentience into her as she had asked.

Her skin became transparent, and for just a moment he could see her veins and bones, the shuddering, laboring heart, the blue-filled lungs, the shriveling tongue and seething brain, all gushing a blinding white light that caused the fires that blazed behind his own eyes to cringe and falter. Then she seemed to explode with a sound like the collision of two suns. Rays of light burst from her, and he shrieked and, hiding his face, ran down the stair. The grass on the plain caught fire, little rivulets of red flame running swiftly over the earth like ribbons. At the foot of the sheer cliff into which the palace had been built, the trees flamed out suddenly like guttering red candles. The uppermost tiers of the city and the spires of the Towers of Peace blackened, crumbled, and began to pitch forward slowly to come crashing down. The sun, bereft of its essence, began to teeter in the sky. Back and forth it wobbled drunkenly, caught up in the throes of its death, and Shol was dragged with it. The earth shook. The mountain cracked and smoked. But the column of wild, whirling energy that was now both the sun and the sun-lord descended the steps, passing steadily through the sparks and falling branches.

At their foot the Unmaker had turned and marshaled all his strength. His own might was like a solid black, jagged iceberg around which his servile dark fire danced. Though he towered high over the whiteness of the thing Sholia had become, she felt nothing. She was consumed, she was one with her sun. She was the fire that burned to light the universe, feeding with magnificent aloofness upon itself yet never diminishing. Apart, sun and sun-lord were as twins. Together, fused into one entity, they were an omnipotent power, filling up the hollows within each other to become perfect.

Behind them the stair broke in two with a sound like a clap of sudden thunder, and the pillars above gave way, but Unmaker and white fire faced each other in silence. The Unmaker reared up, and with a cry he fell upon Sholia. The two fires clashed, and Shol and the empty, tormented sun in the silver sky screamed in agony. The city rocked, toppled, and began to slide toward an ocean that steamed and heaved. A hundred ravines gaped open in the plain, and the exquisite airy bones of the palace melted and fused together. The Unmaker felt as though he also were being shaken apart. Three times he strove to smother the thing that was Sholia and her sun, and three times his black fire shivered and splintered into a thousand shards while pain such as he had never known roared through him and left him shaken and weak. "I made you!" he howled, demented. "I made you!" And though he wanted to smash and maim, tear down, slash open, he knew in an overpowering spasm of hate that Sholia had defeated him.

He turned and strode in the direction of the Gate, but the fire came after him, ripping at his heels, searing his back. Once he looked back and fancied that in the midst of the blinding torrent of energy he saw the outlines of a face he had hoped he would never see again, a face from beyond the universe. Real terror sunk its teeth into his throat, and shrieking, he broke into a run.

Although the Hall of Waiting was on fire, it still stood, for

strong magic protected the Gate on every world from all disasters
save the word of a sun-lord. The gems and bright scenes that had
adorned walls and ceiling had melted and run down to sizzle on
the red-hot stone of the floor, and the room was full of fumes and
a stinging, sulphurous smoke. Here, before the Gate which framed
him with stars and cool darkness, the Unmaker turned for the last
time. "I will not give up!" he croaked. "This is not the end!" And
Sholia and the sun, drawing to themselves the last of the sun's vitality, saw him as small and far away, and infinitely insignificant.

Will I die also? Sholia thought, but no emotion was attached
to the question. Death did not matter, not at all. The Unmaker
must be thrust far from Shol, but even that act was seen by her
against the backdrop of the unrolling of the whole universe's history, from the moment when the Lawmaker had called the Worldmaker into being and the Worldmaker had entered time. Now she
was ready.

For a second they regarded each other, and she spoke to him
with the strange, turgid voice of the sun. *Go back to your own
accursed place, Unmaker*, she said. *Depart from Shol*. She saw the
Unmaker lifted from his feet and flung bodily through the Gate.
She heard him scream as he fell, and the lintel of the Gate buckled
and heaved. But behind the seeing and the hearing was a pain that
rushed upon her with the speed of light itself, and her own scream
mingled with his as the sun exploded and its light was extinguished
forever. Shon and Sumel, sucked into the last conflagration, burned
fiercely and then disintegrated.

Sholia found herself on her hands and knees before the Gate,
her necklet grasped tightly in her fingers, her hair straggling singed
and limp around a face swollen with tears; aching, bruised, and
buffeted, but her own face, her own heavy, paining body. The sudden weight of it dragged her down, and she wanted to collapse and
lie with eyes closed, to go immediately into the near past and live
again and again the few moments when she had been above all, a
thing of unparalleled beauty and unconquerable power, but she was
too weak to take even that journey. Ponderous with blood and bone,
empty of all save her own small thought, she crawled closer to the
Gate, summoning her will to send one last call winging out on the
frail remnants of her immortality. Come to me quickly, she pleaded

to her one remaining sun. My life wanes, yet I ask not for myself but for the closing of the Gate. Still trembling from the force of its companion's dying, it answered her, and its shivering light played shyly around her, beaming through the curling smoke that choked the Hall of Waiting. Sholia could not rise, nor could she find the strength to make the full spell. "I, sun-lord of Shol, order you to close," she whispered at the Gate through charred lips. "In the name of the Lawmaker I beg!"

For a long time nothing happened, and Sholia began to sob, knowing that she was incapable of taking the spell from its solemn beginning. But with a delicate, faint tinkle one and then another tiny silver bell appeared suspended within the Gate, swaying to and fro on an invisible arm, the little clappers tonguing back and forth and filling the ruined Hall of Waiting with sweet, discordant music. The two became twenty, and the twenty multiplied rapidly until uncounted numbers of little bells rang out as though the stars had condensed themselves and their song to fill the Gate. For an age Sholia wept in relief, listening to the voice of Shol as it had been, until one by one the bells fell silent and still, and when the last thin note had ceased to vibrate, they melted cleanly and swiftly to form one glittering, smooth silver wall. The Gate was shut.

Sholia crept slowly to the wall, but when she put out a hand to pull herself upright, it scorched her palm. On hands and knees she struggled to the doors and, finding them cooler, hauled herself to her feet and stood looking out upon Shol. In every direction fire met her gaze. The Towers of Peace had vanished, and she knew that the city was no longer perched on the slope of the cliff, for the convulsed plain was shorter, its new, raw edge visible through the smoke spewing out of the clefts in the mountain. To her left the palace stair lay buried under a rubble of rock, and the entrance to the palace itself was blocked by stone that had come crashing from the heights above. Rivers of lava oozed onto the plain, and apart from the sounds of fire and cracking rock, Shol was silent. Sholia did not allow herself to think of Shon and Sumel, their orchards and the sun-bronzed people. She turned from the desolation around her, away from her palace, away from the Gate, and began to stagger across the plain toward the place where the mountain had sloped down to become forested foothills threaded with rivers. Now the rivers were steam and the foothills a smoldering waste of ash, but beyond them were more valleys, secret places, far from the scene of her agony.

She had taken no more than ten slow steps before a rumble behind her made her turn in time to see a cascade of boulders tear loose from the rock above the door to the Hall of Waiting. When the dust of their passage had cleared, the doorway was no longer there, and the doors themselves had been wrenched from their hinges and buried deep. She looked ahead to the parched devastation on the horizon and back to the place where the Gate now lay hidden in stillness and darkness, and then she flung her necklet to the ground and set out to cross the plain. I am sun-lord no longer, she thought, but it does not matter. I have served my purpose, and Shol does not need me anymore.

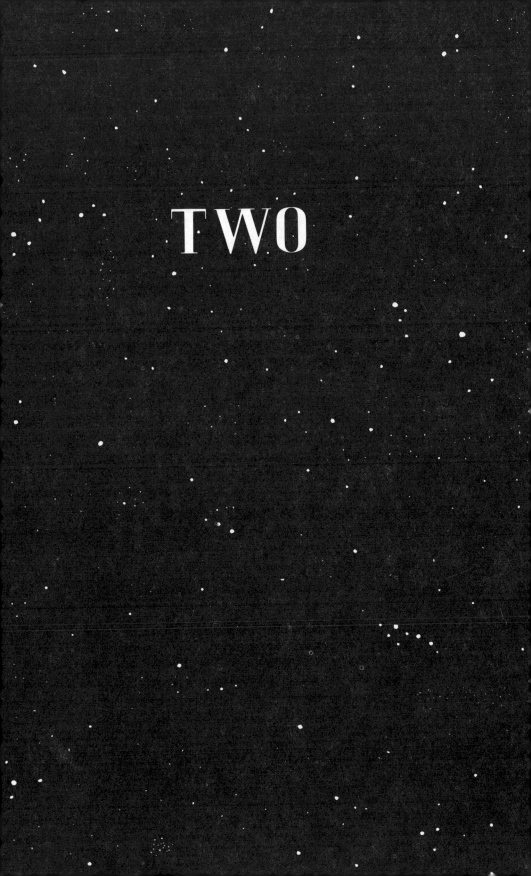

# TWO

# 18

Danarion's small wooden house lay on the outskirts of the city. Three haeli trees clustered together at the foot of his garden, casting a blue and dim golden shade over his lawn and shedding rustling rivers of crisp leaves each autumn, and beyond them was his wall, a gate, and the road beyond that. He could have lived in the palace with Janthis, for Danar was his charge by right and its sun had spawned him, but he preferred to be where he could hear the voices of the city by day and see the lights of the surrounding houses flicker through the dark trees by night.

Each morning he would walk across his dew-heavy grass, go out his gate, and follow the road that took him into the city, and he spent his days wandering, talking to whomever he overtook, entering a house whenever there was an invitation, feeling almost unconsciously for any undercurrents of dark change beneath the slow tidal washing of the usual mortal flow and ebb. He found none. In summer the corions would sail over his wall and lie in the shade of his trees, talking lazily together. In the short winter he gathered up the iridescent feathers dropped by the migrating birds, as his neighbors did, and piled them into vases to mingle with his own sunlight and glow through the still nights. He gardened a little, cooked a little for his mortal neighbors, and even learned to spin and weave. He helped to fell trees in the forest that pressed close to the city, and he gave a hand to the people who crafted houses. The world of mortal life fascinated him; it always had, but now he sought its heart out of his own loneliness.

Sometimes he almost succeeded in believing that he could forget the powers dormant within him. Sometimes, when he became involved in a task or sat beside a mortal's hearth with a family gathered around him, he fancied that his blood flowed red instead of golden, that his place was in just such a house with his own wife and children. But in the nights, when his mortals rested, dreaming their dreams, he stood at his windows and watched the calm, motionless shadows lie over his lawn, knowing that he did nothing more than play a game. Time would not receive him as its servant. Try as he might, it continued to bow before him, step reverently around him, set him apart from the people whose homes hugged close to his own.

He tried not to see the children grow into adults and the adults mature into a strong and vital old age while his reflection in the ruffled pools that lay in the roads after a rain showed him the same face they had given back to him one thousand, six thousand Danar-years ago. He tried to greet the sun as the mortals did, with a cheerful moment of gratitude soon buried under a preoccupation with the business of the day, but dawn after dawn as his brother lipped the horizon his heart leaped within him and he wanted to leave his body and go soaring toward it, to plunge deep into its welcoming embrace, and the frail mirage he had built around him during the previous day vanished and had to be painstakingly erected once more.

He seldom went to the palace, for Janthis had shut himself into his little room and spent the years standing before his walls, calling to him first one lost world and then another or facing the blank solidity of grayness. Danarion dreaded the long walk to the domed council chamber, where the table was mutely laid with a necklet before each empty chair except Sholia's, and only Danar's sun twinkled out in all the solemn silence of the floor which stretched away to the foot of the dais like eternity itself.

Once or twice a year at the time of the seed-fires he went into the Time-forest and sat engulfed in the dry golden leaves which whispered down to rest around him, watching the seeds detach themselves from the trees with tiny explosions and burst into red flames as they whirled to the forest floor. A thin blue smoke like fragrant incense hung between the trees, and Danarion would inhale it and think unwillingly of the members of his kin that he would never see again.

The corions loved the seed-fires. Storn and the other corions stalked the forests, sniffing and watching as though autumn would never come back. Even in the Time-forest Danarion saw them, a deeper, fluid gold amid the light color of the leaves, the shadows slipping over them as they glided out of sight on the periphery of his vision.

He did not know if the years gliding by him so quickly were the peace of a last bastion before the final assault or a prelude to the deeper despair of the winding down of the universe. He only knew, in his more honest moments, that he was a useless anachronism, the last of a unique breed now condemned to exist in a humiliating semblance of contentment, neither mortal nor fully sun-lord, shorn of the weight of the company of his brethren.

His conversations with Janthis were about all the things that had been said and done a million years ago, for the present was an unvarying desert of predictable motion, and the future had ceased to rush toward them when Sholia closed her Gate. But the memories they shared did not draw them together. They reminded them of things that wounded. Janthis suggested that Danar's Gate be closed, but it seemed a pointless, futile gesture and would only serve to sever the mortals on Yantar and Brintar from contact with friends and families on Danar. No Traders came with wares for mortal or corion, and the door of the room containing the Books of Lore remained closed.

Danarion began to be aware of a slight change in the mortals' perception of him as he continued to wander through the city and saw one generation succeed another. In the beginning, in the time when Sholia had closed her own Gate and Danar had become a prisoner of itself, the people had run out to greet him as he passed their houses, touching him with a loving reverence and calling him sun-lord, and he had been unable to move among them and communicate with them for the invisible wall of awe and respect they lived behind. Now he knocked on the doors of their descendants, who called him simply Danarion, inviting him in, offering him food he could not eat and drink he could not swallow, chattering to him as though he were one of them. They no longer gave him his title, although they knew that he was not one of them, that he was different. Their long family memories told them what he was, but with the passing of the centuries the memories, though always vivid and clear, receded and became their history, the true tales of Danar long ago, and the Danarion who smiled at them and shared their fires was no more than a curiosity. The Gate took them to the other planets of their system with smooth efficiency, and they thought no more about the other worlds whose stars hung above them in the night skies than they did of the Gate itself, which had always been there.

He was tempted to erase his own past from his memory, to wipe from himself the times of agony and great power, but often his only companions were the ghosts who crowded him on Ixel, Fallan, Ghaka, and Shol. At first he had visited them out of a need to pretend that nothing had changed. He rode with Falia across Fallan's wide vistas. He stood under Ixel's waterfalls with Ixelion, both of them laughing and gasping as the water pounded against them. But as year succeeded year the past became more distant, and each time he returned to his present, it was like coming home from foreign countries where he had been a stranger.

The centuries multiplied on Danar, became thousands, and it seemed as though the matter of Lawmaker and Unmaker, falling worlds and corrupted sun-lords had slipped into the realm of dreams.

Summer hung still and hot in Danarion's garden when he was called. He had been sitting under his trees, talking with Tandil, his neighbor's small daughter, when Janthis's voice came clear and urgent into his mind: Danarion, come quickly. You are needed.

Surprised, he rose, and sending the girl back to her own garden, he went out his gate and turned right, away from the city. He followed the road until it forked, and he took the narrow, grass-choked path that soon plunged in under the murmuring shade of the Time-forest.

He walked quickly, feeling the strange yet familiar tug at his ankles as mortal time relinquished its hold on him and his own time swirled to meet him. The forest was empty, and before long he could glimpse the wide stone stair glinting white in the sunlight, which did not penetrate the umbrella of soft, pliant haeli leaves. Then he was out under a sun that stood at its zenith, and he saluted it with a word as he mounted the stair, still guarded by corions who stifled yawns and watched him out of the corners of drooping azure eyes.

Halfway up he glanced over the bridge span to the Gate, for Janthis's summons had been curt with an edge of fear to it, and he wondered if something threatening was about to emerge. But the ornate entrance arch shimmered quietly in the heat, and no travelers troubled its sleep.

Cresting the last step, he strode in under the cool gloom, crossing the entrance hall. Pacing steadily he came at last to the drowned silence of the chamber, but before he had reached his own chair, Janthis's door had opened, and Danarion sprang up onto the dais and joined him.

"Come into my room," Janthis said without preamble. "I have something to show you." After Danarion slipped past him, he shut the door and turned to one of the walls. "I call the worlds to me every day," he went on tersely. "I watch for changes, and for the last thousand years there have been none. Until today. Look, Danarion."

At a soft word the wall's grayness dissolved into the wide blackness Danarion knew so well, and at another word the stars began to speed toward him. *I had forgotten*, he thought in wonder. *The ecstasy of the corridors, the freedom of space, the thrill of an easy power, I had forgotten them all, but now it is as though my years with the mortals are fragile visions that fade so fast, so fast.*

"Ixel," Janthis commanded, and obediently Ixel's sun rolled into view, its yellow brilliance encompassed by a ring of tonguing black. Then it had passed them, and Ixel herself hovered, filling the wall, her nimbus of misty atmosphere shot through in blackness. "Closer. I want to see the Gate," Janthis said, and then the Gate was before them, Lix's cold green crystal glittering. "Tell me what you see, Danarion," Janthis snapped, not turning to him.

Danarion answered bewilderedly, "I see the Gate as we left it, closed and sealed with the hands. I see nothing changed."

Curtly Janthis nodded, flung out his fingers, and Ixel vanished. "Ghaka!" he spat, and once more the stars flowed toward them, parted, and Ghaka's sullen purple sun bulged out at them. "Ghaka's Gate," Janthis said, and it was there, the stone birds still frozen in their moment of struggle, the one smooth surface showing Danarion two hands, palms facing outward in a gesture of warning. Again Janthis questioned Danarion, and again Danarion could see nothing untoward, only the cruel and lonely stamp that they had placed on Ghaka's ruin. Janthis flicked his fingers, and Ghaka disappeared. "Watch carefully," he said. "I will call Shol." Shol's one remaining sun careened toward them and was gone, leaving Shol to hang alone in the little room, and where Shon and Sumel had once twinkled in the darkness with reflected light there was only a deeper blackness. "The Gate," Janthis whispered this time, his voice shaking, and the mirror moved inward. Danarion waited to see the glint of Shol's sun on the silver sheet he knew was there, but nothing happened. The wall was blank. Again Janthis ordered, but the mirror did not move. There was no silver, no hands etched deep, no blackened, twisted lintels.

Danarion turned to Janthis. "What does it mean?" he asked. "Where is the Gate? Has the mirror ceased to obey you?"

Janthis glanced at him and then back to the wall. "The mirror has no mind to decide whether to obey or disobey," he replied shortly. "It was made for my use only and shows me exactly what I ask of it. I requested a view of Shol's Gate, and that is what we see."

"But there is no Gate! There is nothing! Where is the Gate?"

Janthis dismissed the vision and turned at last to face Danarion. "The Gate has gone," he said wearily. "If we were standing in Shol's Hall of Waiting looking toward the Gate, we would see the shape of a door set into a wall. The physical parts of the Gate are still there, but its essence is not. And that is a matter for grave concern."

Danarion wanted to laugh in his anxiety. "How can a Gate vanish? What power can move one, and why?"

"I had thought that no power but a Maker's could do such a thing," Janthis said heavily, "and then only if a Gate was open and needed to be moved within a world. Such a thing never happened. The Gates were set down in their ordained places in the beginning. I cannot answer you, Danarion. The Unmaker's will goes on working behind a closed Gate, and who can say what unknown forces that will is able to bring to birth through the use of fallen mortals? Since he ceased to be the Worldmaker, many things have happened that I have not been able to explain."

"Then some new magic has been devised on Shol?"

"I think so. I fear that some dark work may be coming to fruition there, and we must know to what end." Janthis put his arm around Danarion's shoulders, and they passed out into the hall.

Foreboding hung over Danarion, as though he knew what Janthis would say to him next. The touch of the other was neither calming nor reassuring, and when Janthis took his arm away, Danarion saw that in his other hand he held the dim sun-ball. He began to pass it from one hand to the other, his thoughts far away, and Danarion waited.

Presently he sighed and looked up. "You and I have not been much comfort to each other, Danarion," he said softly. "Too many sorrows clothe us. Yet there has been security for me in knowing that I am not an immortal alone on Danar, that you are kin to me." He faltered and then went on more briskly. "We cannot leave the mystery of Shol's Gate unsolved. It would be easy to tell each other that there is not much we can do, but while the power to reassume some of our responsibility lies in us we must not turn away. The time has come for us to part."

Dread stole suddenly over Danarion. "What do you mean?" he said huskily, but he knew, and the knowledge filled him with terror.

"One of us must go to Shol and find the Gate and, if possible, fit it once more into the Hall of Waiting. If it hangs open somewhere, it must be closed again."

Danarion wanted to run away from him and his mirror, to find his own little gate and go through it and shut it, to lie on the grass of his peaceful garden until dusk stole, still and warm, over him. He had not battled the Unmaker. He had not grappled daily with the delicate balance of a world bombarded by greedy flames howling to enter it. He had seen his kin go down one after the other, he had walked for a time on worlds he would never see again, but he had been able to return to Danar, and safety. Danar had rested untouched, ignored by the Unmaker as he plotted to encompass Shol at last, and now Danarion acknowledged to himself the relief he had felt when the long fight for Shol had reached a conclusion. But now it is my turn, he thought grimly. I have received my share of quiet, and the price must be paid. He dared not answer Janthis, and Janthis spoke again.

"Danar is your world," he said slowly, "and ultimately the responsibility for its defense is yours. I can only advise. I cannot order you to Shol. You can refuse this request without damage to your wholeness, but if the Gate on Shol is open, it means danger to Danar, and Danar is all we have left. Will you go?"

"I do not think it is possible to go even if I were to agree," he answered. "You know the words of closing: 'Henceforth neither mortal nor immortal, Maker nor Messenger nor any created thing may enter here.' And if the Gate is missing, there is no way to enter, in any case."

"I did not say you would use the Gate. Of course that would be impossible even if it still fitted its visible confines. A Messenger will take you."

Danarion's fire blazed out in surprise. "What?"

"I have already called one and spoken with it. It tells me that it can carry you to Shol if you are willing to go. It has the power, but until now such a thing has been forbidden. It went to the Law-maker and has returned with his permission.

Danarion glanced quickly about the chamber, but there was no sign of the familiar spiral of whirling light. The heat of summer hung stultifying in the room, and sunlight gleamed through the clerestory windows. A tiny flicker of hope woke in him, and he turned back to Janthis. "So the Lawmaker knows," he said. "He has not forgotten us, he still watches." Janthis nodded, and Danarion turned away from him, gazing down the long hall without seeing. If I go, I may never return, never again walk the crowded, sun-drenched streets of the city, never draw in through eyes and nostrils the wonder of the seed-fires. Yet if I refuse, if I walk out of the palace, Danar's security will be forever threatened. He could not feel resentment toward Janthis, who so easily put this task on his shoulders. He had seen him lose composure when they had watched the closing of Shol's Gate, and did not doubt the depths of hurt he suffered. Yet he cast about in his mind for some alternative that would leave him secure on Danar without compromising his honesty.

Janthis gazed at him quietly, the sun-ball tight in his grasp, and then broke in on Danarion's frantic thought. "You cannot go in your body, if you decide to go at all," he said. "You must know the risks, Danarion. The Messenger will travel outside the corridors, through places where you would not survive, even in such a body as you have. And even if you were able to, the Sholans would see by your body that you are not as they are. The Messenger will put you in a mortal's body. You will be a Sholan."

"My powers?" Danarion whispered, not looking at him, and Janthis told him the truth. "You will not be able to command fully Shol's sun, for only Sholia or I may do that. You will carry with you some of your own sun's power, but how much help it will be to you I do not know. Your body will be a prisoner of Shol-time, but not lightly and willingly, for time on Shol, like everything else there, must be hostile. Your host body will bleed, suffer pain, even die, Danarion, and I cannot tell you whether these things will affect you or not. But be very careful that you do not allow your essence to become fused with the Sholan mind, for then you will lose your wholeness and fall."

"You presume that I shall go!"

Janthis smiled. "If I could go, I would," he replied mildly. "But I cannot. Something must be done, and only you can do it. Have you not sometimes wished that you were mortal?"

"But not a fallen mortal on Shol, not on a world where every step would be for me a torment!"

"Your body stays here in my care. Your feet will not tread the earth of Shol. Will you go, Danarion?"

After a long interval, during which Danarion's light trickled unchecked over the floor, he raised his head. "I recognize the choice," he said formally. "I will go."

Janthis did not thank him but merely nodded. "Then go and sit in your chair and place your necklet on the table in front of you. Do you understand what you must do on Shol?"

"Yes, I understand." Danarion went down the steps and lowered himself into his chair, lifting his necklet over his head and laying it on the table. I did not even sense this coming, he thought, his hands folded on the sun-disc. I have been playing with the mortals for too long. This is my judgment. He felt Janthis move to stand at his elbow, and all at once the room was full of a hot, strong perfume. He did not dare to raise his eyes to the thing whose power roared like a wind through the chamber.

"You have great knowledge of mortal life and thought," Janthis said, his voice seeming to come from far away, and Danarion felt a hand pressed briefly against his forehead. "Inhabiting a mortal's body will diminish you, but it may bring you a measure of contentment also. Farewell, Danarion."

The momentary touch had brought calmness with it, and Danarion felt his mind clear, become cool and alert. He heard receding footsteps and then the closing of Janthis's door. The Messenger came closer. Danarion could see its silver and blue colors throbbing on the polished surface of the table. He tensed in anticipation, and a voice spoke, a voice without the warmth and timbre of breath passing over tongue, without the fiery flow that wove in a sun's speech, a thin, unhuman voice that made him tremble.

*Close your eyes and move out toward your sun*, it said, and Danarion obeyed. For one moment he felt himself speeding to the sun, and it prepared to embrace him eagerly. But then between him and the sun a vast silver curtain was spread, spangled through with shards of blue light. It shook and dissolved to become green, then red. He could not slow his pace and went hurtling toward the net. Then he was in it, and it wrapped him around, and abruptly his vision cleared.

He was not facing his sun after all but was in a cage of transparent fluidity, as though he stood surrounded by waterfalls. Beyond the sliding, shaking curtain the immensity of the universe lay around him, under and over him. He was reminded of Janthis's mirror, for the stars flashed by him, leaving sizzling white trails, and it seemed to him that everything was in motion but himself. Glancing to where his feet ought to have been, he saw that he was hanging inside a column which just below him broke into streamers of blinding colored light that hung for a moment before exploding in a silent shower of rainbowed sparks. He looked up, but as far as he could see, the undulating walls of the column stretched away, and above him the stars were fixed and without movement.

He felt as though his thoughts were dropping with infinite slowness into his mind, each shining with well-being and a brilliant coherence, but he could not hold them. Finally he ceased to think at all. The universe drifted by him, the waterfall shimmered, and he allowed it all to simply be, just as he had relinquished himself to simply being. He did not know whether time was moving backward or forward or had stopped altogether. He began to believe that he had always hung suspended between the stars and would remain so forever.

Then full consciousness returned to him, for the Messenger had paused and was contracting itself. The transparency wavered violently and reformed into the misty silver net Danarion had seen flung out between himself and his sun. Through it, hazy and very far away, he could discern Shol's one sun, trapped in the mist of gray as he had seen it last in the mirror.

Danarion held out arms he did not have in a gesture of supplication, and the sun came closer. He thought he heard it crying, and the slow tendrils of grayness surrounding it licked toward him as the Messenger hurtled toward it, the silver net shrinking to a hard brilliance that broke the starlight into white spears and turned back the questing mouths of the darkness.

For a moment Danarion felt himself buffeted as the Messenger was itself tossed to and fro, but then the sun was behind them, and Shol came into view, a tiny prick of dim light which grew as they sped silently toward it. The Messenger slowed to a long glide, and the stars ceased to move and became single crystals quivering, green and red through the net. Shol was a half-moon whose horizon curved mistily against blackness, and time began to beat against Danarion once more.

The horizon rose and flattened, and the mist became low cloud tinged with the pink of a rising sun. To his left Danarion saw a range of mountains dominated by one massive, blunt peak. Rivers oozed from the rock like gray blood, but he was still too high to see the movement of the water. Below him was a vast plain, also gray but dotted with dark lakes, and to his right the flat expanse of the ocean. He looked ahead so that he might not see the earth come racing toward him, and far in the distance he thought he caught the reflection of a flash of early light. The bells of Shaban, he thought with a stab of relief and anticipation, but then he remembered, and the terror was back. The mountains dipped and reared up beside him. The plain unrolled, flattening the lakes into invisibility, and the Messenger came to rest just above the ground. Danarion looked down.

# 19

Lying on the verge of a lake was a man, his black, untidy head turned to one side, his hands open and reaching for the dark water. Under his legs grew coarse grass which straggled away from him and followed the wandering arc of the beach, and thorny shrubs struggled for rootholds in the sand and rocks beyond him. He was very still. There was no movement in the broad shoulders under the stained brown tunic.

Suddenly Danarion saw metal bands about both thick wrists, each band set with closed hooks, but before he could wonder, the Messenger stirred, and the scene began to blur. "Not this body!" Danarion whispered, horrified. "This mortal is dead!" But the Messenger said nothing, and for a moment a great calm enveloped Danarion, as though at last he might taste mortal sleep. Then it seemed as though the Messenger broke into many pieces. The net shredded and whipped away. The mountains creaked, the rivers roared, the constant thirst of the ugly, dusty bushes was a murmured groaning.

He felt himself propelled downward. Instinctively he called to his sun, but there was no response. Don't leave me! he thought wildly, don't abandon me in this terrible place. When will you come for me again? Where? Will you be able to find me?

Sight and sound were blotted out as he found himself in a place of utter darkness, like a cavern deep under the earth, so empty that even the awareness of it was itself a void that had always existed. This mortal is dead, he thought. His essence is gone. He should have been taken to the Gate, where essence and body would fuse closer together, become a white cargo for a Messenger. In his momentary panic he had forgotten, but then, as he fought to remain calm, a curious thrill, half revulsion and half anticipation, went through him. Of course, death on Shol is different now. But where do the essences go? Where is this man now? Shadowing by a Gate that is no longer in place? I am in a dead body. I am a mortal, and I am dead. This is the body I am to use. I am sorry, so sorry, whoever you were who looked out through these black eyes.

He began to expand himself, searching for the limits of the emptiness. He felt into the marrow of the bones, the secrets of the cells, finding in each the fading imprint of the mortal whose thoughts had warmed them, whose energy had permeated them, saturating them with life and purpose. The nebulous, pervasive force had left a faint aura that was alien to Danarion, but he thought of the time he had spent sitting with his own mortals by their hearths, striving to understand them, to be as one of them, and he did not shrink. There was something in this mortal that would not have been in an inhabitant of Danar, a mingling of wholeness and complexity, a fear for the safety of his body and a suffocating drive to change and destroy, a swirling giddiness of hate, love, pride, and selflessness, all fractured yet intertwined. So this is what it means to be a fallen mortal, he thought. This terrible interior war that can have no resolution. Sholia closed the Gate, but too late to prevent the posing of a threat that can have no end and no victory for either the Unmaker or herself. I must not let it pierce me, although here in this body it is as close to me as an indrawn breath. Now, who am I?

He probed the brain, and a dark flow of fear and defiance beat him back as he struggled to approach, to unlock the frozen memories left by the essence. He knew that the fear belonged to the moment of death, when the man could run no more and had turned at bay, and the captain had raised his bow, and the arrow had found its target. Danarion tasted the terror and found the defiance to be against Ishban, and its Lady, and the emotion was so strong that even the moment of death had not eclipsed it. What is Ishban, he thought. And what Lady? Can Sholia be still in the city? Then why this death, this killing? I do not know enough, I do not know where to start or how to seek. But I must begin. He felt himself tolerated by every cell, a foreign but acceptable presence, and he took the last step and flooded his mind into the brain. He opened the eyes.

Pain burst in him, and he cried out, seeking the blissful shelter of Shol's sun. But it did not recognize the call, and the body still encased him like a clumsy, heavy shroud. He tried to sit up and could not, but he turned the head and saw a crust of dry color on the sand, brownish-red. He made the eyes look along the body. An arrow jutted from its side, the shaft broken off. As he looked at the wound the memories at last sprang to life for Danarion, and this time separate sensations came with them: a gulf of pain that had stilled the heart, and beneath it many lesser throbs—feet and ankles swollen because of the running, the scabbed graze on the left shoulder where the body had fallen while climbing over the city wall in the darkness, the burning ache of punished muscles, the exhaustion of flight.

Danarion moved an arm, and the fingers took the arrow and pulled. It came slowly, the barbs tearing flesh loose, and the fingers dropped it and felt in the hole it had left. Danarion made the head lie back while he coaxed the heart into a flutter, and the wound to begin to knit. The blood began to flow again, cool and sluggish compared to his own. He made the eyes open onto sunlight, but the sight was blinding, and they closed again of their own volition. Behind the lids Danarion saw the dazzle, and with anguish he knew that most of his power was gone, sunk uncontrollable beneath this strange red blood and these slowly working, stiff organs, and all that was left to him was the power to command himself. The ability to order a sun was no longer in him. He felt naked, protected only by this arrangement of softness held up by brittle bones.

He made the body lie still as he quietly observed the new life he had brought, course through it, healing the wound, soothing the muscles, drenching the cells with a foreign vitality. While he watched he became aware of something else, something that reached out from this flesh, that had saturated it and now sought to inundate him, and he let it come. I am no longer outside time, he thought. Now it is within me. I feel it draining me as it does the mortals, a store of sand trickling slowly away, a minute and steady atrophy in these cells that cannot be touched by me. He tried to analyze the feeling. It was not merely a matter of changes in the cells from moment to moment as it would be for mortals on an unfallen world, a flux along the same plane. Time here was an active, hostile participant, interfering with the proper course of the changes, warping them into progressive stages of decay. Each second leeched vitality from the body. Time itself was feeding on life. Tentatively Danarion tried to stop the parasitic feast, but when he did so, the cells ceased to function. He knew he was being devoured. Once again this body is dying, he thought. So this is how it feels. I am set on the path to death, and there is no escape. The last mystery is open to me, and I must find the courage to bear it. Now, what is my name?

The brain cells responded. I am Chilka, slave to Yarne in the House of the Lady. I am a Sholan one-mind. Once again I am running to the mountains, where the remnants of my people live, where my wife and child have waited six years for me to return from hunting. The soldiers pursued me and killed me, and now I am free to go home, no more to see the sickness of the two-minds, to hear their sleepless whispers in the night, to be chained while they wander, vulnerable and mad, through the halls of the House. Free to run home, to run, run! I am Chilka!

The exultation of the thoughts brought Danarion to his knees, and he looked to where the mountains beckoned, the one blunt mass casting a long midmorning shadow. He scrambled to his feet, and now did not need to command the body to obey him. My legs straighten, he said to himself. My head turns. Firmly he fought down the urgent demands of memory and stood swaying, one hand to his side where the new scar had formed. "Of what use are the mountains to me?" he said aloud. It is the Gate that I seek, and Sholia's palace. Perhaps this House is the palace, and she is the Lady. I must go to Shaban, and Chilka must show me the way. Then he laughed. The clumsy mortal body bent and, scooping up the brackish water, drank until its thirst was quenched. It walked, loosely and without coordination, until Danarion realized that he need not speak directly to each muscle. Not it, he told himself. This is me. I am this. He peered into the bushes and found the skin pouch Chilka had worn across his chest. The pursuers had rifled it. The knife had gone, and the coat, but some bread lay baking in the sun beside it. Danarion squatted and broke the loaf, forcing the brittle pieces into his mouth.

A memory of his own came fleetingly. He was sitting at table on Danar in his neighbor's house, the little girl on his knee, and he was refusing the food she held up to him, feeling once again the wall that he wished to break down between himself and the mortals. The memory was indistinct and soon faded, and he crunched the dry bread with satisfaction. Now I know, he thought, and the knowing is good. He swallowed and then swept up the pouch and drew it over his head, noticing as he did so his reflection in the water. A tousled beard, two black, wild eyes, skin lined and filthy. Chilka, he thought, I greet you. The mouth smiled back at him. He stood straight and, turning his back on the lake, set off in the direction of the ocean.

He walked intermittently for a day and a night. He knew that Chilka recognized the land, and he plotted his path by the man's memories, but as Danarion it was all strange to him. He had visited Sholia several times, had known how the city clung to the steep sides of a cliff with the ocean at its foot, and had seen the grassy plain that swept to meet the palace. He knew that forests had grown on the edge of the plain where rivers meandered to the sea, and beyond the forests were miles of rolling, tree-clad country where the nomads camped in summer, and he could only suppose that he was very far from what he had seen then. His feet began to swell with heat that rose from the sand, and the sun made the huge rocks that lay tumbled in his path shimmer and dance. The mountains sent out a spur of land that dwindled to be lost in the distance, and it was toward this spur that he headed, with the mountains themselves behind him and marching on his left, very far away.

He drank from small rock pools hidden in shadow but found nothing to eat. As Danarion that did not concern him, but Chilka's body craved food in spite of Danarion's power to keep it moving. It also needed much sleep, and in the dark hours, when it lay uncomfortably behind some rock or pressed deep into grass, Danarion had time to investigate the memories. Chilka's ancestors were not there. Try as he might, Danarion could find nothing beyond a time when Chilka had been three years old. His birth, his father's life, his grandfather's life had never been a part of his consciousness, and in their absence there was a vast plateau of uneasiness, as though some rough hand had wiped them away and left only a faint pulse of dull pain.

The child had been reared in the mountains. Danarion saw cold dawns and the footprints of wild game clearly in the snow. He saw summer sunsets of red and gray which the boy stood naked to watch, and the heat was a thing he could smell as well as feel. Quickly Danarion sifted down the years. There was a woman, small, fair, and pretty, and Chilka was now a man, already sown with the seeds of bitterness against the two-minds. He listened avidly to the stories of Shol's past, his emotions mixed, longing to believe yet finding no correlation between legend and what he saw with his own eyes. Danarion, listening also to the memories as Chilka's body murmured and sighed in its sleep, heard for the first time of the destruction that had come upon Shol.

Legends told how an army of magicians had come from the stars and had brought a sickness of the mind to Shol, so that the people were no longer whole but divided within themselves, and with the magicians had come fire and death, and a great shaking in the heavens. Some said that Shol had had two suns, and that the magicians had flung giant rocks at one of them and destroyed it. That, the myth-teller had said as Chilka's dark eyes had narrowed in disbelief, was difficult to believe, and harder still to believe was the legend that told of other worlds in the heavens where the people of Shol came and went, worlds the magicians had also destroyed. What were these magicians like? Danarion heard the voice of Chilka's body, a little derisive, a little patronizing, yet with a longing to know. The old man smiled apologetically. The legends tell us that they were shaped like us but had mighty wings, and they flew down to Shol bringing fire and war. They could make a man mad in his sleep, and they caused Sholan to rise against Sholan. Only us, the one-minds, were not touched. Our fathers ran and hid in these mountains. We are the true Sholans. The two-minds belong to the stars. Where did they come from? Chilka asked, the wind howling around the cave and the firelight flickering red on his face. From Raka, the old man said softly, and Chilka had laughed out loud. Raka? A constellation barely visible to the eye, and then only in the depths of winter when the air is dry and cold? How could anyone sprout wings and fly across such a distance? A magician might, the old man replied, smiling faintly. I do not dispute. My task is only to keep the legends alive. Is there a child born who does not fear the birds? We kill and eat them reciting words that will fill us with their magic. Why? The people listening murmured among themselves. One did not speak lightly of such things. One killed and whispered the words, and ate, and one did not think too much. The two-minds are not happy, the old man went on. They fear the stars as we fear the birds. That is why we kill them in the dark, when their minds are clouded with terror and sickness. Perhaps they fear a punishment from the stars. Who knows? The legends say that their Lady who never dies was once one of us, and she let the magicians come in exchange for her immortality, and it was she who loosed fire on Ishban and made the mountains split and the forests burn. There is, of course, a happy ending to this child's tale, Chilka sneered loudly, and the old man looked at him mildly and nodded. Not happy, perhaps, for nothing can be as it once was. Sholans will never again go to worlds beyond the sun. But the legend says that a god will come and heal the two-minds. From another constellation, I suppose, Chilka said, and the old man smiled. From Danic, he said. Chilka yawned. I am more interested in your news from the city, he said. Stop telling stories and give me some facts. The old man complied, but the people listened without true concentration, their thoughts full of the old lore, their faces bright in the fire's leaping, reflecting their hope.

That memory, so clear in Chilka's brain, gave Danarion much to ponder as the body trudged toward the spur of rock that grew steadily larger. He had remembered the old man's words with such clarity that Danarion knew, in spite of the scoffing, that Chilka longed deeply for the legends to be true. But I know the truth, Danarion thought, or most of it. Is it the Unmaker himself who lives in Sholia's body in the palace? Then where is Ghakazian? His essences took possession of Sholan bodies, that much is obvious, and they are trapped here. Such knowledge is of no use to me, for it will not help me find the Gate. Must I face the Unmaker alone, in a mortal body, with no power to speak of? Surely he is not here. Surely it is only his breath, not his presence, that has infected Shol. My only task is to find the Gate and render it safe for Danar if I can. If I become caught up in the mortals' struggles with one another, I will lose the distance that separates me so narrowly from this flesh and become half-mortal myself. My concerns must be for Danar and Janthis.

The body was sweating and stumbling. Its side ached where the scar ran, raised and an angry red, and thirst swelled the throat. It mutely demanded more rest, and water, and for one blinding second Danarion hated it. Then, trembling, he sat it down and passed the hands over it gently in a gesture of apology, the hate turning to pity. He looked out over the landscape and realized he was sitting in the shadow of the spur, which had now taken on definition and ran like jagged teeth into a haze in the distance that Danarion knew was the ocean. The sand had largely given way to a coarse, gray grass and straggling clumps of trees, and the end of the spur was fuzzed in green growth. As he sat, the body ceased to pant, and the heartbeat slowed. Sighing, he rose and had begun to pick his way forward when he heard a shout.

"Chilka!" It struck him like a blow and echoed from the shaking, heat-seared slope of the mountain.

He turned. Six men were running toward him, and in Chilka's brain the need to flee was a surge of energy and panic that gave way to relief as their faces wavered and came into focus. He stood still and let them come. But ten paces from him they stopped. Danarion read their uncertainty, a doubt tinged with awe and fear. He smiled.

"Yes, it is I," he said steadily. "I am so glad to see you."

They still did not speak. Finally a young man stepped forward. He lifted Chilka's arm and ran his fingers down the scar, and his touch smoothed wonderingly over the scabbed shoulder and drifted hesitantly along the cheek and over the lined mouth.

"What is the matter, Sadal?" Danarion said, and the hand dropped. Sadal shook his head.

"We saw them shoot you," he said flatly. "We saw you running by the lake. I couldn't believe it was you so soon after the last escape. We saw the arrow go in. After they had taken your coat and knife, they rode away, and we came to look." He swallowed, and Danarion felt the eyes of the others fixed on him darkly, suspiciously. "You were dead," Sadal said flatly. "Candar tried to pull out the arrow, but the flesh was ripping too badly, and even though you were dead, we did not want to . . . to mutilate . . ." He broke off and looked at the ground.

"I broke the arrow," Candar's harsh voice almost shouted. "Your eyes were open and filling with sand. You no longer bled. Your chest was still. The breath had gone. What in the name of Sholia are you?"

The old oath jolted Danarion. "What happened then?" he said quietly.

Sadal shrugged. "We did not dare to carry you away just then for fear the soldiers might come back. We withdrew a little and waited. When we returned, you had gone. We thought they might have come back and thrown your body in the lake, but the tracks said no. We followed your footsteps, not knowing what we might find."

"And here I am," Danarion finished for him. "Did it not occur to you that I might be merely wounded?"

Candar laughed. "Even if there was life in that body, it would have needed more than Lallin's care to get up and walk away. Who are you?"

Immediately the true fear sprang to life behind their eyes, and Danarion saw their hands move cautiously to rest on their weapons. "You think that somehow in the House they have turned me into a two-mind," he said slowly, "or that it happened there by the lake. And I am now an enemy. You are wrong." What shall I tell them? he thought dismally. They would twist the truth in their minds because mine is too nearly the condition of the Shol-Ghakans, and they would not take long to decide to kill Chilka. I could once more knit the body together, but such an effort would serve no purpose.

"Where were you going?" Candar asked sharply. "Only Ishban lies that way."

Danarion feigned surprise. "Does it?" he said. "I was in such pain of mind and body when I got up from the lake that I lost my bearings. Think for a moment, Candar! If I had become a two-mind charged with spying on you, would I then get up and go back to Ishban? In any case the two-minds cannot increase their numbers."

"You do not talk like Chilka," Candar growled, "yet it is true that the two-minds cannot multiply. Sadal?"

The younger man smiled, and his blue eyes lit up. "Lallin will tell us." He grinned, and the others laughed. Danarion found a face in the body's brain, small, framed in fair hair, with brown eyes and a quick, large smile. Chilka's wife, Lallin. With her was a boy, and the memory embraced him lovingly. "If this is a mystery, then it is a sweet one," Sadal went on. He touched Chilka's mouth again. "We all knew that they could not hold you for long. Welcome back to the mountains, Chilka one-mind!"

"But not to this mountain." Candar glanced up at it and then to the sinking sun, still high in the heavens but beginning to lose its midafternoon heat. "The dead crowd this place. I can feel them." He turned away, and the others followed. Sadal fell into step with Danarion and offered him bread and a flask of water as they walked, but Danarion found it difficult to follow the man's sporadic conversation. There was other vital knowledge to be gleaned from Chilka's remains, and he put a name to the bulky jut of blunt mountain. The Mountain of Mourning. The place where the dead were brought. The place, Danarion surmised with a pity for mortals he had never felt before, where the essences, denied a Gate, were condemned to wait down all the long years. Was it so on other worlds, Fallan, Ixel, Ghaka? No, not Ghaka. What is happening to my own memory? he worried. Here the Sholan essences are released while those of the Ghakan invaders find other bodies to inhabit. How? Chilka's brain could supply no answer.

"What did Yarne say to you when they dragged you back a year ago?" Sadal was saying. "Two escapes in six years must have made him angry."

"Yarne is never angry," Danarion replied automatically, and realized that he was nestling ever more deeply into Chilka's consciousness. "He warned me that the next would mean my death and said he would be sorry to lose me."

"Is it true that he's a renegade one-mind? Is that why he's so high in their Lady's favor?"

"There are many rumors about him," Danarion found himself replying. "Some say that she had a brother once of the same name, but he was mortal and died, and she used her magic to make Yarne in his image. Others say that there have been many Yarnes, that she sends secretly to the slavers for young men who match her dead brother's likeness and then puts their essences to sleep and gives them his memories. I myself cannot say what is true. I only know that she loves him profoundly and sends for him often, and that he does not age. Perhaps she gives him potions in the night, to keep him young. Perhaps he is immortal after all. I cannot help liking him."

"I know you cannot," Sadal said grimly, "and I wonder why. In the mountains we say that he is nothing more than a renegade who caught the Lady's eye and now goes softly clad, with all freedom and much authority, and does nothing to help his own people."

"That may be true," Danarion replied, "but it cannot be held against him. He only cares for his dabblings in history. He is an innocent. Immortal or sham, he understands nothing else. He wanders happily and obliviously in the past."

Sadal glanced across at him sharply. "You never cared to understand much yourself, Chilka," he said, "and all you cared to know about a man was whether he was for or against us. You have changed."

"I have been away for a long time," Danarion said lightly, "and perhaps I have been learning caution. Forget about Yarne. He is harmless."

"He cannot be harmless if the Lady thinks so highly of him. I think he is a clever one-mind traitor taking advantage of her obsession with a dead brother, hiding behind a mask of inoffensiveness."

"You have never met him," Danarion retorted shortly, and they lapsed into silence, walking swiftly with the long red arm of early sunset laid over them and the Mountain of Mourning once again sinking into a blur behind them.

# 20

In the five days it took to retrace their steps past the shallow, stagnant lakes and enter the cover of the mountains, the men watched
Danarion carefully. At night, as he deliberately lay under full starlight, he felt their eyes on him, and while he kept Chilka's eyes
closed and body limp, he himself gazed into the heavens. Ghaka's
sun was indeed barely visible, as Chilka had pointed out so skepti-
cally to the old man, a sullen reddish star that pulsed unevenly
through Shol's atmosphere, and Danarion could only just make out
Ghaka itself if he concentrated. Looking west, farther down the sky,
Ixel's sun was a faded creamy color and Ixel itself a steady dull
white, and only Lix sparkled coldly and cheerfully through the
blackness.

Danarion studied the jeweled blackness, naming the other constellations to himself, remembering the soul of each one. It seemed
to him that the sky was tired, that the heavens hung wearily in place
in a kind of stupor. The soft sounds of sleep around him, the warm
breaths of men, their mutters, the still moon-shadows cast by the
rocks, the far calling of some night creature were like a cloak of
security and peace, while the faces of his true kin seemed pale and
unearthly, like ripples on far water.

He watched the sun rise, and with it came the daily hope that
light brought to the world of men. He struggled but could not
imagine himself buried deep in the heart of that searing fire. He
thought of his own sun, and the Messenger who had brought him
to Shol across the deeps of space, and by the time he had risen, fed
and watered Chilka's heavy body, and picked up the skin bag, he
had renewed his consciousness of his immortality.

Before noon they had arrived. The mountains were not sheer
and unbroken, as Danarion had thought. Between each range there
were wide, river-slashed valleys full of trees and small fields of crops,
and one or two villages always wandered along the banks of the

water. They walked through three such valleys and then came out of a shadowed cleft that funneled the river, to stand high above a fourth. "Home again!" Sadal said and smiled at Danarion. An uprush of pride and release flooded Danarion, and he grinned back, jogging down the steep path and entering a grove of trees that he knew. His eyes, Chilka's eyes, picked out his own cottage, far below, and he found he was trembling. Chilka's legs began to run. The trees fled behind him. It was as though some quiet force still left in Chilka's brain had woken to joyous life and was forcing Danarion into submission.

Finally Chilka had to slow. His side ached, and his chest heaved. He strode through the ripening crops, and all around him birds started up with alarm and flew away screaming. Chilka winced, but Danarion ignored them, feeling this body, this brain tense with one desire only. The fields came to an end, and flowers burst into view, blue and scarlet. He turned between the cottages that lined the river. By each door hung a cluster of small bells, and with a rush of nostalgia Danarion heard them tinkle as Chilka went by. Sholia's face sprang to him on the vibrations of that ancient music, pouring light that drenched her golden hair and flowed from her eyes, her nostrils, her parted mouth. She was laughing. So strong was the vision that he was almost unaware when Chilka stopped, turned, and ran up to a door, lifting the latch and almost tumbling inside.

A woman sitting in the light from the one small window rose in astonishment, one hand going to the spear propped in the corner, but then the hand came up to her face and she shouted, "Chilka!" Danarion was jolted back to the present, and in place of Sholia's immortal and unchanging loveliness another face flew toward him, small, wrinkled about the eyes, the hair short and untidy, whose mortality was like a blow to him. No! he thought in revulsion. Don't touch me, for I am a god. Don't sully me! But Chilka's arms rose, widened, and the woman flung herself upon him.

"Chilka! I cannot believe . . . You got away after six years . . . I cannot believe!"

He folded her in upon himself, holding the warm, tiny body, and in spite of himself Danarion was infected with the overwhelming relief and pleasure that filled Chilka's body. That so much should remain once the essence is gone! he marveled. All else has faded but this! For a long time they cradled each other, and then Danarion lifted his head and stood her away from him.

"Nenan?" he asked huskily.

"He is grown now," she replied in a whisper. "Six years is a long time, Chilka. He has gone hunting for us. He has cared for me very well. They said you had escaped once before but got no farther than the wall. Six years . . ."

An odd formality fell on them, and for a while they simply smiled at each other, until Chilka motioned to the fire.

"Make me some of your stew," he said, "and fill my cup with water from the river. I do not want to speak. I just want to watch you." She came to him shyly, kissed him on his bearded cheek, and busied herself by the fire. Danarion sat in the chair by the window and observed her. The room was stark in its simplicity but comfortable, the floor covered in thick, handwoven rugs, the fireplace pointed in gray fieldstone, the furniture carved skillfully from mountain trees. "Have there been many raids since I was taken?" he asked. She paused, knife in hand, and smiled at him again long and gleefully before she replied.

"Ah, Chilka! To hear your voice again in this house, and to see you sitting by the window and smiling at me. We have not lost many in this valley because we are so far into the mountains, but the other villages have been raided twice a year. Not always successfully. The two-minds cannot always reach the safety of the lowlands before nightfall, and our men often see to it that they do not. Nenan has done his share. He went with Sadal three months ago and caught a party of them at sunset. There was a rock fall blocking the way to the plain, so the two-minds had to dig. Nenan said that as soon as the sun went, the madness came on them, and they stood on the edge of the cliff, holding out their arms and wailing. Sadal and his men pushed them all over."

Danarion was absorbed in thought. It had taken five days to come here by way of the foothills and lakes, but as he sought further in Chilka's mind he found an alternative route. It was a path leading directly down the other side of the mountain to the plain, two days and a night of hard walking from the village, but once on the plain, the city was only a three-hour ride away. Excitement stirred in him, for this time there was something familiar about the scene passing swiftly from Chilka to him. But with it came the fear of great plunging heights and hawks and eagles. Lallin turned away again, and Danarion spoke no more.

When the food was ready, she placed it before him on a small table and, unhooking a large wooden cup from the mantel, went out, leaving the door open. Sunlight streamed into the room in a great shaft. Danarion saw her walk to the river, hitch up her skirt with one hand, and bend to fill the cup. There was a man sitting on the bank, his back to the water, his eyes fixed on the cottage, and Lallin's high, excited voice came floating to Danarion. The man nodded once or twice, but if he spoke to her, Danarion did not hear. It was Candar, grim and suspicious still, keeping a guard over him. Lallin came back, placing the brimming cup beside the stew and sitting opposite him. Danarion lifted the cup, hesitated, and then dipped in his fingers and sprinkled droplets of water on the floor. "For Sholia, wherever she may be," he said before he drank.

Lallin went white. "You have never done that before," she said softly. "It is a tale, a fable to quiet children and soothe the dreams of old men, or so you always told me. What has happened to you?"

Danarion shrugged and smiled at her, picking up the spoon. "Perhaps I have become superstitious after all," he replied. "Perhaps I am just taking no chances. It is as though I have come back from the dead, Lallin."

"The longer I listen to you, the more I am aware of changes in you," she said again, her face still pale. "The words you choose, the way you say them, gentler, less sharply. Six years have given me back a different man." She was trying to smile, but Danarion sensed the uncertainty beneath. He touched her hand and went back to his meal.

He did not stir from the chair all the long afternoon. People came knocking at the door to welcome him home, their voices hesitant, their hands cold in his, and Danarion quickly realized that the story of his seeming resurrection had been spreading. He knew that he could not stay, that soon he must slip away and find the city, go down that impossible path that snaked like a black thread of terror through Chilka's memory, but the lassitude of the body had seeped into him, and he was content to sit by the window, acknowledging the greetings of Chilka's fellows. Sadal came, bringing none of the doubt that had circled the others, and sat before him, knee to knee.

"We can take up where we left off now, Chilka." He smiled. "I have not forgotten the plans we used to make. Establish better communication with our fellows scattered over Shol, build an army, and eventually wipe out every two-mind in the world. They say that Ishban once belonged to us. Well, we'll take it back, now that you've come home."

"Ishban never belonged to you," Danarion said quietly, absently. "It was Shaban, the city under the sea, that was inhabited by one-minds."

Sadal blinked and was very still, and Danarion suddenly realized what he had said. Lallin was hovering behind him, and he saw Sadal glance at her in puzzlement. "You are no believer in legend, Chilka, and neither am I," Sadal said kindly, and Danarion understood that Sadal had decided to humor a wounded and weary man. "If Shaban ever existed, it cannot be proved, unless we find a way to breathe under the water. Chilka, don't tell me that you have been infected by them in the years of your captivity!" he finished in a burst of irritation.

Danarion, with great effort, lifted a hand and smiled. "No, Sadal. I'm sorry. It is just that the two-minds believe so strongly and fearfully in the old city's existence, almost as though they think that one day it may rise from the ocean and somehow destroy them all, that it is difficult for any man to withstand such foolishness day after day."

"Well, it has nothing to do with us," Sadal grumbled, mollified. "You're back. I give us five years to defeat them now, eh, Lallin?" But she was staring at Chilka and had not heard him. Sadal went home cheerfully some time later after planning a campaign to defeat the Lady and occupy the city, and Lallin took the chair he had left.

"Chilka," she said hoarsely, "what did you mean when you spoke to Sadal as though he and you were not one? There is something here I do not understand." But she got no further, for the door was flung open, bringing a gust of cold night air into the house, and with a start Danarion realized that the sun had long since set. A young man came bounding across the floor, and Danarion barely had time to rise before he was crushed.

"Father!" the young man shouted. "I ran right through the village when they told me! Oh, welcome, welcome!"

So this was Nenan. Danarion freed himself, fighting against the webs of caring and belonging that were beginning to form around him in this place, and took the eager face between his palms. Chilka showed him a gangling stripling of twelve, all dark eyes, but he found himself looking at a broad-shouldered, lithe man of eighteen.

"Nenan, my son," he said, and a curious thrill went through him. "Six years do not change a man much, but they turn boys into men. You are as tall as I now."

Nenan twisted away but held to Chilka's arm in a gesture of delighted disbelief. "You got away! I always knew you would. Ishban won't hold my father for long, I used to tell myself when the nights were long and cold on the slopes and the game wouldn't show. I've looked after Mother as well as I could."

"She's told me." Danarion found that the lump in Chilka's throat had been formed by his own strange emotion. "You have done very well."

Nenan released him. "Mother, there are two rabbits outside, and I'm hungry." He grinned at his father. "Oh, so hungry! I'll have some of that stew. Are they hunting you, Father? Do you want to talk, or will it hurt you for a while?"

So he had not heard of the killing. Danarion lowered himself opposite his son and suddenly felt his responsibility for these two mortals, their unearned love, their happy trust rise up to condemn him. What have I to do with them? he tried to tell himself. I am not concerned with the strife of mortals. I am here to secure the Gate, wait for a Messenger, and go home to Danar. He saw his house there, ringed by grass and fragrant blue haeli trees, but the vision was lifeless. Around him Lallin's large candles flickered, and the smell of the stew was in his nostrils, and Nenan was shaking his head in wonderment and smiling still. Danarion knew real fear then, the fear of dislocation, of irrevocable commitment and change. "I think that tonight I want only peace," he said slowly.

Nenan nodded agreeably.

"Then I'll sleep at Sadal's place. Mother will want you to herself."

"Is Candar still outside?" Danarion asked.

"Yes, he is. Your return must have given him a shock. He could hardly speak to me as I passed him." Nenan finished the food and stood. "I'll go now," he said, embracing Chilka again, "but I'll be back early in the morning." He went out whistling, and Lallin began to clear the table. He watched her deft fingers, her economical movements. She did not look at him. When she had finished, she paused, then came to him and, putting her hands against his neck, kissed him on the mouth.

Danarion's whole essence cringed. Avenues of intimacy and possession that Chilka's mind had not shown him before opened under him like a gulf of hot darkness. He was horrified and repulsed, yet under Lallin's soft lips the body of Chilka responded, and Danarion found he could not forbid it. Presently she drew away, pulling him to his feet, and kissed him again, her arms around him, her own body tight against him. Then she abruptly pushed him away, and her hand found her mouth.

"The moment I heard you speak, I knew you had changed," she said dully. "Every word and movement spoke to me of six years acting on you like some spell that had twisted you into someone I no longer know. To kiss you is like kissing a stranger. Is there a woman in Ishban, Chilka my husband, who looks for you in vain tonight?" She was struggling to hide the hurt, but to Danarion it was evident. "I will understand," she said more loudly. "I cannot expect your continence for six long years. You are home, and that is all I must see."

It was fully dark now. The window no longer gave out onto fields and the blunt peaks of the mountains, but had become a mirror. Danarion, glancing at it, saw her reflection distorted and pale, a long, grotesque face, a misshapen body. Candlelight flickered around the image, and it seemed to him that she was burning with this doubt, this jealousy against which she fought. He turned back to her deliberately, took her hands, and forced her gently into the chair.

"Lallin," he said quietly, "I must tell you the truth. Candar suspects that I am a two-mind come to spy on you all, and he is right in a way, but to you I owe the whole truth, because you loved Chilka, and he would have died for you—indeed, in a way he did." Her expression did not change, but a stillness came over her, an inward stiffening against more hurt. He dropped her hands. "I am not Chilka," he went on heavily. "I use his mouth, his eyes, I dip into his memories so that I may know where to go, what to expect, but the thing you love, your husband's flame, his essence, is gone."

She smiled wryly, and her face fell once more into lines of tense control. "What you are trying to tell me, Chilka, is that I no longer have your heart, that it has gone to some Ishban woman who has cared for you. Is she another slave, a two-mind, perhaps a friend of Yarne?"

"No!" He did not want to see her like this, encased in brittle calmness. "If Chilka had found another love in the city, it would be here"—he tapped the black, untidy head—"in his memories, his brain, his mind's echo. He loved only you. He was running to you when he died. He escaped twice before, and it was only for you. The soldiers rode after him and caught up with him by one of the lakes and shot him dead with an arrow. Ask Candar or Sadal if this is true."

"Obviously it is not," she retorted, still calm, "or you would not be standing there telling me nonsense. Your captivity has turned your brain, Chilka." Suddenly her face softened. "Oh, my love," she said gently. "It is not important. You cannot be hurt anymore."

For answer he lifted his shirt, and the scar was red and raised against the brown skin. "This is where the arrow entered," he said. "It pierced Chilka's stomach and nicked his heart."

For the first time she showed alarm. She put one finger on the scar. "This is new," she admitted, "but so is the graze on your shoulder." She lifted his arm, and her fingers found another scar by his armpit, smooth, old, and painless now. "You are Chilka," she said definitely. "I will have to teach you that you are."

"Lallin, a moment ago you were suspicious of me. Can the truth be so preposterous that you cannot understand it? I am not Chilka, I am not a Sholan. I am an immortal, a god if you like. I fell from the sky into Chilka's body and must use it for a while. Your husband is dead."

She stood. "Slavery does strange things to a man," she said slowly. "A woman may shrug and accept it, but a man's dignity, particularly yours, demands immediate escape. Inwards, if it cannot be over the real wall. Your escape has been inwards, to the legends. Chilka, you have gone mad." Her mouth trembled, and she came to him and put her arms around him again, laying her head against his chest. "It doesn't matter. I don't care. One day you will recover."

Danarion allowed his arms to respond, but despair filled him. She would believe nothing he might tell her. It was all too far-fetched. He thought for a long while of Shol in the days of security, when multitudes poured through the Gate to and from Shon or Sumel, when he and the other sun-lords had mingled with them openly and gladly and the Worldmaker himself had trailed his feet in the ocean. How long ago? he wondered. Ten thousand Shol-years? A hundred thousand? I must go. I cannot stay here. His haste was rooted in fear of Lallin herself and Chilka's unbreakable ties to her.

He set her away carefully and, taking her face in both hands, he drew from himself what power he could. "Lallin," he whispered, "I want you to rest now. Go to sleep. I will give you a dream of my world, of Danar, and when you wake, you will not fret that I have gone. I will come back if I can, I swear it. I do not blame you for your disbelief." Her eyes widened, and she would have spoken, but he willed her mind to blur with a need for sleep.

"Lie me down, Chilka," she murmured. "I'm so tired. We can talk in the morning."

He caught her as she fell, laid her on the bed, and covered her. He blew out the candles and let himself out without a sound.

Candar had gone. The riverbank lay peaceful and deserted, and the water chattered as it flowed swiftly with starlight caught in its froth. Danarion crept along by the cottages, and soon the village was behind him and he was wading once more through some tall crop that swished against his thighs. As he went he forced Chilka's mind to yield to him the way down the other side of the mountain, the precipitous route the two-minds took when they came slaving, but only portions of the path were locked in the mortal's brain. The blanks were full of darkness and fear. Down through the valley, the forest, a short drop to where a waterfall gushed out, then rock and a looming shape on the right that was, Danarion surmised because of Chilka's terror, the backside of the Mountain of Mourning. Here the memories ceased to flow, and only trickled through again when the plain was reached and the pinnacles of Ishban shivered on the horizon.

Danarion walked on. The valley began to narrow, and the dark, fuzzed blur of a forest loomed. He left the fields and struck into the trees, following a faint but distinct track. Danarion was conscious of the body's extreme weariness. It had been under much stress since morning and needed rest to face the perpendicular horror of the mountain. Reluctantly he turned off the little path and curled into a nest of moss and last year's leaves. He closed Chilka's eyes. For a while his thoughts were wandering and chaotic, with no purpose. He remembered the feel of Lallin's lips against his own. Then there was nothing to remember or forget.

# 21

He came to himself with a start. Where have I been? he thought anxiously. I was on Danar with Storn, but that was eons ago, for Storn has long since gone with a Messenger. Is that sleep? Are Chilka's cells absorbing me and conquering? With a shudder he sat up to see the first indifferent light of dawn bathing the mist around him and a man kneeling beside him. He exclaimed, still in a strange, foreign fog of sluggish thought and heaviness, and saw that the man was Nenan.

"I've been watching you for two hours," Nenan said huskily. "You babble strange things in your sleep, Father. Why did you run away?" His voice was strained, and Danarion saw Nenan choke in the effort to control himself.

"How did you know I had run away?"

"Sadal and I had been to see Candar in his house and were walking back when I heard the bells. They rang as you passed them. Sadal did not hear, but I know the note. I followed you, not believing. Where are you going? What did you say to Mother?"

Tears were not far away, Danarion could see that. Oh, let me go! he thought suddenly. I am tormented in this body, I only want to do the task set to me and then spend a thousand years sheltering and healing in my sun. Wearily he stood, brushing leaves from his clothes and hair.

"I am going to Ishban," he said curtly. "Don't worry about your mother. I put her to sleep, and when she wakes, she will be at peace. I am not your father, Nenan."

The young man hissed, a sigh of speculation but not surprise. "So Candar was right," he said loudly. "I know the story. He told me. He and Sadal argued for most of the night about you, and then Sadal said that Mother would know and we only had to wait until morning. I was ashamed of Candar, and angry with him also. Now I don't know what to do. I should try and kill you, I suppose . . ."

His voice trailed off, thick with tears, and he turned his head away.

"You could not kill me, Nenan, even if you tried," Danarion said more gently. "You could pierce this body, your father's body, but I would knit it together again and go on. Do not do it more hurt, I beg you. I need it. It has become a home to me, and your father's memories are my friends."

"You're a two-mind!" Nenan's head was still averted.

"No," Danarion said patiently. "I come from the stars. I am on Shol to perform a task. I could not travel through space in my own body, so when I arrived, I was put into your father's."

"The two-minds talk that way when the madness is on them," Nenan retorted grimly. "They believe they've fallen from the stars and don't belong on Shol. I remember your telling Lallin so, the first time you escaped. Prove to me that you are not one of them!"

Danarion thought, Why should I? It would serve no purpose. If he will not believe my words even though he sees and hears that I am not Chilka, then he will not believe anything that I show him. His acceptance or rejection is nothing to me, and I am wasting time. But something of the love he had felt for Nenan when he had first seen him came back to him. My son.

"I have little power away from my sun," he said slowly. "I cannot ask Shol's sun to rise more quickly for you. But perhaps I can show you myself in your father's flesh."

"You had better not be less than a god," Nenan choked, tears flooding his eyes, making them even larger and more luminous than they already were. "Only a god will do. If you fail to appease me, then I shall hack my . . . my father into such tiny pieces that they will never knit again, and bury them all!"

Danarion was not tempted to laugh at this mortal's impudent defiance. He was learning a respect for them, these complex, prideful beings. "Then I should have to find another body, and you would have done your father a grave insult," he said. "Watch, Nenan."

Nenan stood stiffly rebellious and looked at Chilka. Six years had put more lines around the mouth and the dark eyes than he had remembered, he thought with an ache, and the skin was coarser. The black beard was new, and the length of the hair. Chilka was thinner, more used up, somehow, battered and old. A protective love flooded Nenan. He wanted to take this deranged being, his father, and lead him home by the hand like a blind man and tell him that all would be well. He had opened his mouth to speak when Chilka seemed to loosen. A peace like death stole over him. Nenan found himself looking into mild golden eyes set in a face more beautiful than any he had ever seen. The hair that framed it was a deeper gold, alive and lifting with some unseen, hot wind. The body was straight, the limbs youthful and vigorous. Under the skin a white light pulsed, filling the morning coolness of the forest with heat and a delirious, heady odor that made Nenan want to laugh aloud and dance about. A necklet of gold and blue went around the dazzling throat. Nenan, blinded and yet seeing more clearly than ever before in his life, fell to his knees. "Are you the essence of a two-mind?" he faltered, the old doubt and fear still hovering.

The voice that spoke to him was deep and strong. "The two-minds have two essences, and one of those essences has wings. Am I winged, mortal?"

"No." Nenan covered his eyes. Instantly the fire and light died, and his father's voice said kindly, "I am here to harm no one. You have a choice now, Nenan. You can go home to your mother and tell her what you have seen, or you can come with me."

Nenan looked up, and Chilka's dark eyes smiled into his own. "A god," he whispered. "So the legends are true."

"They are—that is, they contain much of the truth. I am not a god, Nenan. I am made, as you are. But I live forever, until my sun burns out, and my gifts are the gifts of a sun. Yours are the gifts of the earth, from which you are made. I have to go to Ishban." He rose and extended a hand to Nenan. "I must go by way of the Mountain of Mourning because there is something in your father's memories I must see for myself. You know the way. You can show me those parts of the climb that your father refuses to remember."

Nenan shivered. "They would take me for a slave," he said, troubled, "like . . . like Chilka. He *is* really dead, isn't he?"

"Yes, he is. Will you come? I will let nothing harm you in Ishban."

"If, as you say, my mother will suffer no grief, then I will come."

Nenan took his hand and rose. "I know the way. It is very terrible. But with you I will be safe, I think."

Danarion was suddenly glad of the inexplicable urge that had prompted him to ask for Nenan's company. "You will be safe. I would like to be on the plains by sunset, so we must move on. The forest is waiting."

By noon they had come to the edge of the forest and out under a hot sun, where they began to pick their way toward the waterfall that they had heard long before they saw it, a ceaseless rumble that trembled in the ground under their feet. They stood on its brink, and Nenan pointed. "We go down there!" he shouted over the noise of the water, "and hope we do not meet soldiers coming up! Will you pick me up and fly with me?"

Danarion laughed. "No. We must climb." He scanned the almost vertical drop to the river below and saw a slim, winding track zigzagging along the side of the cliff. "The two-minds have no fear of heights," Nenan shouted again, "particularly at night."

Danarion nodded. "I will go first," he shouted back and stepped gingerly over the edge, bracing himself with hands and taut calves. Nenan followed with less confidence. Once on the slope Danarion found it to be less steep than it had appeared. The danger lay in the wetness of the rock, the drenching spray, and the unvarying noise of the waterfall, a tremor under the feet and a threat to balance. But within the hour he and Nenan stood beside the swirling white water, grinning at each other.

"That was easy," Nenan said. "The hard part is only beginning. I have never been farther than this and only I know the way, but you have been along the whole route." He flushed and bit his lip, and Danarion shook his head.

"Your father blotted it out," he said. "There are no memories."

Nenan made no response. He turned abruptly. There was a crude wooden bridge, logs rolled together and a rope for hands, through which the water sloshed up to wet the feet of the travelers.

"Why have you never broken this bridge?" Danarion asked curiously. Nenan replied without turning around, "Because we do not want them to find another route into the valleys. This one is the quickest and most dangerous, even for them. We can kill many this way."

Danarion joined him on the farther bank. There, hardly visible in the black shadow of a crease in the rock, was an opening. Nenan hesitated, and Danarion caught a gleam of challenge in his eyes. "The tunnel is not long, or so the older men say, but it is very rough and completely dark. I have no light. You are a sun-god. Can you give us light?"

Belief was fading under fresh doubts. Danarion sighed inwardly. "I think so. My own light will be sufficient." He walked in under the overhang and paused, and a dull yellow light began to trickle from Chilka's outstretched hands. Nenan said nothing more.

The tunnel was indeed not long, but the weight of stone and thick darkness held feebly at bay and the uneven, chip-strewn floor made it seem much longer. When they emerged, Danarion stood on a narrow lip of rock that reminded him suddenly and forcefully of Ghakazian's great rock Gate and was momentarily stunned. The Mountain of Mourning was so close on his right that it could almost be touched, a huge, rearing bulk of barrenness that permanently shut out the sun. Strange gray thistles grew haphazardly on its steep sandy slope. Over it all lay a palpable, frowning hostility.

Nenan shuddered. "I do not fear the dead," he said in a high voice. "It is the other, the presence, the unknown thing that haunts the Mountain. The two-minds cannot bear it either, but their need of slaves overcomes their fear."

Danarion took a closer look at the Mountain, trying to ignore the clamor of retreat, pain, and dread that swirled in Chilka's mind as the memories woke. The visible cliffs were not unbroken. Buttresses, slanting ledges, smooth slides that slowed to flat places became clearer the longer he looked. It was difficult to make out any detail without direct sunlight, but it seemed to Danarion that irregularities in the rock were in fact patches of faint white or jumbles of gray sticks. Mutely he enquired of Chilka, and past the drumming of fear and the birth of courage the answer came. The dead— brought to the Mountain, wrapped in white linen, and carried by those who afterward ate a small farewell meal beside the bier and then crept away, leaving the body on the slopes for the few wild animals that might prey upon the rotting flesh. It was a pitiful, crude parody of a Sholan death, Danarion reflected. The white garment, the Hall of Waiting filled with happy well-wishers, the Messenger waiting beyond the Gate reduced to this unthinkable deforming. Why here? he wondered. Why here? And Chilka's heart beat faster.

"Chilka was taken by that route," Danarion said to Nenan, pointing down the slope. "It comes out at the foot of the plain opposite the city. But I want to end up farther to the south. We must go over the Mountain."

Nenan shook his head and backed away. "No one climbs the Mountain," he whispered. "Funerals come up from the other side, or so I believe, early in the morning so that they may be off the Mountain by dark. We would still be there when sunset comes! I will not go!"

"Very well," Danarion said gently. "Go home if you must. The dead cannot hurt you and would not wish to even if they could, and if there is something else up there other than fear itself, Nenan, it cannot hurt me. Don't you understand? Nothing on Shol can destroy me, and if you are with me, you are safe."

Nenan hesitated, torn between fear and pride. "My father would have been afraid, but he would have gone with you, I know, if he were here," he said finally. "Very well. I have nothing in this whole world to lose." Danarion touched him briefly on the arm, a gesture of approval and support, but Nenan shrugged away. They stepped from the shelter of the tunnel mouth onto the cold sand and turned their faces to the Mountain.

By early afternoon they were struggling up the barren slopes. By sunset they were standing on the summit, a flat, slightly rolling height bare of all but black and gray rock and an evening wind with a night chill in it. Ahead lay the plain, green and tree-dotted, and beyond that the ocean, lying pink and blue-gray at the horizon. To the left was the city of Ishban, hidden by evening haze and the miles between.

Nenan shivered. "It's cold up here," he said, "and I am hungry and very thirsty. I came after you with nothing."

"I have no food or water either." Danarion drew him down into a little dip in the rock. "Tomorrow I will find us something on the plain."

"The plain is full of two-minds who tend fruit trees and vines. They say it is warmer down there by night, and cooler by day."

Danarion knew that Nenan's calm voice hid a terror that was growing as the sun hovered, a half-disc on the ocean, and he settled closer to the young man. "Would you like me to put you to sleep like Lallin?" he asked gently.

Nenan thought, then shook his head with weak defiance. "I will not run, not now. Tell me about where you come from. Fill the legends for me."

So as night fell and the stars appeared, so close in the black arc above them that Danarion felt he could reach out and caress them, he told Nenan of Danar, the palace of the immortals, the mighty Gate. He spoke of Shol in the days when it was new and unsullied, of Sholia, of Shaban with its steep streets, its dream-weavers, its many bells. Nenan listened, entranced, now and then breathing, "I do not believe! I cannot!" in a voice thick with thrall. Once he asked, "Do you mean that all the worlds had Gates? That Shol had a Gate through which the people could go to the stars?"

"Not to the stars," Danarion replied. "Only to Shon and Sumel, but they were destroyed when Shol's other sun exploded."

"And if you find this Gate, will you open it once more so that the people can go through?"

Sadly Danarion realized that Nenan had not fully understood, that he had been asked to comprehend too much. "The people can no longer go through," he said. "I want to find it only so that I may know it is safely shut forever."

"If I had been a god, I would not have let it happen, any of it!" Nenan said bitterly. "We mortal people have done nothing, we were innocent. Why should we suffer the evils of beings we know nothing of except in stories?"

"Everything that was made suffered," Danarion answered heavily, "because nothing was made to stand alone except the Law-maker himself. I have told you enough, my son. Go to sleep now." Nenan muttered a protest, but Danarion touched his eyes, and he exhaled and fell into a deep slumber.

Danarion sat looking into the darkness. Chilka's body demanded sleep also, but Danarion was afraid to relax for fear he should sink into the well of not-knowing that had overtaken him the night before, so he ignored the exhausted flesh encasing him. For a while he studied the stars, and gradually he became aware that he was not alone. A wind that was not moving air sighed on the Mountain, full of the far voices of invisible hosts drifting to and fro across the summit, from nowhere to nowhere and back again.

The wailings of the essences did not frighten him. He listened to them absently, random thoughts passing through his mind, until he was suddenly aware of someone standing before him. The impression was so strong that he glanced sharply up expecting to see a bulk that would blot out the stars, but Chilka's eyes and his own inner sight showed him nothing. Only his instinct told him that someone stood near his feet, and a terrible pleading came to him, washing over him as he sat tensed and listening. *Come please, please* . . . The urge to rise, to follow nothing to some unknown place was very strong, but he resisted it. "I cannot help the dead," he whispered. "There is nothing I can do. I seek the Gate and nothing more." For the rest of the night the presence remained beseeching, mute, and cold, but when the sky began to lighten, Danarion felt it leave him. Was it Chilka he wondered suddenly, looking at his body with longing? All at once he was possessive of the flesh surrounding him, and he hugged himself tightly as Nenan sat up, shivering.

"The sun's rising," he murmured, "and I am even hungrier than before. I would give anything for Lallin's hot stew." He gazed about him, half-astonished that he should still be on the Mountain yet unharmed.

Danarion rose abruptly. "It is not far now to the fruit trees," he said. "We must go."

But Nenan had grasped his arm and pointed. "Look! A funeral procession coming this way! If we run, we will be seen, but if we stay, they will walk right up to us!"

The silent party was almost up to them, toiling without sound, heads bowed, not in grief, Danarion thought, but against the effort of the stiff climb. The man who led was dressed in a long red sleeveless garment emblazoned down the front with two suns, a yellow one overlapping a black. Behind him came two men bowed under the weight of a huge metal sun which glinted in the early, fresh light. A family followed them: a man in late middle age, gray-bearded and with a stately carriage; a woman heavily veiled; a young man, very fair and slightly older than Nenan, by the look of him; and two little boys. Bringing up the rear were a half-dozen servants, each carrying a load of wood and jars on his back. Nenan was panting with fear and clutching Danarion's arm. "If they see us, they'll kill us! This is no ordinary funeral." Danarion glanced at the sun, now striking full into his eyes. It was well clear of the horizon and climbing steadily. "Take my hand," he said to Nenan, "and do not move or speak. We will try to be thin, you and I, to change color, to merge with the sun." Danarion gazed straight ahead, feeding himself into the young man through his tight fingers, willing Shol's sun to enter and smooth them, camouflage them.

The procession halted within a stone's throw of Danarion. There was still no sound, as though the people were sleepwalkers. The long-robed man pointed, and the servants began to pile the wood and douse it with oil, their movements fluid and unconscious. The sun-disc was laid on a rock a little distance from the pyre. Then they all stood in a stillness so profound that Danarion wondered if they were drugged or tranced. Some minutes had gone by when the first man to appear made a small gesture with his hand, and the father of the family went to the pile of oily, glistening wood and laid himself upon it. The eldest son stretched himself face down on the copper sun. More puzzled than ever, Danarion watched, unease growing in him. There was no corpse to burn. Was this an execution of some kind? He dared not retreat into Chilka's brain, for Shol's sun had answered his request only grudgingly, as though it had been barely heard, and he was forced to concentrate on the link with it.

The robed man produced a light and calmly, almost indifferently, touched it to the wood. The man on the pyre did not struggle or cry out as the flames, the only vibrant, speaking things on the windy Mountain, leaped and crackled. For an age they all watched, their faces blank, and Danarion held to Nenan tightly for fear he should cry out. The form on the disc did not stir but lay supine and loose with eyes closed. Although he did not know at what point the old man died, Danarion, watching through the wind-ripped, swirling smoke, thought he saw pale wings unfolding like a crumpled petal opening to the light. The flesh on the pyre began to crack and snap, and Nenan grunted, the small sound lost in the larger noises of the fire.

Then Danarion's grip on the sun faltered for a moment, for the young man lying on the disc had begun to struggle. His arms and legs flailed. His eyes opened suddenly and widened in horror. "No!" he screamed. "Please, no! Not to me!" Though nothing visible held him, he seemed to be pinned between the shoulder blades. The others watched in complete passivity as sweat drenched him, blossoming on his white tunic and running down his cheeks.

As abruptly as he had begun to scream he fell silent. The robed man gestured again, and servants moved to lift the young man and set him on his feet. As he stood and turned Danarion saw that his blue eyes were clear, calm, and brilliant, glittering with new life and vigor. The procession reformed, turned from the fire, and filed away.

Trembling, Danarion loosed his hold on the sun and sank to the ground, finding Chilka's own body bathed in sweat. Nenan lurched forward with a groan and vomited. "No one-mind has ever seen it," he croaked as he wiped his mouth on his sleeve. "Such insanity, such vicious, incomprehensible rottenness. The rumors say that only the most highly placed two-minds do this. For the rest it is different."

Danarion did not reply. He took the boy's arm, hauling himself up on legs that seemed too weak to bear him, and they started down the Mountain. Not incomprehensible, Danarion thought, after searching Chilka and finding no memories to connect to what he had just seen. The winged Ghakans must have found it easier to move from an old body to a young before death, and it would not serve them to go into the body of a young child. Better the young men and girls who had reached their first maturity.

"Tell me," Nenan said shakily, "is the sun a living, thinking being, or am I as mad as the two-minds? I felt something, there beside you."

"The suns are the Worldmaker's children," Danarion replied, glad that Nenan was trying to occupy his mind with something other than the horror he had just witnessed. "They are immensely powerful but shy and obedient to us, their kin."

Nenan managed a short laugh. "They always told us that the two suns on Shol's flag meant night and day, but I know better now."

# 22

Before long they were walking on lush grass, soft and yielding under feet that had felt nothing but rock for so long. Trees closed over their heads, clad in a summer richness, and Danarion finally sat with his back against a wide trunk as Nenan went in search of fruit, bringing back enough to stave off his hunger. He sucked at the juice thirstily while Danarion ate swiftly and without tasting, ransacking Chilka's memories. The trees were not part of a forest but had been planted in orderly precision, covering several square miles. Between them and the city was more rock and gray, hard-packed sand, sliced by a road along which the privileged might ride to enjoy shade and fruit on hot summer afternoons.

That road passed a place he wanted very much to see, for he was oriented at last. Somewhere between here and Ishban, in the side of the Mountain, lay Sholia's palace and the Hall of Waiting. If he walked straight on through the trees, the ocean would be there, lying at the foot of the cliff that had swept unbroken by all save the steep bay upon which Shaban had been built.

Nenan squinted to where the sunlight filtered down through green leaves. "Greetings, sun," he said half to himself. "You're beautiful."

Danarion came to himself with a start and smiled. "It is time to be moving," he said. "We must walk along the road now."

"I think we should wait for night," Nenan said doubtfully. "The road is very exposed. What do you plan to do when you reach Ishban, anyway?"

"I'm not sure," Danarion replied carefully. "I will follow whatever opportunity presents itself. First I must get into the House."

Nenan's eyebrows rose. "In that case, by all means let us go. We are sure to be arrested on the road."

Danarion smiled at the cheerful sarcasm. "I want to see what I can in daylight," he said, rising, "if you have guzzled enough fruit, Nenan."

They left the shade and passed under the trees, walking steadily to where a line of bright sunlight marked the edge of the grove. On their right the ocean could be heard, a pleasant susurration of low sound which mingled with the cries of sea birds. "My ancestors were fishermen," Nenan said suddenly, "yet I have never so much as placed a foot in the ocean, and there are no boats in Ishban. The two-minds fear everything, even the sea."

"They fear Shaban, under the sea," Danarion responded, and Nenan shot him a dark, respectful look and was silent.

They came to the end of the trees and stepped out into the full glare of Shol's summer noon. Nenan shaded his eyes and looked down the road, but Danarion, seeing the towers of Ishban shimmering white-gray in the sea haze, was afflicted with sudden awe. For the first time since he had stood with Janthis and watched a distrait and almost unrecognizable Sholia close the Gate of this world, he retreated into full memory. He and Sholia were walking along the plain, talking together. One sun had set. The other, farther away, was slipping also, and Shaban was casting long streamers of pointed shadow over a calm vermilion ocean. The palace steps gleamed white as Sholia's light, spilling from every high window, lay on them. Far down at the foot of the city the fishing boats with their bright little sails were crowded like eager puppies at the docks, and the Towers of Peace were being lit. Men walked behind the stone parapets. He could hear their voices and smell the brisk, briny evening wind that had sprung up to ruffle the long grass under his feet and set the many bells of the city chiming and tinkling. Sholia had ceased to speak, and they walked in a contented quiet.

"Chilka?" Nenan was patting his arm. "Chilka!"

Danarion found himself sweating under a hot sun. The view before him now mingled briefly with the living memory, so that Shaban seemed to hang in the air where there was no longer rock to hold it, and Ishban was superimposed on the Towers of Peace. Then memory was gone, but the feeling of fracture remained. The city was too close, the cliff's slope on his left too jagged, the plain impossibly foreshortened. He scanned it all slowly. Where the palace had been was jumbled rock. The city itself squatted safely on the plain, and where the plain had been sliced away in the cataclysm that had slipped Shaban into the sea, the city's wall rose to a vast height and had no gates, for below it was a sickening drop and the grind of the surf. "The road is empty," Nenan said, looking at him anxiously. "We cannot stand here all afternoon."

Danarion nodded, and they set off along it, feeling exposed as the trees dropped away behind them. He wondered at the emptiness. Surely slaves should have been basketing fruit, horses and men coming and going, women in litters swaying toward the coolness of dewed grass and dappled shade.

They made good time, trudging rhythmically side by side. Danarion's gaze played often on the walls of the cliff that rose on his left, but Nenan kept his head down and flinched at every bird's cry. Then, an hour before sunset, the gulls began to stream inland, and Nenan blanched and came to a shaking halt.

"I'm sorry," he said breathlessly. "I cannot bear them. I cannot go on until sunset."

"Don't you know that they are harmless," Danarion snapped, dragging his thoughts from the coils of Chilka's memory. "Your fear is of other winged beings, not birds. It is memory, Nenan, only the long memory of your people!"

Danarion looked up at the cliff and saw that they had come abreast of some massive excavation in its side. A hole braced with timber gaped dark, and outside it the plain was littered with piles of stone debris. He looked again and sucked in a startled breath. "Very well," he said. "We can rest in there." He pointed. "The birds go to their nests in the cliff face, that is all. Soon the plain will be clear of them."

Nenan began to run, panic at his heels, and Danarion walked after him. Yarne's obsession, Chilka's brain told him. Always the seeking, the laborious poring over the book, the digging here that drains many slaves from the mountains, the need to pierce the dark veils of Shol's history. What book? Danarion queried sharply. A book full of riddles and incomprehensible myths, Chilka's brain showed him. The line dividing late afternoon sun from coolness and dimness was immediate, and Danarion began to shiver. Cold blood, he thought. So cold!

"There's water here," Nenan said, his voice echoing. "In tubs. I suppose for slaves to wash in. It's dirty, but I don't care." He bent and cupped his hands, and Danarion looked about him.

He was in a vast, square hall. At first he thought it was nothing but a cave and was crushed with disappointment, but then Chilka's eyes became adjusted to the dimness. The late light began to wink on walls and ceiling, little flickers of dull color that came and went as Danarion slowly turned his head. Rubble and dust lay about the floor, and the walls were uneven, but where they had been chipped back deeply, the stone revealed the imprints of an artist's work. Nenan had finished drinking and was studying the lintel under which they had passed. His hand went out. "Oh, come and look!" he said wonderingly. "What does it mean?" Danarion ran to him. The copper was black with age and decay, gouged and streaked. In places it had suffered some terrible conflagration, for it had melted and the reliefs had run into one another, but in patches the old Sholan artistry could still be seen, and a metal Shaban rose, tier upon mighty tier, to the roof.

Danarion craned upward. The constellations winked at him, black, stone-bound, yet in places showing clearly where the workmen had labored to expose the grooves some ancient hand had carved. Danarion fell to his knees and, taking up a stone, began to chip at the uneven stoop of the door. All Chilka's strength went into his blows, and presently a small slab of stone cracked and lifted. Danarion threw it behind him. There was a Sholan ship sailing a copper ocean, serene, hot, the color of bronze in a drowsy noon. When Danarion rose, he found his legs trembling. He peered into the hall. "There will be other doors," he breathed aloud. They were never closed, and beyond them the universe hung, black and crystal. He walked deliberately to the opposite wall, Nenan stumbling after, and found to his surprise that his cheeks were wet. He knew that Chilka had no share in this grief.

The excavators had found the doorway. Nothing remained but the lintel. The huge copper doors emblazoned with Sholia's likeness and the twin suns had gone, whether melted away or broken and mixed with the floor or carried into the city, he did not know. He ran his hands over rough stone, and his fingers glided and bumped as they encountered the cold smoothness of copper. The diggers had eagerly pierced the rock that had blocked the door, thinking perhaps to find some ancient treasure beyond, but there had been nothing. Only the solid finality of more rock. The marks and hollows of their tools showed they had picked at it halfheartedly for a while, but they had apparently sensed that only mountain lay beyond. How foolish, they must have thought. How pointless to build a door giving onto nothing but stone. The ancestors were an enigma, were madmen who said and did things without purpose. Yet, Danarion thought, his hands caressing the door, if they had but known it, Shol's greatest treasure did indeed lie beyond this tall doorway. Above his head there were notches in the wall, and grooves in the ceiling. The roof had been of haeli wood, he remembered.

"What is this place?" Nenan whispered with awe. "Some vast royal house? How was it buried? Is it so old that time has covered it with the mountain?"

"It is indeed old," Danarion forced himself to reply past the lump in his throat. "It was built at the dawning of this world, tens of thousands of your years ago. But time meant nothing to it, once. It was protected from decay by spells."

"What is it? What spells? Are we safe, so close to it?"

Danarion turned to him, wanting suddenly to embrace his ignorance, his innocence. He himself felt old and thin in his essence. Nenan was fresh and young in this ravaged place. He did not deserve the fruits of what had occurred here long before he was born. For all our talk of protecting and saving, he thought, did we really know how to care for the mortals under us? Was our love really only a blind love of ourselves? Did all our spending of ourselves, our frantic efforts at defense mean only a cosmic selfishness in the end? I love you, Nenan, but it is not the love of sun-lord for mortal. It is something greater, for in Chilka I am no longer perfect. I love you as my son, as like to like, the wounded clasping the wounded. Your own small sufferings mean more to me now than the eternal pain of my own sun-kin. I do not know if I have the strength to simply find the Gate and then go away.

"It was Shol's Hall of Waiting," he answered. "This"—he slapped the twisted frame of the door—"was the Gate itself."

"I do not understand," Nenan said. "There is nothing. Only mountain." He looked at Danarion, and even in the half-light the skepticism of his father was evident in his eyes.

"This was the physical Gate," Danarion tried to explain. "To expect to step from a physical Shol into space would be impossible.

But as well as a physical Gate there was the essence of a Gate, which took the people into another dimension and set them on Shon or Sumel, where there were other Gates."

"Then why can't I see the stars through here?" Nenan's voice was harsh, unforgiving.

"Because Sholia closed the Gate. But more—if she had closed it and its essence was still here, we should see the door filled with a silver wall set with Shol's symbols, the bells of Shaban. And you would be unable to approach it."

"You talk very glibly," Nenan retorted. "You have such tricks as perhaps the philosopher-priests of the two-minds have, but I still wonder just who you really are."

Danarion did not reply. He stood back from the Gate, raised his arms, and touching the buckled lintel, uttered a word. There was a low rumble which rolled through the ground, making the lintel quiver gently, but nothing else. Again he spoke, more loudly this time, but again there was only a vibration in the rock. He sighed. "The Gate is not here, just as Janthis feared."

"Then this was not a House?" Nenan was still grappling with Danarion's words.

"No. The palace was there"—Danarion waved at the rock wall—"some hundred steps."

"Strange," Nenan murmured, "this is not a haunted place. I feel safe here."

"You can be certain that the people of Ishban do not!" Danarion smiled grimly. "Only Yarne would have dared to uncover this place. It is your inheritance, Nenan, but to the two-minds it means the terror of their first coming and their long imprisonment here."

"Then they did not come willingly?"

"No, and neither did they really wish to conquer Shol. Their sun-lord and their own need drove them. They belong to Ghaka."

Nenan's shoulders drooped. "It all seems like a jumbled child's tale," he said. "They are there in the city, and I am here in this ruin, and that is all I know."

"I can do no more here." Danarion turned from the blackened lintels, the picked and broken rock. "We must go. I think the birds will be settled on their nests now, Nenan. We can hug the foot of the cliff and then skirt the wall and climb over it in the dark."

Nenan said nothing. Deep in thought, he followed Danarion

out under a late afternoon sky. The sun was westering softly. The road lay quiet and empty. Danarion turned sharply, and soon he and Nenan were walking with the cliff on the left and half a mile of scree, jumbled stones, and sand on their right between them and the road. The land lay peaceful around them, and in the hours it took them to walk to the city they saw no other being.

The sun went from yellow to a fat, shimmering purple and slid over the horizon, and with its going a vagrant breeze cooled them and put new life into their step. Light slanted over the plain, turning the road to a ribbon of blood, striking the wall of the city and painting it also an ominous and sullen red. Danarion watched it grow taller. Only the tops of its towers showed over the wall, and they seemed to be modeled artlessly on the saw-toothed, jagged tips of the mountains themselves. Spires huddled together as if jostling for space. They reminded Danarion, suddenly and vividly, of the crystal icicles of Lix, but they were undressed stone and did not sparkle in the last sunlight. They were full of tall, thin windows, and their walls were spiraled by curling, guardless ramps and walkways that made him, aware as never before of his body, slightly dizzy. Familiarity nagged at him. He had seen just such an arrangement of unblunted peaks before. Then he knew. The city had been built to resemble the cave-hollowed peaks of Ghaka. With the knowledge came cold shock that such a small thing could be so hard to bring to mind. To whose mind? he wondered. As Danarion my recall is perfect. But as Chilka . . . I am allowing myself to meld with Chilka, even as Janthis warned.

Darkness came, and they reached the wall. Danarion laid a hand on it.

"It is far too high to climb," Nenan whispered, "and must surely be guarded."

Danarion searched his mind. "The guards are one-minds trained from birth and are therefore alert at night," he said. "There is only one gate, the one that leads out onto the plain, and it is already shut, but on the ocean side, where the fall is very steep, the wall is not watched. That is where I climbed over when I escaped. The wall seems high there, but inside it the houses are built right against it, and because of the lay of the land the roofs come almost to its top. We can get in there."

It took them an hour to half-circle the wall, and when they

came to the lip of the plain, where the ground suddenly fell away and far below, invisible save for a thin line of crooked white foam, was the ocean, they sat with their backs to the wall and rested. There was no sound from the other side, no bark of dogs or rattle of carts, no torchlit crowds pattering laughing in the streets. Yet Danarion, senses keened to any movement, could hear an undercurrent of whispering, private and constant, a low rise and fall like the soft hiss of water on pebbles far below on the beach. Finally he stood and craned upward. The wall was not well maintained here. The people's fear of the ocean had battled with their love of heights, and the fear had won. The wall was eaten by salt winds and time and though terrifyingly high was not unscalable. "You go first," he told Nenan, "and I will be right behind in case you fall."

Nenan was standing also, peering into the darkness with eyes wide open and a small smile on his face. "The smell of the ocean," he said. "It is sweet and very winsome, and it beckons me like an old friend. I would like to have been a fisherman like my fathers." He turned and began to climb, fitting fingers and feet into the crumbling stone, Danarion following. Strange, he thought. I risked my life to get away from the city only a few days ago, and here I am struggling to reenter it, my hands and feet using the selfsame cracks and niches.

It seemed to him that he had been reaching forever, fingers prying and testing, arm muscles beginning to ache and the sweat to run, breath rasping and coming quick and hard, when he heard Nenan grunt. There was a scrabble of sound, and he found himself lying on top of the wall. For a moment he closed his eyes and let himself loosen, and then he rolled under Nenan's steadying hands onto the roof of a small house.

Suddenly Nenan clapped a hand over his mouth and pointed. They were not alone. The dark silhouette of a man stood out against the stars. He was perched loosely and easily on the slates with feet apart and arms hanging at his sides, and the wind stirred in his long hair. Nenan's grip trembled, and Danarion put his own fingers over Nenan's cold ones. He understood the fear. It was not of discovery but of something intangible, and though the eye saw a man, a shape without detail in the starry darkness, yet the mind heard a frantic flurry of wings against a cage. "I don't think he can hear or see us," Danarion said. "Take heart, Nenan. We will ignore him."

He led Nenan to the eaves and sprang lightly into the garden. Nenan followed, then turned and looked up. The man still had not moved. "You should pity them, not fear them," Danarion said aloud, but that part of him which was Chilka thought of a swift knife sliding through the unresisting flesh. "We must press on." Chilka knew the way. He slipped quickly along the streets with Nenan huddled close to him.

Ishban at night was a city of walking dead. They thronged the streets with sightless eyes. They stood on roofs, in the spreading trees, and high on the tight-twisting spires of the towers, and the sound of their despair was a moaning of loss and misery that fanned Nenan's fear into panic. "It is a city of birds!" he whispered hoarsely to Chilka, hardly able to walk for the weakness in his legs. Chilka nodded, his own eyes, Danarion's shocked mind on the frilled iron gates, the shop fronts, the fretted iron fences. Everywhere there were wings where once there had been bells, and Danarion realized that it was the absence of Shaban's constant trilling that had been nagging at him ever since they had scaled the wall.

Often they walked alone through star-silvered, deserted streets whose unlit buildings stood like hollow mounds in a graveyard, but just as often they would turn a corner to find themselves in the middle of a quiet, slow-weaving throng. Yet they were ignored.

They stopped once. There was a woman standing alone before her gate, face lifted to the dark sky, and Danarion took her hand and stroked her cheek, murmuring in some language that Nenan did not understand. But though the woman strove to answer, her lips working, her eyes remained opaque, and no words came. Danarion kissed the hand and let it fall, and it was then that Nenan's fear left him.

Much later they came to a halt before a wall within the city, gated in copper doors upon which two vast wings reared. Chilka drew Nenan back into shadow. "This gate is guarded by one-minds," he whispered. "Beyond it is the House. To get in we must overpower the men but not kill them, for they are our kin. Can you do this?" Nenan nodded. Together they approached, and Chilka unhooked the massive padded striker that hung on the wall and struck the gate. The boom reverberated through the street and the courtyard beyond, then faded. They waited.

Presently one of the doors inched open, slowly and cautiously, and Chilka did not wait to be scrutinized. He put his foot to it and leaped inside, taking the man with him. His hands found the throat, and he slammed the body onto the ground. Only when he stood did he remember who he was and that he could have quieted the guard with one soft word. Aghast, Danarion looked at Chilka's flexing fingers and then to the man groaning and half-conscious at his feet.

Nenan came swiftly, rubbing his shoulder. "I got kicked," he said ruefully, yet there was a light in his eye. "The other guard is sleeping by the wall. What will happen when they recover, Chilka? Perhaps we should kill them."

Danarion, still confused, shook his head. "No! It will not matter by then. I only wanted to get inside. By the time the alarm is given and they see that no attack is coming, I will be no threat to them."

"What of me?" Nenan looked around him uneasily. The courtyard was full of shadows, and the House reared up sheer and jagged from the ground to end in peaks that seemed to climax among the stars. "How long will you stay here? Is it best that I go home?"

Danarion hesitated. "I don't know, Nenan. I may find all my answers here or I may not. It could take a long time. I only know that I must resume my work as slave to Yarne. I wish that you would stay with me. Yarne will give you a bed with me and will not question my motives. You will understand when you see him. He is . . . strange."

"If I can be of any use to you, I will stay," Nenan said simply. "Whatever you are, and I do not entirely believe your stories, I want to be with you, because six years is a long time."

Danarion impulsively stepped forward and embraced him. "My son," he said, eyes closed. "Whatever else you believe or choose to disbelieve, you are still my son. Now follow me." He led the way across the courtyard and around to the side of the House. Here there was a smaller door without guard or lock. Chilka pushed it open and drew Nenan into a dark passage lined with similar doors, but all these were closed and hung with three and four great locks. "The slaves live here," he said in a low voice. "Every night they must be locked in, or they could simply walk away. Not enough one-minds are trainable as guards. This is my cell. I see they have not yet given it to another." He pushed open the door, which had been standing ajar, and Nenan followed him in. Chilka closed it behind them. "You may sleep on the bed," he said. "I will take the floor. I do not tire as you do."

Nenan looked about. There was no window. The only light came from under the door, and it showed him only a bed and a stool. He went to the bed, conscious all at once of great weariness, and lay down, pulling the one blanket over himself. "I hope Mother is not fretting," he said drowsily, and Danarion felt an immediate twinge of worry and regret for Lallin. "No, she is not fretting," he said, and the young man fell instantly asleep.

Danarion stretched out on the floor. For a while he tried to think of Ghakazian and Sholia and the missing Gate, to speculate on who the mysterious Lady of this House might be, but Chilka was bone-weary, and Chilka's memories of this place were too fresh and powerful for him to stand away from them. He found his mind drifting on a sea of half-formed thoughts and the nebulous edges of dreams. The road was empty because of the funeral, he thought lazily. Of course. Lallin, my love, I miss you so much. He slept.

# 23

He did not wake until his door flew open, when he sat up with a jerk, his body a mass of odd aches and strains from his climb. Nenan was swinging his legs onto the floor.

"Chilka!" said a man with a red tunic emblazoned with the yellow and black suns. His face had gone livid with shock. "You're dead. They shot you while you ran. I know. The captain told me he shot you dead. What magic is this?"

Chilka grinned at him. "Not dead enough, Sigran. The captain is a bad shot on horseback. I crawled away and licked my wounds and decided to come back and stick my head once more into the two-headed beasts' lair. The mountains are harsh masters. I'm tired of running."

Sigran backed away as Chilka rose and stretched. "Keep away from me! This time we'll make sure! Three escapes means execution, and I will bury you with my own hands. You were dead!"

Chilka yawned. "This is Nenan, my son," he said. "Nenan dragged me home, and when I decided to come back, he came too. Where is Yarne?"

The man was too shocked to ponder the glib story. At the mention of Yarne's name he slumped. "You're right," he snarled. "Yarne will never let you be shot. He's with his precious relics."

"Good. Nenan, stay here until I send for you. Sigran, get the boy some food, and see he is not molested."

"Who are you to give orders to me, one-mind?" the man blustered, but awe was still in him, and he made no move to stop Chilka as he pushed past him and into the passage.

The House was full of bustling life. Chatter and laughter, the sound of many feet coming and going, sunlight pooling bright through the slit windows, the smell of cooking—it was as if, Danarion thought, two Houses existed in two different dimensions on the same spot, and there was no point of contact between them.

He went out into the sunny courtyard, crossed to the big doors which stood open, and entered the hall. Here voices echoed, and feet slapped on the mighty stone stair that lifted dizzily to be lost in the height of the roof. A fire was burning, and though the day was young, petitioners and administrators already jostled around it, gossiping, waiting to see the three judges who ruled Ishban. Chilka named them as he began to mount the stair. Melfidor. Veltim. Fitrec. Ancient and honorable Sholan names, to be carried by foreign scum.

He circled higher, and the babbling crowd in the hall shrank to small, gaily capped heads nodding against one another. The smoke from the fire thinned to a gray haze up here and made him cough. He passed one small door set into the curved wall on his left and then another, his shoulder grazing the stone as he hugged the wall, for though the stair was as wide as his full height, there was no rail on the outer side. At the third door he stopped and knocked and pushed it open.

As he entered, the smoke and the booming echo of voices from below vanished. He shut the door quietly, and the cessation of noise was like a blanket flung over him as he advanced into the room. The silence was more than an absence of sound. It was a climate of deep thought, a cup full of the still, purposeful peace of mental industry. Chilka remembered this and found it natural, but Danarion sensed another quiet here, the passionless enigmas of ancient mysteries, the invisible eddies of the past. Two tall windows looked out upon the winding streets of the city, now full of people hurrying to and fro about the day's business. Flags ripped and fluttered in the wind, carts piled with merchandise rattled over stone, shopkeepers leaned against the lintels of their establishments and gossiped, and almost out of sight a faint white glitter told of the ocean. The walls of the room were lined with waist-high cases, some open, all bathed in sunlight, and light lay also on the smooth stone floor, shafting across the wooden desk piled with paper at which a young man sat, facing the thin windows.

He was slim, with a small waist and delicate shoulders sloping evenly under his white tunic. The skin of his sun-touched face and the graceful hands poised before him was exquisitely fine-grained and so transparent that it had a faint bluish tinge. He turned his head abruptly at the closing of the door, his white-gold hair waving loosely around a smooth neck. His eyes were the pale, brilliant blue of sapphires. He embodies all that I remember of the Shol that once was, Danarion thought in surprise. He is pure Sholan, all white, blue, and gold.

Yarne showed no surprise. "So you came back," he said, rising, a mild reproach in his light voice. "And looking older and more tired than when you ran away. I suppose they will want to shoot you now. This is your third attempt, you know. But I won't let them. I missed you. Are you ready to go to work this morning? You had better wash your hands, and bring me fresh ink." When he had finished speaking, he stood perfectly still, one long-fingered hand flat on the desk, a smile on the delicate mouth. The only movement lay in his throat, where the slow, regular flutter of his heartbeat showed against the collar of his tunic. It was as though some contact had been made deep inside him, and he had spoken, and then the contact had been broken, leaving him lifeless and stiff until he might be required to speak or move again. His head was on one side. The smile did not slip.

"I have missed you, too," Chilka said. "I reached the mountains, Yarne, but I am no longer as willing to endure their hardships as I once was, so I came back."

Yarne nodded, and the silken hair fell over his shoulders. "I have heard that you encountered more than hardship in the mountains," he said. "I heard that they had killed you. By sunset the whole city will be talking of the one-mind who came back from the dead. Did you?"

Danarion looked at him in amazement. He might have been asking cheerfully how well his slave had slept. "Yes," he found himself answering. "I did, in a way."

"Only in a way? But I understand. I myself am born again every morning. I think of death a great deal, I suppose because my sister and I are immortal and never die. It is like a game to me, imagining what it must be like. The two-minds never die either, but that is different, not true immortality, because they put on the bodies of their sons or daughters. Like giant birds of prey, aren't they, Chilka? But you have the same body, a bit more battered than before. Do the one-minds somehow refresh their essences? Is that what you mean?"

"You are a one-mind yourself," Chilka retorted. "You were born in the mountains."

"So they say." Yarne sat down. "But it is not true. I have no memories of the mountains. I think we will work now."

"One thing before we do." Chilka came to the desk and faced again that odd, sudden suspension of vitality in Yarne. "I have brought my son, Nenan, with me. Without your protection he will be sold to someone in the House. Will you take him?"

"How extraordinary!" Yarne said, but again without surprise. "If you one-minds begin to bring your families into voluntary slavery, we shall have an embarrassing situation in Ishban. If I don't take him, he will doubtless be given to Maltor, who burned his father yesterday and, as master of his house, now needs a slave. All right, Chilka. He needn't do anything, but I will let it be known that he is under my cloak. They grumble at me already for treating you more like a brother than a witless slave." He grasped Chilka's arm, and his touch was cold, but his eyes were full of a timid affection. "They laughed at me each time you ran away," he said. "They do not dare to do it to my face, but I know. I felt betrayed, yet I do not hate you. I cannot tell you how glad I am that you have come home."

Chilka recoiled in mingled love and shame, like a man driven to treason against his nation yet seeing clearly the necessity of betrayal, and it was Danarion who bent and kissed the transparent knuckles that lay like white flowers against the grime and roughness of his shirt. He felt a warmth for this youth, who reminded him of the Traders who once used to move between the worlds. Like them he seemed apart from both good and evil, simple and guileless. "I would not willingly cause you grief, my old friend," he said. "Thank you on behalf of my son. Now I will wash my hands and bring you ink."

Yarne smiled. Chilka went to a door behind the desk which let onto an anteroom containing a washbasin, jug, and walls lined with cupboards. He washed quickly, took down two small pots, mixed powder, added water, and carried extra pens with him when he went back to Yarne.

"Now bring me the book," Yarne said. "Set it on the pedestal."

Chilka went to one of the cases and, lifting the lid, took the book carefully in his hands. His memory of this room, this work, this book had told Danarion nothing unusual. To Chilka the book was simply his master's passion. But Danarion, as he looked down on its thick red cover spidered in gold lettering, felt those memories grow brittle and sift away like pieces of scattered autumn leaves, and for a moment he forgot that he was in Chilka's body. He saw his own golden hands cradling the book, bathing it in light that brought the faded lettering to a brief semblance of life. Again, as when standing in the ruins of the Hall of Waiting, he felt unbearably old. I am more ancient than the stone of this House, he thought, older than the mountains from which it was wrenched. This book, as yet unstained by Sholia's pen, was on Shol before the Worldmaker formed the ocean and set the mountains in their places. The weight of such an unimaginable accumulation of time was suffocating him, pressing above and around him. I am imprisoned in my own immortality while the whole universe has shuddered into other shapes around me, leaving me stranded here in this strange room, on this strange planet that I once dreamed was different. I dreamed I was a sun-lord, one among a thousand bright immortals, that there was war in the heavens, a million million years of slow attrition. Did I dream? There is only this book to link me with my dreams. I am a slave, but to what? To whom?

*The Annals of Shol,* he read and turned back the cover. *Before the beginning was the Lawmaker,* he read in Sholia's flowing, sure hand, *and the Lawmaker made the Worldmaker and commanded him to make according to his nature. And the Worldmaker made the worlds . . .* The shock receded, leaving him shivering. He turned the page hurriedly, clumsily, and it tore with a tiny rasping sound. No spells of protection could last through the eons since her last entry. Yarne gave a cry. "Chilka, what is the matter with you? It is priceless, without value! For Sholia's sake, put it down!" Again the old oath, meaningless now, as much an anachronism as Danarion felt himself to be. Unsteadily he walked to the reading pedestal and set the book upon it. "I have done nothing since you left," Yarne grumbled quietly. "The slaves work in the strange room in the mountain, but what they uncover simply adds to the mystery." He had risen and glided to the pedestal, and Chilka knew what he had to do.

He walked to the desk and lowered himself behind it, setting out clean paper, dipping a pen into the ink. "So little progress, though I think about it night and day," Yarne was whispering half to himself as he gingerly turned the pages. "Legends for the folk historians, myths and stories for the one-minds, death for the two-minds who dare even to begin to believe. And for me a tangle of all three, with no link to the Shol of today, none at all. What do we labor over, Chilka? A clever riddle to hide a truth so terrible that the words could not be set down uncovered? A cipher?" He had found his place. "Are you ready? I forgot to tell you that the diggers in the sand to the east have unearthed a jar, and in it a love poem, or a song. I have not yet decided which it is. I will show it to you later, and you can set my thoughts about it on a separate sheet." His glittering eyes found the window for a moment. "A hundred years of digging," he said sadly, "and what do we have? Love poems. A few stories that seem ridiculous, like the one about the four men sitting under a tree like no tree on Shol and touching fingers for a day. No sagas of war, no accounts of strife, yet war there must have been, and *something* fell from the heavens to bury Shaban. If Shaban ever existed." He sighed and cleared his throat. "Begin."

Danarion began to write with a trembling hand as Yarne read from the book and interspersed his reading with his own observations. " 'Sholia went through the Gate to Danar. Janthis refused her pleas for help. In the room the Book of What Will Be was guarded by Chilorn, yet Sholia was tempted and almost fell . . .' At least we know that by Danar the writer must mean the constellation Danic, though what the symbolism of the Gate is we can as yet only guess. Perhaps it was a matter of religion. If the ancients worshiped the stars of Danic as a god and had built a temple to it with a sacred Gate, the problem is partially solved, and perhaps the vast hall the new digging has uncovered in the mountain may be such a temple." Danarion wrote the words. A sickness was on him, and if Yarne had asked him a question, he would not have been able to reply.

At noon a bell rang, very clear and sweet in the room, and Yarne closed the book and stretched. "My Lady calls me," he said. "Put the book away, Chilka, and go and eat. Bring your son to me later. Take care to cover the ink." He went out, and Danarion went to the book, placed it back in the case, and then walked slowly along the other cases.

Yarne's gleanings were small. Scraps of brocaded cloth, bells corroded and thickened with age, the flue of a fountain made in the likeness of a corion of Danar, some timber from a ship, now crystallized but still with the haeli wood's faint glow of blue, and most incongruous of all, a sea-rotted roof tile from Shaban. Fuel for an obsession, Danarion thought, fuzzy with emotional exhaustion. Why is Yarne so obsessed? Why do I sense some lack in him, something unfocused? And why is he, so wealthy and favored, unable to write? Chilka had no answers. Danarion's essence ached with pain. He covered the ink pots and went out into the echo of ceaseless babble and the miasma of smoke which columned from the hall below to the unseen ceiling.

Nenan's familiar voice happily recounting his adventures of the morning served to spread balm over Danarion's hurts. Together they crossed the courtyard and entered the blackened dining room where the slaves ate under the eye of several guards, and Nenan greeted first one and then another slave with an easy grace that told Chilka how the young man had spent his time. "It is not altogether a place of nightmare," Nenan said to him between mouthfuls of soup. "It seems to me that the slaves are not ill-used and have much freedom, limited of course. I have seen no two-minds yet, but how beautiful and populous the city looks through the cracks in the gate!"

"And how beckoning!" Chilka grinned. "The girls are fair, Nenan, and the fruit ripe. The wine is sweet, and the sun is hot. But wait until night comes, when you and I are locked in our cell, not loose in the streets as we were last night, and you cannot run away."

That afternoon Chilka took Nenan to meet Yarne. Yarne seemed content to smile and nod at him and ask him what he wished to do, setting him a few small tasks around his own quarters and sending him away. Chilka spent the remaining hours of daylight at the desk while Yarne translated the ancient language of the book and added his musings, later preparing the young man's food for him and serving it on the desk. Yarne slept next door to the relic room, where he had a bed, a chest for his clothes, and a table, all expensively appointed, yet he did no more than sleep there. He lived among the relics when he was not riding to one of his diggings.

At sunset the guards came for Chilka, and he surrendered himself to them with a polite word of good-night to his master. As he was marched down the stair he heard the bell in the relic room tinkle once and knew that the Lady had summoned her brother again.

Night fell. Chilka lit a candle, and by its light he and Nenan sat on the floor talking. Ishban was suddenly silent.

"I wish the cell had a window," Nenan complained, and Chilka shook his head.

"I think when you have spent many nights here, you will be glad you cannot see out, even into the courtyard. At first it is not bad, but after a while the sickness of Ishban begins to prey on you. Sometimes it follows you into your dreams. And the two-minds are not always as harmless as they seemed to us last night. Once, just before I was taken for the first time, the cells were unlocked in the middle of the night. The slaves were dragged to the top of the House, up that winding parapet we saw, and dropped one by one into the courtyard. They say the two-minds did not speak. They simply disposed of all their slaves."

Nenan shuddered. "Surely the guards could have stopped them!"

"The guards were taken also. Listen, Nenan. It has begun."

They sat for a while in silence while beyond the wall thin wails broke on the air and from above in the House the sounds of despair filtered down to them.

In the cell next to theirs a man began to melody. He had a strong, lusty voice, full of life and sunlight, and the tune was a rollicking drinking song that drowned out the sighings and shufflings above. But soon he had exhausted his medley, and once more the madness seeped through their cell's walls. Nenan played with the candle, picking off melted wax and passing his finger through the flame, and he was very pale.

"What did you think of Yarne?" Chilka asked to take his mind off the insanity around them, and Nenan managed a smile.

"He is very beautiful, but not womanish, although I have never seen a woman as lovely as he. Is he as gentle as he seems?"

"I don't think it is gentleness. Yarne simply does not think like anyone else I know."

"What does he do at night?"

Chilka's gaze focused slowly on the yellow beam of the candle. "He spends most of the dark hours with the Lady. His sister."

In the morning the sun shone, the cells were unlocked, and the life of the House resumed its cheerful, chaotic way. After they had eaten, Chilka took Nenan and a guard and went into the city to the nearest market, where the produce from the surrounding countryside was brought in fresh at daybreak. He chose food for Yarne carefully, and Nenan was allowed to wander in sight of the guard. He looked into the dark entrances of shops, teased smiles from the girls, and gaped like the country boy he was at the crowds pushing around him while the farmers stood behind their mounds of vegetables and their hanging rabbits and barked their invitations to buy.

His purchases made, Chilka was lingering among the stalls when he heard someone say, "Isn't that him?" Heads turned in uncomprehending curiosity. "That's the one-mind!" someone else shouted, and before long they were jostling around Chilka, trying to touch him, pulling his hair, all talking at once.

"He came back from the dead!"

"He took an arrow that opened his heart, my husband told me."

"The Lady was there disguised as a soldier, and she breathed life into him again . . ."

"The Lady has made him a two-mind . . ."

"No, he's a god in disguise. He's come to Shol to learn wisdom from her."

The guard had jumped to protect Chilka, and Nenan was elbowing his way through the excited people.

"Is it true? How did you do it? Have you seen the Lady? What does she look like?"

Chilka tried to prevent his basket from being upset and looked around with a momentary bewilderment.

Above the noise of the crowd came a louder, more insistent cry. "Save us!" The shouting ceased. Quiet pooled out, and the people suddenly became still. Then someone else took it up, and the square became full of chanting. "Save us! Save us! Save us!" The sound had an undercurrent of both desperation and an ominous threat. Chilka, catching Nenan's eye at last, saw that the young man's reserve had dropped around him again. His glance was frightened and respectful, the regard of a stranger. Chilka reached out and grasped his arm.

"Begin to walk slowly toward the House," the guard said, himself white under the bluster. "Whatever you do, don't run." Nenan shouldered his way to lead. Chilka followed him, careful to look only at his straight back, and the guard brought up the rear. Slowly they left the market, but the crowd surged after them, still chanting. Bystanders joined it, not knowing what was happening but happy to shout and wave also, and it was a flood of humanity that washed up against the gate and broke when the three men slipped through.

The guard mopped his brow. "God indeed!" he snapped. "I don't know how these rumors get started. Not from the captain, but from his soldiers, I suppose. Go about your business, Chilka. They'll soon get tired of wasting time, and besides, when night comes, they'll go home quickly enough."

Chilka and Nenan walked unsteadily to the kitchens. "I had almost forgotten," Nenan said in a low voice. "I wanted to forget!"

Chilka stopped and turned to him. "I want you to forget also, Nenan," he replied, deeply troubled. "Sometimes I myself forget, and it is good to be Chilka alone. Let us both forget, until the time comes when I must act."

Nenan smiled tremulously, but Danarion sensed the distance in him, the drawing away, and was hurt beyond measure.

The crowd scattered just before sunset, but that night it seemed to Chilka that the sounds of loss and anguish were louder than before in the shadows beyond the sheltering gate, and he fancied that he heard his name called in the House several times. Nenan lay on the bed and answered his attempts at conversation with noncommittal grunts. Presently he slept, but his sleep was troubled, and Chilka sat and watched him twitch and moan.

"Are you really a god?" Yarne asked him the next morning before they began their work, and Chilka laughed.

"No, master. I am Chilka, your slave."

"Well, why do the people stand outside the gate and shout for you? The captain went out and told them how you were only wounded."

"They do not believe it. They have a need to believe something else."

"What?"

"That I have come to save them from themselves."

Yarne did not reply. Again that curious stillness fell on him, the seeming absence of all the tiny movements that show life in even the most motionless of men. In his throat the heartbeat throbbed, unchanging and unvarying in its ponderous rhythm. When he did speak again, it was to begin the dictation.

# 24

For many days crowds continued to gather at the gate. Soldiers tried to drive them away, but they always came back. The three judges, Melfidor, Veltim, and Fitrec, who processed across the courtyard in their stiff brocaded robes of gold and blue with their guards before and their slaves behind, spoke to them scornfully, but it made little difference. At night it often seemed to Chilka that the whole of Ishban was congregated just outside the frail protection of his cell, moaning and wailing for him in reproach and longing. Time finally did what soldier and ruler could not. Chilka took care to stay in the House unseen by them, and eventually they forgot why they had come, lost interest, and went home. Only a handful stubbornly came every day, convinced that behind a slave's lined face there was a thing of exotic power or an example of miracle, but Chilka was able to slip past them with Nenan unremarked.

As day flowed into day Danarion felt himself tied ever more strongly to the man that had been, his essence nestling closer into Chilka's warm cells. With an increasing effort he tried to remember his purpose in Ishban. He suspected that the mysterious Lady would hold the answer to the whereabouts of the Gate if only he could reach her. He prowled the House in the evenings before his guard came for him, climbing the stair to the door without handles or lock behind which she lived, following little-used passages that might reveal another entrance to her chamber but which always ended in dusty storerooms or forgotten balconies. Sometimes he stood outside the House, craning upward to the slitted windows of her room, overcome with frustration at the sheerness of the rock wall. He read Shol's Annals in the hours when Yarne was with his sister, hoping that Sholia's words might provide a clue. He listened to the gossip of the streets and the often incoherent babbling of the two-minds in the night but heard nothing of consequence. Gradually his sense of urgency began to fade, until a moment came when he stood facing the Lady's door and wondered why he was there. He knew he wanted to see her, that somehow she was connected to the thing that had happened to him by the lake, but Chilka whispered in his mind, You were so badly wounded. Death entered you for a second, bringing strange visions, changing you. There is a scar on your mind to match the visible weal on your body. This insanity will heal, this dream of sun-lords and worlds in space, this spurious other self who has such power will slowly weaken as the memory of death recedes. Lallin was right when she told you you had gone mad. His hand slid under his shirt, fingering the scar, and the feel of it was reassuring. Fate was kind to me, he thought as he turned back down the stair. It gave me back my life.

Summer faded into autumn, a brief season of rain and strong winds that collapsed into light snow and watery skies. Something told Chilka that Shol was a stranger to such seasonal definition, that snow was a new thing, that once the seasons could only be measured by a changing color on the trees and in the ocean and by the smell of the air, but he did not follow the thought.

He missed Lallin more as time went by, thinking of her sitting alone in the cottage, her shawl around her shoulders, her face turned placidly to the firelight, and sometimes he thought of her naked, that same firelight playing on her small, compact limbs and soft breasts, but those thoughts were old, dark memories, broken by the thing that had happened to him in the summer, by the lake.

Only at work with Yarne in the muffled quiet of the relic room did he reflect. Yarne puzzled him in a way he could not remember being puzzled before. The routine of his life had not dulled that nagging doubt. Yarne was a man distressed as much by a slave's empty belly as by the occasional execution in the city. He was easy to love, warm in his concern for Chilka and Nenan, uncomplicated in his devotion to the task he had been allowed to take on himself by the Lady. His beauty made one hold one's breath, and every morning Chilka was struck anew by the smooth transparency of the skin, the glittering blue eyes, the grace of hand, voice, and walk, the shining paleness of the matchless hair.

Yet under all this was a mystery, a sea of things unknown. Sometimes Yarne seemed like an object caused to move and speak, smile and laugh, and between these things to be shut off, like the closing and opening of a gate. He seemed to feel neither heat nor cold, and when the snow fell and Chilka shivered at the desk, he would be garbed in a thin, sleeveless white tunic, and his feet on the stone would be bare. Yet when he touched his slave in affection or gentle remonstrance, his long fingers were always cold. He was a man, Chilka reflected, without emotions, save the slight ripples of convention. Chilka knew that he must know Yarne, that it was important to pierce to the heart that caused the steady flicker in the white throat, but it often occurred to him that perhaps within Yarne there was nothing.

He worked and watched and was unaware that he also waited. He cooked and served, washed Yarne's clothes and made his bed, mixed his inks and took his notes. Twice a day the tiny bell would send out its polite summons, and Yarne would tell him to tidy the room, leaving to climb the stair to its summit, where, under the ragged roof of the House, the Lady lived.

No one ever saw her, but she was everywhere. Nothing was done without reference to her. She dominated every conversation in the city and in the cells of the slaves. She was the subject of worship, conjecture, oath-making, and fear. Sometimes Chilka would go to the door to watch his master run lightly up the stair, and to peer into the shadows that always seemed to lie inside the great summit spires of the House, but though he often saw the vast double doors open to admit Yarne, he caught no glimpse of the hand that swung them inward.

Ishban by day was endlessly fascinating to Nenan. He and Chilka explored it from wall to gate and back again, the only slaves within the House to be given that privilege. But a restlessness had begun in Nenan, growing with his increasing fear of Ishban's haunted nights, and one evening in their cell he asked Chilka diffidently, "Father, isn't it time we went back to the mountains? You can run away anytime you choose, you know you can. Have you done what you came back for?"

Why did I come back? Chilka wondered. Wings, bells, and a Gate. I promised Yarne that I would not hurt him again. But is it worth leaving Lallin to wait uncomprehendingly for me and allowing my son to grow to manhood in Ishban? What am I waiting for? He shrugged and managed a wry smile. "I do not think so," he said. "I'm not sure."

Nenan's face mirrored frustration, anger. "Perhaps it is a cunning lie," he whispered. "Perhaps they have put a spell on you, these past six years, so that no matter how you try, you can never tear Ishban out of your essence. Can the two-minds drug the essences of their slaves with words? Are fear and hatred themselves drugs? I have come to feel both. You were right. Ishban is a mirage, a vision just out of reach of my understanding. I am beginning to doubt my own memories."

"So am I." Chilka tried to smile. "I know I have been on Shol all my life. I know I have a wife in the mountains who still waits for me with a damning patience. But sometimes I am equally sure that I only came to Shol last summer and I have an overlord on Danar who paces by my empty body and peers into his mirror at a Gate that is no longer there." He sighed and lay on the bed. "Perhaps I am mad, but there is something within me that compels me to see my madness through to its end. I must wait, Nenan."

Nenan scowled. "You showed me visions on the mountain, and then I believed. But visions fade with time, and now I only want to go home." He sat on the floor, prepared to argue, but saw that his father had fallen asleep.

In the morning Yarne sent for Chilka. He climbed the stairs that seemed to hang suspended over the terrifying void of the hollow House and knocked on the little door, hearing Yarne's permission to enter as he swung it open. He had not slept well. He had dreamed vividly and frighteningly of nothingness, of the space between the stars, black and awesomely empty, and his dream came back to him as he advanced into the room. No sunlight fell through the straight, thin windows. The sky was sullen and heavy with unshed snow. Yarne stood by the window, lit palely, and Chilka fancied that the wanness of the day had somehow entered the blue-tinged skin and dulled the sparkling eyes.

"I have ordered our notes," Yarne said. "Today we will begin a discussion on the scrap of poem that was found in the jar. I am tired of the book. I don't want to see it today."

Chilka was shocked. The book was Yarne's family, his lover, his friend. "Very well," he said and moved to the desk, uncovering the ink and picking up a pen. Clean paper lay before him. He lifted the mantle of the lamp and lit it and then sat waiting. The moments ticked by. Yarne still gazed abstractedly out the window, and presently a few flakes of snow drifted past his set face, gray and silent. Chilka noticed that he wore a white cloak, and his feet were booted. Then Yarne spoke, still without turning his head.

"I had a dream last night," he said. "I have never dreamed before. I dreamed that I was dead, that I was not immortal, that I had died a thousand times, over and over. My life was a thousand lives, all the same, and at the end, a thousand deaths, all the same. I dreamed a great nothingness, out among the stars. I dreamed of you." Then he turned, and Chilka saw that he was shivering under the thick warmth of the cloak. "I dreamed of you," he repeated, leaning wearily against the window frame, his face no longer in shadow but yellow in the lamp's glow. "You were the book, and the book was you, out there where there is no life, only black nothingness. Tell me, Chilka, what is it like to die?"

The snow was falling faster, swirling with a faint hiss against the window. Chilka felt his mouth go dry. "I did not die, Yarne. I have told you. I was only deeply wounded."

Yarne sighed. "You are the only one who believes so," he said, his words slow and inexact. "When I woke, I was oppressed by the nothingness of my dream. I tried to fill it with memories, but I do not remember a father or mother, a childhood in the mountains, as some say I had, or a house other than this House. There are only my sister and I, forever. I am a nothingness, Chilka. I am a mystery even to myself."

There was a lonely vulnerability about the youth that tugged at Chilka's heart. "Did you tell your sister the dream?"

Yarne smiled wanly. "I did. She said nothing for a long time. She just looked at me. And then she asked me about you." Chilka's heartbeat quickened. He laid down the pen but kept silent. "She spoke sharply to me. I had to tell her all I have learned of you since you first stood before me in your chains."

"It was only a dream, Yarne," Chilka said gently. "In sleep the mind wanders, that is all, and today it is cold and gray. Tomorrow the sun will shine on the snow, and you will have forgotten this thing."

But Yarne was looking at him through narrowed eyes. "I have already forgotten everything," he replied hoarsely. "I have no memories, Chilka. Only the book and my sister thread my life together.

Today, for the first time, I wish the rumors that I was a one-mind stolen from the mountains to be my Lady's kin were true. I wish you were my father and Nenan my brother."

"But you have a sister who is the most powerful woman in the world," Chilka reminded him, his heart still tripping and racing in his chest. "You are loved, Yarne."

Yarne turned away so that his face was hidden. "Though she and I go on forever," he said forlornly, "I do not think she loves me."

Something strong and familiar began to stir in Chilka. "Tell me what she is like."

The stillness of death fell on Yarne. Chilka waited for the odd moment to pass. When it did, Yarne put one curved finger against the pane and followed the erratic path of a stray snowflake. Suddenly Danarion, half-blind and somnolent behind the wall of Chilka's mind, which had been strengthening so rapidly over the months, saw that the finger's passage left no trail of warmth to melt the frost on the pane. Who are you? he shouted silently, struggling to push aside Chilka's thoughts. Chilka resisted stubbornly, fighting to hold to the reality of a wound, a healing that had left him dislocated in mind, while Danarion, with all his powers, strove to give substance to the truth. No, Chilka, he said emphatically within himself. You are dead. Nothing is left but memories that have no life of their own. Your mind is fostering a delusion of vitality you no longer have. You walk without limbs on the Mountain of Mourning. All your emotions, all your thoughts come from the past. You cannot make them new anymore.

"What she is like." Yarne repeated Chilka's words tonelessly and then took his finger away from the pane. "She is beautiful. She touches me, and I am young again. She . . ." He shrugged helplessly. "She is."

She is. Danarion cut savagely at Chilka's last despairing, self-delusions. She is who, she is what? She is the key. He rose and went to Yarne, taking the head between his hands, forcing the eyes to meet his own. As always, the flesh was cold and dead to the touch. "Yarne, I want to see her. Take me to her." Looking into those pale blue eyes was like peering into space itself, like standing on the lip of the universe before launching himself through a Gate.

Yarne withdrew himself from Chilka's grasp, and with a consciousness of deepening mystery Danarion realized that he could not influence Yarne by an imposition of the will.

"No, I cannot, unless she wants to see you," Yarne said. "Very
few mortals have ever seen her face. If you have a petition, take it
to the judges or tell me. I thought we were friends, Chilka."

"I have told you that we are." Danarion had moved away from
the white-clad figure. "But you are unhappy. The Lady spoke sharply
to you when you wanted comfort. Why did she do that?" He had
gentled his tone, and Yarne managed a brief smile.

"I suppose that I made her angry with my dream."

"Do you think that something in the dream made her afraid?"

Yarne stared at him, uncomprehending. "Nothing can make
her afraid. You do not understand about her. She is like me. She
feels nothing beyond the small movements of convention. But last
night . . ." He shuddered and plucked his cloak more tightly around
him. "Last night I knew fear. It was my fear that made her angry."

And insecure? Danarion wondered silently. He closed his eyes
in defeat. There were riddles within riddles here. "Perhaps if you
and I went to her together . . ."

"Why?" Yarne swung from the window, and his boots clicked
on the stone floor as he gestured toward the desk and began to pace,
one hand raised. "We will work now. I should not have told you of
my dream. It was a foolish thing to do. Sit and write my words."

Danarion did as he was told, and while Chilka moved the pen
over the pristine paper he retreated behind the Sholan and began to
consider ways of reaching the Lady who dwelt like the Lawmaker
himself, alone and unapproachable.

The morning wore on. Several times Yarne ceased his musings
and came to the desk, asking to have read back to him what had
been written. Each time Danarion watched him closely, the pulse
in his throat, the empty eyes, the breath of cold as he leaned toward
him.

Noon came, and Danarion's preoccupied glance strayed to the
small silver knife used for slicing paper which was lying under the
lamp's steady flame. He picked it up and made a show of drawing
a sheaf toward him. Yarne paused and came to the desk. "Seeing
you have come to the end of the page, we can stop here," he said.

"My sister will be sending for me soon." He put out a hand, and Danarion swiftly changed his grip on the knife and drew it savagely across the unlined palm. He sprang up, ready words of excuse and apology on his lips, but they died unspoken. Yarne did not so much as flinch. He looked at his palm, flexed the fingers, and smiled. "You will have to sharpen it again if you want it to cut paper," he said calmly. Danarion stared back at him. The wound was ugly, a bone-deep gash from wrist to forefinger, but it did not bleed. The lips were dry where they had parted, and the flesh within was purple. Yarne drew the fingers of his other hand across it, and before Danarion's startled gaze it closed, leaving no scar. "Don't look so terrified, Chilka," Yarne said affectionately. "It was my fault for getting between knife and paper. No harm is done."

Far down in Chilka's body Danarion felt his fire dim. Small things impressed themselves vividly upon his consciousness: the sound of the snow hissing against the window, the lamplight pooling like a golden net on Yarne's long hair, the rustle of paper under Chilka's shaking hand. Yarne was not mortal, for there was no blood in his delicate blue veins. He was not immortal, for he had not prevented the knife from piercing his skin, nor did he have the golden blood of the sun-people. The beat of his throat, so strong, so indicative of the warm, dark runnels of life Danarion knew so intimately in Chilka's own body, was a sham, a deception. For Danarion knew what Yarne was. He was a dead man, a corpse like those rotting on the Mountain of Mourning, and whatever inhabited him was no longer human. "I dreamed that I was dead," he had said, "that I had died a thousand times, over and over . . ." Danarion's eyes dropped to the knife. It was clean and dry. He released it, and it fell against the lamp with a tinkle. Yarne continued to stand motionless, the sympathetic smile still fixed on his exquisitely formed mouth, and the silence in the room deepened as Danarion searched his own vast knowledge with a reckless speed that bordered on panic. What are you?

Then from some invisible shadow the bell chimed, sweet and loud. Yarne reached out and laid a hand on Chilka's. "Go and eat with your son," he said. "I must go also. Don't forget to cover the ink. I will see you in two hours." He went out, the cloak brushing the floor with a soft swish, the boots clicking. Danarion looked at the knife again, and it seemed to grin up at him with insolence. Unsteadily he walked to the window and, opening it, leaned out, letting the tart, cold air rush over him. Snow settled eagerly on his black hair and began to sift against his shirt. He could see nothing of the city sprawled out below him, but every sound was magnified in the cold air. I have never seen him eat, he thought suddenly. Like us he has no need of food. I prepare it and go away, and when I return, the dishes are scoured. Something else sustains that body. Something powerful forces life through the ancient limbs, moves the tongue to speech, lights whatever memory is left, but whatever it is, it does not operate as I do in Chilka. Not with compassion.

. . . *She touches me, and I am young again.* . . .

I am beginning to be afraid of this Lady. He pulled the window closed and was standing absently brushing snow from his chest and shoulders when the door opened. The captain who had felled Chilka glanced in, and Nenan was behind him.

"You won't escape that way," he snapped, seeing the little pool of water forming at Chilka's feet. "The Lady herself has summoned you into her presence, together with your son and me. Hurry up." Danarion saw the fear behind the bluff words. Fear of the Lady and fear of this, the man whom he knew without doubt he had killed.

Chilka went to him, and he backed onto the stair. Nenan stepped to his father with anxious eyes, but before he could speak, Chilka smiled, shook his head, and led the way to where the double doors stood shut, high in the darkness of the jagged roof where neither smoke nor any sound from the hall below could reach.

# 25

The captain was breathing heavily by the time the three of them gathered in a small, frightened huddle at the top of the stair. On their left the stair spiraled away into nothingness. Behind them there was only the vast hollow core of the House, funneling down to the unseen floor below, and to the right a tiny locked door had been let into the undressed rock. Nenan was trembling. "This is not at all like climbing the mountains," he whispered to his father. Danarion took his hand, and with the other struck the copper doors. The sound was faint and muffled, but in instant obedience they swung inward. More steps mounted into the timeless dimness of a gray winter afternoon made darker by walls and a roof of black rock.

Hesitantly they went forward, and as their feet found the sixth and last step the doors closed with a click behind them. They were standing at one end of a long, dark hall. Under their feet massive flagstones glided away into distance, their gloom broken only twice by pools of pale, indistinct light that fell from two thin, arched windows high in one wall. The roof, almost lost in shadow, was the jumbled, jostling interior of the sharp spires Danarion had seen rising over the wall as he and Nenan had approached the city. There were no coverings on the cold floor or hangings on the rough, somehow hostile brutishness of the thick walls, but at the far end they could make out a raised dais running the width of the hall and, in the center of it, an enormous chair. Something or someone sat in the chair, but nothing could be made of the shapeless shadow.

"Come forward." It was Yarne's voice, a drifting, cold echo. "Don't be afraid. You are not criminals here to have your execution pronounced. My Lady wants to ask you some questions, that is all."

The captain winced, as though Yarne's voice had caused him pain, and wiped his sweating palms against his shirt. Nenan let go of Chilka's hand, and all three of them began the long walk to the foot of the dais. Familiarity tugged at Danarion's mind as the vastness filled with the echoes of their feet. He remembered Ghakazian's mighty mountain fastness with its rock funnel diving straight to the mountain's roots, its long hall and stone dais. Light washed over him for a moment, and he glanced up at the thin window, its sill heaped with snow, but then he was in half-light again, Nenan beside him, the captain behind, his breath ragged with fear. Danarion knew that he must not endanger himself by remaining in control of Chilka. He was facing an unknown in the Lady, and her powers were great. Carefully he relinquished the body to Chilka's memories, the mind that had been his guide for so long now that every corner of it was as familiar to him as his own. Chilka my brother, he said to it gently, be careful. Remember all you have lived for, all we have been through together. Hold on to your temper and your courage for both our sakes. As always when he gave Chilka's body back to its mind, he was filled with a desolation for Lallin. It was the one overriding purpose in Chilka's life, the one unstanchable wound.

As they approached it the dais seemed to widen and gain height. The chair became solid and held the tall form of a woman. When they were only a few feet away, Yarne uncurled from its foot and came striding toward them. They halted, and he patted Chilka reassuringly on the shoulder. The slackness of the morning had gone. Once more he was tight-skinned and lithely graceful, and even in the dimness his eyes sparkled and glittered ice-blue. "You wanted to see her," he said triumphantly, "and she sends for you! There is nothing she does not know." Chilka smiled weakly. The captain bent his knee to the figure in the chair. Nenan held his breath, his eyes riveted on the small movement there.

Then a cold light began to grow. It seemed to seep sluggishly from the walls, the floor, the chair itself, an orange-yellow, heavy sulkiness that made Chilka feel all at once very tired. Slowly it grew in strength until there were no more shadows, yet it was hard to pierce, as though one were gazing through murky water. The figure moved, sat upright, and leaned forward, and Chilka looked for the first time on the Lady of Shol.

Danarion quickly suppressed the second of uncontrollable shock, for hanging from the long neck was a necklet sparking dully in the low, colored light, its gold almost orange in the distortion, its bells blue as the deep ocean. It was stained and broken in places, but it was recognizably Sholia's. Wild hope engulfed Danarion, but it quickly faded. This creature was not Sholia. The Lady was swathed in a stiff brocaded robe of bright red, high at the neck, with voluminous, stiff sleeves that fell from her thin wrists and met the hem of her garment where it touched small black-clad feet. Her face was stark white and so smooth that her light found no lines or hollows to shade and so slid over the skin like soft oils. Blue-black hair coiled about her small skull, heavy and thickly shining, and it was matched by her eyes. They were large, black, and utterly level in their appraisal as her gaze was fixed on each of them in turn. She looked at Chilka for a long time, and try as he might, he could not hold her gaze. His eyes dropped, and she laughed, a high, tinkling sound that shattered around him like breaking icicles.

"Welcome to my hall," she said. "You are more honored than you know. Only judges and criminals on their last day of life have seen me. Are you then judges, or are you malefactors? We shall see." Her voice fluted into the softly moving airs of the great room, the tones high and brittle like her laugh, and white fingers tipped in long, curving nails fanned and circled as she spoke. "It has come to my ears that a certain extraordinary event has taken place. I dismissed it as foolish rumor of the marketplaces, but it did not die away. It grew and would not be dispelled. Still I put it from my mind, having greater things to ponder than the lies that feed my housewives and my gullible young men. Today my brother comes to me in distress. He has dreamed, he tells me. I cannot have a single anxiety trouble the mind of my dearest kin, so I must investigate this unquenchable story. Captain, tell me how you killed a slave."

The man stepped forward on shaking legs. He tried to speak, but his voice broke. He swallowed, and all the time the Lady sat watching him, a tiny smile on her red mouth, her hands now resting on the arms of her chair. Then he tested his voice again, and it finally obeyed him, a husky rumble that strengthened as he went on.

"Chilka the slave ran away," he said, not looking at her. "It was the third time, and it meant his death." He cast a sidelong glance to Yarne, who was once more perched immobile at his Lady's feet. "I did not consult your brother. I took four soldiers and rode after the slave. I was angry, because Chilka had always been treated with more consideration than any slave has a right to be, and he rewarded your brother by constantly trying to escape. I took the road that foots the cliff and then skirted the Mountain of Mourning, and I came upon Chilka by a lake, close to the foothills. He had been running and was near spent. I took an arrow, fitted it to my bow, and shot him as he lay to drink." He paused and licked his lips. The Lady still smiled encouragingly. Yarne had not moved. Nenan was staring at the ground, his expression unreadable. "My men and I dismounted and walked to the body, turning it over. The eyes were already filling with sand, and the mouth also. The heart did not beat. There was no more breath. I have killed many times," he insisted, his voice rising emphatically, "and this man was dead! We took his knife and his coat, but the afternoon had begun, and I did not wish to be close to the Mountain after sunset. I should have brought the body back to the city, but I was afraid to tarry, afraid to be slowed by it. We left it in the sand. That is all."

The Lady had stopped smiling. Her curving nails rattled against one another as she clasped and unclasped her hands. "Captain," she fluted sweetly, "will you swear an oath on my name that, to the best of your knowledge, Chilka the slave was slain by you, there on the verge of the lake?" She did not need to add a threat to her words. It was said in the city that her anger could slay a mortal though she did not touch him.

The captain pursed his lips, but his speech had given him confidence. "I swear on your immortality, Lady, that what I have told you is true."

She nodded. "To the best of his knowledge," she whispered half to herself, and her gaze left him and traveled to Nenan. "Nenan one-mind!" she called suddenly, some deeper, more vibrant note beneath the fragile splintering of her ice-voice. "Is this man your father?" The nails clicked together as she pointed at Chilka. Nenan lifted his head and met Chilka's eye. He tried to read his father's message but saw only love and puzzlement. Nothing alien flickered behind the dark eyes.

"Tell her the truth," Chilka said quietly.

Nenan looked at her face, and then his gaze slid to her black feet. "He is."

"He cannot be. You have heard the captain swear an oath. Your father is dead. Who is this man?"

"He is my father. He was not killed, only wounded. The captain feared the coming of night and did not wait to verify the death. When he had gone, my father's friends found him and took him home."

"Yet you had not seen him for six years, in which time you grew from child into man. You are deluded."

"No." Nenan stepped closer to Chilka. "My mother knew him. The people of the village knew him."

She stirred pettishly. "It is no use asking an oath from you, one-mind. You have nothing sacred to swear by, and I do not trust you."

"I will swear by Sholia."

The name galvanized her. She stood suddenly, and they saw that she was very tall. Her arms went rigid, and her eyes blazed. "You will not swear by that name! A name of myth, of dreams! To speak it is death!"

"You have given Yarne permission to speak it, for he is Shol's history-reader." The voice was Chilka's. He had pushed Nenan behind him and was facing her with courage. Her anger died as swiftly as it had come, and she lowered herself onto the chair.

"Be quiet!" she snapped and fell to brooding, her eyes gliding from one man to the other, her tiny pointed chin resting in one pale palm. Chilka could feel her will questing him, and Danarion, buried deep, walled himself further from the feather-light brushes of her mind. "Where did you shoot this man?" she asked finally, and the captain croaked, "In his left side."

Chilka felt Nenan stiffen against him. That's right, in the left side, he told himself feverishly. A bloody wound. Why do I feel such anguish, such confusion? I remember the pain and the blood on my hands and striving to pull out the arrow.

The Lady gestured, and slowly Chilka pulled up his shirt to reveal the long, jagged scar, now whitening. She raised her eyebrows and made a small, polite grimace. "So," she said. "I have finished with you all, except Chilka. Wait outside the doors." The captain bowed and stumbled eagerly away, and Nenan followed unwillingly after meeting his father's smile. Yarne did not stir.

It was a long time before the doors at the far end creaked open and then clicked shut, and during the wait Chilka fought against his awe and panic. The sullen orange light still hung about the dais, but out of its reach the noon shadows had begun to lengthen as Shol's sun began its western journey. The echo of the closing door rolled toward him and was dissipated in the lofty ceiling. The Lady rose and began to pace the dais with noiseless, catlike steps.

Presently she said, "Why did you cut his hand?" Her own hand rested briefly on Yarne's silken head as she passed him, still slumped on the dais. He did not acknowledge her touch but sat with head bowed, unseeing and unhearing, motionless as the dead.

"It was an accident, Lady."

She turned to face him. "Why did you cut his hand?" The tone was harder now.

Chilka shook his head helplessly. "I did not do it on purpose," he reiterated desperately. "It was . . ."

"It was no accident!" she roared at him suddenly. "You sneaking, crawling, one-mind liar. Liar! Everything about you is a lie, your words, your eyes, your body. Yes, that lying body." Her voice dropped to a whisper, the rustle of ice rain against cold windows. She sprang from the dais and came to him, and he shrank away in terror. "I know who you are," she hissed, and her breath in his face was cold and odorless. "You are Tagar. Tagar, my wingless one, old traitor. Ages beyond ages ago I hurled you from the sky because of your disobedience. Do you remember how it felt? The rush of air, the horror of falling, the crunch of your bones against the road?" She put a hand to his throat, and her nails dug viciously into his skin. "Still you defy me, your lord. They fear you, skulking forever on the Mountain of Mourning. A presence, they say, a hovering evil. Impotent old fool! You brought agony to no one but yourself when you would not take a body in the palace. But you have weakened at last." She shook him and flung him to the ground, her strength irresistible. Her voice no longer fluted but rang through the hall, deep and masculine, like the howling of a winter wind. Chilka cowered on the floor, his hands over his ears. Yarne sat on, eyes glazed, oblivious. "I do not understand, Lady," Chilka cried out, and she kicked him and began to pace again.

"You do," she said. "You saw a dying man fall with an arrow in his side. You, gliding invisible and friendless on the Mountain. You could bear it no longer. Oh, the feel of warm flesh around you, eh, Tagar? Ground beneath strong feet, odor of hot sand and dank water in quivering nostrils! I know your lust. Maker, I know it! And this time you could not resist. It happened so quickly. Tagar." She began to laugh, peal upon peal of harsh laughter. "Tagar!"

"I am Chilka one-mind!" Chilka sobbed, his face to the cold stone. "Chilka one-mind!"

But behind the man's bewildered terror Danarion watched, numb and sick. Ghakazian, he whispered to himself. Ghakazian, sun-lord, my old friend. The despoiler of Shol. He did not dare to think, for fear Ghakazian might sense him. The Lady came close and, taking Chilka by one arm, pulled him to his feet. Holding his tear-streaked face, she probed behind his eyes with her own. Deeper and further she scoured him, and Chilka screamed as she ripped into his memories and tore through his mind. It was as though she had reached into him with her sharp fingernails and had slashed blood from his essence.

"You are hiding!" she snarled, letting him go and swinging to the chair. "I know your tricks. Tell me, Tagar, how has your patience rewarded you? What have you learned, wandering on the Mountain? Have you seen her?" But Chilka was past thought or answering. He swayed on his feet, eyes closed. "Or have you stayed on the Mountain by an empty Hall of Waiting, hoping that someday rescue might come to you through the Gate?" She sat and regarded him dispassionately. "Sholia closed the Gate, and then I took it away. But by now you have become accustomed to waiting, so you will not mind going back to the Mountain and giving the people a few thousand more years of superstitious dread. Yarne, recall the captain." Instantly the blond head jerked up, the infectious smile lit the beautiful face, and Yarne uncurled and went striding down the hall.

Evening had come. The sun had set, and Chilka, trembling with fatigue, realized how much time had passed since he, Nenan, and the captain had stood before the door. He wanted to lie down at the Lady's feet, those same feet that had bruised and blackened his chest, and fall into an eternal unconsciousness. The doors groaned. Presently Yarne came into the orange light, and the captain bowed and stood waiting anxiously. Once more the Lady's nails crackled against themselves.

"Take Chilka out to the foot of the Mountain of Mourning," she said gently, "and kill him. This time, cut off his head and bring it to me. I want to see it myself."

Chilka tried to speak, but his tongue would not obey him. After one frightened, defiant glance at him the captain nodded. "But I dare not go in darkness, Lady," he said pleadingly. "Give me leave to take him at dawn."

She shrugged her narrow shoulders. "It does not matter, but guard him well tonight. Now take him away." The captain went to Chilka and took his arm. Chilka staggered down the hall beside him. The light from the windows that had gleamed gray on the huge flagstones now lay softly pink, and the Lady's magic light dimmed and was extinguished. In the second it took for the heavy doors to swing open, Chilka turned a throbbing head. The Lady had an arm across Yarne's slim shoulders and was smiling into his face.

Nenan supported his father down the never-ending steps which reverberated under their feet, echoing down the darkness like hollow bells, while the captain ran behind. With nightfall the mood of the House had changed, become melancholy and mysterious. They made their way slowly toward the hall, passing many closed doors let into the curving wall. Glancing through one that was ajar, Nenan saw a far window, an arch of lighter darkness, and pressed against it were faces, peering in with blank eyes that saw nothing but their own interior torment, their bodies teetering on the thin ledge outside. He shuddered, and then the hall was there, firm under his longing feet, and the courtyard, empty and snow-filled, and the passage with its row of locked cell doors. Thankfully he pulled Chilka inside, and the captain jingled his keys. "Until the morning," he said, the sweetness of a just revenge on his face. "I will send a soldier to guard you." He closed the door, and Nenan heard the keys grind in the locks, one after the other. Chilka was sitting on the floor where he had fallen, and Nenan went to him and put his arms around him. "What did she do to you?" he said angrily, but Chilka pulled the arms away. "Not now," he said. "I am to be executed in the morning. I must think." Nenan cried out and sat on the bed, and Chilka closed his eyes.

Nenan watched as he began to rock, his arms about his knees, lost in the meditation of healing and solving. Nothing seemed real to him this night. Not his father's drawn face, not the wails and shuffling outside, not the time creeping by, taking Chilka to his death, not the repellent beauty of the Lady in her vast hall. He felt detached from himself, a spectator at a curious ritual in which he had been taking part all his life and which had twisted and lashed him this way and that, bending and beating him into a shape he hardly recognized. That man was his father or perhaps was not. This youth was himself, yet somehow he had ceased to be himself when he had walked into his mother's cottage and seen that man sitting at the table, very large in the small room, his presence an overpowering thing. That same presence now filled the cell, more real and vital than foolish words about death in the morning, more unquenchable than ever.

After several hours had passed, Danarion suddenly stopped rocking and opened his eyes. "I do not know where it is," he murmured wearily. "I cannot think anymore. He took it away, and where it is now only the Lawmaker knows. Surely I have failed, and I am doomed to be Chilka forever." He rubbed his eyes and passed a hand through his tangled hair. "Nenan, my son, you must go home. If I put you over the wall tonight, can you find your own way?"

Nenan slipped to the floor. "Are you saying that I must leave you to whatever the morning brings and climb the Mountain of Mourning in the dark?" He shivered. "I don't know if I can do this."

"Nothing on the Mountain can hurt you."

"That was because you were with me. Come home with me, Chilka! Back to Lallin and the river and your old friends. Why are we still here, at the mercy of that witch? You know how to get out of the cell. We can go together! I am afraid of the Mountain on my own."

Danarion's eyes were swollen and red with tiredness and the tears of fear Chilka had not been able to keep back. He rubbed them again and looked at Nenan blearily. "Very well. I will take you over the Mountain, and you must go home. I don't know what will happen then, Nenan. I have no intention of dying, but I must keep looking."

"For what?" Nenan grasped his arm.

"For the Gate, the Gate, the stupid, meaningless, useless Gate! Start banging on the door, Nenan. The guard is uneasy enough as it is. When he unlocks it, pull the door open."

"Chilka . . ."

"Do as I say!"

Nenan went to the door and began to beat on it with both fists, and Danarion hauled himself sluggishly to his feet. He went to stand just out of sight of the door, and Nenan shouted.

"Be quiet!" The guard's voice was muffled, but they could hear the edge of panic to it. "I am not to open for any reason." But Nenan went on pounding and screaming, and soon there was a rasp of metal on metal. "Hush!" the guard shrieked like a woman. "I don't want any two-minds down here!"

The door opened a crack, and Nenan heaved. The guard tumbled into the room, and Danarion swung, his fist clenched. The guard went down and was silent. That felt good, Danarion thought, his fingers throbbing, but I hope I didn't misjudge my strength and kill him. Almost unthinkingly he bent and tugged a long knife from the guard's belt, and thrusting it inside his shirt, he followed Nenan out into the passage. Together they ran to the courtyard.

It was snowing again, and the night was blanketed in a moving grayness. The gate was closed. Nenan flung himself on the man who stood before it, glad to be acting recklessly, doing anything so long as it was something definite, and Danarion fumbled to release its great locks. They fled into the streets of the city, the buildings unlit and foreign-looking under their clothing of snow.

They walked quickly away from the House and were soon lost in the cold, crooked shadows of Ishban. The sound of their footfalls was muffled in snow. Dark grilled gates, deserted shop fronts, a low wall over which naked tree branches hung glided past them. By now Nenan knew the city as well as his father, and its dangers were delineated. The people hung about the streets like homeless ghosts, standing silently in twos and threes or keening quietly alone at their upper windows. Snow blew around them in glancing flurries. Once Nenan stopped walking and flung his arms wide, his head back. "Farewell, Ishban, black joke of the universe!" he hooted. "Your madness is like a blind man who tumbles into a hole and sets the children laughing."

"That's enough, Nenan!" Danarion said sharply, pulling him out of the lonely square and hurrying him toward the wall. "You don't know what you are saying." Nenan fell silent as the wall loomed above them, a hump of blackness through a gray curtain.

Above the city it was cold. As they climbed down they could not see the ocean, but they could hear it grinding on the rocks below. No summer salt smell rose from it, only a dampness that chilled them, numbing their bare hands and laying ice against the crevices their questing feet sought. It took them a long time to reach the bottom, and when they did, the cold drove them quickly away from the corner where they had rested on their way into the city. They circled the wall, found the road, and set out upon it, knowing that nothing would be moving on it. As they walked the snow thinned and finally ceased to fall, although the night sky remained thick with cloud, and no stars could be seen. Grimly they trudged, not speaking, and when Danarion summoned the will to look back, there was no sign that a mighty city lay behind them. No lights glinted, and no sound but the whisper of a tired wind broke the calm of the night. Ishban was a mirage, a spell that held him captive, and when he broke loose from it, it vanished as though it had never been. He smiled to himself without humor at the fancy and pushed on.

Three hours later the fruit trees loomed up, ragged shadows into whose silent shelter he fell gratefully, and he and Nenan rested briefly and uncomfortably. Danarion's eyes strayed to Nenan, who was scanning the sky. He is not only the son of my time in Ishban, he thought. I no longer simply watch Chilka's memories of him as a young boy, I feel them also. Now it is more than a sharing of emotion with Chilka, it is a blending. I know I have loved Nenan since he was born.

"There are the stars," Nenan said suddenly. Looking through the trellis of black branches overhead, Danarion saw them twinkling frostily. "How long till the dawn?" Nenan whispered again.

His body already cooling rapidly now that he was still, Danarion shivered. "Perhaps an hour, and we still have to reach the face of the Mountain. We will not be safe until we have scrambled onto the plateau and out of sight."

They came to their feet and veered right. The orchard seemed to go on forever, but eventually the trees drew back as though awed, and by silver starlight the face of the Mountain of Mourning was a nightmare pattern of black shadow and stark slopes. "Dawn comes," Nenan panted, and indeed, the sky seemed a little less densely black between the nets of the constellations.

They had started across the open mile that in summer was thick grass and nodding red flowers when Danarion stopped abruptly and turned his ear into the wind. He strained to listen, and Nenan, watching him anxiously, thought he caught the far-off neighing of horses and clink of bits.

"Only the Lady could have driven them out before dawn," he said bitterly. "They are following our tracks in the snow."

"Can you run?" Danarion asked swiftly. Nenan nodded. "Then run!"

They burst from the trees and fled over the snow, their shadows racing beside them. Now they could see each other faintly, and visibility lent dark wings to their feet. The sun was rolling imperceptibly toward its birth. Nenan counted his steps under his breath, trying to forget the pain in his ankles. Danarion could not ignore his weakness. Chilka's body was slow to respond. His chest was tender where the Lady's foot had bruised it, and the nagging ache in his head where she had forced open his mind had spread to his back and was shooting down his legs. He pounded heavily after Nenan.

Now the horses and the shouts of several men could be plainly heard. Danarion threw a glance over his shoulder and saw three riders break from the trees and point excitedly. I saw them, he thought fleetingly. The sun is close. He tried to draw himself away from Chilka's laboring breath and ailing body but found he could not. He flowed with the streaming blood; he was present in every frantic beat of the punished heart.

Yet he tried to think. *I took it away,* she had said. *I took it away.* He heard the horses start across the plain, but the face of the Mountain was nearer now. He made a rhythm out of the words, for his feet. *I took-it-away, I took-it-away.* Then he slowed.

*I took . . .*

*I took . . .*

The truth exploded in his mind, a burst of light. He howled like an animal and came to a halt. "Of course!" he cried.

"Of course!"

"Father, run!" Nenan screamed, but for a moment Danarion was blind to his danger, the Mountain, the chill bite of snow on his feet.

"Yarne!" he shouted. "Yarne is the Gate! I must go back to Ishban!" But Nenan had flung back and was shaking him, shouting at him, dragging him forward. He was dazed. "It's Yarne, it's Yarne," he sobbed, and his body stumbled after Nenan, not knowing where it was going.

They reached the foot of the Mountain, and Nenan pushed him violently onto the winding path up which the grotesque funeral procession had climbed. Hooves thrummed behind them. He was both laughing and crying, Nenan scrabbling ahead of him, urging him on. He followed almost blindly. There was shouting below, and the clatter of hooves on rock. Nenan had almost reached the plateau and was turning, a hand outstretched, his face twisted into a grimace, when Danarion heard a quick twanging, like the tuning of a harp string. He could not place it, but Chilka knew, and flung his body flat against the path with a scream. Nenan shouted. And just as the sun's rays topped the Mountain, glimmering red and new, pain flared in Chilka and burst along his veins like the white fire dancing around him. But this time the pain was not his alone. It engulfed Danarion also. Mind touched essence, meshed, and in the extremity of mortal anguish, they became one. He screamed, the taste of sand gritty in his mouth, his knees folding upward to his chest, trying to cradle the pain, to enclose it, his fingers digging deep. Again the lake shimmered before his eyes, tantalizing water just out of reach, and his throat swelled with the need for it. The sun is burning me up, he shrieked in his mind. I am on fire. Lallin, Lallin . . . Danarion had never known such agony. The Messenger was the Unmaker's tool, it had brought him to Shol to destroy him, burn him, Janthis was a traitor, left to rule Danar alone and unchallenged forever. A raucous yell of triumph went up. They are rifling my bag. I can smell my own blood, steaming in the sun, yet before my eyes there is darkness. Lallin. I am Chilka-Danarion, and I am dying.

He felt himself lifted. He did not want to move, he wanted to stay lying on the Mountain, curled in upon himself, but someone was panting, crying, pulling him upward, and then there were other hands and a low voice, his son answering with breathless hope, but the ocean slapped against him, buffeting him without mercy, and he sank beneath its surface and was at peace.

# 26

He woke to a raging thirst and a body throbbing with aches and stiff along the left side. For a long while he lay looking at yellow light that flickered across a low ceiling, content to be hypnotized by its slow, comfortable movement, his mind half-dreaming, half-sleeping. He had decided that the light was a fire's welcome glow and that he was warm and lying on a low, soft bed when there was a whisper of movement and someone sat beside him, cutting off the fire's somnolent, silent lullaby. He blinked.

"So you are Chilka one-mind, the man who would not die," a voice said. The tone was soft, amused. "I have heard of you. You are lucky I was out on the Mountain yesterday morning, or you certainly would have died this time. Are you thirsty? Lift your head so I can guide the cup to your mouth."

Everything in him seemed to falter. His labored heartbeat slowed. His breath stopped, and a tingle shivered over his body. Slowly, fearfully he turned his head, and when he saw her face, he tried to speak and could not. She hushed him, still with the amused lilt to her voice.

"Don't try to say anything until you have drunk. Your son is safe. I sent him home to tell your wife that you will be with her in three days. I promise it."

His hands lifted. His throat worked. "Sholia!" he whispered. She started violently, and water splashed from the cup onto her lap. "Sholia, it is I, Danarion, I Chilka. Chilka-Danarion . . ." With a convulsive movement he turned his face into her bosom and wept like a child.

When he was spent and she had helped him to drink, cradling his head and lifting the cup to his lips, he lay back, and they talked quietly together, their hands linked, their eyes meeting with a bewildered joy. For a while they spoke of the past, of days of power and endless freedoms, but too many years of darkness lay between that time and this, and it hurt both of them. Finally Danarion told her why he had come to Shol, and how. She listened soberly, her head averted, the white-streaked golden hair laid in neat coils against her neck, the firelight playing on one cheek and the fan of tiny lines radiating across her temple. When he had finished, she sighed, and her body sagged. "I knew about Ghakazian," she said in a low voice, "even before . . . before the Unmaker came to my Gate, I suspected. There was something about Rilla. She made me afraid. And later, when I had made this cave my home and heard how she had gathered the two-minds around her and was building a new city, I was certain. I mourned for the Rilla I had known, and for many years I heard nothing of her brother, Yarne. When word did begin to spread, the rumors about him were contradictory."

Danarion nodded. "I've heard some of them. Sholia, why did you do nothing? Why hide here in a cave when you have command of Shol's remaining sun? Couldn't you have imprisoned Ghakazian?"

"No." She turned to face him, her lips quivering. This was the first time she had been able to speak of the years since she had closed the Gate, and Danarion saw tears gather in her eyes. Like me, he thought wonderingly. Like any common mortal. "After I drove the Unmaker back and closed the Gate, I ran away. I was tired, Danarion, more tired than you can possibly imagine. I had been a sun, *been* a sun, and until Shol ceases to turn, I shall never forget the ecstasy of that moment. But for a body, even an immortal one, to open itself to the full power of a sun was a kind of death. I wandered for many years. I could not rest. Often I longed for mortal sleep. I could not rid myself of that terrible exhaustion. I tried to go into my other sun and discovered to my horror that it no longer heard me or recognized me. I had burned myself out. Do you understand?"

"Yes," he whispered, thinking of the sufferings he had shared with Chilka. "I do."

"I am scarred inside, hollowed out. It shows on my face, my hair. I am still tired, but not with the unbearable weight I carried for so long. It seems to be abating slowly. But all my power has gone. I cannot command the sun to restrain Ghakazian, and even if I could, what profit would there be? The Gate is closed. The

Ghakans cannot return to their home. In the end I returned to the Hall of Waiting and found a great city and a ruling Lady, and a precarious balance worked out between two minds in one body. I found something else. We were not healers, were we, Danarion? Our mandate was to preserve, to maintain. Yet in place of the power I have lost, I have gained the ability to heal. I am careful not to make myself obvious, for I am afraid of Ghakazian. He still searches for me once in a while. But people come to me if they dare. They fear the Mountain."

"Is it the rumor of you that they fear?"

She smiled through her unshed tears. "No. There is something else here, something pathetic and yet threatening, some great essence that cannot escape."

"Tagar," Danarion murmured. "He accused me of being an essence called Tagar."

"Perhaps. I still have some small tricks left, like the one you played when the funeral came past you, which I used to hide you and your son from the soldiers who were seeking your body. But we needn't discuss this now, for the news you bring of Yarne is very serious. Are you certain?"

He moved against the tight bandages, and pain rippled through him. "Yes. He can't be explained in any other way. He is dead, a corpse. Whatever lives in him is not the essence of mortal or immortal but is something with sentience. Ghakazian gives him words to say and the key to unlock Yarne's memories when he needs to. How did Ghakazian do it? And why?"

"Lie still. I can heal quickly, but not if you thrash about. I don't know how he did it, but then, how did he learn that he was able to take the essences of his people through his Gate and across space? He must have studied the Book of Lore. Perhaps he learned other things there."

Silence fell on them. Danarion drifted into a light sleep, the sudden loss of identity that comes to the injured, and dreamed that Lallin sat beside him, holding his hand. Sholia watched him, getting up sometimes to replenish the fire and stand at the cave mouth, where snow was melting and running in cold rivulets down the Mountain. When he woke again, he was stronger, able to sit and eat. "If I had completed the task I was set, a Messenger would have come for me," he said as he ate the food that she had prepared. "I have found the Gate, but I am still on Shol, and therefore I am required to undo the evil as best I can. To tell you the truth, Sholia," he confessed, smiling at her, "I am strangely reluctant to go back to Danar. I think of Janthis and see only Nenan's face. Danar is like a fading dream in my mind."

"I dare not think of Danar at all," she replied, a catch in her voice. "It is forever unattainable to me now. I shall never again greet Janthis. I shall grow old on Shol. I have been . . . lonely, Danarion."

He wanted to embrace her, kiss her on the mouth, drive the loneliness away with his body. But remembering his dream, he knew that it was Lallin he wanted to hold, not Sholia. "What shall we do?" he said unsteadily.

"Tomorrow you will be able to walk. The next day you will feel well again. The arrow pierced your left side, did you know? I think Ghakazian will come looking for you himself. He will know by now that an arrow struck you but that your body has disappeared. He will be frightened. He will bring many soldiers and will come to the Mountain."

"Then we will go down and wait for him in the proper place, by the Hall of Waiting. You will come with me?"

She sat still for a long time, her expression unreadable, and he thought how fear had ruled her life since the moment when the Worldmaker had stood before them on Danar and claimed all the worlds of making for his own. Her one act of desperate courage had been to cast him from Shol, an act of lunatic bravery he did not think he himself could ever have accomplished, and she should have been purged by it, but he saw that she was not. Fear was still there, a residue in her essence that would never be washed away. At last she pressed her hands together, a gesture of pain, and glanced across at him and away. "I will come," she said.

The next day, as she had promised, he was able to walk about the cave. He felt weak but whole again. She removed the bandages, and he saw the swollen red welt, almost identical to the older scar, before she covered it again with one thin strip of linen. She had washed his clothes, and he struggled into them and felt immediately himself.

That night they sat by the fire and talked of inconsequential things: the changing weather, the people she had cured. He slept long and deeply while she sat outside and watched the constellations appear in the night sky, a dusting of sparkling shapes that did little to alleviate the loneliness Danarion had rekindled in her.

In the morning they prepared to leave the cave. Danarion took the knife he had stolen from the guard and hesitated, turning it over in his fingers, but then shrugged and tucked it inside his shirt. Sholia wrapped herself in a short, sleeved cloak, and they went out into the dawn.

The sky was a clear, watery blue, and gulls rustled overhead on their way to the beaches. The ground was wet with melted snow, although here and there in the places of perpetual mountain shadow small patches of white remained. The cave was a natural hollow, its entrance hidden by a short slope that rose at its mouth and then plunged away to join the main sweep of the Mountain, and Danarion saw that it was not far from the tunnel through which he had groped with Nenan, lit by his own small light.

He and Sholia skirted the slope and began the short climb to the uneven, rounded plateau where the funeral had taken place. The path they took was narrow but well-worn. Beside it, wherever there was a hollow in the rock or a hint of shelter, bones lay on the tattered remains of woven mats, bleached and worn by summer sun and winter rains, often drifted over with the always-moving sand. Many of the corpses had been wrapped in white shrouds, which had loosened and blown away to hang netted against the tough mountain scrub and be picked at by birds eager for threads to line their nests.

Once on the plateau Danarion breathed a sigh of relief. He paused to look out upon the plain, miles of sand and rock to the left, its brown grass ahead leading to the dark blur of the orchards out of which the road ran, and far away to the haze of the ocean. He missed Nenan, and in that moment Sholia was more of a stranger to him than his son. "Nothing is moving," Sholia remarked, and he did not reply, his eyes traveling slowly over the view. The snow he and Nenan had floundered through on their wild dash for safety was gone, melted away into the dead grasses, taking with it the reality of that night, that dawn. "He may not come today," Sholia went on. "The wait could be long."

I don't care, Danarion thought mutinously. I don't care about anything anymore but the well-being of my wife, my child. He touched the knife resting against his skin and started down the Mountain.

By noon they had angled across the plain, avoiding the orchards in order to strike the road where it began to hug the long side of the Mountain. When they reached the road, Danarion stopped. "I'm hungry," he said. "Is there any bread?"

Wordlessly she sank to the ground and opened the pouch she carried, and he wolfed down the bread and herbs she offered. Thirst began to trouble him and he found a small pool of melted snow caught in a dip in the grass. Kneeling, he lifted the freezing water to his mouth, lapping it up like a dog, aware of Sholia's eyes on his back.

By sunset they stood outside the excavation in the cliff, and Ishban itself reared from the plain in the distance, its walls and leaping spires stained blood-red, as he had seen them with Nenan by his side. The gulls that had flapped overhead on their way to the ocean in the morning now streamed inland against the placid pink sky, and Danarion winced at the sight and strident sound of them. "We will wait in the Hall," he said peremptorily. "At least we will have shelter there." He led the way into the darkness, under the timber props and beside a clutter of workmen's tools. The sunset followed him, laying a shaft of red light under his feet.

Once in the Hall he turned to face the entrance and lowered himself to the floor, his back against a wall. He was tired. Sholia dropped her pouch beside him and began to wander, touching the places where the copper reliefs lay exposed to the last of the daylight. When she came to the lintels of the door that led so irrationally onto the raw rock face, she stood very still gazing at it, her hands loose at her sides. "Sun-lord," she whispered. "It was all so long ago. I can no longer believe that it was I." She stayed there until full darkness overflowed from the world outside and washed up the walls in a soundless tide, blotting them out, and then she came and sat beside Danarion. He held out a hand, groping in the darkness, and she took it. He thought of giving a little of his own light to make the darkness more bearable, but he was too weary to make the effort and had almost forgotten how. In any case, neither of them had anything to fear from this place. They were a part of it. Their time had been its time. They felt as quietly, calmly useless as it was now and sat clasping hands, each sunk in far dreams. At last Danarion's eyes grew heavy, and his head slid onto her shoulder. It is ridiculous, an insult, for two such as us to face a sun-lord, he thought drowsily as her arm went around him. We are two children whose spirit of make-believe has led them into realms of unknown danger. He slept and dreamed of Nenan and Lallin again, and the feel of the mountain stream against his skin on hot summer afternoons, but something of the ancient magic of the Hall drifted softly over him as the night wore away, and his dream changed to one of Janthis waiting by his body in the jeweled council hall on Danar and a Messenger flashing like white starlight through space, coming to take him home.

When he opened his eyes, morning light filled the room, drab and colorless on the chipped and broken stone, and Sholia was alert, shaking him gently. "I can hear something on the road," she said. He scrambled to his feet, and they ran to the entrance. Sunlight dazzled on the sand, blinding them for a moment, but then their eyes adjusted and they turned to the road. They saw pennants waving, yellow and black suns on a red background, and the muffled booming of a drum rolled toward them. Like a black ribbon a procession of horsemen wound along the road, and as it came slowly closer they saw a break in the stream, a large litter of yellow and black carried by slaves with its curtains tightly drawn. Danarion heard Sholia's breath sucked in beside him, and his own breath came fast hard. "He came, he came," she whispered tensely. Danarion took her arm and drew her out from the shadow of the doorway, and together they stood with the sun beating on their heads and the wind whipping at their clothes.

The drumbeat advanced, no longer muffled but a clear, sharp *toom, toom* that vibrated in the cliff behind them. The outriders with their fluttering pennants were now close enough to reveal stern faces under yellow and black caps. Danarion and Sholia did not stir. The outriders passed without noticing them, followed by soldiers on lean black horses, two by two.

As the litter finally came abreast, a swaying, silken box which shone in the sun, Danarion stepped forward. "I am here!" he called. Instantly there was confusion. The outriders reined in and wheeled.

The drumbeat ceased abruptly. The soldiers milled about but soon saw him and came thundering down upon him, and in a second he was ringed. The captain looked down on him, his face pale, the trembling hands clutching the reins. The slaves carrying the litter had obeyed some unheard command and had lowered it to the ground, and Sholia saw the curtain twitch and pull back. The slaves averted their faces. A long white leg appeared, topped at thigh length by a pleated tunic of silver, and Yarne slid from the litter and came striding over the sand. The ring of horsemen parted to let him through, and he came up to Danarion and halted. He gave Sholia one disinterested glance, and his eyes, brighter and paler than the sky that poured light into his shining blond hair, returned to the man fronting him.

"You ran away again," he said reproachfully. "You promised not to hurt me, but you did."

Sholia stared at him, and Danarion laid a hand gently on the slim, silver-hung shoulder.

"I am sorry, Yarne," he said quietly. "They were going to kill me. I had to leave."

"They would never have done it," Yarne insisted. "I would not have let them. Please come back with me. I need you very much."

"I cannot," Danarion answered. "In a moment they will receive an order to shoot me down, and nothing you can say will change that. That Lady wishes me dead."

"I don't see why," Yarne said evenly. "She said I could have you for as long as I wanted if we found you."

"She lied. Please go to her, Yarne, quickly, before she tires of waiting, and tell her that Sholia wishes to speak to her."

Yarne looked at Sholia with more interest and then nodded. "All right, but that name will make her very angry. What game are you playing? Where is Nenan?"

"He went home. Please go."

Yarne swung back, and once more the soldiers made a path for him. The captain sat motionless, an arrow already fitted to his bow, watchfulness and a resigned horror on his face. Yarne had reached the litter. He pulled aside the curtain and bent, and for a while no one moved. But then a white hand came out, gripping his shoulder, and the soldiers and slaves around the litter murmured and turned their faces away. Slowly the Lady emerged, a black foot, a swing of stiff red gown that glittered with gold thread in the sunlight, a small head swathed in coiled hair. At a sharp word from the captain the ring around the two prisoners broke up, and Yarne and the Lady walked toward the cliff. Sholia steadily watched them come, her eyes on the Lady, and at the moment of recognition she saw the little feet stumble and the head droop toward Yarne.

Brother and sister came to a halt. The Lady's skin still showed no hint of a line, but looking at her carefully under the pitiless sun, Danarion received the impression of an age so great that it was carried by her like a measurelessly heavy burden and encased her like walls of iron. It was most clearly revealed in her eyes, now narrowed and appraising, a black accumulation of years, uncounted, stale, and endless.

"So, Tagar, you have found her," she said, the little hands with their cruel nails mincing through the cold air. "Or she has found you, which is more likely. Where have you spent the long ages, Sholia? I have searched for you."

"I did not want to be found, Ghakazian," Sholia replied, her voice teetering on the verge of breaking.

At the mention of his name Ghakazian put up a white hand and stepped back against Yarne's tall body as though for protection. "And now you do," the sweet, high voice went on. "Why? Have you tired of being hunted? I shall prepare a special cell for you, deep in the rock under my House, where you may meditate upon the time stretching ahead of you." The little oval face was lifted briefly to the sun, and the red mouth curved. "I think there is much life left in your sun. Much life."

The threat was so like the one the Unmaker had hurled at her centuries earlier that Sholia faltered. Her hand found Danarion's, and she clutched at him, but her voice had gained strength, and she looked at Ghakazian calmly.

"More life than in your own, shining dimly over Ghaka," she replied. "I shall live longer than you, sun-lord."

The listening soldiers muttered, shocked at her impudence yet not understanding, and for a moment Ghakazian remained silent, thinking. Then the nails clicked, and the spine straightened under the heavy brocaded covering.

"I cannot stand here in the cold all day. Captain, shoot that stupid body. I will send Tagar gibbering back onto the Mountain, and you and I, Sholia, will return to the House. I am relieved to finally have you in my hands."

But Danarion swiftly raised an arm, and with one savage movement he thrust his face close to hers. "Look at me, Ghakazian," he ordered. "Look deep into me before the captain shoots, for his effort will be wasted. You cannot destroy me with an arrow. Look well!"

Startled, she turned the velvet-black eyes to his and at once was caught. Behind Chilka's gaze Danarion's essence unfolded, tendriling through Chilka's mind. As she staggered Yarne's body suddenly loosened and swayed. "Danarion!" she whispered. "Danarion . . ." Recovering her dignity, though her skin was like chalk and her eyes seemed to fill her small face, she slashed an arm at the soldiers. "Go!" she screamed, and they pulled back, afraid. She clung to Yarne, and with her reviving strength he stiffened.

Danarion pointed behind him. "We will go into the Hall," he said curtly. "What must be said is not for mortal ears." He did not know if it was Sholia's presence or Chilka's quick anger, but he felt confidence flow into him, pumping through him on Chilka's strong heart. He swung about and strode under the shadow of the passage, Sholia beside him, and the Lady and her brother followed.

# 27

Inside the Hall it was dim and very cold, full of a brooding quiet that rendered them all momentarily speechless. Then Ghakazian rounded, shouting.

"How did you get here? It has been ages beyond ages! You did not come through the Gate, none knows that better than I!" His voice boomed in the enclosed space, waking echoes that expanded it and threw it against Danarion like an avalanche of sound.

"Janthis looked in the mirror," he answered quietly. "He saw that Shol's Gate was missing, and with a Messenger's permission he sent me to find it."

Ghakazian stopped still and stared at him. "So Chilka *was* slain by the lake! You took his body! Poor, clumsy Chilka one-mind, the dupe of the immortals! For all your fine talk around the council table you had no qualms about using him, did you?"

"I did not kill him to gain his body!" Danarion shouted back hotly, stung into a defense, not of himself but of Chilka. "I love him! He is my brother!"

Ghakazian peered at him and began to laugh. The long fingers twirled and dipped. The feminine lines of the little mouth opened wide on white teeth. But as quickly as it had begun, his shiver of mirth was gone. "So," he said softly. "You have been absorbing him, have you? How well I know the feeling! Poor little Rilla, the dream-weaver. You remember Rilla, don't you, Sholia? I gave her a dream that she has been unable to forget. The greatest dream of her long life." He swung carelessly to the wall and struck it, and his nails scratched over the stone like sharp teeth on the bones of a slain prey. "But you need not have troubled yourself, Danarion, you and Janthis with your heads together, a little council of worry. The Gate is safe. Nothing"—he licked his lips nervously—"nothing can go out or come in. It is seldom out of my sight. It comes when I call."

"But why, Ghakazian, why?" Sholia cried out. "It was closed. You were safe behind it!"

"Safe?" He closed his eyes for a moment and shuddered. "Safe. I had to be sure he could not come in to take me. I had become his lawful prey. It haunted me, the thought that the Gate was here untended year after year."

"So you stole it." Danarion walked to him, rage and anguish brimming in him. He took the soft shoulders and shook the graceful body, his teeth clenched. "You stole it! You caused me to live this torture! What happened to Yarne? How did you get possession of the Gate?"

Ghakazian wrenched himself away and ran to the motionless sliver of paleness that stood with head bowed. "Look at him!" he cried out, thrusting a hand under the chin and lifting it so that they could see the blank, changeless face. "Isn't he lovely! The most beautiful thing on Shol, and the most lifeless." His voice rose, harsh and strong, and then broke into pain. "Rilla loved him. I loved him. Do you think I wanted to do him harm?" His hands stroked the smooth cheeks and pushed back the waving hair. "I sacrificed his essence to the Gate. I made an exchange. I ripped it from him and flung it out into the stars, and in its place I set the essence of the Gate. Every night I breathe life into this thick flesh, mouth pressed to mouth, so that by day it might smile with those cold lips and glide about the House with a grace that makes men stare, all so that the Gate might remain under my eye. Do you hear it?" He brushed a finger across the smooth throat. His voice had fallen to a whisper as he struggled for control. "The pulse of a Gate against eternity. The sound I have lived with night and day for a thousand years." At his touch the flutter in the young man's throat could be heard, a dull, regular throbbing, its rhythm unvarying. Danarion listened to that ominous beat, more terrifying than any drum, and Sholia covered her face with both hands. "Smile, Yarne!" Ghakazian shouted shrilly. "Smile at Chilka, your friend!" and Yarne's mouth curved warmly, his eyes turning slowly to find the face of the Sholan.

"Stop it!" Danarion shouted back, horrified. Ghakazian touched Yarne's face gently, and Yarne slumped. "Ghakazian," Danarion said urgently, "you must put the Gate back. If you put Yarne's essence out among the stars, then there must have been a moment when the Gate was open. Reverse it all! Call out your people and let them go. Let the Messengers judge you."

Ghakazian shook his head. "I was deceived by the accursed Book," he said sadly. "I fell. Unknowingly, but I still fell. The Messengers are just, but their justice is never tempered with mercy. I am afraid of them. Perhaps I could return to Ghaka if a way were found, but what is there for me on Ghaka? My body is a blackened ruin, lying by my Gate. The bodies óf my people have crumbled to dust long ago. You have only been in Chilka a short time, but I have been Rilla and she me for many Shol-years. I am no longer Ghakazian, sun-lord. I am Rilla-Ghakazian, undying ruler of this place, and oh, it weighs heavily on me, without the joy of true immortality or the small pleasures of passing time that the mortals delight in! I am as much a prisoner of this body as of the Gate itself."

"Do you know how to replace the Gate?" Danarion asked.

An expression of cunning flitted swiftly across Ghakazian's pretty face, and he backed away. "No," he said promptly.

But Sholia came forward. "Yes, you do," she said loudly, her voice ringing against the walls. "And so do I. Another sacrifice is required, isn't that right, Ghakazian? But this time it must be you. Think about it, Danarion. Time can be reversed only at the expense of life." She was very pale but held her head erect. In the dimness the lines of her face were gentled away, and he saw her as she had been, imperious and very beautiful.

Ghakazian saw it too. He backed away until he came to a wall. "You would not dare!" he said loudly. "An act like that would be murder. It is forbidden!"

"It was forbidden you, too, but that did not stop you," she responded easily, "and it would make no difference to me because Shol is now a fallen world . . ." Her strength failed then, and she swallowed and looked away.

Ghakazian pressed his advantage. "You and I were very close," he said quickly. "You could not slay me even if the sun was still yours to command, which I doubt, or you would still be glowing with its health. And Danarion will do nothing to endanger Danar. He will not strike either." He came away from the wall with mincing steps, his hands fanning around him. "Call a Messenger and go home, Danarion," he urged. "You have seen that the Gate is safe. Sholia, I will let you go free, I swear. Leave all as it is, both of you." He scanned their faces eagerly, and Sholia looked at Danarion.

Does he lie? Danarion wondered, the full weight of his decision beginning to settle on him. If, as Chilka, I strike him down, will I carry back to Danar a tainted essence? Of course he lies! How can he do anything else, faced with what he sees? He loses nothing by deluding me into weakness, and I know without doubt that my innocence is gone, lost forever in the memories I share with Chilka, and no matter what happens, I must return to Danar irreparably changed. He did not feel the horror of what he was acknowledging to himself and strove to think without emotion. I will do it, Chilka whispered. I have killed before, I am able. But Danarion shook his head. No, he thought. He felt the cool blade of the knife against his belly, and he reached into his shirt and drew it out slowly. For a moment he looked at it, almost surprised to find it lying in his hand.

"The purpose will be mine," he said grimly, "but the hand will not be mortal. Yarne, come here."

For a second Ghakazian was puzzled, but then he sprang between them. "Yarne does what I command," he said coldly. "He does nothing of his own volition except the small things that belong to Yarne's memory. I command the Gate!"

"Wait." Sholia's voice came low under the echoes of Ghakazian's. "This Gate is on my world, and therefore it is under my direct jurisdiction." She seemed to be speaking to herself, frowning. "You were able to move it only because I was not here to stop you. It will obey me now, as it has in the past, and I need no sun's power. I cannot keep it open as it once was, but I can override your demands, Ghakazian, if I choose."

"But you will not choose, will you?" Ghakazian said, and all at once it seemed to Danarion that the Hall, long asleep, had suddenly woken and was listening avidly. "You will not harm me, Sholia. Remember how I used to come to Shol, and we would walk arm in arm by the water, watching the ships? And you came to Ghaka, and I took you on my back and flew with you down my long valleys. We loved each other. Will you betray me now?" He flung his arms wide, and the brocade rustled. "This is all I have, the only life I will ever know. If the Messengers take me, they will annihilate me. Let me live, Sholia, let me live!"

All the old compelling sweetness was in his voice then, all the strength and vibrant beauty that he had once been, and it brought vividly to Danarion a picture of him standing in his own hall on Ghaka, wings spread wide, brown hair blowing in the draughts of the funnel, feet planted solidly against the rock, his face alive with the joy of his being. Sholia's eyes were closed and her hands outstretched in pleading.

Danarion knew then that he must not interfere. The situation had gone beyond his authority, and this final scene must be played out without him. He had been nothing but a catalyst after all, come to Shol to draw these two together as though his part had been foreordained. He held the knife and waited.

"You speak to me of betrayal," she said, still with eyes closed. "You came to Shol with my destruction in your heart, and you broke me and rocked my world to its foundations."

"I did not know! I was deceived!"

"And did you never doubt?"

At that he was silent. She opened her eyes and, walking to Danarion, took the knife from between his fingers and held it out to Yarne. "Take it and kill the Lady," she said curtly, but her tears continued to fall. Ghakazian made as if to speak and then changed his mind. He drew himself up, and his eyes began to deepen and glow. Danarion felt the power of his will bent now on Yarne, and Sholia was oppressed by it also. She put a hand on Yarne's throat and stood firm. The room seemed to heat with their silent battle, and sweat ran suddenly down Danarion's back. Ghakazian spoke once. "Pitiless!" he whispered, and Sholia answered, "My trust in you is long dead."

Yarne had begun to tremble. Groans broke from him as he swayed to and fro, and his empty eyes swiveled to his Lady and back again. Slowly, every inch an agony, his hand came out, and he took the knife. For a long moment its point wavered; then, with a shriek of torment, Yarne flung himself upon Ghakazian. The blade glimmered dully as he raised it and struck, and Ghakazian staggered back and fell to his knees, blood gushing from his throat. The Hall was immediately filled with the sound of the beating of the Gate, and each stroke was like the colliding of worlds. Danarion could not bear it, and he cowered down, his hands over his ears, but Sholia was unmoved.

A wind came howling, dashing against the walls, slamming against the frail bodies. Glancing up through wind-blurred eyes, Danarion saw that a hole had opened in Yarne and was rapidly growing, a black vortex of power out of which the wind screamed and the pulse slammed louder and faster. Then Danarion was engulfed. He found himself clinging to the lip of the Gate, sick with terror, for below him was the awesome nothingness of space. He fought to retain his hold, fingers and toes scrabbling frantically against stone.

From inside the Hall Sholia cried out in wonder. "The stars! And an open Gate! Oh, I want to go home, I want to fall through, even though I should die!"

Then Danarion found himself being hurtled bodily back into the Hall, falling and rolling, crying out as his body struck rock. A Messenger stood blocking the Gate, its colors writhing green, blue, and gold against the cold backdrop of the stars. It said nothing but simply waited. Pulling himself painfully to his feet beside Sholia, Danarion saw that Yarne was still the Gate, his arms stretched out, his head tilted back, his features contorted in agony. The emptiness within him that Danarion had sensed so many times was now ablaze with stars. The torment was not of his body. The Gate itself was wracked. Danarion turned to Ghakazian. The small corpse lay huddled at Sholia's feet, looking as frail and light as an autumn leaf, a crumpled pile of garish red brocade from which a white head lolled. The hair had loosed and now fell in a black silken shower over Sholia's feet. Over it an image towered, dark and indistinct to Chilka's mortal eyes but clear to Danarion who saw the lordly sweep of Ghakazian's wings framing Rilla's sad, shadowed face. "Now call them out, Ghakazian," Sholia commanded. "Let them go wherever the Messenger decrees. Will you go also?"

The image smiled with Ghakazian's wry twist to the nebulous mouth, and Danarion heard its answer in his mind. I have no choice anymore. I will go. The wings suddenly flared, a canopy of darkness. The eyes closed. Danarion felt the power of Ghakazian's call go rushing by him, increasing in strength as it went, and for what seemed an eternity there was peace in the Hall. The Messenger veiled the stars, and they shimmered many-colored in its net. The others were still.

Presently Sholia whispered, "Stand aside, Danarion," and he obeyed.

The air in the Hall became colder, and eddies trembled through it like swirling currents of icy water. The light, already dim, became murky, and Danarion realized that darkly transparent shapes were moving between him and the small square of sun at the entrance, their outlines barely visible. The Hall began to fill with a murmuring host. Frail wings rose and fell, flickers like dust motes catching light in the chill breeze. Faces hovered on the edge of his vision, there and gone before he could make out what he had seen. He pressed himself against the wall as winged and wingless flowed past him to the Gate, their thoughts a river of timidity, relief, eagerness, and regret washing over him. He did not know how long he stood afraid to move, stiff and numb. It could have been a day or a Shol-year, and still the essences came.

Just when he was certain he could bear the cold and his aching body no longer, the Hall began to brighten and warm. He bent to rub his shaking knees, glancing at Ghakazian, and saw one last wingless shape quivering before the Gate. The Messenger had glided forward to prevent its leaving, and its bewilderment rippled in Danarion's mind.

So you are the victor after all, Tagar, Ghakazian said, though the mouth remained closed. Your integrity has outlasted the fall of two worlds, and you are here to see the one who cast you down destroyed in his turn. It seems you are to receive what I may not. I wish you joy of it.

Tagar had no time to reply, for the Messenger was changing, having thinned and begun to curl around the man-shaped blur, its color deepening to a rich blue shot through with gold. Danarion stared, holding his breath. The gold splinters slowly formed ribs, a spine, the long bones of limbs, and curved gracefully to form a skull, and he found himself gazing at a golden skeleton that gleamed in the dim Hall. The blue of the Messenger gradually solidified, shrinking and lightening in color to lay itself over the bones, forming muscles, tendons, sinews. A heart began to beat, and Danarion could see the sudden rush of new blood along the myriad arteries. The Messenger withdrew, pulling itself away from its work and resuming its normal state, pulsing gently. Then a flare of brilliant red leaped from it, and a flush of skin spread over the body, hiding the bones and organs, clothing the outflung hands and fine-sculpted face, and Danarion saw eyes appear suddenly, burning with astonishment and delight. A young man turned to them, laughing, his hands flying over his thick brown hair, his unlined cheeks, the straight set of his shoulders. "It is I, Tagar!" he shouted. "Look at me!" He fell on his knees before the Messenger and then looked up at Ghakazian. "I love you still," he whispered. Bounding to his feet, he ran joyously from the Hall and into Shol's bright, warming sunlight.

At last only Ghakazian, Sholia, and Danarion remained. Ghakazian looked to the Gate and then to the others, and gravely he smiled. Farewell forever, he rustled in their minds. They saw the Messenger lean inward, and Ghakazian incline himself toward the Gate, wings folding slowly, and he was gone. The Gate was clear. Sholia gazed through it and could not speak, and Danarion strained to catch a last glimpse of the one he had loved.

Scarcely had Ghakazian vanished when a voice came from behind them, and they whirled. Another Messenger waited, its smoke filling the Hall with haze and a whiff of far realms.

*It is your turn, Danarion,* it said without inflection. *Your task is over. I will take you back to Danar.*

"But I am not ready!" he blurted, fighting to recover. "I need time, I must prepare myself, I . . ."

*There is no time. He is aware.*

Sholia blanched, and fear lanced at Danarion. He is aware. Of course. The Gate is open, and the way into Shol is once more paved for him. But I am not ready!

He turned his back on Messenger and Gate, unleashing a flood of emotions. To go, leaving Chilka's body on the floor of the Hall like something used up, something worthless. No, not Chilka's body only. My body as well. He fingered his scars, the tender bruises on his chest. He ran a hand through his wiry hair and touched the contours of his face. "Give me an hour," he said haltingly, grief strangling him.

No, the Messenger said. *You endanger me as well as Shol.*

Something in Danarion broke then. "I care nothing for you," he shouted, "as you care nothing for me! What is your danger to me? Nothing, nothing! It is my blood flowing beneath this skin, my heart beating under the bruises I have suffered, my voice rich with the life that throbs through my body. My body! My own! You ask me to leave a son I love, a woman I know only in memories and will never hold in my arms again. Give me one hour, you creature without mercy!" The spectrum of bright colors shifted, dimmed, became swirls of misty gray. "I have sacrificed my innocence on Shol," he finished brokenly. "Grant me one hour."

*Very well.* The reply came in the same timbreless half-whisper. *I will take you to the lake.*

Sholia stepped to him, and they embraced. For the last time he held her tightly, inhaling her warmth, her hair against his mouth, and then he pushed her gently away. "Hang bells in Shaban," he said. "I would like to know that they are ringing when I think of the wind coming in off the ocean." He kissed her and surrendered himself to the Messenger.

The lake lay as he had first seen it, a dank, rough oval on whose banks sullen bushes straggled, the sparse grass on its edge giving way to churned sand pitted with scattered rocks. In the distance loomed the mountains where Nenan and Lallin waited for him, where Sadal and Candar and the others had come seeking game and finding a mystery. He smiled wryly and began to pace slowly, his eyes on the spot where Chilka had lain dead, his agony past. He fancied that the bushes were still snapped and broken where the soldiers had trampled them, looking for his bag, but of course it could not be. Spring was coming. It had been high summer then, the earth parched, the sun pitilessly hot. He had been so thirsty . . . Danarion stood still. The lake smelled stagnant, but the odor of the wind was very good, bracing and cold with the flavor of the season in it and a hint of the ocean, and he shook back his hair and let it play on his neck. He bent and dug his hands into the sand, big hands, able to draw a bow and write notes, touch a son's face, draw passion from a woman, lift water to his mouth. He stood again and turned. "I am ready," he said simply. He waited while the Messenger reached for him, its hot net snaking around him. The landscape began to slip out of focus as he was torn from Chilka's body. In an instant of panic he tried to cling to the warm friendliness of the cells that were relinquishing him so painfully, but the Messenger could not be resisted, and with a last jolt Danarion found himself standing on the grass, Chilka face down beside him.

Chilka wriggled forward, his bag tossed aside, his hands straining eagerly. Water at last, he thought, but before he drank, he lay with his face to the sand until his breath had slowed and his legs ceased to throb. I have run a long way, he thought. Not much farther now, and I'll be safe. Farewell, Ishban, may every two-mind in you rot. I'm so thirsty! The sun on my head is burning. He had stopped panting. He pulled himself to the very edge of the lake, leaning out to where his reflection met him, dark in the brackish water, and although he wrinkled his nose in disgust, he dipped his hands, and the reflection broke, rippling into fragments. He lifted the water to his mouth. So good, he thought, sucking at it and cupping his hands for more. So very good.

"Water tastes good when you're thirsty, no matter where it's from," a voice from above him said. Chilka cried out in shock, rolled over, and leaped to his feet. He looked about wildly for his bag and the knife it contained, and the stranger chuckled. "No need for it now," he said. "And you can stop running and walk home. There will be no pursuit, Chilka, I promise you."

Chilka blinked at him suspiciously. He was tall, with golden eyes and long brown hair. Across his breast he wore a rich jewel that blazed in the cold sunlight. He was smiling warmly, and somehow Chilka found himself smiling back, his suspicions dissipating.

"Is that so?" Chilka said. His eye caught the strap of his bag, hooked over a low shrub, and he bent and swept it up, passing it over his head and settling it on his hip. He had begun to shiver. Strange, he thought. It feels more like winter now than summer, yet I was so hot and thirsty. "How do you know my name?" he asked. "Are you from the House?"

"No, I am not. And you are right, it is winter."

Something stirred in Chilka. Dark memories flew across his mind and were gone, leaving him puzzled and shaken. "Winter," he repeated stupidly. "But that cannot be. All the trees were in leaf when I left Ishban four days ago." He frowned at Danarion. "I think I know you," he said slowly, "but I cannot remember where or how."

"It does not matter." The stranger was no longer smiling, yet even in repose his face was full of warmth. The golden eyes held Chilka's, and there was sorrow in them and something more. Complicity, perhaps. "I know you very well. You might say we are brothers. You should be on your way if you want to reach the valley by sunset. Greet Lallin for me. Look after her well, Chilka. Take her to Shaban sometimes. She will like that."

Chilka took one step away and then another. He was not afraid. Although he could not understand, he knew somewhere deep inside him that this man was his friend. "I will," he replied haltingly, "if you say so." Their eyes met, and suddenly they smiled at each other. Chilka turned away, but he had not gone far when the stranger called.

"Chilka!"

"Yes?"

"Tell Nenan I love him. He will understand."

"Madman." Chilka laughed under his breath and strode away whistling. Danarion watched him go. He knew what the Messenger had done, and he was full of wonder.

The Messenger did not tarry. Before Chilka was out of sight, it gathered up Danarion and raced across Shol. The Mountain of Mourning grew from a jumbled speck on the horizon to a towering breadth of rock with the entrance to the Gate a shadow at its foot. Swooping low, the Messenger went in. The Hall of Waiting was empty, the stars still sparking cold where Yarne stood. The Messenger flashed through, out into blackness, and Danarion, looking back, heard a great crash. His eyes found the Gate, a dwindling square of silver, and etched on its surface was Yarne's face, gazing out onto the universe with grave eyes and a slight smile, framed in waving silver hair. Above Danarion was the transparent column that had brought him to Shol. Then he had been awed but not afraid. Now he was terrified. That part of him that was Chilka and always would be cowered away from the silent immensity around him and longed for solid earth under its feet. Shol was a faint mist, soon lost to sight, and in its place Danarion saw a vague cloud of blackness that was blotting out the stars. He felt the Messenger quiver and fling itself faster into the void. The cloud began to coalesce. It acquired a shape and came speeding after them. The Unmaker. He had hoped that his angry words to the Messenger in the Hall had been a lie, but, they were not. His innocence, his wholeness, was gone. He was bringing a stain with him to Danar. Violence and deception, envy and hatred were all in him, in his essence, where Chilka's memories were shared. Danar would fall, and he would be the instrument of its change. It would not be a catastrophe, a thing of violence, though, like Shol's topple into ruin, but a slow change, a gradual tightening of time's grip, a slipping into the arbitrary. He would not think of it now. He forced himself to watch the Unmaker come. Around him the sky exploded, star merging into star as the Messenger's speed increased, but still the dark blot with the shape of a man clung to their fiery wake. The Messenger roared and suddenly slowed, and Danarion saw his own sun flash by. Then he was toppling toward Danar, a pinprick of reflected light, a white ball, a colored hemisphere, and the dearly familiar towers of his own palace careened to meet him.

There was a moment of confusion when he felt the Messenger toss him away, and he cried out and clutched at nothing. But soon he was lying across the black marble table in the council hall. Mild sunlight pooled across his hands. Shakily he pulled himself into a sitting position and sat staring at those hands, impossibly long-fingered, incredibly, limpidly golden. Above him birds fluttered in and out the clerestory windows, twittering. He pushed back his chair and rose, almost falling. He was so light. He felt he might float away if he let go of the edge of the table.

*Close the Gate, Danarion.*

He started. The Messenger was behind him, rose-red and glimmering. Danarion stared at it through the quiet, long room.

"Where is Janthis?" he said, his head feeling hollow. "Janthis!"

*Close the Gate,* the Messenger repeated. *Hurry, or it will be too late.*

Danarion remembered, and his heart constricted. Stumbling, he began to run. Down the room and along a passage, out onto the terrace where the corions yawned and cocked sharp eyes at him. He flung himself at the stair, leaped onto the arch that soared to the mouth of the Gate, and fled along the stone passageway. The Gate stood open. Danarion fell against the frame. Out where the stars should have been there was only the towering shape of the Unmaker, and an icy wind blew in through the Gate. Danarion did not pause to think but flung out his arms and shouted, "I close the Gate of Danar! I, sun-lord, command you to close. Your service is at an end. Henceforth neither Messenger nor Unmaker nor any created thing may enter here! Close! Close!"

With a ponderous slowness the Gate began to fill with smoke. Through the scented haze Danarion could see the enemy almost upon him, and he bit his lip to keep from screaming. The haze thickened, the heavy, sweet smell of flaming haeli seeds filling the space before the Gate, and then the whole area burst into red flame. For a moment it burned brightly, sending tongues of harmless flame and billowing sweet smoke into Danarion's face, and then it began to die, until only a glow remained. That too dimmed and went out, and Danarion found himself looking at a wall of gold upon which a thousand burning haeli seeds were spiraling to the ground. Reclining under them, its face lifted to receive their scent, was a golden corion with wings outspread. It is done, Danarion thought weakly. It is over. Danar is the last world to be sealed in upon itself.

He turned and went back the way he had come, one hand against the wall to support himself. He crossed the arch, climbed the stair, and spoke to the corions on the terrace, though afterward he did not remember what he had said to them. In the cool passages and ringing echoes of the palace Danarion searched for Janthis. He could not believe that he was not there. He had promised to wait. He called his name as he wandered from room to room among the bright gems and costly hangings, the flowing arches and tinkling fountains where the sun-people used to walk, but the city within a city gave him no sound but the tinkling water and quiet wind.

He went back to the council hall. Its floor was dark. No world was left to prick its light bravely up at him as he strode along behind the chairs drawn up to the shining black surface of the table. One beside another, the necklets lay in perfect symmetry, and he knew that they would rest so until the end of time. He stood on the dais, looking back down the hall. "Janthis!" he shouted. "Janthis, where are you?" There was no answer.

He left the palace and went out onto the steps. He enquired of the corions, but they could tell him nothing. They had not seen Janthis for a long time. Danarion went down into the Time-forest, scuffing through the carpet of leaves that always lay there, but now when he felt the mortal time rush to meet him, it embraced him as though he were one of its own children, and he slid into it with absentminded ease.

His small house had not changed. One window was open as he had left it. The grass was lush and springy under his feet as he crossed from the swinging gate to the door, and he entered with a feeling of utter unreality. He thought Janthis might have left a message for him here, but there was nothing. Next door he heard children laughing, and he went out again, his eyes searching for the little girl he had been talking with when Janthis's summons had come, but the children were strangers who paused in their play to stare at him with interest.

"I am looking for Tandil," he said to them. "Is she at home today?"

One child with dark hair and large eyes came to the hedge. "Tandil was my grandmother," she said politely. "She went through the Gate a long time ago. Who are you?"

"Oh, no one," Danarion managed, turning away, and he found himself running, over his lawn, out his gate, along the path under the trees, not caring where he was going. In some quiet moment the child might search her memories and find her grandmother sitting on the knee of a stranger whose name was Danarion, he thought, and the thought brought him an unbearable hurt. I am not Danarion anymore.

# 28

He wandered over Danar as day followed long, sunlit day. He had no desire to go into his sun or to escape from himself. His eyes watched the people, and sometimes he would run after some mortal whose color of hair or straight walk made him think it might be Janthis, but it never was.

He walked in the empty places, too, where there were pools that reminded him of Chilka drinking avidly, and low mountains that he invested with height and valleys with rivers along whose banks small cottages clustered.

At last he stood again at the foot of the long stair that swept to the terrace. It was winter. The corions had gone to sleep their long sleep, and the pillars fronting the shadowed audience hall were nakedly empty. He climbed to them and faced out, his eyes traveling the forest, the silhouette of the city beyond, sharp against a blue sky, and the arch that led to a silent passage and a blind Gate. I lack, he whispered to himself. I lack, and I am lonely. I miss Chilka's mortality, the swift numbering of his days, the challenges, the choices for good or evil, the opportunities for heroism or baseness. Who would have thought that out of a disfigured, fallen world could rise such precious things? The perfection of the worlds before the Worldmaker became the Unmaker was a bland, tasteless state, as Danar seems to me now, stale in its changelessness, stifling in its orderedness. I am wounded, my immortality is decaying, and I embrace this wound, I welcome it. How much time has gone by on Shol? Is Chilka dead and Nenan gone from youth into old age? Yet Chilka will live on in me, a seed of ruin to Danar, and it is good. I am Chilka. I am Danarion. I am Chilka-Danarion, and I would not have it any other way.

He left the terrace and wended his way toward the council hall. No dust drifted in the empty rooms. Precious metals from the far corners of the universe gleamed as softly as ever. The stonework was as fresh and clean as it had been on the day it was set in place. He reached the hall and went up onto the dais and paused.

"Janthis," he said. "What happened to you?"

*A Messenger took him away, Danarion.* The voice was quiet yet filled the hall with its presence. Danarion swung round. The door on the left stood open, and within the tiny room where Janthis used to peer into his mirror a white light burned. *Come in,* the voice went on. *You have nothing to fear.*

But he did fear. It was not a fear of some terrible darkness but an awe that had fallen on him, and he went toward the light on trembling legs. Janthis's mirror-wall was blank and gray, but the opposite wall had vanished in an outpouring of splendor that dazzled him so that he had to avert his eyes.

"Who are you?" he choked, though suddenly he knew, and the voice woke rivers of joy in him.

*You know who I am. I stand on the edge. I am outside time and beyond all space. For me there is no such thing as a beginning, for beginning and ending are one and the same. There is no future and no past. There is only an eternal now. I have been waiting for you to understand.*

"Why did the Messenger take Janthis?" He knew he should not ask. He really did not want to, for he felt completely at peace, but his question was answered immediately, as though he had asked it of an equal.

*Janthis surrendered himself to the Messenger because he had allowed corruption to enter Danar. It is the Law.*

Janthis must have known, Danarion thought. Even as he was calling to me to come to him he must have been measuring the price he would pay for sending a sun-lord out onto a shadowed world, knowing that someone changed and maimed would return.

*The day of the sun-lords is over, Danarion,* the light went on. *The universe belongs now to the mortals. Sun-lords were part of the dawn, and it is now full morning. You have done well, all of you, against a terror that is stronger than anything but me. You do not yet recognize the fruit of your long battle, but you will. Your powers will be in healing that which is wounded.*

"But it could have been different!" Danarion burst out, overwhelmed suddenly by the futility of all that lay behind him, the pain and change of what lay ahead.

The voice answered gently. *Yes, it could have been different. The hall behind you could still be full of sun-lords with the World-maker sitting smiling in his chair. The Gates could still be open, spilling life over the universe. You yourself could still be without the knowledge of pain. But that is not the way that was chosen.*

"I did not make the choice," Danarion whispered.

*I know you did not. It will be remembered. Now go to the ledge by the window and bring the Book.*

He could no more refuse the voice than he could refuse to breathe. He felt as though every desire had been fulfilled before he had felt it, every doubt and terror burned away. He went to the ledge and a book was there, its white cover gleaming, its silver lettering sparkling in the light that continued to flood the room and spill out to gild the bare branches of the trees far below. He picked it up and gave a low cry.

"This is the Book of What Will Be!"

*Of course. Open it.*

Danarion hesitated. "It is forbidden."

*I made it. I tell you to open and read.*

This thing destroyed Fallan, Danarion thought, and Ixel and Ghaka. With a beating heart and clumsy fingers he lifted back the cover. The pages were transparently thin and fluttered with his breath. He glanced at the pages hesitantly, riffling through them. He went back and turned them again. Then he closed the cover and stared down at it.

"The pages are blank," he said wonderingly. "There is no writing."

The voice laughed, and the light in the room shook and shivered. *Yes, they are blank, Danarion. That is my gift to all that is made. There is a key beside the Book. Take it and the Book and go down to your house. Lock the sun-people's palace and do not look back. You do not belong in it anymore. Remember Chilka and his gift to you. The future is yours and his and every mortal's until I speak the final word. Go now.* The light vanished. Danarion ran forward, but the wall was gray and solid. Pale sunlight lay across the window ledge and spattered on the floor, and he could hear a wind stirring in the hall beyond. With a dazed, uncomprehending wonder he picked up the massive golden key that lay waiting for him. "Thank you," he whispered. "Thank you."

He walked through the hall for the last time, the Book and the key in his hands. One by one he named them, the sun-lords, his kin, but hope was in his heart as he did so. He passed under the great copper dome studded with gems, paced the corridors, and so stepped out at last onto the terrace where the high doors had stood open since the beginning. Laying down the Book, he reached in and pulled them closed. They moved soundlessly and fitted together without a chink. He turned the key in the huge carven lock and then removed it and retrieved the Book. On impulse he leaned forward and pressed his cheek to the warmth of the golden-veined haeli wood, thinking of the shadowed labyrinth of silent rooms beyond that would stand empty and indestructible forever, and then he ran down the steps and into the brooding silence of the Time-forest. He did not look back.

## About the Author

Pauline Gedge was born in Auckland, New Zealand, in 1945. She spent part of her childhood in Oxfordshire, England, and now lives in Alberta, Canada. She is the author of two previous books, both historical fiction: *Child of the Morning* (1977) and *The Eagle and the Raven* (1978).